ALSO BY EVAN GRAVER

<u>Ryan Weller Thrillers</u>

Dark Water

Dark Ship

Dark Horse

Dark Shadows

Dark Paradise

Dark Fury

Dark Hunt

Dark Path

Dark Prey

Dark Fraud

Dark Drone

Dark Country

Dark Order

Dark Cover-up

Dark Angel

<u>Stand Alone</u>

Liberty Brigade

<u>John Phoenix Thrillers</u>

Rising Phoenix

Target Phoenix

Target Phoenix

© 2024 Evan Graver

www.evangraver.com

ISBN-13: 979-8-9899997-1-2

Cover: Cover2Book

This is a work of fiction. Any resemblance to any person, living or dead, business, companies, events, or locales is entirely coincidental.

Printed and bound in the United States of America

First Printed February 2024

Published by Third Reef Publishing, LLC

Hollywood, Florida

www.thirdreefpublishing.com

TARGET PHOENIX
A JOHN PHOENIX THRILLER

EVAN GRAVER

CHAPTER 1

Ankoko Island
Guyana

Captain Tyler Verdin peered through the night vision goggles mounted on his helmet as he knelt in the sand at the edge of the Cuyuní River. He had the stock of his suppressed Colt M4A1 pressed to his shoulder, ready for battle. He studied the tin shack on stilts as his five teammates moved out of the water and closed the five meters between Verdin and the shack.

Once they'd stacked up in a gun train at the base of the stairs, Verdin left his position at the beachhead and moved to the front of the line. Each man gave him the signal they were ready to move, and without hesitation, he went up the steps with the others right behind him.

They came to a wide veranda at the top of the stairs, moving as quietly as they could over the ancient, squeaky planks. Verdin stopped at the front door. As soon as the gun train collapsed into a tight knot behind him, he kicked through the door and swept to his right, knowing the men behind him would sweep left and straight ahead.

Verdin saw a shadowy figure move. He pressed the trigger on his M4, sending a burst of bullets into the man. Verdin heard more gunfire from his teammates as they eliminated the Venezuelan soldiers in the shack.

A chorus of "Clear" rang through the building moments later.

Verdin lifted his night vision goggles and glanced around. His blue eyes swept the room before he pushed off his helmet and ran a hand through his sweaty blonde hair. At just five feet four inches tall, or 162cm, Verdin wasn't a giant by any means, but he could hold his own in any combat situation. Over the years, he found that it was short guys like himself with something to prove who made it through Special Forces training. The big guys were an anomaly stereotyped by the movies. Arnold would have never made it through Hell Week.

With the building clear, Guyana Defence Force (GDF) Major John Yaw, a Guyanese native with a craggy face, thick black mustache, and dark bushy eyebrows, ordered his men to police the weapons from the dead Venezuelans. Once they'd collected the loot of Kalashnikov AK-103s, the men retreated from the house and signaled the two waiting boats to come ashore.

In all, the mixture of Guyanese from the 31 Special Forces Squadron and mercenaries hired to fight the Venezuelans totaled twenty-four. As they formed up into Red and Blue Teams at the edge of the jungle, Major Yaw took control of the first squad, and Verdin softly commanded his Blue Team to move out. They would form a pincher movement by crossing Ankoko Island and flanking the military barracks on the far side of the runway.

The going was easy for the first eight hundred meters as they patrolled along a narrow dirt road from the waterside hut to the airstrip. Moving cautiously up the jungle trail, Verdin listened to the chirp of insects and other jungle night sounds as he reflected on his path to Guyana.

Three weeks ago, he'd been working for Constellis, a private security contractor, when the call went out for men of his special skillset to join the GDF as contractors. He'd jumped at the chance to fight in the jungle and do something besides babysitting high-value diplomats on overseas junkets. He'd packed his bags, flown to Guyana, and volunteered. Within twenty-four hours, the former Navy SEAL found himself at the Colonel Robert Mitchell Jungle and Amphibious Training School in Makouria. Soon after, he'd become embroiled in planning the mission to recapture Ankoko Island.

Verdin had joined for the money and the adventure, but he'd quickly realized how much he'd missed the operational tempo of planning and executing special warfare operations, a specialty during his tenure as a SEAL officer.

Just before they reached the airstrip, the two teams split and moved parallel to the active construction site. From intelligence gathered by locals and provided to them by GDF headquarters, Verdin knew the Venezuelans had brought in Russian contractors to pave the runway on Ankoko pursuant to stationing Sukhoi Su-30 Flanker fighter jets and Mi-35 Hind attack helicopters there. The GDF knew that having a Venezuelan base right on their border was a horrible idea, so they wanted to reclaim the island for their own use.

As any good ops officer would, Verdin had studied the history of the conflict between the two warring nation-states. In accordance with the 1899 Paris Arbitral Award, Venezuela and Guyana had divided Ankoko Island in two, but no sooner had the ink dried on the award than the Venezuelans declared it void. In 1966, after Guyana had won independence from Britain, Venezuela, in a display of strength, sent Army troops to occupy the seven-square-kilometer island, and they'd established a military base and later carved out the airstrip.

The Guyanese government, for its part, had lodged a *strong* protest. The Venezuelans had rejected it out of hand, claiming the entire island as Venezuelan property along with the entire Essequibo Region. They asserted that when Spain created the Kingdom of Venezuela in 1777, they established the Essequibo River as a dividing line between the Spanish and Dutch colonies.

Since then, various international courts had tried to settle the dispute, but to no avail. Both countries wanted the riches that lay within the Essequibo Region, from gold to oil. With ExxonMobil's find off the coast of Guyana in 2015, Venezuelan President Michel Zarate had ratcheted up the rhetoric and sent naval vessels to patrol the waters off the Essequibo Region, harassing fishermen and oil workers.

Things had finally come to blows when the GDFS *Essequibo*, one of Guyana's newest patrol boats, had torpedoed and sank the PC-21 *Guaiqueri*, a Venezuelan offshore patrol vessel, after the *Guaiqueri* had fired upon them. In retaliation, the Venezuelans had sent a flight of Flankers to bomb Base Camp Seweyo, one of the GDF's primary technical and training facilities.

Now, the GDF Special Forces were moving through the jungle, ready to retake the island for Guyana and establish their own forward operating base. Instead of sending a couple of their new A-29 Super Tucano warplanes to bomb the base into oblivion, the GDF had decided on a more surgical strike.

Once they had occupied the island, the GDF planned to use the barracks, headquarters building, chow hall, and various maintenance and storage facilities scattered among the trees to quarter GDF troops. Brigadier General Wesley Patrick, head of the GDF, had also ordered the A-team not to destroy any of the construction equipment and to try to capture the Russian advisors alive as he didn't want to piss off the Kremlin any more than necessary.

Reaching their staging point in a clearing off to the side of the runway, Verdin checked with his men, ensuring they all arrived.

Once everyone had moved into a semi-circular formation, guns out and ready, Verdin instructed his sniper to check for sentries on the far side of the landing strip. Bianka Nascimento, a young Guyanese female trooper, climbed onto a nearby dump truck and sprawled on the cab before setting up her rifle.

Staring through the scope, Nascimento reported, "Two men are standing near the road to the camp just inside the tree line."

"You copy, Red One?" Verdin asked Major Yaw over their secure comms unit. The Florida National Guard had sent a batch of the latest L3Harris Technologies comms units, and Yaw had quickly commandeered them for this raid and the future needs of the 31 Special Forces Squadron.

"Copy and set. Snipers are free to fire," Yaw replied.

"I've got the one on the left," the Blue Team sniper stated.

"Roger that. I've got right," Red Team's sniper replied. "Go on three." She softly counted down, and the two snipers fired.

Verdin heard the cough of the suppressed high-powered rifle and waited breathlessly for the report from the snipers. Seconds later, both snipers stated their targets were down.

"Move!" Yaw commanded over the net.

Preset teams of two raced across the 99-meter-wide strip of open ground until only the snipers remained behind as rear guard.

Verdin was the last to cross the airfield with his battle

buddy, a young man named Weaver Smith from Corriverton on the Suriname border. Smittie, as all the guys called him, was a handsome kid with dusky skin and coal-black eyes. He had joined the Army at seventeen and volunteered for Special Forces training at twenty-one. Once Verdin arrived in-country, Smittie glued himself to his hip, and the two had become fast friends.

What had pissed Verdin off was Smittie's nickname for him—Fight Club. The others in the squadron had picked it, and it had become his call sign. While his name was scandalously close to Brad Pitt's character, Tyler Durden, Verdin *hated* the nickname, especially when someone told him to punch himself in the face.

Formed up on the northern side of the runway, Blue One ordered his troops to head for the squad barracks as Red One led his team toward the headquarters building and officer huts.

As soon as a team of six Guyanese entered the clearing in front of the barracks, gunfire rang out. More AK-103s joined the fight. Verdin saw two of his troops cut down in the initial volley. He raised his rifle and fired at shadowy figures as they charged out of the barracks.

Satellite photos showed seven buildings, and the intelligence clowns had claimed there were no more than one hundred members of the *Fuerza Armada Nacional Bolivariana* (FANB), or National Bolivarian Armed Forces, stationed on Ankoko. Verdin and his fellow mercs had taken to calling the Venezuelan forces "Fanboys," and, at the moment, there seemed to be a never-ending supply of them.

"Red One, we are taking heavy fire from the barracks. Request use of the SLIM," Verdin said into his comms. He understood the GDF's desire to keep the buildings intact, but if he needed to knock the barracks flat with the Shoulder-Launched Individual Munition (SLIM) to save his men,

Verdin had no qualms about it. One of the things Verdin enjoyed about this shitty little war was that it was a test bed for all kinds of new tech, like the SLIM, a 6.8-kilogram, disposable, shoulder-fired rocket made by Aerojet Rocketdyne.

"Negative. Stand your ground," Yaw replied. "We need those buildings."

"Son of a bitch," Verdin muttered to himself, then called out, "Reloading!"

Major Yaw could have his buildings intact, but they'd be perforated with more holes than a colander.

Smith took up the slack in firing as Verdin replenished his rifle. With a fresh mag in the well, Verdin targeted a man who had just ducked out from behind the barracks and hoisted a rocket-propelled grenade launcher to his shoulder. Verdin sent a trio of rounds the man's way before diving to the ground as he shouted, "RPG! RPG!"

The RPG went wide, smacking into a tree trunk about twenty feet above the heads of the invaders, and toppled the massive canopy to the ground with a thunderous crack. Verdin popped up and shouldered his rifle, scanning through the optics for more Fanboys. He idly noted the man who'd fired the RPG lay dead. Someone had killed him and, in the process, deflected the gunner's shot. Verdin hoped it had been his bullets that had sent the man to meet his maker.

All around the military base, pockets of resistance continued to launch RPGs and fire automatic weapons at the 31 Special Forces Squadron. Verdin listened to the radio calls and tried to cement in his mind an accurate picture of the action. Once he had a plan, he turned to his battle buddy, "We need to move toward the docks and circle back—pincer the pincer."

Smittie nodded with a grin. Despite Smittie giving him a stupid call sign, Verdin liked having the kid around. He was an eager student and constantly picked Verdin's brain for tactics and strategy.

The two men began moving north through the trees, recruiting more Blue Team members into their new plan.

"Red One, this is Blue One," Verdin said over the radio. "Can you hold them at the south tree line?"

"Copy, Blue One. Can do."

Verdin told Yaw his plan as he scrambled through the darkness away from the gunfight. During the initial advance, Verdin had sent a four-man team to the river dock to secure it, and as he approached, one of the men ran out to greet him.

"We have movement across the river," Johnson reported. Like Verdin, he was an American merc, but he'd come through the 75th Ranger Regiment. Johnson, a sawed-off runt with red hair and freckles, looked more like a high school freshman than a hardened warrior.

"Can you blast them with the SLIM?" Verdin asked.

"Yeah," Johson said with a smile. "We can knock their asses out flat."

"Do it. Light 'em, Sergeant. And then you and Colbert link up with me. We're flanking the barracks. The Fanboys are holed up there."

Johnson gave a chipper, "Roger that, sir."

Verdin led his team across a narrow dirt road and entered the woods on the far side. The Fanboys had knocked down most of the brush over the years, and the going was quick and smooth. Behind him, Verdin heard his men engage the Fanboys on the far side of the Cuyuní River, rippling off three SLIM shots that blossomed flame into the air and ignited the wooden structures around the Venezuelan ferry dock.

Not long after that, Johnson and his partner linked up with Verdin's force as they spread out in the woods. Verdin radioed Major Yaw to tell him his team was set and to take cover so they wouldn't get hit by friendly fire. Once Yaw confirmed his men were down, Verdin and his team engaged, killing every last Venezuelan and Russian holding a weapon.

"Cease fire!" Major Yaw called over the radio, but almost everyone had stopped shooting when the last of the enemy had fallen. A few GDF soldiers walked through the dead and wounded, firing a bullet into each enemy head.

Verdin joined Major Yaw in front of the headquarters building, where the two men raised a Guyanese Golden Arrowhead flag over the island for the first time in fifty-eight years.

Yaw stepped back, saluted the flag, and then picked up his satellite phone. He called Brigadier Patrick to report the outcome of the battle. "We have secured the island, sir. Send the reinforcements." For a moment, he was silent, then said, "No, sir. The Russians helped to defend the base. Everyone is dead."

Once Yaw ended the call, he turned to his second in command. "Helicopters are in-bound to deliver reinforce-ments and take out our wounded. Let's make sure we're set for when they arrive."

Verdin walked off to find the members of his Blue Team.

"Six casualties, sir," Smittie reported when Verdin walked up. "Four KIA and two wounded. One needs an evac."

"Choppers are on the way," Verdin replied. "Get him stabilized and move him to the airstrip along with the dead." Turning to Johnson, he said, "I want you to move some of that heavy equipment. Turn their lights on so the choppers have a safe place to land."

As the men dispersed to carry out his orders, Verdin walked over to a sergeant from Red Team. "Take two men and reinforce the dock. Call in your sniper and take him with you."

"Yes, sir," the man said and trotted away, hailing the Red Team sniper over the radio as he went.

Verdin continued to coordinate the Special Forces troops

into defensive positions and assist in bringing dead and wounded Guyanese and American mercs to the airstrip. He wondered if the surprise attack was enough to keep the Venezuelans at bay for the moment or if they had another trick up their sleeve.

CHAPTER 2

Twenty minutes after Major Yaw had called Brigadier General Patrick to report that Ankoko Island was back in Guyanese hands, the sound of inbound helicopters reached Verdin's ears.

Four brand-new AgustaWestland AW149 troop transporters swept in from the Kaikan GDF base forty miles south along the Pilima River that marked the western border between Guyana and Venezuela.

The first bird disgorged its ground forces and took the wounded soldiers to Georgetown. Each successive helicopter landed in the zone lit up by the construction equipment and disembarked twelve soldiers until forty-eight fresh troops from the 3rd Infantry Battalion were on the ground, with another thirty-six on their way.

Major Yaw stood near the landing zone, directing troops to take over the positions of the 31 Special Forces Squadron and to start collecting the dead Venezuelans and Russians.

"What do you want us to do with them?" Verdin asked Yaw.

"Use one of those dozers and dig a hole. We'll put them underground."

"Yes, sir. I'll have to separate the Russians," Verdin replied. "Those commie bastards always want their boys back."

Before Verdin could walk off, he heard Johnson shout over the comms. "Yeehaw! We got ourselves a fucking gunboat. Yo! Fight Club. Come check this shit out."

"Where are you?" Verdin asked.

"The boat's anchored off the island's west end in a little cove," Johnson replied.

"I'll be there in a few minutes," Verdin said into the mic, then signed off the net.

Major Yaw walked over to where Verdin stood beside an excavator. "Go check out the boat. Take a couple of your Blue Team. I've got things here."

"Yes, sir," Verdin replied. He turned to find Smith practically in his shadow. "Shit, Smittie! Why the hell do you do that to me?"

Smittie grinned boyishly as Verdin spoke into his radio mic. "Moore. Douglas. Rally at the construction equipment."

Moments later, two men came running up. The rest of the team had started calling them "The Twins." Although they didn't look anything alike, their brown, burly beards were, however, nearly identical.

The four men jogged to the end of the runway and beat their way through the bush along a narrow, winding path. Verdin and the others flipped their night vision goggles into place to help guide them around the low, swampy areas.

Three hundred meters off the end of the runway, Verdin and his small contingent from Blue Team stepped onto the riverbank. Johnson and Colbert hooted to them, drawing Verdin's attention to a gunboat surrounded by heavy brush in a narrow, hand-dug canal.

Verdin quickly appraised the machine. It seemed fairly new, and the Fanboys had kept it in excellent shape. The ten-meter rigid hull inflatable boat (RHIB) came equipped with twin Mercury Verado four-hundred-horsepower outboards and a 12.7mm machine gun on a swivel mount at the bow.

A new voice came over the radio before Verdin and his men could investigate the boat further.

"Red One, this is Air Base Mobil One. Be advised. We have inbound Mi-35 Hind helicopters from the La Camorra Territorial Security Airbase. We've scrambled the Flying Jaguars. They'll be overhead in less than twenty minutes."

"How long until our bandits are on station?" Yaw asked.

"Ten minutes," Air Mobil responded.

Verdin cursed. Air Base Mobil was one of two twin-turboprop Northrop Grumman E-2D Hawkeyes that the American government had gifted to the Guyana Air Force. They'd even trained several crews to fly the former U.S. Navy's all-weather, tactical airborne early warning and control aircraft. One of AWACS had launched to keep tabs on the Venezuelans while the 31 Special Forces invaded Ankoko Island.

Tuning to Johnson, who was in the patrol boat, Verdin asked, "What's the status on that gun? We got bullets for it?"

"I found five full cans of ammo in a locker, and there's a partial in the gun."

"Can we get the boat started?" Verdin asked Colbert, who sat behind the wheel.

To answer the captain's question, Colbert twisted the key and fired up the motors.

"Let's get aboard," Verdin said to Smith and The Twins.

The men waded through the water and climbed onto the RHIB. Once they were sitting in the suspension seats, Verdin ordered Colbert to drive the boat around to the dock. As Colbert drove, he radioed Major Yaw and told him the plan. Yaw gathered and divided the remaining SLIMs between his land force and his newly formed naval crew, sending five SLIMs to the dock for Verdin. While the SLIM hadn't been designed for surface-to-air use, Verdin hoped it would hold off the helicopters until the Flying Jaguars arrived to provide air cover.

Once the crew in the RHIB had picked up the SLIMs, Verdin told his driver to head downriver. "Let's get a better sightline so we can kick some Hindends."

"Roger that, boss," Colbert replied. The Guyana native pushed the throttles forward, and the patrol craft shot away from the dock.

As they ran east along the Cuyuní River, the sun was just beginning to glow on the horizon. Verdin liked their chances. He planned to park the boat where they had a better view of the sky and try to pick off the helicopters with their SLIMs, although he wished he had some FIM-92 Stinger missiles that operated with infrared homing devices. They would make shooting down the Hind much easier than with the unguided SLIMs. Hopefully, the Super Tucanos would arrive on station before Verdin's meager crew needed to use the missiles, but it was better to be prepared than caught unaware.

Approximately seven hundred meters downstream, just before the river bent to the east, Verdin ordered Colbert to turn the boat around and idle in place. The sun was just a bit higher, and Verdin could make out the shit brown color of the river and the verdant green of the surrounding jungle on both sides of the waterway. He removed his night vision goggles and tucked them into his pack as the others did the same.

Moving forward to the open bow, Verdin picked up one of the SLIMs, then joined Johnson at the 12.7mm gun. "You ready?" he asked.

"Not sure what good we're going to do, but I'm as ready as I can be," Johnson said.

"All we can do is try," Verdin replied. They had all been in tough spots before, especially the American former servicemen who had experienced war firsthand in Iraq or Afghanistan. Their Guyanese counterparts were a little less practiced but ready, nonetheless.

Verdin heard the faint sound of helicopter rotors over the low hum of the idling Mercury outboards. His heart rate increased, and he had to wipe the sweat from his palms. If the Hinds spotted them on the open river, they could give chase, and Verdin's crew might end up dead or swimming for their lives within the next few minutes.

You wanted adventure. You fucking got it, brother. In spades.

CHAPTER 3

Cheddi Jagan International Airport
Timehri, Guayana

Lieutenant Will Pounder heard the emergency alert as he stood at the urinal, draining the copious amount of coffee he'd drank over the last four hours.

He zipped up his green flight suit and turned to the sink to wash his hands. Glancing in the mirror over the white porcelain sink, Pounder ran a damp hand through his thick brown hair and examined the bags under his green eyes. He wasn't quite the thin, muscular youth he'd been when he'd first joined the U.S. Army at eighteen. As a civilian, he'd gained weight over the last few years, sitting on his ass in the cockpit of an airplane, either teaching new students to fly or dusting crops from a bright yellow Air Tractor.

Now, he was about to take off in an Embraer A-29 Super Tucano light attack aircraft powered by a 1,604-horsepower turboprop engine. The emergency alert meant the 31 Special

Forces Squadron needed their help in wrangling the Venezuelans off Ankoko Island.

Before Pounder could leave the restroom, the door opened, and Tammy "Stitches" Dorn called out, "Yo, Dumpster, you comin' or you too busy jerking off?"

"Can't a guy take a leak in peace, or do you wanna come shake it for me?" Pounder shot back.

Stitches laughed. "In your dreams."

Pounder stepped out of the restroom and put his arm around the shorter brunette. At six feet tall, he had five inches on the gray-eyed navigator. She had been a backseater in U.S. Air Force F-15EX Eagle IIs, and now she was Pounder's navigator. Stitches claimed to have lost a bet to become Dumpster's navigator, but he knew better. She was the best the motley crew of flying mercenaries had to offer. They both were.

After picking up their flight gear, they joined his squadron mates in the bed of an M35 Deuce and a Half truck for the ride from the GDF base to the airport. It was warm even with the sun just coming up, and under his survival vest, Pounder's flight suit clung to his sweaty skin. It had been a long time since Pounder had been in combat, and he could feel the old responses coming back—the heightening of the senses for battle. When he'd last fought, it had been on foot in Iraq with the 82nd Airborne for patriotic duty. Now, it was for money and adventure. As his buddy Steve Gruber had put it, "We're grabbing life by the balls."

Pounder, Stitches, and the other pilots, including their illustrious leader, Colonel Jorge Mansoor—a wiry Black man with close-cropped hair who had learned to fly planes in England after distinguishing himself at the Royal Military Academy at Sandhurst—had trained to fly the Super Tucanos at Moody Air Force Base in Valdosta, Georgia. The course, normally a year-long, had been condensed into two weeks of intensive study. Once the two South American countries had exchanged blows, Guyana had wanted their planes and mercenary pilots on the ground at Camp Stephenson, ready to fight.

To get the flight of five Super Tucanos from Moody AFB to Guyana, the pilots had followed the old "Southern Air Route" established during World War II to get U.S. bombers and fighter planes to Africa, Europe, China, and Russia. Since the old bombers and fighters only had a range of two thousand miles, the U.S. military had flown the planes in short hops from Homestead Air Force Base in Florida across the Caribbean and into South America, stopping at various air bases along the way to refuel.

The Super Tucano crews had flown a grueling three-day hop across the open ocean in sight of tantalizingly beautiful Caribbean Islands to reach Timehri, one of the old U.S. bases. Once there, the pilots had parked the planes on the ramp outside the civilian fixed-base operator for fuel and maintenance.

Across the runway, Pounder saw that construction contractors had partially erected a brand-new hangar for the two Tucano squadrons the GDF would eventually field with twelve planes each. Since the GDF didn't have enough personnel to combat the Venezuelans, they had offered top dollar to hire pilots, groundcrew, and infantrymen to supplement their meager force. And with the influx of oil money from the newly discovered offshore deposits, they could afford the best.

Pounder hopped out of the truck, his pulse quickening at the sight of the airplanes. Overnight, someone had painted shark teeth as nose art on the sleek gray crafts, reminiscent of U.S. fighter planes from World War II. Walking over to his plane, he caressed her nose just behind the prop and whispered, "All right, sweetheart, this is the real deal. Let's get home to Max."

"You know what I like about you, Dumpster?" Stitches

asked as they did a quick walk-around inspection of their aircraft.

"No, but I bet you're gonna tell me," Pounder said.

"You haven't hit on me once," she said. "Max must be pretty special."

"I think she is," he said, giving the airplane another gentle pat before climbing into the cockpit. From the walk-around, Pounder knew his plane carried four Brazilian-made MAA-1 Piranha air-to-air missiles, twin gun pods containing Dillon Aero M134 Miniguns with three thousand rounds of 7.62mm each, and a full complement of five hundred 12.7mm rounds for the internal wing-mounted FN Herstal machine guns.

Cory Anderson, a former U.S. Navy submariner with a bushy beard and thick shock of light brown hair, climbed up to help strap the aviators into their seats. He and the other maintainers had flown down on a commercial jet to meet the pilots and navigators in Guyana. After leaving the military, Anderson had gotten his airframe and powerplant license. He had been fixing Cessnas at a little airport in Texas before being lured away by the GDF's more lucrative pay scale.

"How's she looking, Chief?" Pounder asked.

"She's in top shape even with all the hours you put on her. I've pulled all the ordnance pins, and you're ready for flight. Just try to keep her in one piece, yeah?"

"Will do," Pounder said, pulling his restraints tight. Mansoor ordered them to start engines, and four Pratt & Witney Canada PT6A turboprop engines cranked to life.

Slowly, they taxied to the end of the runway, where the tower cleared them for a routine training flight amid the commercial air traffic. Their fifth plane remained on standby. Mansoor didn't want to take all his aircraft into battle when he might need one for backup. Pounder thought it was wise, but the plane's crew didn't. They were as hungry to get into the fight as the other pilots and navigators.

Once they were in the air, the four planes lined up on

Mansoor, who flew at the front of the V-shaped formation. Pounder took a last look at Camp Stephenson and thought about the base's history. During World War II, when the Americans established the Lend-Lease program, the British gave the U.S. authority to use its overseas territories as bases.

Guyana had become an integral part of the "Southern Air Route," with the Americans building Atkinson Field, now Cheddi Jagan International, on the east bank of the Demerara River. Camp Stephenson still contained some of the old buildings, with the former hospital complex currently serving as the GDF's headquarters. Pounder and the others occupied bungalows initially built for married couples, and the GDF troops lived in the old barracks buildings. The Americans had built the facility to be self-sufficient with a power station, water filtration plant, a swimming pool—the first built in the tiny nation—an ice-making plant, and a large vegetable and animal farm to feed the passing crews and the 44th Reconnaissance Squadron that flew recon missions to intercept hostile naval forces with B-17 Flying Fortresses and other lighter bombers.

Now, the base camp was at war again. This time, it was not to protect faraway lands but the sovereignty of Guyana.

Pounder glanced out the canopy at the carpet of green jungle interspersed with strips of ocher where the Guyanese had carved dirt roads and tiny farms out of the forest. Far to the west, low mountains rose to meet the Brazilian and Venezuelan borders. It was a beautiful landscape filled with rainforests, flat-topped mountains, and sweeping savannas.

The pilot closed his eyes, allowing the autopilot to fly the plane as his senses felt the aircraft for any vibration or abnormality. When he felt none, Pounder opened his eyes and scanned the instruments and then the skies ahead. He checked their time in-flight, then pulled out his Glock 19 and jacked a round into the chamber. If they got shot down, he wanted a fighting chance after ejecting. In the rear seat, Stitches did the same with her sidearm.

Mansoor led them across the fertile countryside and called out the time to target.

This is a milk run, Pounder told himself, trying to maintain his brash exterior. Inside, he was praying he didn't screw up. Pounder had flown crop dusters for years, priding himself on laying down the spray in just the right area and feeling his butthole pucker as he flew nap-of-the-earth. In bomb training, he'd had to learn to pickle off his rounds with even greater precision, and despite his limited practice, he'd discovered how to hit the bullseye.

It was time to test himself once again.

"Armed, hot, and ready," Stitches said into the intercom.

"You know what I like about you, Stitches?" Pounder asked.

"What's that Dumpster?"

"You haven't hit on me yet."

"Well, Colonel Romano back at the training squadron in Georgia said it best, and I quote, 'You're just one big fucking dumpster fire,' end quote."

"I appreciate that, Stitches. You're too kind."

"Just hit the target today, okay?"

"I've four missiles and plenty of lead," Pounder replied, reminding her of their loadout.

"Even a blind hog can find an acorn, Dumpster."

"Well, let's hope we get to root around in the slope," Pounder replied.

Mansoor's call over the radio broke their banter. "Separate for aerial combat."

Behind them, Steve "Hans" Gruber, the fifty-year-old, ex-Navy Tomcat fighter jock who had talked Pounder into joining the GDF mercenary squadron, and Roger "The Big Dog" Clifford, a lean bumpkin from West Virginia with a Cro-Magnon brow, separated toward the southwest.

All Pounder had to do was follow Mansoor's lead and protect the old man's six. He concentrated on staying in formation with Mansoor's plane as they crossed the Cuyuní River. Their original orders had been to remain in Guyana, if possible, but with the Venezuelans sending Hind helicopters toward Ankoko, Mansoor must have felt justified in breaking the rules.

Pounder listened to the radio traffic between Mansoor and the E-2 Hawkeye, vectoring them toward the flight of four Russian-made Mi-35 Hind helicopters. The Hinds had the shortest route to Ankoko and were already strafing the Special Forces squadron on the ground.

The pilot of the Hawkeye had one last piece of information for the Flying Jaguars. "Be advised there is a patrol boat on the river. It belongs to our team. Let's not have any friendly fire incidents."

The Super Tucanos were five minutes from Ankoko, and Pounder strained against his belts, tightening them one last time as he scanned the skies ahead.

"I've got tone lock," Stitches reported from the backseat.

Suddenly, Mansoor broke to the left and screamed, "Pull up!"

Instinctively, Pounder hauled back on the stick, and the A-29 went into a steep climb. Out of the corner of his eye, Pounder saw the flash of a missile as it passed by, and his thumb automatically hit the button to release chaff and flares to distract what he figured was a heat-seeking missile.

Pounder shoved the stick forward and saw a Hind hovering above the trees almost two miles out. The tone sounded in his ear to signal a missile lock, and he fired. The Piranha leaped off the pylon beneath the Super Tucano's wing. It streaked out and smacked the Hind in the cockpit before Pounder could even blink. The big attack helicopter seemed to buckle in mid-air, and then it exploded, raining debris down on the jungle.

"One down, motherfuckers, three to go," Pounder muttered to himself as he banked toward a Hind flying low over the runway on Ankoko, its Yakushev-Borzov machine gun spitting red tracers among the unseen 12.7mm rounds.

Instead of rippling off a second Piranha, Pounder flicked his switch to guns, arming the Dillon Aero Miniguns in the wing pods. He lined his sights up on the Hind and dove straight for it.

"Mansoor is on our wing," Stitches commented. "Light 'em up, Dumpster."

Pounder didn't bother to check over his shoulder. He concentrated on his sights and engaged his trigger. The Super Tucano shuddered as the miniguns spit a hail of lead into the Hind. The big helicopter pitched forward and slammed into the middle of the runway. Its rotor blades snapped off and whistled through the trees like giant scythes, mowing down everything in their paths.

Someone yelled over the radio, "Yeehaw! Jester's dead."

Pounder climbed with Mansoor still on his wing. He liked this down-and-dirty battle. It reminded him of crop dusting, swooping in on the target, and then getting out in a hurry. Mansoor might have been rated to fly all five types of aircraft in the GDF arsenal, but they weren't warplanes, and he was used to flying high and clean. He was glad Mansoor was on his hip and not the other way around.

Air Base Mobil One came over the radio. "Be advised, the patrol boat is being chased by a Hind. Anyone in the vicinity, please engage."

"Where they at Stitches?" Pounder asked, craning his neck to see the ground.

"We've got them!" Gruber called over the radio.

With two Hinds down, Pounder led Mansoor into a climb to gain a better view of the battlespace. Far below, he saw the patrol boat racing full speed down the brown river with a Hind on its tail. The gunner in the boat had swiveled the machine gun around to face aft and was firing bursts at the Hind, his rounds marked by green tracers. The bouncing of the boat made hitting the Hind nearly impossible, but the fire caused the Hind to swerve back and forth, keeping the Fanboys from hitting their target, too.

Tailing the first Hind was its buddy, flying a loose formation. Pounder thought about putting missiles into each of them, but he'd already downed two birds today. He'd let the other pilots have some fun.

He saw Gruber and Clifford come up behind the trailing Hind. Gruber downed it with bursts from his internal FN machine guns. The Hind that was firing on the patrol boat turned north, presumably to save his own skin. Naturally, Gruber and Clifford turned with it.

Out of the corner of his eye, Pounder saw something that made his blood run cold. Out of nowhere, another Hind had joined the fight, launching a missile at Gruber and Clifford.

"Where the hell did that son of a bitch come from?" Pounder muttered, hauling over the stick to turn this little plane as hard as he could. Over the radio, he called, "We've got another bandit inbound at our ten o'clock!"

"Missiles armed!" Stitches shouted. "I'm tracking him!"

The Hind's heat-seeking missile smacked Clifford's plane in the cockpit. The Super Tucano exploded in mid-air and fell smoking toward the earth.

"Get out of there, old man!" Pounder yelled at Gruber as the tone continued to sound in his ear, indicating his own heat-seeking missile had locked on.

The Hind had turned away from the fight below as Gruber had raced away from Clifford's wreckage.

A new warning sound buzzed in Pounder's ears as the Hind locked onto his plane.

"He's gonna hit us, Dumpster!" Stitches screamed.

"Fuck that," Pounder muttered, touching the trigger to launch his missile.

The Hind tried to bank away, but the heat-seeking Piranha struck the helicopter just aft of the exhaust port and shattered it into pieces.

"Nice one, kid," Gruber called over the air. "Two more, and you'll be an ace."

Pounder didn't respond. His hands shook from adrenaline and freight. He took a deep breath and strained against his safety belts, trying to push the fury and the hate from his body, but that motherfucker deserved everything he'd gotten for shooting down Roger Clifford. The Big Dog would bark no more.

Mansoor triggered his missile to kill the remaining attack helicopter, and five Venezuela Hinds lay dead on the jungle floor.

"An eye for an eye," Pounder whispered.

CHAPTER 4

CIA Headquarters
Washington, D.C.

John Phoenix rubbed his forehead in consternation, trying to keep his annoyance in check.

He sat in a windowless conference room with ten other Central Intelligence Agency (CIA) technical operatives, targeting analysts, and cyber geeks. Phoenix glanced over at his handler, Leslie Connelly, who had hoped to spearhead their upcoming operation in Mexico City. Sandy Delacroix, their boss at the Latin American Division, had relegated Connelly to second chair.

It seemed to Phoenix that there were too many fucking cooks in the kitchen.

Operation Unicorn had started as an assignment for him to try to turn the new Venezuelan Vice President, Evelyn Acevedo, into a CIA asset. In typical bureaucratic fashion, it had grown from an intimate group of four to this cluster fuck of a crowded conference room.

Standing, Phoenix went to the refreshment table, poured more coffee into a paper cup, and selected a glazed doughnut from the box before he returned to his seat. He glanced at Connelly again as he sat back down. She looked amazing in a black pantsuit with a royal purple blouse that offset her lustrous espresso skin, long black hair pulled into a low bun, and warm brown eyes. Her high-arched brows and full lips fit perfectly on her oval face.

Despite their differing career ambitions, Phoenix still carried a torch for her even though she had ended their brief affair with hopes of ascending to the Seventh Floor. Right then, Phoenix wished he was back in the field, recruiting another asset to help combat the spread of communism or end some brushfire war, instead of being stuck inside the Beltway and thinking lustful thoughts about his handler.

A hush fell over the room as the conference door opened, bringing Phoenix back to the present just in time to see Sandy Delacroix enter the room. Phoenix trusted Delacroix as much as he trusted anyone. He had first met her when she was station chief in Santiago, Chile, and he'd been running and gunning with Ground Branch. She'd pulled him out of paramilitary ops and brought him into the National Clandestine Service. He felt protective of her and would do almost anything she asked.

Delacroix was taller than average and in excellent shape for being almost fifty. She maintained a grueling fitness regime despite her long hours at the office. Her layered honey blonde hair was parted to the left and hung to her shoulders. She kept using the tip of her index finger to remove a lock from in front of her electric blue eyes. Some would call her a classic beauty with an oval face, thin pale lips, high cheekbones, and an aquiline nose. She had two teenage children, a photo of which she kept on her desk, and—in Phoenix's opinion—a rather *large* douchebag for a husband.

Phoenix had met Phillip, a high-ranking foreign service

officer at the State Department, when he and his Army Special Forces team had escorted the pompous ass through Afghanistan on a handshaking tour with some of the local warlords. After being ambushed by the Taliban, Phillip had literally shit his pants. Phoenix had never said anything to Delacroix, and he doubted Phillip had ever told her.

Delacroix trained her gaze first on Connelly and then on Phoenix. He gave her a half-hearted smile. The chief moved to the head of the table and smoothed the seat of her gray plaid midi sheath dress as she took her chair.

"I think we can start now," Delacroix said. "Leslie, I want you to run the show. This was your operation before anyone else got involved. Bring us up to speed and tell us what you plan to do going forward."

Connelly stood beside her boss and gave a PowerPoint presentation on what had happened thus far. On orders from the Director of the Central Intelligence Agency (D/CIA) Cole Stratten and blessed by President Randy Mercia, Phoenix had snuck into Venezuela with a brown leather satchel bearing two-hundred-fifty-thousand dollars U.S. He had hoped to create a bump—finding Acevedo in some public place and manufacturing a reason to talk to her. The bump would naturally lead to a second meeting where Phoenix had planned to convince Acevedo to help the CIA and use the money as a payoff to get things started. That had not been the case.

After becoming VP, Hector Calderón, the director of Venezuela's ruthless internal security apparatus, *Servicio Bolivariano de Inteligencia Nacional* (SEBIN), had surrounded Acevedo with agents to protect her. The SEBIN's constant presence had necessitated a change in tactics for Phoenix.

Eventually, he'd settled on breaking into Acevedo's apartment and planting the money in her desk drawer with a note asking her to contact her old CIA handler. While Acevedo had never been a trained ops officer, she had nevertheless advised the CIA on various developments in the countries where she'd worked as a medical doctor for Doctors Without Borders. Whether it was counting guns or providing economic information, her intelligence had always been direct and to the point. The CIA hoped she would return to the fold now that she was in a position of power in Venezuela, even if dictator Michel Zarate suppressed that power.

Phoenix had taken pictures of the staged money, believing he could use the photos as blackmail if Acevedo didn't cooperate. He'd sent the photos to Connelly via the Signal app to prove he had gotten into Acevedo's apartment and had a path forward.

Connelly displayed the photos on a screen behind her as she continued speaking to the crowded room.

Phoenix didn't need to listen to her brief. He could just replay the action in his mind.

After planting the money in her desk, Phoenix had retreated to an apartment he'd rented across the street. From there, he'd watched Acevedo through binoculars as she'd first discovered the cash and then called Hector Calderón, and the director arrived shortly after. The two had a brief discussion in the apartment before retreating to the roof of her building for a lengthier conversation. What the outcome of their talk had been, Phoenix didn't know.

Once Acevedo had called Calderón, Phoenix had known the game was over, and he'd fled the country, taking Coralina Blanco, a beautiful Venezuelan Special Forces soldier, who he'd turned into an agent-in-place on an earlier mission.

Blanco had provided him with plans for "Operation Takeback," Venezuela's strategy for war against its neighbor, Guyana. During their escape from Venezuela, Blanco had been shot to death by National Guard troops. He'd hated himself for leaving her to die in their bullet-riddled SUV as he ran for his life, but Phoenix had a job to do, and getting the plans back to Washington meant he could salvage something from his failed operation to recruit Acevedo. But back at

Headquarters, Phoenix learned Blanco had double-crossed him, swapping out the SD card in the spy pen she'd used to photograph Operation Takeback.

While Phoenix knew he should have been righteously angry at Blanco's misdeeds, he couldn't bring himself to hate her. Blanco had been the first woman to turn his head since Connelly had dumped him. And while the CIA frowned upon its case officers sleeping with their assets, Phoenix had tumbled into bed with her and made his life even more complicated.

"Bowie?" Connelly said, using Phoenix's codename.

He cleared his throat. "Yeah."

"Anything you would like to elaborate on about Unicorn?" she asked, using the codename assigned to the vice president. He could tell by the tone of her voice that she felt annoyed by his distance. She always seemed to be irritated over some minor infraction when it came to him. Phoenix liked to think it was because she still had the hots for him but would never admit it. At least, that's what his ego boasted.

"No, ma'am," Phoenix replied. "You covered it all."

It didn't mean anything if she had missed a few minor details. They had no way of knowing if Acevedo would even turn, yet they had a room full of people sitting on their hands, hoping she would.

Just before Connelly moved to the next slide in her presentation, Phoenix remembered a pertinent question. Connelly had told Phoenix that Acevedo had a handler at the agency, but she had never told him who it was. If he could pick their brain about the new VP, he might gain valuable insight into how to approach and handle her.

"Leslie, could you tell us who Unicorn's previous handler was?" Phoenix asked.

Delacroix leaned forward in her seat. "I was her handler, Bowie. We'll talk more about it later."

"Yes, ma'am." He leaned back in his chair and contemplated the meaning of Delacroix leading the team. At least she would be in Mexico City if he did land the whale of his career, but on the other hand, Delacroix's presence could also mean she planned to handle Acevedo herself. Either way, Phoenix would be happy. Having Delacroix take Acevedo off his plate meant he could do other things, like sneak back into Venezuela and learn the latest scuttlebutt about the GDF retaking Ankoko Island.

He checked his watch as Connelly got the briefing back underway. The team would fly to Mexico City and work with embassy officers already there. Phoenix would attempt to contact Acevedo again to get a definitive answer from her. The job of everyone on the task force hinged on Acevedo saying yes. If she said no, then they'd have wasted a lot of time, money, and effort for nothing, which, in Phoenix's opinion, was how things usually went.

The more he became embroiled in this clusterfuck of an operation, the more he thought about getting out of the agency and going back to Texas to be a hunting guide. But in his soul, he knew he wouldn't leave. He'd miss the action and the intrigue too much. If the CIA was a drug, then Phoenix was an addict. There was something thrilling about being in constant mortal danger as he walked darkened streets, running a surveillance detection route (SDR) on the way to meet an asset. Hunting white-tailed deer had been a thrill when he was a kid, but hunting man was a much better challenge for Phoenix now.

While Phoenix wanted to be in the field, targeting new assets, the reality of the situation was that the CIA was just a bunch of people in sensible shoes sitting in cubicles, reading reports. If that was where the powers that be would eventually pigeonhole him, then Phoenix was out. He'd take his ball and go home. With another glance around the room, he realized most of the people there would never run an asset or put themselves at risk. Yet, honestly, it was the asset who risked everything to gather information and bring it to the case officer. Their life was on the line while the case officer sat and waited for the contact.

Connelly finally wrapped up her briefing, and Phoenix allowed the room to clear so he could speak privately to Delacroix about Unicorn.

When only Delacroix, Connelly, and Phoenix remained, he moved closer to address the chief. "What can you tell me about Unicorn?"

"There will be plenty of time for that," Delacroix responded. "First, you need to take a polygraph." She held up her hands in defense. "Company policy. You know that."

Phoenix did. And he would go to the appointment.

"After the poly, I want you to see the shrink," Delacroix added. "Leslie will take the task force to Mexico City. You and I will fly down after you've made the rounds. We'll have a chance to talk on the plane."

Phoenix's eyebrows rose.

"You suffered the death of an asset, Bowie," his boss added. "We can all use someone to talk to after that happens. And it's not a request. It's an order."

CHAPTER 5

Seeing a shrink made most people nervous.

Sitting on the couch across from Tom Lester, Phoenix knew whatever he said would end up on Delacroix's desk. Nothing was confidential in the CIA. Lester smiled broadly and tried to reassure Phoenix that he was in good company. Phoenix knew the man rarely left his office and wouldn't know how to run an asset or hit a bullseye if his life depended on it, but those things weren't part of his job description. Lester's job was to probe deep into the minds of CIA employees and evaluate their readiness for duty.

Phoenix had gotten used to seeing shrinks a long time ago. He'd seen more than his fair share.

After his parents had been killed by a drunk driver, Child Protective Services had sent Phoenix to talk to Bernard Winston. Phoenix had been fifteen at the time. He could still visualize their first meeting. The old guy had leaned back in his chair as he'd lit a cigarette. After smoothing down his wisps of thinning gray hair, the psychiatrist had puffed away in silence. Phoenix recalled staring out the window at the leafy green trees beyond, wishing he could escape.

The wrinkly old man had finished his cigarette in silence, then stubbed it out in an ashtray. Winston slowly leaned forward with a creak of chair springs and placed his forearms on the desk. He'd let out a weary sigh and said, "I'm not going to lie to you, son. Losing parents at an early age can affect a man. I say man, because you are one. Whatever you want to tell me will stay here between us. Yes, I have to report to CPS about your mental health, but not about the specifics of our discussions. That's called doctor-patient confidentiality. I'm bound by the law to adhere to it. And I can see you're chewin' on something. Take your time and get it right in your mind so you can put it into words, and if you can't, well, that's okay, too. I'm here for you, son, whenever you're ready."

He'd leaned back in the chair and lit another cigarette. On the night Phoenix's parents had died, he'd been on a hunting trip. Young Phoenix had gotten home just in time to see the sheriff's deputy arrive and knock on the front door. Not wanting to get jammed up with the law, Phoenix had hidden in the woods. After the deputy had driven off, Phoenix had gone into the house. When his parents didn't come home, he'd made some calls and learned the truth. He stayed in the woods for months, skipping school, living off the land, and grieving the loss of his parents in his own way, but he was still angry.

Come to think of it, he still had a beef with the cops for not finding the low-life son of a bitch that had destroyed his happy childhood. Phoenix had strong memories of his father. They'd spent plenty of time together in the bush as he'd learned his father's trade—being a hunting and fishing guide. Memories of his mother were more fleeting. Some days, he couldn't remember her face, but she'd been a beautiful woman, full of life and love.

Hank Phoenix had found Marisol in the desert, badly

dehydrated and malnourished, left for dead by the coyote who'd trafficked her up from Colombia. After taking her home, Hank had nursed Marisol back to health. She had rewarded him with her undying love and gratitude, giving birth to a healthy baby boy. Phoenix had gotten his permanently tanned skin, black hair, and brown eyes from her. From his father, who was part Comanche, he'd gotten a warrior's spirit and the ability to hunt and track game. His parents had both been gregarious and easygoing, so Phoenix had learned early not to let things bother him. He knew how to roll with the punches, but he could punch right back when he needed to.

When Phoenix finally opened up to the old shrink back in Texas, it was like a dam bursting. He'd poured out his heart and soul because no one else would listen. During their sessions together, Phoenix had come to think of Winston as a father figure, but it wasn't enough to keep Phoenix's anger in check or to avoid the law.

"What do you want to talk about today, Bowie?" Lester asked.

"You ever think about the value of a T-Rex?" Phoenix asked.

"New or used? Those trucks are pretty expensive," Lester replied wistfully.

"You a truck guy, Tom? I figured you'd drive a minivan."

"You're not wrong, but I've got kids."

"They make trucks with four doors now, but they're not as fuel efficient, which brings me back to the T-Rex." Phoenix pulled his arms tight to his body and let his hands hang like claws. "You know. Big teeth. Short arms."

Lester chuckled. "I can't say I've ever thought about what one costs. What do you think they do?"

"Let's say you're a caveman, right?" Phoenix said. "You manage to slay the mighty beast, and you've got food for maybe four or five days at the most. That's not the whole carcass. It's just what they can eat. Family of four, maybe have some friends over for a barbeque—who knows? The point is that cavemen can't refrigerate the meat. They don't smoke it, or turn it into jerky, or have any other way to preserve it, so the T-Rex just rots away in the jungle. Relative value of the T-Rex to the caveman is three or four days of food—unless he gets sick of the leftovers."

Lester chuckled again.

"That same T-Rex turns into a pile of sunbaked bones, and a century or two later, some guy with a whip and a fedora comes along and finds the skeleton buried in the ground. That guy spends an entire year digging out the bones, dusting them off, and gluing them back together so they can be displayed in a museum. To the archaeologist, the value of that T-Rex is probably the salary he's being paid by some university in the Midwest. Hundred twenty K before taxes, if he's lucky."

Lester nodded intently, but Phoenix could see he needed to pull his thoughts together.

"Now, take that T-Rex's brother and a half dozen of his friends, bury them way down, turn them into black goo, and let some guy named Rockefeller come along and pump them out of the ground. Relative value of the T-Rex—billions."

"Is there a point to this diatribe, Bowie, or are you just ranting to avoid talking to me about what happened in Venezuela?"

"That T-Rex is why I was in Venezuela, Tom. Do you think the U.S. would care about Venezuela if it wasn't for those dinosaurs? Case in point: Cuba. What's Cuba got to offer us—tropical beaches and sugar cane? We can get those on any Caribbean Island. Castro kills his own people … Who cares, right? But if Cuba had oil, you could bet your sweet ass we'd have knocked Castro flat to get to it, or at least capitulated to him like we do with every other tin horn dictator with a barrel of oil to sell. The relative value of the T-Rex to Cuba is zero."

"Tell me about her," Lester prompted, changing the politically charged subject.

"Who?"

"The woman you recruited in Venezuela, Cobra. Tell me about your decision to leave her as an agent in place when you could have brought her out with you the first time."

"Bad call," Phoenix replied flatly.

"Would you bring her out if you had to do it over again?" the psychiatrist asked.

"This isn't a game of second guesses, Doc. I can't change what I did. Do I regret it? Maybe. But I thought she could get us information. It didn't pan out. I'm not happy she's dead, if that's what you're asking. I liked her, and I will freely admit that I made the mistake of sleeping with her, but damn, Doc … You should have seen her. You'd have slept with her, too."

"You were attracted to her?"

"I wasn't pulling a raven." Phoenix knew Lester understood the language of the agency and that a raven was a male agent employed to seduce people to gather intelligence.

"I wasn't suggesting it," Lester replied. "I'm asking if you felt romantically inclined toward her. She's the first woman you've mentioned since we spoke about Leslie."

Phoenix rolled his shoulders. The knot in his muscles between his shoulder blade and spine had loosened since he'd been in D.C. He'd seen a masseuse, an acupuncturist, and a chiropractor. As Lester drilled him, the tension knot tightened. If he harbored resentment in the knot, then he resented the line of questioning. He resented Blanco for lying to him and for dying on him. He resented Connelly for foisting Operation Unicorn on him.

And he resented himself for being the cause of his current

career path. After eluding the cops and CPS for months, Phoenix had found an old family friend on his doorstep. Paul Schaffer had spoken to CPS, and they had agreed to allow Phoenix to move in with the Schaffers instead of being placed in the foster care system. It was a bad move for everyone.

Adrift in a sea of pain and loneliness, Phoenix started having sex with Angela, the Shaffers' youngest daughter. Angela, trying to cope with her own demons, joined some friends for a night of partying and underage drinking in Abilene to celebrate their high school graduation, but the night had taken a wrong turn, and she'd called Phoenix for help.

When Phoenix had finally found her in a college frat house, Angela was semi-conscious and half-naked, being humped by some pencil dick with his pants around his ankles. Phoenix had beaten him mercilessly and, in the process, knocked over a candle someone had lit to diffuse the stench of marijuana smoke. The candle flame had licked the curtains and set them ablaze.

Phoenix stopped beating the frat asshole, pulled Angela's jeans back up, and carried her out of the house. It didn't take the cops long to track the license plate on the car Phoenix had been driving or to arrest him for arson. After much stalling on his part, the court-appointed attorney had turned to Bernard Winston for help. Winston had coaxed the story from Phoenix. The attorney had gone to the judge and asked for leniency. The judge had offered John Phoenix a way out. He could go to jail, or he could join the Army. Phoenix had signed his Army indoc papers in handcuffs.

Maybe he resented the judge for not letting him take the cuffs off his wrists, and Angela for putting herself in that situation, and the Shaffers for never speaking to him again. Fine Christian folks, they turned out to be.

But the only person Phoenix had to blame was himself. Winston had taught him to accept responsibility for his actions. Not only was sitting down with an agency shrink cathartic for him, but the agency demanded to know everyone's secrets. It was like being in a cult. Phoenix, however, would never admit that he enjoyed talking to a shrink. He had a reputation to maintain as a tough guy. And if Connelly walked into the room right then, handed him a gun, and told him to kill Tom Lester because Lester was a traitor, then Phoenix would put a bullet between the bastard's eyes.

Does that make me a patriot or a ruthless assassin?

When Phoenix, lost in the swirl of his past drama, didn't elaborate on his relationship with Blanco or Connelly, Lester asked, "So, Cobra was beautiful. What else attracted you to her?"

"She was smart, strong, capable. She was everything we look for in a case officer or an asset."

"Dig deep, Bowie. Tell me what was so special about her that you ignored your training."

Phoenix shrugged. "I liked her. She made me feel something for the first time in a long time. And she wanted to be with me, or at least I thought she did. After replaying everything, maybe she was just a 'swallow.' You know, the opposite of a raven. Maybe she was working me. I just don't know." He shrugged again. "I never will."

"Why do you think she might have been a swallow?"

"Her behavior at times. There is nothing I can pinpoint other than that I came up empty-handed regarding the information she supposedly gathered for me." He didn't think Lester had been read in on Unicorn and didn't want to divulge sensitive information to the shrink, so he didn't elaborate on the fact that he'd sent Cobra to photograph the plans for Venezuela's Operation Takeback.

"You think she acted as a double agent?" Lester asked.

Phoenix shrugged. "You gonna put all this in a report to Sandy?"

"Contrary to what you knuckle draggers think, Bowie, I'm

not the Gestapo," Lester replied with a condescending smile that told Phoenix they had covered all this ground before. "You know exactly what my job entails. We have a confidentiality agreement."

Phoenix liked that about Lester. He gave as good as he got and pulled no punches when it came to his assessment. He smiled to let Lester know he thought he was full of bullshit but said, "Good. I was hoping you would say that."

"Do you take Cobra's death personally?" Lester probed.

"I take the death of my assets very personally, *Tom*. I am solely responsible for sending them into harm's way. I recruit them. I handle them. I become friends with them."

In many cases, Phoenix had spent long hours with his assets and gotten to know their intimate hopes and dreams. Building a rapport with a targeted asset wasn't always easy. Still, a well-rounded case officer often found it easier to connect with someone over shared hobbies or interests, instantly turning from a stranger to a peer. The CIA called it: "You, Me, Same Same."

Over his years in Army Special Forces and then as a CIA officer, Phoenix had participated in just about every extreme action sport available, took driving lessons to race cars and motorcycles, studied at a culinary institute, shadowed a sommelier to learn wines and whiskeys, practiced his language skills, and keyed in on whatever passions a possible asset might have to leverage during his recruitment of them. If he needed to learn a new skill, he would. It was all about building a network of assets and gathering human intelligence (HUMIT) to send back to Headquarters.

Whether anyone actually read the laborious reports he typed and forwarded was another story altogether. Since he was a part of the Directorate of Operations and the Directorate of Intelligence collated the reports for dissemination, he didn't know if anything ever came from some of his clandestine cables.

Lester cleared his throat to bring his patient back to the present. Phoenix stared at his hands and once again thought of quitting the agency. He wondered if he could find peace in the wilderness or if trouble would find him like it had his entire life.

"What's bothering you, Bowie? I can see it on your face, and your body language is throwing off all sorts of strange vibes."

"I'm worried about an upcoming op."

"Life is full of unknowns, Bowie. You're more aware of that than most. I suggest you keep your head down and not embroil yourself romantically with any more of your assets."

"That's not going to be a problem, Doc. I'll be well-supervised during this shit show."

"Why do you think it will go so poorly for you?"

"My gut says it's a waste of time."

"I would tell you to follow that instinct, but I also know you have to follow orders."

Phoenix nodded.

"You still thinking about quitting the agency?"

"Every damn day, Doc. But you and I both know I won't. I'm an addict."

"Anyone can break an addiction, Bowie. You just have to figure out what you want to do next."

Phoenix let out a sigh and adjusted himself in the chair. "Right now, I want to go back to South America and do my job. Maybe I'll figure something out between now and then."

Lester checked his watch. "Our time is about up for the day, Bowie. Anything else you want to discuss?"

"How many dinosaurs do you think roamed the earth before the asteroid killed them all? We've been pumping oil out of the ground for over one hundred fifty years. That's a *lot* of dinosaurs, right?"

"Oil is made from more than dinosaurs. Mostly, its decayed plant life turned to goo."

At the door, Bowie paused. He glanced over his shoulder. "My gut says you should buy the truck."

Outside the shrink's office, Phoenix rolled his right shoulder to try to loosen the knot behind it. His gut told him Mexico City was a dead end, but he'd already set events in motion, and he had to follow through.

CHAPTER 6

Oval Office
Washington, D.C.

President Randy Mercia paced across the presidential seal woven into the blue carpet of his office. As the supposed leader of the free world, he felt hemmed in on all sides.

He had only a few moments of privacy to collect his thoughts before meeting with his national security staff to discuss the ongoing hostilities between Guyana and Venezuela. He assumed they would also talk about their support for the war in Ukraine and the actions Israel had initiated against Hamas.

As Mercia continued to wear a circuit in the carpet, he ran his hands over his face and tried to come up with a plan. As if he were straight out of central casting, women often described Mercia as tall, dark, and handsome with his chestnut brown hair and sea-blue eyes. He was the son of Charlie Mercia, a wealthy oilman from Oklahoma. But Mercia had turned down a job at his father's company for politics.

Despite his choice of career path, Mercia often leaned on Charlie when he needed to know about the geopolitics of oil and frequently heeded his advice on domestic and foreign matters concerning oil production. Mercia had made Oklahoma energy independent despite his presidential predecessor's copious attempts to stop energy production in America, and he had dreams of making America energy independent again.

From the onset of his announcement to run for the presidency, Mercia hadn't had much support, but during a Republican debate, one of his fellow candidates had made a slip of the tongue and called him Randy 'Merica. The nickname had become a rallying cry for Mercia's campaign, and donations, including special interest funds, had poured in. Mercia had wanted to become president so badly that he could taste it, and while he'd prided himself on being an incorruptible straight arrow who tried to do what was best for his constituents, he had made the mistake of "lying down with the pigs" as his daddy had put it.

His old man had also told him that any man who ran for president had to be out of their mind. Charlie had pointed to photographic evidence of how men had aged rapidly behind the Resolute desk. He'd also told Randy that he'd be on the hook for every dollar his campaign spent. *Oh, how right you were, Pops.*

The first thing Mercia's shadow donors had done was saddle Mercia with his chief of staff, Carlton Choi, a fourth-generation Korean American who had grown up in the liberal incubator of San Francisco and was a dyed-in-the-wool socialist. To Mercia, his choice of Choi signaled to the American people that he was an outright liar after he'd promised to combat liberalism on the campaign trail. Choi was there to keep Mercia in check. Mercia hadn't been the shadow money's handpicked candidate from the start. The American people had forced them to endorse Mercia simply because he'd ridden the patriotic wave to popularity over their candidate. Mercia, who could play the redneck rube to perfection, now ended his speeches and press conferences by shouting, "'Merica!" as a fuck you to his masters.

When Choi had learned that Mercia had green-lit a clandestine operation for the CIA to try to turn Venezuelan Vice President Evelyn Acevedo into an asset, he'd gone ballistic, screaming that they were to maintain the status quo. Mercia wasn't to do anything to rock the boat. He was simply a placeholder until the special interest money could put in their candidate of choice during the next election cycle.

"Fuck those guys," Mercia muttered to himself as he continued to pace. "Randy 'Merica is President."

He had his own idea of how to deal with Venezuela, and it was completely different from how America had handled anything since the end of World War II. The United States needed a win, and it was time to stop pussyfooting around. And it was for that reason he'd excluded Choi from the meetings he'd had on the growing South American conflict.

A knock on the door interrupted his thoughts. Spinning, he found Tabitha Crowley at the door. She had knotted her dirty blonde hair into a French braid, and the overhead lights glinted off the lenses of her black-framed glasses. "Sir, Asbury and Stratten are here."

"Send them in," Mercia said to his executive assistant.

Petite and pretty, Tabby was one of the few staffers Mercia had been allowed to bring with him from Oklahoma. The rest had come from the Council on Foreign Relations (CFR), megabanks, and lawyers from major D.C. firms.

The CFR billed itself as a foreign policy think tank composed of academics, businessmen, and politicians, and many of their "views" or "opinions" often shaped U.S. actions overseas. Established in June 1921 by J.P. Morgan and John D. Rockefeller, the council's legacy often lent itself to conspiracy theories. The theorists liked to claim that the

CFR's true objective was to consolidate economic power into the hands of the elite global banking system. They frequently referred to the CFR as an "invisible government" with the ultimate goal of creating a one-world socialist system.

Interestingly enough, Mercia had received a lot of pressure to appoint CFR members to his cabinet, including his Secretary of State, Mike Asbury, an elder statesman who had devoted his life to international diplomacy. At sixty-five, Asbury still had a full head of salt-and-pepper hair above his rectangular face, and the CFR's international policy magazine, *Foreign Affairs,* had frequently featured his op-eds. As the head of State, Asbury now had the dubious pleasure of trying to implement the policies he'd boasted so much about.

But the world was turning to shit in a handbag, and Mercia had decided enough was enough.

Cole Stratten strode in behind his colleague, a distinguished-looking gentleman in his fifties with a hint of gray at the temples of his black hair. He and Mercia had been friends for years. Mercia had appointed Stratten as D/CIA because Stratten had once been a case officer before joining a more financially lucrative private defense consulting company.

Following on the heels of the two men was another CFR representative, Maggie Green, a chunky woman of average height with curly red hair and green eyes. The Michigan native had earned the position of National Security Advisor after serving as an FBI agent and an assistant secretary at the Department of Homeland Security. Green had a reputation for being a no-nonsense power broker. She frequently gave honest pushback on some of Mercia's or the State Department's national security recommendations, but Mercia was still wary of her.

The fourth person to enter the Oval Office was Rex Scott, the Secretary of Defense. Of Germanic descent, Scott carried his tall, lean frame with rigid military pride. He was one of only a handful of generals to head the Department of Defense

(DOD). After his retirement, Scott had served as a consultant for Lockheed Martin and acted as a talking head on the various cable news programs before landing a starring role in Mercia's cabinet. Bald as a newborn baby, he accented his chrome dome with a thin mustache under his bulbous nose and warm gray eyes. Scott wasn't considered a hawk, but he was a huge advocate for rebuilding and reshaping the military into a modern fighting force to combat growing threats from China and other foreign terrorists.

Once the four advisors had taken seats around the central coffee table, Tabby delivered a Red Bull for Stratten and coffee for Asbury, Green, and Scott, and then she disappeared out the door as the meeting got underway.

"What's the latest news?" Mercia asked.

Green was the first to speak after exchanging glances with the other three. It was her job to have a handle on all national security issues and act as a go-between with the various agencies. "Guyana initiated a raid on Ankoko Island and recaptured it. They killed all the Venezuelan soldiers and some Russian advisors who joined the firefight. Venezuela then launched a counter-offensive with a fleet of Hind attack helicopters. Guyana's Flying Jaguars shot down all five with only one lost plane on their side."

"Remind me who the Flying Jaguars are again," Mercia said.

"They're Guyana's mercenary squadron composed of foreign pilots flying A-29 Super Tucanos," Scott explained. "We trained, and are still training them, at Moody Air Force Base."

Mercia remembered the briefing he'd received from Stratten and Leslie Connelly on the Flying Jaguars and that he had authorized the training in Georgia, wanting to do whatever he could to aid Guyana in its struggle against the bully to their west.

"I thought they'd agreed to halt all hostilities until we

could sit down in Mexico City. What happened to that?" Mercia asked.

Asbury fielded this question. "They did agree to those terms, but then Zarate decided he wanted to strike a retaliatory blow for the sinking of the PC-21 *Guaiqueri,* so he sent Su-30 Flankers to bomb a training base in Guyana."

"Then Guyana sent their 31 Special Forces Squadron to retake Ankoko," Stratten clarified.

"I don't think talks will work," Mercia stated. "Zarate is beating the war drum with that referendum vote to retake the Essequibo."

"It's a bullshit vote," Stratten said. "Zarate is trying to distract the people from the fact that he's doing a shit job of running the country. It's just a way to rally nationalistic sentiment and provide a barometer for Zarate to gauge voter turnout. I think he's looking for a way to suspend the election and stay in power."

"The International Court of Justice has asked Venezuela to refrain from escalating tensions," Asbury added. "But we still need to give the peace talks a shot."

"What are you going to talk about?" Mercia asked, finally sitting down on the couch across from his advisors. "The way I see it, is that no matter what they agree to in Mexico City, there will always be tension between the two countries. If Venezuela refuses to acknowledge that the Essequibo Region is part of Guyana, there will never be peace. Whatever you guys hammer out, it has to be based on Guyana retaining the Essequibo."

"And if Zarate refuses?" Green asked.

"Then we back Guyana to the hilt," Mercia replied, and Rex Scott nodded.

Asbury cleared his throat in disapproval.

"What, Mike? What policy are you pushing today from the CFR?"

"Peaceful resolution."

"And how do we do that?" Scott asked in disgust. "Last time you clowns negotiated with Zarate, you gave him a license to print money by allowing Chevron to step up oil production. And you failed to get any concessions from him. Do you really think he will come to the table in any position other than one of strength? Let's face it, you guys blinked, and he laughed all the way to the bank." Scott cupped his hand to his ear. "In fact, I can still hear him laughing."

"That was the previous administration, Rex," Asbury replied dryly. "I *was not* the Secretary of State."

"No, you weren't," Scott scoffed, "but your buddy from the CFR was, and I think you guys would lick Zarate's asshole just to be cozy with him."

"Don't be so crude, Rex," Stratten said. "There's a lady present."

Scott chuckled. "Like you haven't heard her cuss a blue streak. All those DHS guys think they can cuss like sailors because the Coast Guard falls under their umbrella."

"Fuck you, Rex," Green said, leaning forward to give him a joking smile.

"Thank you for making my point, Maggie, but the reality of the situation is that the president is right. There won't be peace in the Essequibo until Venezuela recognizes the border on the Cuyuní River."

CHAPTER 7

"I NEED TO CATCH MY FLIGHT TO MEXICO CITY," ASBURY SAID after checking his Breitling Navitimer.

The presidential advisory group had spent the last thirty minutes speaking about various issues concerning national security, always circling back to the Essequibo Region.

Asbury had a private jet on standby to take him to the summit between Guyana and Venezuela, with officials from Turkey, Switzerland, and the U.S. as referees. China and Brazil had also agreed to send representatives since China had major financial stakes in both countries, and Brazil shared a common border with them. As Guyana and Venezuela continued to strike at each other, Brazil had reinforced its border with a surge of armored vehicles and troops.

A representative from the Regional Security Service—a mutual cooperative of Caribbean countries committed to island defense and combating drug smuggling and human trafficking—as well as a delegate from the Organization of American States—a multilateral, regional body focused on human rights, electoral oversight, social and economic development, and security in the Western Hemisphere—had agreed to attend the conference to voice their concerns about the humanitarian and economic crises in Venezuela and how a war would aggravate them.

Asbury stood and buttoned his suit coat. "I understand your desire to rush headlong into this brushfire," he said to President Mercia. "War, however, can make or break you. I don't want you to do anything until after the conference, understand?"

Mercia nodded. The masters from the CFR had spoken.

As the others stood, Mercia motioned for Stratten to stay behind.

Once the Oval Office had cleared, Stratten moved closer to the president. "What is it, Randy?"

The two men were old friends, and Stratten didn't bother with the honorific title.

"How's the mole hunt going?" Mercia asked.

"We've had to prioritize the conference so we can run Operation Unicorn, but I still have Connelly working on it."

"What's the point if … what did you call the mole before?"

"Dragonfly?" Stratten said.

"What's the point of Operation Unicorn if Dragonfly has access to CIA information?" Mercia asked. "He'll know Acevedo is your asset."

"We'll just have to take that chance," Stratten replied. "But what's the deal with busting Asbury's ass? You sound like you're ready to send troops down there."

Mercia rubbed his chin thoughtfully as he considered his answer. "I'd love to, but we'll see how things go in Mexico City."

"I have to stay in Washington, but I'll monitor things down there and keep you apprised on the talks and Operation Unicorn," Stratten said.

"Thank you, Cole. Come over tomorrow night. I'll get the chef to whip us up some barbeque, and we'll drink a few beers like the old days."

"I'd love that, Randy. I'll see you around seven."

"Better make it eight," Mercia said. "I'm sure they'll find something for me to do around here."

Stratten chuckled. "Call me when you're free, and I'll come over."

The two men shook hands, and Stratten headed for the door.

"Send Tabby in here, would you, Cole," Mercia called after him.

Stratten called for Tabby to enter the Oval Office as he walked out. Calton Choi followed Tabby into the room.

Mercia felt annoyed at the sight of Choi but spoke calmly to his EO. "Tabby, see if you can catch General Scott before he leaves the building. I want to speak to him privately."

"Yes, sir," she said, ducking out of the office.

"Mister President, I need to be at these meetings. You can't keep shutting me out," Choi chided after Tabby had closed the office door.

Mercia snorted. "Asbury was here. He'll make a full report to the CFR. And I'm sure you listened in on our conversation through the audio recorder in your office, so what is it that you need?"

"I *need* to be in your meetings," Choi pleaded. "I'm your chief of staff, for crying out loud."

"It sounds like you are crying," Mercia muttered.

Choi continued unabated, an edge of hostility in his voice. "As the man who is *supposed* to be your closest advisor, I should be privy at all your meetings and agendas."

"You and I both know you would never be my chief of staff if it wasn't for the money I took to run my campaign."

The chief of staff smirked. "Then you understand the reality of the situation, so stop fighting it."

"Okay, tough guy," Mercia said. "What's the council's action plan? How does this skirmish fit into their plan for global domination?"

Choi slid his hands into his pockets and stared at the floor momentarily. In a more civilized tone, he said, "You know I'm not privy to that information, sir. I'm only here to advise you on policy."

"Then advise me, Carlton. What are you going to tell the Guyanese about the Essequibo Region? Should they give it up like Ukraine gave up Crimea, or should they fight?"

"Neither, sir. Diplomatic relations are the way forward."

"Do you remember when I first asked you about this dispute?" Mercia said. "You told me the two countries have been fighting over this region for over two hundred years. How many times have they been to court in all those years?"

"A dozen or so," Choi replied with a shrug.

"The other tool in the box is sanctions, right?" Mercia asked.

Choi nodded.

"How can we sanction Venezuela any further than we already have?" Mercia asked.

"I'm not sure, but I would also sanction Guyana," Choi replied.

"And what would be the purpose of that?" Mercia asked incredulously. "Venezuela was the aggressor. If your logic holds true, then we should sanction Ukraine and Israel."

Before Choi could respond, Tabby opened the door and said, "I have General Scott for you, sir."

"Thank you, Tabby. Show him in. Oh, and have Agent Starling step in here, please."

Seconds later, the retired general entered, followed by the Secret Service agent. Tabby started to close the door, but Mercia stopped her by saying, "Tabby, come in here and leave the door open. Agent Starling, please escort Carlton Choi off the premises. He is no longer my chief of staff."

"What are you saying?" Choi asked in confusion.

Mercia smiled mirthlessly. "In the infamous words of one of my predecessors, *'You're fired.'* Agent Starling will help pack your personnel items and escort you out of the building. Starling, you will revoke Mister Choi's credentials and put him on a list to never be allowed inside the White House again unless it's with a fucking tour group."

"But Mister President …" Choi tried to object.

"Get out, Choi," Mercia growled.

Agent Starling, a beefy ex-cop from Des Moines, hooked Choi under the arm and said, "Let's go, son. The president just gave you an order."

Starling marched the former chief of staff out of the room, and it seemed as if both Tabby and General Scott breathed a sigh of relief at the confrontation ending.

"I'm sorry about that," Mercia said. "I can't stand that fucking guy." Pausing to put his hands on Tabby's shoulders, he said, "Tabby, you've been with me from the start of my career, and you've been invaluable to me. How would you like to be my new chief of staff?"

Tabby's eyebrows shot up in surprise, and her green eyes widened in delight. "Thank you, sir. I would be honored."

"Good. After all these years of service, I think you deserve it. You can have Carlton's office as soon as he's out of the building. Now, General …" Mercia turned to face Scott and rubbed his chin as he appraised the man.

Scott tried to beat him to the punch. "You can have my resignation, sir. I never liked the direction you were taking the country, anyway."

Mercia shook his head. "No. I won't accept your resignation, Rex. We're going in a new direction. That's why I asked you to come back."

The head of the DOD straightened as if pleased to be back in the game. "I'm listening, sir."

"Before I get into this, Tabby, get Stratten on the phone."

Tabby called the D/CIA and put Mercia on the line. "Cole. Who are you sending to Mexico City? That guy, Bowie, right?"

"Yes, sir. And Sandy Delacroix. She's the chief on the Latin America desk."

"Have they left D.C. yet?" Mercia asked.

"Uh … I'm not sure, sir," Stratten replied. "I think they have a flight today."

"Can you catch them and send them to my office?" the president asked.

"I'd do my best, sir," Stratten said. "Let me call Sandy while I have you on the line. Is that all right?"

Mercia gave his acceptance, and Stratten phoned Delacroix. Mercia overheard the conversation, and when Stratten came back on the line, he told Mercia that the two case officers would be at the Oval Office within thirty minutes. The president could tell by Scott's cocked eyebrow that the general would dearly love to know why two spooks needed to join the conversation, but he never asked.

While Mercia, General Scott, and Tabby Crowley waited for the two case officers to arrive, they discussed rebuilding the military and what legislation they needed to push in Congress to get their military and energy agendas through. Crowley figured most Republicans would favor the legislation, and they would need to build a coalition of moderate Democrats to help pass the appropriations.

Once Delacroix and Bowie arrived at the Oval Office, Agent Starling showed them in.

"Please sit," Mercia ordered, gesturing to the sofa where Scott was already waiting. As the two settled in, the president asked, "What has been the foundation of American foreign policy for the last century?"

Scott reached for the coffee cup that was still sitting on the table, but it was empty. Out of habit, Tabby stepped to the urn on a silver cart and poured a fresh cup for all of them. Even she could tell this was a turning point and that they needed a strong dose of caffeine for what lay ahead.

"Well, Randy … Can I call you Randy?" Scott asked. "Since I feel like we're just spitballing here."

"Sure, Rex. I'm a good old boy from Oklahoma. We don't always stand on formality. That goes for you as well," he said to Bowie and Delacroix. He could tell the male case officer was highly uncomfortable in the setting, even though he'd been to the Oval Office once before. Mercia needed them to be as relaxed as possible so they would be receptive to his plan.

Scott chuckled. "Just don't shout 'Merica! at the end of your speech."

Mercia chuckled. "I promise you that you'll be shouting it once I'm done telling you the plan, but back to my question on foreign policy. What do you think the foundation of U.S. foreign policy has been over the last several decades?"

"I always felt it was a carrot and stick approach," Scott replied vaguely as if he didn't understand the president's question.

Neither Bowie nor Delacroix responded.

"Let me enlighten you as to what I've learned doing a little research on my own," Mercia said. "The U.S. has used three basic tools—isolationism, sanctions, and war. All three bring pain and suffering to the citizens of our target countries and to our own. Those policies also produce hatred and distrust of the U.S., as evidenced by the radical terrorists who believe we are the 'Great Satan' for our lack of caring, our abusive policies, and our outright underhanded manipulation of situations, governments, and currencies."

Scott nodded as if he understood. Bowie remained stoic, although he seemed to be trying to relieve an ache in his shoulder by subtly rolling it about.

"Are you all right, Bowie?" Mercia asked, wondering if he'd been wounded during his latest incursion into Venezuela.

"Yes, sir," Bowie grunted. "Just an old injury acting up. Continue with what you were saying. I'm deeply interested."

"As am I, sir," Delacroix added.

"You're a proponent of change, right, General?" Mercia asked.

"Meaningful change, sir. Yes," Scott replied.

Mercia nodded. He stood to pace the floor, doing his thinking on his feet. "I want to propose a change of course, but first, we'll have to be drawn into a war that I really don't want any part of. By my own admission, we need to back Guyana with the military might of the U.S. government." He glanced at his audience to gauge their reaction but saw their faces remained blank.

"In other words," Mercia continued, "I want to send troops to effect regime change in Venezuela. I know what I said earlier about foreign policy, but Zarate isn't going to deal with us, and he only cares about remaining in power and reacquiring the Essequibo Region. This is where I'll deviate from the traditional way we've always done things.

"In the last two wars that we've fought—namely Iraq and Afghanistan—we missed vital opportunities to benefit both the people of those countries and the U.S. By that, I mean, we could have worked to improve infrastructure, manufacturing, mining, drilling, and a lot of other jobs that would have taken rifles out of our enemies hands and exchanged them for paychecks.

"Venezuela is the perfect incubator to try this new method. Think of all the cheap oil we could fill our pumps with. We can eliminate their humanitarian crisis and become their number-one trading partner.

"This will have a couple of benefits. One: it will strengthen Venezuela through expanded economic growth beyond dependency on oil sales. Two: it will bring cheap oil to the U.S. from both Guyana and Venezuela, and three: we kick China in the nuts and start taking back the Western Hemisphere."

"If you can remove Zarate and provide fair and open elections, I think the Venezuelan people will be very receptive," Bowie said. "They're desperate for change. All we need to do is light the powder keg. But I need to caution you, sir. Your approach will not right the ship overnight. There is *a lot* of criminal activity in Venezuela, everything from corrupt military officers to roving gangs of *colectivos*. Getting those guys to surrender their power will be tough sledding."

"I agree with Bowie," Delacroix said. "Zarate is the tip of the iceberg."

"Recommendations?" Mercia said.

"Put a gun store on every corner and legalize firearms," Bowie said. "Give the Venezuelans a fighting chance. We know that the 2A protects the rest of our Constitution. Take away our guns, and we'll be in the same boat that Venezuela is in now."

"General?" Mercia asked.

"I agree with … Bowie, is it?" Scott said.

"Like the knife, sir," Phoenix replied. "Or Jim Bowie. Remember the Alamo."

Scott cleared his throat. "Tip of the spear then. Good to know." He turned to Mercia. "I've proposed this same plan to State multiple times, but they wanted Afghanistan and Iraq to stand on their own feet and didn't want to put in the work. Or they didn't want us to look like imperialists."

"It's no different than what we did for Japan or South Korea," Delacroix said. "I think if you can do what you're talking about, we can sway the balance of power."

"I'm on board," General Scott stated. "I'll start working with the Joint Chiefs to draw up invasion plans."

"I want this to remain lowkey," Mercia replied. "I want Guyana to lead the fight. Let's aid them in whatever way possible. If we can build a coalition, then we should."

"I agree," Scott said. "I'll call Brigadier General Patrick at the GDF and see what he needs."

Bowie spoke up again. "You need to take out their air

defense missile batteries and the fighter jets. The Venezuelans only have a handful of functioning ones, but they'll blast those Super Tucs out of the sky if they get the chance. The other thing Guyana needs is naval power, both brown water and blue. The Cuyuní and, to a lesser extent, the Essequibo Rivers will need constant patrols."

"Good thinking, Bowie," Mercia said.

"I'll speak to Admiral Garrison, Chief of Naval Operations, and see what we've got on the scrap heap to give them," Scott said.

"Lend-lease, Rex," Mercia corrected. "I want oil as payment. A *lot* of it."

"Yes, sir." Rex Scott headed for the door with a grin on his face. Before he twisted the knob, he turned back to the president. "Don't screw us like Kennedy screwed the Bay of Pigs, sir. There's no coming back from that."

"Thank you for the advice, General. You have my word," Mercia said truthfully.

Once the head of the DOD had departed, Mercia turned to the two spooks. "Convey the message to Acevedo. If she wants to be Venezuela's president, she needs to get on board. Otherwise, we'll find someone else."

CHAPTER 8

CIA private jet
Over the Gulf of Mexico

JOHN PHOENIX KEPT MULLING OVER THE PRESIDENT'S WORDS, trying to get a grasp on the man's overall plan.

Mercia was right in the fact that Zarate didn't care about negotiating for control over the Essequibo Region. He'd rejected the International Court of Justice's right to rule on the dispute. He forcefully boasted that he wouldn't stop until the Essequibo was back in Venezuelan hands, going so far as to announce that he considered *Guyana Esequiba* to be the twenty-fourth state of Venezuela.

Phoenix felt Zarate had only agreed to the Mexico City talks to get the U.S. to lift more sanctions.

Phoenix swiveled in his seat and studied the sharp planes of Sandy Delacroix's face. She must have sensed his observations when she looked up from the file she'd been intently reading.

"If the U.S. invades Venezuela, what is the purpose of meeting with Acevedo?" Phoenix asked.

Delacroix took off her glasses and rubbed her eyes. "You heard President Mercia. It sounds like he wants her to be the next president."

"Wouldn't the Venezuelans want Juan Guaidó?" Phoenix asked. "After all, he supposedly won the last election before Zarate voided it."

"Correction," Delacroix replied. "Guaidó declared himself the winner, and the U.S. and other governments backed him, hoping to oust Zarate from office. My sense is that Mercia sees Guaidó as a loser since Zarate expelled him from Venezuela. Acevedo makes sense as she won her seat in the National Assembly by an overwhelming majority, and she's publicly bucked Zarate on several key issues."

"Yet, he trusts her enough to be his envoy to Mexico City."

"Does he?" Delacroix asked in a motherly fashion as if Phoenix was a young boy in need of correction.

"I don't know where she stands," Phoenix replied. "She looked pretty chummy with Hector Calderón."

"She is his boss, according to the SEBIN's charter," Delacroix stated.

"I still don't get why she told him about the money," Phoenix said. "You ran her. What's your sense of the situation? Will she come back to the fold, or is she too patriotic now?"

Delacroix closed her folder and gazed out the window for a moment at the clouds below. When she turned back to her case officer, she said, "My gut always told me that she withheld information. I was never sure she wanted to work for the CIA, and I think she felt pressured into doing it."

"By whom?"

"Certainly not by me," Delacroix responded. "I was part of a recruitment team back then. You know, working on the college campuses. I thought she would make an excellent case officer, but she declined my offer of employment. I could see she wasn't a fan, so I didn't pursue her."

Since Acevedo wasn't a U.S. citizen, the CIA would have fast-tracked her citizenship application so she could become a case officer.

Delacroix ran a hand through her blonde hair, bunching it between her fingers before continuing. "After she turned me down, I offered her a position with USAID in the Humanitarian Assistance department, but she declined that, too, and took a job with Doctors Without Borders."

Phoenix knew firsthand about the United States Agency for International Development. Initially created in 1961, USAID had been designed to help the U.S. win the "hearts and minds" of citizens in poor countries through civic action, economic aid, and humanitarian assistance. At times, the agency had been a front for CIA operations, and they'd inserted case officers into the program to infiltrate foreign countries. Phoenix had gone into Guatemala under the guise of USAID's specialized technical office to provide counter-narcotics assistance to the local police forces back when he was a paramilitary operations officer.

"What did she do for the CIA while she was with Doctors Without Borders?" Phoenix asked.

"She reported on economic and sanitary conditions in the African countries she worked in. Sometimes, she would count rifles if she was in hostile territory."

"Why do you feel she held out on you?" Phoenix persisted.

"We're trained to detect microexpressions," Delacroix said. "Some of her answers were flat-out lies. I don't know why, and I didn't care at the time. Most of the intelligence she brought back was excellent—operational even. I let the lies slip as long as she provided good HUMIT."

"How receptive do you think she'll be to our offer to force regime change?" Phoenix asked.

"It's a coin flip. If Unicorn is under Calderón's thumb or acting as Zarate's minion, she'll go straight to the press and out us to everyone she knows. I would if I were her. It would be a strategic move to insulate herself from Zarate's wrath, or she might think it's a good move to save her country from U.S. imperialism."

Phoenix nodded. He'd hoped Delacroix would provide some deeper insight into the targeted asset, but he'd yet to grasp anything he could latch on to so he could form that "you, me same same" bond.

"What was her attitude regarding the U.S. and the CIA?" Phoenix asked. "Obviously, she worked for you, but did you get a sense of her loyalty?"

"Like I said earlier, I think she felt pressured to work with us. I had the NSA pull her phone, text, and email logs when she was overseas—she was never a U.S. citizen, so it wasn't illegal."

"Did you find anything?" the case officer asked.

Delacroix shook her head as she continued to fuss with her hair, a sure sign to Phoenix that she was self-soothing. "No. I never did. She missed her family in Venezuela, and she planned to return as soon as her contract with Doctors Without Borders ended."

"So where do you think the pressure came from, if there was any?" Phoenix asked.

Delacroix spread her hands in frustration. "I don't know, Bowie. Maybe my gut was wrong."

"Who's going to run her if she agrees to spy for us?" he asked.

"I think that's her choice. If she's comfortable with me, then I should handle her. My guess is that she'll feel slighted since you tried to blackmail her by leaving the money."

Phoenix rubbed the back of his neck, then rolled his shoulder.

"Are you okay?" his boss asked. "You've been contorting yourself all over the place for the last couple of days."

"I've got this stress knot in my shoulder. Nothing seems to make it go away. Painkillers don't make a dent."

"Why didn't you see an agency doc?" Delacroix asked.

"I saw an acupuncturist and got three massages," Phoenix replied. "The only thing it did was make the pain migrate into my shoulder. My whole fucking arm aches. Sorry, ma'am." He immediately apologized for his foul language.

Delacroix reached for her folder. She opened it on her lap and slipped her glasses back on. Phoenix took her actions to mean their conversation was over. He leaned back in his seat and stared out the window at the blue water far below.

He wasn't going to hold his breath that Acevedo would turn. He flashed back to the Venezuelan vice president standing on the roof with Hector Calderón. They looked like coconspirators. In his mind's eye, he turned his head and saw the beautiful face of Coralina Blanco, her brown hair shining in the light from the window they were peering out, and her gray eyes bright with excitement. He pictured her full lips puckering to press against his.

Phoenix wanted revenge on the men who'd killed her, but that would have to wait. There was too much on his plate with Operation Unicorn and the mole hunt for Dragonfly, the seller of case officer names to the highest bidder.

The stress knot tightened. Phoenix settled into the seat and closed his eyes to sleep, but all he saw was blood bubbling from Blanco's chest, and felt the phantom grasp of her hand on his forearm as she whispered, "I love you."

"Bowie," Delacroix said, drawing his attention. "This op will work. Have faith."

CHAPTER 9

SEBIN Headquarters
Caracas, Venezuela

"I want you to meet someone," Hector Calderón said.

Coralina Blanco lifted her head from between her arms, where she sat in the corner of the tiny cell, knees to her chest. The Venezuelan Special Forces lieutenant didn't know how long she'd been in the cell nor if anyone would ever come for her. She believed the SEBIN had arrested her as a traitor to her country and that she would never see the light of day again.

"Don't be shy, Coralina. I'm not here to hurt you," Calderón reassured her. He introduced himself to the prisoner, so she understood the power of his position. "I want you to work with me."

Blanco stared at the director of the secret police. Calderón was in his late fifties with coppery skin and deep-set brown eyes beneath jet-black hair. He wore an expensively tailored civilian suit as if he were trying to impress Blanco with his fashion sense. Blanco knew he wore Prada. Fashion had been her trade when she had participated in beauty pageants. After the collapse of Venezuela's economy, she had joined the Army.

"Get up, Lieutenant!" Calderón barked when she didn't move. "That's an order."

Blanco rose unsteadily to her feet, keeping her back pressed against the cold concrete wall. Other than the occasional guard who would open the window in the cell door to leer in at her naked body, Calderón was the only other person Blanco had seen, and he was the only one to set foot in her cell.

The director appraised her naked body with a wary eye.

"Who … who are we going to see?" Blanco's voice trembled with fear as she thought about coming face to face with Terry Martin, the man who had been her handler when she'd acted as a double agent against the CIA case officer she knew only as Bowie.

As if reading her mind, Calderón replied, "Not Terry Martin. Since you faked your death and your *friend* escaped our country, Martin has been in the wind."

"I thought he was …"

Calderón gave her a tired smile. "Señor Martin serves his own self-interests." He turned to the cell door and rapped his knuckle against the thick steel. Blue paint flaked off the metal, tiny pieces landing on Calderón's pant leg. As he waited for the guard, he pulled a handkerchief from his pocket and dusted the flakes off his trousers.

A female guard opened the door. She carried a baton in her hand and had a holstered pistol on her hip. Blanco sized her up immediately. The guard was shorter than Blanco's five feet, nine inches, or 175cm, and Blanco could tell she had an attitude about her. She couldn't help but think one had to be a sadistic bitch to work in a prison like this, especially when the screams of tortured prisoners reached her ears at all hours of the day.

"Escort Lieutenant Blanco to the showers," Calderón ordered the guard. "See that she gets cleaned up and dressed in the things I have provided her."

The guard slapped the baton into her palm. "With pleasure, sir."

"I'm warning you now, Sergeant Tranquillo, if anything happens to Blanco, it will be you who is in this cell. *Comprendo?*"

Tranquillo nodded and holstered her baton.

"When Lieutenant Blanco is dressed, bring her to my office."

The sergeant nodded again and then motioned for Blanco to follow her. Together, the two women exited the cell. They walked down a long concrete corridor with many blue doors set into the wall. Blanco trembled at the sound of an agonizing scream that came from behind one. Tranquillo glanced over her shoulder at Blanco, a brutal curl to her lip. Another shudder coursed up Blanco's spine at the thought of what lay ahead.

Tranquillo led her into a locker room and retrieved a bag from a locker. She set it on a bench and told Blanco to get cleaned up. Blanco found a towel, a new bar of soap, shampoo, disposable safety razors, and other toiletries inside the bag. She immediately recognized her own clothing and realized they must have taken it from her apartment in Maracay.

Blanco stepped under the shower, letting the water turn from cold to hot as it beat down upon her. She spent the next thirty minutes scrubbing her body, washing her hair, and shaving her legs and armpits. Once she'd finished, Blanco stepped to the sink and wiped away the steam from the mirror above it. Her gray eyes were beset with fatigue, and the tips of her brown hair now brushed her shoulders.

"Speed it up," Tranquillo barked.

"I am your superior," Blanco replied. "Do not order me around."

"You are a regular army soldier," Tranquillo shot back. "I am a member of the SEBIN. You have no authority over me in this prison, *traitor*."

Even though Blanco wore only a towel wrapped around her body, she stepped over to Tranquillo and stood toe to toe with her, peering down at the shorter woman. "I am a member of the 97th Special Forces Brigade. You pose no threat to me."

"I assure you, *traitor*, that it will be my pleasure to pluck out your fingernails and tear your teeth from your mouth."

"Try it, bitch," Blanco urged.

Tranquillo reached for her baton. Blanco hit her on the chin with an open-hand strike, knocking Tranquillo back against the wall. Sensing her opponent's weakness, Blanco continued the attack, delivering several rapid punches to the sergeant's midsection. Tranquillo screamed in pain and grabbed Blanco in a headlock, trying to reverse her position into a rear naked choke. Blanco felt the towel slip from her body as she smashed an elbow into Tranquillo's ribcage.

The two women continued to struggle for control, toppling over when their feet tangled. They landed hard on the tile floor, and Blanco rolled on top of her attacker. She managed to punch Tranquillo two times in the face before strong hands seized her about the waist and arms and wrenched her off the struggling sergeant.

Slowly, Tranquillo rose to her feet, rubbing her jaw. The area beneath her left eye had started to turn purple and swell from the last punch Blanco had thrown.

"Hold her," Tranquillo ordered, reaching again for her baton.

Blanco lashed out with her foot, striking Tranquillo's hand and knocking it away from the baton. The two men holding

Blanco pulled her backward, away from the fight, but Blanco continued to lash out.

"Enough!" the man on her right bellowed. "Stand down, Sergeant Tranquillo. We have our orders, and they do not include fighting with the prisoner."

Blanco tried to wrestle herself free, but the men's hands were like vises on her arms. She felt one of them slide his hand across her body, cupping her breast and getting a good feel. Incensed, Blanco stomped on the man's instep. He let go of her as he yelped in pain. Before the other guard could react, Blanco spun out of his grasp, kneed her groper in the crotch, and then slammed her knee into his face as he doubled over in pain. Bleeding from the nose, the guard fell over, clutching his nut sack.

"Fuck you!" Blanco shouted. "Don't ever touch a woman like that."

The other male guard picked up the towel from the floor and handed it to Blanco before he escorted his bleeding companion out of the locker room. Blanco wrapped the towel around herself while giving Tranquillo a withering glance. Then she walked over to the bag that contained her clothing and pulled on her underwear before donning her military uniform. Once she tied the laces of her combat boots, Blanco stood and straightened her blouse.

"Let's go," she said to Tranquillo, who stood by with baton in hand.

Tranquillo led the way to the elevator and typed a code into the keypad to open the doors. Despite being back in uniform, Blanco didn't feel as confident as usual. As they stepped into the elevator and it started to rise, a Metro train rumbled past. Blanco asked, "Are we in The Tomb?"

"*Sí,*" Tranquillo replied.

Blanco stared straight ahead, watching the numbers flash on the control panel as the elevator rose. The Tomb was an infamous underground prison in the basement of SEBIN headquarters, a skyscraper near Plaza Venezuela. Originally designed for Metro Caracas, the SEBIN had taken control of the building in 2013, and they'd turned the underground parking levels into tiny cells just two meters by three meters in size. To torture and confuse the prisoners, the guards left the bright lights on inside the cells twenty-four hours a day, and, occasionally, they blared punk rock music at unbearable volumes for hours on end.

The elevator stopped on the sixteenth floor, and the two women stepped out into a marbled corridor that led to a reception desk at the end of an opulent lobby. Behind a wood and granite counter sat a woman in uniform, her blonde hair pulled back in a severe bun. She glanced up as the two women approached, saying, "Director Calderón is expecting you. Go on in."

Tranquillo held the door for Blanco, then posted herself beside it in the lobby to act as a guard.

Blanco glanced around the spacious office. Through the large windows, she had a sweeping view of Caracas. Calderón kept his workspace fastidiously neat, his desk devoid of any paperwork or clutter, preferring to keep his office electronics on a separate workstation.

Calderón started immediately with his instructions. "I know you want to help Venezuela rise from the depths of depravity we have stumbled into, so I am sending you to Mexico City with Vice President Acevedo as part of her security team. I also know your previous handler, Bowie, will be there to recruit Acevedo back into the CIA's fold. I want you to facilitate a meeting between them. This is for the future of our country, Coralina."

Blanco nodded, feeling excitement rising in her at the prospect of seeing Bowie.

"Do you understand?" Calderón asked, and Blanco replied that she did. "Excellent," he continued. "I have told you what I want you to do. Tranquillo is not privy to our plans. What I say to her will be to throw her off the scent. Am I clear?"

"Yes, sir," Blanco replied.

Caldron opened the door and instructed Tranquillo to come inside. She entered and stood beside Lieutenant Blanco.

"Can I pour you ladies a drink?" Calderón asked.

Coming to attention, Tranquillo barked, "No, sir. I'm on duty, sir."

Blanco wasn't as particular. These assholes had held her in a cell for who knows how long, and she deserved a drink, figuring whatever Caldron served her would be top-shelf quality. With a genuine smile of enthusiasm for her new assignment, she said, "I'll have whatever you're having, sir."

Calderón poured brown liquid into two rocks glasses. He handed one to Blanco and sat the other on the corner of his desk after placing a coaster beneath it. "For you, Sergeant, when you're ready."

"Thank you, sir," Tranquillo replied but didn't reach for the glass.

Blanco sipped the liquor, which turned out to be excellent tasting rum. She knew she had to pace herself after being deprived of food and water for however long she'd been in the cell. The alcohol would go straight to her head if she wasn't careful.

And she knew she had to keep her wits about her. Everything about this situation seemed a little surreal. From faking her own death to now standing in the office of the director of the SEBIN, it felt like a crazy roller coaster ride. She hoped that being back in uniform meant Zarate wouldn't hang her as a traitor.

"Please sit." Calderón directed the women to chairs in front of his desk. "We have a few minutes before our special guest arrives."

Blanco slid into the seat, thankful to be off her feet, but Tranquillo remained at attention.

Calderón pointed at the chair. "Sit, Tranquillo. That's an order."

Reluctantly, the female SEBIN agent took her place beside Blanco. Calderón perched himself on the corner of his desk and examined Tranquillo's black eye. "I see you ladies have been getting to know one another."

The two women remained silent, keeping their own secrets. Blanco thought Calderón didn't need to know any more about their altercation than he already did. She had a few bruises from where the two male guards had handled her roughly, but nothing like what she had done to Tranquillo's face.

Calderón stepped around his desk, produced a bottle of acetaminophen from a drawer, and shook two tablets into his hand. He handed them to Tranquillo, noting they would help ease the pain and swelling around her eye. The SEBIN agent swallowed them without taking a drink.

There was a gentle knock on the door, and Calderón called for the visitor to enter as he stowed the pill bottle.

As Vice President Evelyn Acevedo entered the room, Blanco immediately stood and came to attention. Tranquillo followed her lead an instant later.

"At ease," Acevedo said to them.

Blanco's gut fluttered at the sight of the VP. The last time she'd seen Acevedo, the woman had been on the rooftop of her apartment building, speaking to Calderón about the satchel full of money Bowie had planted in her desk drawer. Moments after that, Blanco and Bowie had gone on the run, fleeing the country.

Acevedo extended her hand to both women and personally introduced herself. Blanco smiled as she shook the VP's hand, wondering if Acevedo knew about her role in the scheme.

"Please sit," Calderón said after the introductions. Once Blanco and Tranquillo had returned to their seats and

Acevedo had a tumbler of Aviator Gin in her hand, the director continued. "As you know, a peace negotiation is scheduled in Mexico City to try to normalize relations with Guyana over the Essequibo Region. Your orders are to escort Vice President Acevedo to the meeting and act as her personal bodyguards."

"Yes, sir," Tranquillo replied.

"And you, Lieutenant?" Calderón asked when Blanco made no reply.

"Permission to speak freely, sir?" the Special Forces operator asked.

Calderón nodded.

Blanco figured Tranquillo knew all about her and her work as a double agent for the CIA and for whatever agency or country Terry Martin had affiliated himself with, so she decided to speak her mind. "The Americans will know who I am. Am I the best choice to accompany Madam Acevedo to Mexico?"

"You're the perfect choice," Calderón stated. "My theory is that your friend Bowie will try to contact Evelyn again. I want you there to throw him off his game. From what I understand, you two had an intimate relationship, and he now thinks you're dead. If we can distract him even a little, we can give the vice president a better chance of avoiding contact with the Criminal Imperialist Agency."

I understand, sir," Blanco replied, feeling her heart flutter at the mention of Bowie's name. Going to Mexico City also gave her another chance to defect—if the Americans would have her.

"I don't like it, sir," Tranquillo said, obviously emboldened by Blanco's blunt address. "She's a traitor! What if she decides to go rogue again? You're putting Madam Acevedo in danger."

Calderón held his hands up to thwart Tranquillo's objections. "I understand your point of view, Sergeant. That's why you're going. I know you're loyal to the SEBIN and to Venezuela. I expect you to be my emissary on this mission."

"Is she supposed to spy on me?" Blanco asked derisively.

"She's supposed to spy on both of us," Acevedo retorted.

The director of the SEBIN smiled. "We all want what's best for our country. We just have different ways of going about it. You two, however, will work together to ensure Madam Acevedo's safety and bring her safely back to Caracas. Am I understood?"

"Yes, sir," the two bodyguards replied almost in unison. They both recognized the benefit of a firm chain of command and the value of the orders they received, even if they didn't like the person they had to work with along the way.

"Any special instructions?" Calderón asked the vice president.

"Leave your military uniforms at home, girls," Acevedo said. "We'll be dressing business casual for this trip. If you need clothes, the shopping will be better in Mexico City. I have a government-issued credit card to cover hotel rooms, food, and incidentals."

Tranquillo's head drooped as she softly said, "I don't have any business casual clothing, ma'am."

"I have something that might fit you," Blanco volunteered, feeling that she needed to befriend the sergeant in the spirit of keeping friends close and your enemies closer. "We might have to take in the pant leg hem, but that won't be a problem."

"Excellent," Calderón said, with a clap of his hands. "You ladies take care of that while Evelyn and I have a chat. You're both excused. Agent de los Rios will brief you and escort you around the city to get what you need for the trip. He should be waiting for you outside."

As Blanco stood, she wondered if her things were still in her apartment. She paused at the door and spoke to Calderón.

"I will need to go to Maracay, Director General. My clothing is still in my apartment there."

"Ah … I forgot," Calderón said with a wagging finger. "I had several agents move your things to the apartment across the street from the Vice President's. The one you so generously told us about during your stay downstairs."

Blanco's face flushed. She felt the heat rise to her skin and strained with every ounce of her being not to scratch at her neck.

Tranquillo flashed an evil grin. Her dark eyes leered at Blanco under thick brows and long, luxurious lashes.

Blanco would have killed for those lashes when she was a pageant model.

Calderón pointed to the door to speed them along. "Agent de los Rios is waiting."

Blanco didn't know what she had gotten herself into, but suddenly, she longed for the simple life of an Army lieutenant. What they were about to do seemed imminently more dangerous than even the limited spying she had already done, but hopefully seeing Bowie again would make it all worthwhile.

Blanco couldn't wait to see the look on his face when he saw she was alive.

CHAPTER 10

Calderón closed the door to his office after Lieutenant Blanco and Sergeant Tranquillo stepped into the hallway. He turned back to the vice president and asked if she wanted him to refresh her drink.

"Certainly," Acevedo agreed. "After learning those two will be with me in Mexico City, I think I need one. What happened to Tranquillo's eye?"

"A matter of disagreement between them, apparently," Calderón said. The director had received a call from the guards after they'd broken up the fight between the two women. "I gather Blanco got the best of her. She also bloodied the nose of a guard who tried to break up the altercation."

"She must be feisty, especially to have worked as a double agent. Do you trust her?" Acevedo asked.

"Blanco is a trained operator, and her record speaks for itself with exemplary service and training—"

Acevedo cut the director general off with a wave of her hand. "But she aided the CIA and tried to defect."

Calderón chuckled. "Apparently, you aided the CIA as well, Evelyn. I believe they left you a message in your desk to that effect."

Acevedo didn't join in with Calderón's chuckling. She had hoped to keep her work for the agency a secret from the Venezuelan government. If Zarate had known that she had been a CIA asset, he would have thrown her into prison and tortured her for the rest of her life. She shuddered at the notion.

Contrary to the admonition Calderón had given to the two female two soldiers about keeping her away from the CIA, he wanted Acevedo to use the agency as a "back door" to the U.S. government so they could hash out sanction relief, acquire foreign aid, and normalize relations.

Calderón turned serious. "Has Zarate given you any orders concerning your trip?"

"He's going there himself. After the referendum, he believes it's imperative that he and President Fredricks speak face to face."

"And tell him to bend over and take it?" Calderón asked. "Fredricks isn't a pushover. He's building a military full of mercenaries and whipping the U.S. president into a frenzy."

"I think Zarate is doing a pretty good job of that himself," Acevedo said. "He's beating the war drums so he can distract the people from what a shitty job he's doing."

"Easy, Evelyn. Let's keep things civil."

Acevedo drew in a ragged breath, trying to control her anger. She had urged Zarate that there were better uses for the funds he pumped into the weeks-long build-up to the Essequibo referendum. As usual, he ignored her pleadings and planned to rally people to his cause by playing Esse-quibo-themed music, nationally televising history lessons about the tensions between the two countries, painting murals, holding street rallies, and posting social media content.

"Tell me you have a plan," Acevedo finally said to Calderón.

"I do, but now isn't the time to discuss it, nor do I want

you to know the particulars. What I want you to do is meet with the American and listen to what he has to say."

"And then what?" she asked.

The spy chief shot back the rest of his rum in one gulp. He stepped to the cabinet and put his rocks glass on the top. "Keep your head down in Mexico City. If at all possible, stay away from Zarate."

"Is there a particular reason why I should stay away from him?" she asked. Typically, she would keep her distance from the egomaniac even though her appointment to the position of VP looked to some like a millstone around her neck, threatening to drown her in the pool of Zarate's deceit.

"Just keep your head down," Calderón reiterated.

"I leave tomorrow," she replied. "Are those girls supposed to protect me from whatever is going to happen?"

"They're both trained in executive protection, and Blanco is a skilled fighter. She learned from the Black Wasps."

The Black Wasps were Cuba's premier special forces unit, trained for direct action, special reconnaissance, and psychological operations. They also received training in parachuting, underwater operations, target interceptions, and intelligence operations. When not making their bones in brushfire wars around the globe, the Black Wasps trained military and paramilitary groups for deployment in South America.

Cuba's communist tentacles wove deep into Venezuela's political, economic, and military machinations, and Acevedo wondered if Calderón had accounted for the blowback that might occur from the Cuban regime if Zarate were to die mysteriously. Maybe he was counting on her taking the governmental reins and dealing with Cuba in her own particular style?

After digesting the fact that the Cuban-trained Blanco hid deadly warfighting skills beneath a body worthy of a Playboy cover, Acevedo asked, "And Tranquillo? What is her training?"

"She has trained with Wagner Group."

Acevedo nodded, knowing the Wagner Group was a Russian-owned private military contractor (PMC) brought in by Zarate to help train elite Venezuelan combat units, protect oil refineries for Russian state oil giant Rosneft, and to aid in smuggling thorium, a naturally radioactive metal, out of the mines in the Orinoco Mining Arc.

"Why aren't you sending Marcus with me?" she asked. "He's done an excellent job so far."

"He's busy doing other things," Calderón replied cryptically.

Acevedo folded her arms across her chest and adopted a slightly defensive posture with a cocked hip. "I think you should explain your plan to me, Hector."

"No," he replied flatly. "Just keep your distance from Zarate outside of any conferences."

"But we're all staying at the Four Seasons. How should I keep my distance in a hotel?" Acevedo wondered.

"He has made plans to travel outside the hotel. Don't go with him."

Acevedo nodded with a tilted head, pondering the warning Calderón had given her. He had told her not long ago that he planned a "revolution." Calderón had never given her the details, only drawing her into a conspiracy to remove Zarate from office by force. She had only gone along with it because she had confided in him about the two-hundred-fifty-thousand dollars that Bowie had planted in her apartment. Between the money and the note for her to call her former handler at the CIA, Calderón could burn her to the ground. The benefit to playing along, however, meant she would step into the most powerful office in Venezuela and have complete control of the system.

That thought almost made her drool.

She believed she could do a much better job running the government than Zarate could ever hope to do. As a medical doctor who had practiced in various third-world countries before returning to Venezuela to work at the University Hospital of Caracas, Acevedo had seen firsthand the lack of medical supplies, running water, electricity, and basic food staples to provide for her patients. She'd seen the gaunt eyes and hollow cheeks of the starving citizens. The lack of care Zarate showed for anything other than maintaining his power sickened Acevedo.

Acevedo had once heard a joke made by a fellow student back at Duke University that still caused her blood to boil. The man had laughingly said to his companion, "Dark humor is like food in Venezuela—most people don't get it."

The opportunity to step into the office of the President of Venezuela was the morsel Calderón had originally tempted her with. But all that really mattered was helping the people of Venezuela, and the best way to do that was to attend the peace talks in Mexico City and possibly get the U.S. to lift sanctions.

While the increase in oil revenue would be a boon for the country, Acevedo knew that to truly thrive, Venezuela needed to diversify away from being singularly dependent on fossil fuels and the mining industry. Oil revenue could, however, fuel the expansion of the economy. With the push for green energy, Acevedo knew she needed to act quickly before the world moved away from dependency on her economic driver.

Acevedo also understood Calderón's warning. If harm befell the president, then she needed to be as far away from the action as possible. She would let Calderón get his hands dirty to avoid any impropriety on her part.

"Do not be naïve in this, Evelyn. Should we fail, our heads will be first to roll. Zarate will clean house," Calderón warned.

"I understand, Hector," Acevedo replied. "So, you better not miss."

CHAPTER 11

Lieutenant Luis del Valle García Air Base
Barcelona, Venezuela

Colonel Carlos Xavier relished the thought of revenge.

He slid the throttle forward, adding fuel to the twin turbofan engines that powered his Sukhoi Su-30MKK fighter jet. Three other fighters from Air Hunting Group 13 flew on his wingtips in a diamond formation. The planes were only a handful of operational units among the twenty-two aircraft that composed two squadrons of Flankers, and President Zarate deemed them worthy of another mission. He'd ordered Air Hunting Group 13 to strike another blow against the Guyanese forces for overrunning the Isla de Ankoko Territorial Security Base.

Their target today was the GDF's Special Forces training base in Makouria, and the pilots planned to bomb the island base back into the Stone Age, where it belonged. Eliminating the Guyanese training cadre and recruits there would severely hamper the country's response to Venezuela's impending reclamation. And there would be no need for the base when Venezuela took over the Essequibo Region.

The flight today was a short hop for the Air Hunting Group, and Xavier planned to make a long sweeping turn over Timehri, just twenty-three miles south of the Makouria base, where he would "accidentally" pickle off a couple of bombs onto the Super Tucanos that he hoped would be parked at the airport.

On his wings, Xavier carried a loadout of R-73 air-to-air missiles and KAB-1500L laser-guided bombs. While the Flanker had an onboard laser designator so the bombs could "ride the beam" to their target, the KABs also contained a GPS receiver for backup, so the weapon would continue to home in on the GPS coordinates if the laser illumination was lost or broken. Xavier believed the Super Tucanos posed no threat to his aircraft, but the ground crew had still given him a full complement of one-hundred-fifty rounds for his GSh-30-1 autocannon.

It didn't take long for Xavier and his fellow fighters to cross into the Essequibo Region. Xavier, a tall, lean man with a full head of wavy black hair, called for his fellow pilots to arm their weapons and prepare for combat. He searched the cockpit gauges with clear, green eyes and gripped the smooth black plastic of the plane's stick and throttle with a tender caress that implied the plane was more of his lover than a war machine. He did love this bird, and together they had bombed the shit out of Base Camp Seweyo near Low Wood, Guyana, not that long ago.

That flight had been a retaliatory blow as well. Xavier hoped Zarate would stop pussyfooting around, so they weren't continually being caught flatfooted by the GDF. They *needed* to take the fight to those fuckers in Georgetown.

For now, Xavier had to be content with Zarate's orders and allow the satisfaction of flying this marvelous machine to be his reward for his steadfast loyalty to the Zarate regime.

"Target in sight," Xavier called over the radio. "Laser designator is on and painting. Tiger Flight, you have the lead."

The two planes on Xavier's right peeled off and zoomed down toward the target, dropping their beam riders straight into the heart of the island and the military complex shadowed beneath the trees.

As Xavier flipped off his laser, he glanced down to see fireballs blossoming from the jungle below. One of the bombs had missed the mark, falling into the muddy water of the Essequibo River. It blasted a giant pit into the sandy bottom, causing the water to part like Moses was holding back the Red Sea.

Xavier nudged his control stick just a hair to deviate from the preplanned flight path and vectored in on the Cheddi Jagan International Airport tower. He felt sure he would find the Super Tucanos belonging to the Flying Jaguars on the apron nearby.

With a smile of satisfaction, he noted three sleek, gray turboprop planes on the ground. He switched on the laser designator and dropped two bombs on the defenseless Super Tucanos before leading his Flanker flight out of harm's way and scurrying low for home.

Xavier had dealt another blow to the GDF, but the thrill was short-lived as a missile warning tone sounded in his ears. His smile of satisfaction slipped from his face as he twisted in his seat to spot the incoming missile. His thumb automatically punched the button on his control stick to deploy chaff and flares as decoys for the heat-seeker.

"Mach 2, now!" Xavier screamed over the radio.

CHAPTER 12

THE AVIATION GODS HAD SMILED ON WILL POUNDER AND clutched him in their favorable embrace.

Pounder and his backseater, Stitches, were flying a routine patrol from Cheddi Jagan International Airport to Ankoko Island with Colonel Jorge "Papa" Mansoor on their wing.

They were on their way back to Camp Stephenson when Stitches piped up. "Hey, Dumpster, I'm getting a strange reading on the radar. It looks like a flight of four fast movers coming from the north."

"How far are we from them?" Pounder asked.

"About forty kilometers," she replied.

"Yo, Papa, you see anything out there?" Pounder asked over the radio while straining his eyes to see the fast movers. He loved having Mansoor on his wing. The colonel had always treated him with respect, and Pounder had found the man to be an aviation father figure. Mansoor kept his cool under pressure, was an excellent pilot, and always had a kind word to say, even if he backed them up with a bit of steel in his voice to let his pilots know he wasn't fucking around. And Mansoor had a love affair with Greg "Pappy" Boyington, the hard-drinking American World War II ace. So, naturally, when Pounder had started calling the older man Papa, the rest of the crew had picked it up.

"I've got them on radar," the colonel responded in his chipper British accent, having retained the vestiges of his officer and pilot training in Great Britain.

"Should we pursue?" Pounder asked, deferring his decision-making to the older man.

"Let's see what those jolly blokes are up to, Dumpster."

"Roger that, Papa," Pounder replied.

He turned slightly onto an intercept bearing and increased his speed from a sedate 280-knot cruising speed to the 320-knot maximum speed of the aircraft.

"Missiles are armed," Stitches said from the back seat.

The four Piranha air-to-air missiles on his wing hardpoints were more than capable of striking down a jet fighter, but it was up to Pounder to put them into a position to do so.

"This is bad," Stitches muttered.

"What?" Pounder demanded.

"Those jets just bombed the base at Makouria and are headed for Camp Stephenson."

"Oh shit," Pounder groaned.

They flew in silence as Pounder calculated an intercept route in his head. Once he had it plotted, he turned his plane farther to the north and descended toward the treetops.

"Where are we going, Dumpster?" Stitches asked.

Pounder keyed the radio mic so Mansoor could also hear his response. "I think they'll head for the airbase in Barcelona like the last time those jets bombed a GDF base. My plan is to slice the pie and gain the advantage by catching them as they pass us."

"They're making the turn from Camp Stephenson," Stitches called out. "Currently headed east and coming around."

Pounder strained to see anything at the limit of his vision. He didn't have the eyesight of an eagle, but he hoped to catch a glint of sun off the metal bodies of the fighter jets. He bumped the throttle with his hand, willing the Pratt & Whitney turboprop engine to go faster and wishing he had an F-35 strapped to his ass so he could really take the fight to the Fanboys.

The theoretical range of his Piranhas was eight to ten kilometers at Mach 2, the same speed the fighters could go if they were Sukhois, as Pounder suspected. He had studied up on the aircraft in the Venezuelan Air Force and knew where the various squadrons were based around the country. Barcelona was the closest fighter base, and Pounder knew he had to head deep into enemy territory if he stood a chance in hell of shooting down a Sukhoi.

"Our targets have completed their turn and are headed northwest," Stitches reported.

"Copy that," Pounder replied. He glanced down at the snapshot of Maxine Gilespie that he'd wedged into a gap in the instrument screen. Her long dark hair framed her round face, and her growing bangs draped seductively in front of her brown right eye as she gazed up at him. He had fallen in love with her when he'd first met her at Airport Steakhouse at Hutchinson Regional Airport in a town with the same fucking name in Kansas. Hutchinson this. Hutchinson that.

I got out and ain't ever going back. Let me root for the GDF. I love flying for my meager paycheck!

Pounder kept scanning the horizon as he made up his little ditty to the tune of "Take Me Out to the Ball Game."

Take me out to the war zone. Give me a fast plane and a heat-seeker to boot. We'll carve up them Fanboys, and we'll win us the game. Root, root, root for the Flying Tigers of the GDF.

"Ten kilometers out," Stiches called. "They'll be passing right to left at Angels Ten."

Pounder checked his altimeter. They were at Angels One, a thousand feet above mean sea level. Beneath them, the land undulated in rolling hills. Ahead, the jet fighters were clocking in at 1455 kilometers per hour.

"Engaging missiles," Stitches confirmed.

Seconds later, there was a lock-up tone in Pounder's ear, and he stroked the trigger on his stick, sending two Piranhas on their way.

"Come on, babies," Pounder muttered, urging the missiles to find their targets.

Suddenly, he saw the bright blaze of flares being jettisoned by the fighters as they tried to evade the missiles.

Someone was a little slow in responding to the threat as one of Pounder's Piranhas slammed its twelve-kilogram, blast fragmentation-type warhead into the engine of a Flanker, exploding it in midair.

"Score one for the Dumpster!" Pounder shouted.

Mansoor had also triggered two of his missiles. One of them burst harmlessly on a puff of chaff while the other smoked up the tailpipe of another Sukhoi.

"Splash two! I repeat, splash two Flankers!" Pounder shouted in uproarious joy. He had goosebumps flushed across his skin. One more kill, and he'd be a fucking ace. He would be the first American ace since Captain Richard "Steve" Ritchie became one in 1972.

Rolling hard to the left, Pounder knew his two-ship flight needed to get back to base before their fuel ran out and they lost all of the Super Tucanos in one day, figuring the Flanker flight over Camp Stephenson had been to destroy the three planes on the ground.

As Pounder flew in a giant arc to circle back toward Guyana, he spotted a C-130 scuttling along the treetops many kilometers out. Missile lock-up sounded in his ears.

"You see that Hercules down there, Max?"

"Max?" Stitches said.

"Sorry, Stiches," Pounder said. "You see that Herc on the radar?"

"I've got it," Stitches said. "The GDF doesn't have any C-130s, so it's gotta belong to the Fanboys."

"Hey, Papa, you want to knock that bird out of the sky?" Pounder asked, not wanting to hog the glory.

"Go for it, Dumpster," Papa Mansoor said. "Get your five kills. I'm proud to have you in my squadron."

Mansoor didn't have to tell him twice. Pounder triggered the Piranha off the rail and sent it hunting for the C-130. Seconds later, the Venezuelan bird disappeared from the sky in a flash of high explosives and black smoke.

"Good shot, Ace!" Mansoor cried.

Pounder wanted to phone Colonel Ceasar "Salad" Romano, the man who had bestowed the nickname Dumpster on him, and tell him to go fuck himself. He was an ace with a kill shot on a Flanker fighter jet—from a prop plane, no less.

Trying desperately to keep his voice calm and even like the professional pilot he was, Pounder clicked the transmit button and said, "Thanks, Papa. Let's go home."

Pounder knew the Fanboys would be hopping mad at losing their jets, and he figured they'd retaliate soon.

CHAPTER 13

Four Seasons Hotel
Mexico City

"LOOKS LIKE THE GANGS ALL HERE," LESLIE CONNELLY SAID AS the Operation Unicorn team watched Vice President Evelyn Acevedo step out of her limousine.

John Phoenix, Connelly, Sandy Delacroix, and a phalanx of other officers from various CIA divisions huddled in a suite, staring at the camera feeds. The techs had tapped into the hotel's security cameras and placed their own in the suites belonging to Acevedo, Presidents Fredricks and Zarate, and in the conference room where the high-level talks would take place to discuss the escalating hostilities over the Essequibo Region.

The suite had two bedrooms, which the targeting officers and techs occupied. The techs had quickly turned the main living area into a high-tech operations center with multiple portable workstations that accommodated access to both the U.S. government's Non-Secure Internet Protocol Router

Network (NIPRnet) and the Secret Internet Protocol Router Network. The SIPRnet provided secure voice, video, and data communications to allow the nation's defense and intelligence agencies to communicate without fear of interception. Phoenix, however, wondered if Dragonfly had gotten his hands on the protocols and released them to the highest bidder.

Each workstation consisted of a desk with high privacy panels on each side, separate data communications lines for network security, and a computer with dual monitors covered with screen panels to prevent those who didn't have proper security clearances from reading the screen. The team had also set up a portable shielding tent that blocked radiofrequency (RF) and electromagnetic interference around a console for accessing Top Secret/Sensitive Compartmented Information (TS/SCI) files. They had also hung RF shields over the windows to prevent eavesdropping via parabolic or laser microphones.

With everything up and running, the suite was a secure hub of the Central Intelligence Agency with direct access to D/CIA Stratten's office. As the techs began to log online, a technical operations officer named Mark Schwartz informed Phoenix that Venezuelan fighter jets had attacked the base at Makouria and that pilots from Guyana's Flying Jaguar squadron had shot down two of the Sukhois.

"There goes all pretexts of peace," Phoenix muttered.

"This guy, Will Pounder, he's the first ace in over fifty years!" Schwartz enthused.

Connelly cut in. "How did they shoot down fighter jets?"

"They were Su-30 Flankers, ma'am," Schwartz replied. "The report says the Guyanese pilots were flying Super Tucanos and used heat-seeking Piranhas to knock them down."

"Lucky shot," Connelly said.

"From a fucking turboprop to boot," Schwartz added. "It's more than lucky. The odds are like a million to one."

"That's not going to make Zarate happy at all," Phoenix said. "Why does he keep kicking the hornets' nest? He's lost an offshore patrol boat, two fighter jets, a handful of helicopters, and the base on Ankoko Island. He's not going to take this lying down."

"What are you thinking?" Connelly asked.

Phoenix didn't answer. His breath caught in his throat as he studied the images on the video monitor. Three women had stepped out of a shiny, black stretch Lincoln behind the Venezuelan vice president. While Phoenix didn't recognize the woman in the lead, he knew the third woman intimately.

"What is it?" Connelly asked, reading the expression on his face.

"Uh … Nothing. I just … Uh … Can you bring up the lobby feed?" Phoenix stammered.

Schwartz changed the camera feed to show the richly appointed lobby. The trio of officers watched Acevedo and her two female bodyguards, all dressed in business casual wear, cross the black-and-white checked tile at the hotel's entrance and entered the lobby while a bellman held the door. The camera fully caught Coralina Blanco's face, and Phoenix felt like someone had just punched him in the gut. He had held her hand as she'd died, and he'd told her that he loved her.

Phoenix tried to swallow the massive lump in his throat.

"What is it, Bowie?" Connelly asked.

He tried to keep his voice level as his heart rate continued to spike. "I thought I recognized one of her bodyguards, but it's nothing."

"Run facial recognition on them, Mark," Connelly ordered. "Let's see who they are."

"I'm going for a walk," Phoenix said. "I need some fresh air, and I'll check the perimeter security."

"Be careful, Bowie," Connelly admonished.

Phoenix walked away without replying. As he stepped into the hallway, Delacroix followed him. They walked to the elevator in silence. After Phoenix had pressed the down button, Delacroix asked, "Who is she, Bowie?"

"The taller of the bodyguards is, *was*, my old asset, Cobra."

"The one you said died during your escape from Venezuela?"

"Yes, ma'am," he replied.

"How is she alive?" Delacroix asked.

"I don't know, but I intend to find out," Phoenix replied.

The elevator doors opened as Delacroix clutched Phoenix by the arm. "You need to keep a level head about this, Bowie. Keep your emotions in check."

"I know, ma'am," he stated flatly, stepping out of her grasp and into the elevator. He punched the button for the lobby and tried to avoid Delacroix's steely gaze. Thankfully, she didn't get into the elevator with him, and the closing doors blocked her incriminating glare.

When the elevator doors next opened, Phoenix entered the lobby, searching for his former lover, but he had missed her. The VP and her entourage had apparently gone up as he had come down. Now alone in the lobby, he was at a loss as to what to do. Part of him was thankful that he hadn't caught up to her, otherwise there might have been a public scene, and neither of them needed that. Phoenix needed to clear his head and try to wrap his brain around all the implications that Blanco had staged her death.

He walked out of the lobby onto the busy street. Glancing both ways, he saw multiple armed policemen wearing black battle dress uniforms (BDU), complete with helmets, face masks, and bulletproof vests. They all carried handguns and M4 rifles courtesy of the U.S. government. Some of the men were Mexican national police, better known as the *Federales*, while others were members of the Mexico City Traffic Police. Interspersed among them were FBI agents, U.S. Special Forces members, and CIA paramilitary officers.

Traffic was nonexistent on the streets around the hotel as several of them had been blocked off with wooden sawhorses to prevent attacks from vehicle-borne improvised explosive devices. Beyond the barricades, a continued blaring of horns sounded from the snarl of traffic. Even the pedestrians had to find new avenues of travel around the barricaded streets. Phoenix fingered the pass in his pocket that would allow him to reenter the secure perimeter as he walked past a sawhorse and wondered why they hadn't set up concrete jersey barriers.

Moving quickly down Burdeos Street, Phoenix turned onto Hamburgo, angling toward a small restaurant with ample patio seating under broad verandas. El Pialadero de Guadalajara offered excellent cuisine, but the only thing Phoenix ordered was a cold Corona beer, which the waiter brought along with a bowl of tortilla chips and salsa. The first sip of beer went down smoothly. Phoenix ordered a second before the waiter could turn away from the table, slipping him a five-hundred peso note, about twenty-five bucks U.S. With an enthusiastic smile, the handsome young Mexican headed for the bar.

Phoenix leaned his back against the wall, finding a small sharp point in the stucco to press his stress knot against to try to relieve the pain. Seeing Blanco had caught him completely by surprise, and his heart ached for her.

To distract himself from thinking about her, he engaged in one of his favorite pastimes—people-watching. He could glean a lot of information about how people dressed, their mannerisms, speech patterns, and local slang, and pick up a few strains of gossip just by sitting in place and having a beer. And tipping the help generously often led them to be more talkative, which could also prove to be beneficial in the intelligence world. Phoenix found that tipping the server before-hand often got him preferential treatment and better service, including tidbits of information.

He drank the first beer almost too quickly, and by the time the waiter delivered the second, Phoenix had eaten nearly all of the chips in the bowl, enjoying the bite of the spicy salsa on his tongue.

"More chips, *señor*?"

"No, thanks, Emilio. I'm good," Phoenix replied in Spanish.

Just as Emilio turned away, the rumble of motorcycles filled the street. Emilio paused to watch as ten motorcycles paraded up Lieja Street. Phoenix noted they were primarily dual sport bikes, a street-legal version of a dirt bike, mixed with a few cruisers and high-performance sport bikes. All the riders wore black garb and full-face helmets with tinted visors. Only a handful of the riders had passengers.

"Who are those guys?" Phoenix asked, his senses on high alert.

"The *Los Perros Negros* Motorcycle Club—The Black Dogs."

"Do they normally come through here?" Phoenix asked.

"Sometimes." Emilio shrugged. "I don't see them often. They stay in Ciudad Neza mostly. It is our largest slum at four million people."

Phoenix knew bikers of this caliber almost always carried weapons, and he wondered why they were cruising past the barricaded streets around the Four Seasons. He left his perch on the stool and stepped to the curb to gain a better vantage point. Suddenly, two bikes split off from the pack, wove through the barricade past stunned policemen, and disappeared behind the BBVA Mexico Tower.

Before Phoenix could react, the staccato echo of gunfire reverberated through the concrete canyons. Pulling another banknote from his pocket, Phoenix pressed it into Emilio's hand to pay for his beers and then sprinted up the street toward the action.

By the time he arrived at the barricade, Phoenix had his credentials dangling from his neck on a chain. He flashed them at the closest uniform and dodged around the herd of men rushing toward the street to pursue the bikers, but the *Los Perros Negros* MC was long gone, having scattered as soon as the two bikers had split off from the pack.

Phoenix saw Connelly standing near the hotel entrance and jogged over to her. "What happened?"

"Where were you?" she demanded.

"Taking a stroll. I needed to clear my head."

Phoenix edged closer to the men in civilian clothes who kneeling beside a dead man whose chest had been riddled with bullets. Bright blood pooled under him on the faded gray cement sidewalk. Phoenix could smell the distinct odor of blood, cordite, and excrement.

"Who is he?" Phoenix asked, squatting beside a plain-clothes Mexican policeman with a badge around his neck and a pistol on his left hip.

"He is Luis Gardoqui, Colombia's National Defence Minister," the mustachioed cop said.

"Those bikers shot him?" Phoenix asked to confirm his theory since he hadn't seen the actual event.

"Yes, but at least our men took out two of the bikers," the cop replied, pointing at a motorcycle lying on its side farther down the street. Two dead bodies sprawled on the blacktop beside it.

"Why'd they kill him?" Phoenix asked, motioning toward Gardoqui.

"That you will have to ask the bikers," the mustachioed cop's partner replied.

Phoenix glanced around at what should have been heightened security. The men in BDUs seemed unfazed by the action that had just taken place.

"We need to get upstairs," Connelly said, tugging at Phoenix's arm. "There's nothing we can do here."

He followed her into the hotel toward the elevator, wondering why the bikers had killed the defense secretary in front of the hotel. It made no sense. At least the guys in BDUs had reacted quickly enough to shoot a pair of the bikers.

Acevedo and her entourage walked up as the elevator doors opened, and Phoenix came face to face with Coralina Blanco.

Phoenix froze for a moment, taking in her presence, happy to see her alive but wondering just what the hell kinda con job she had run on him. His mind reeled back to the scene on the bridge as he and Blanco sat in the bullet-riddled Nissan Patrol. Blood poured from between her fingers as she tried to stymie the flow by pressing her hand to the wound in her chest. She had peered at him through dulling gray eyes and clutched his arm as she'd whispered that she loved him.

He had felt insanely guilty for leaving her, but seeing her in the hallway, all Phoenix felt was a desire to hold her in his arms again.

"Excuse me, *señor*," Blanco said, then stepped around him into the open car, her expression giving nothing away. "Madam," she said over her shoulder to Acevedo.

Phoenix moved out of the way. He never took his eyes off Blanco as he blocked the door with his hand until Acevedo and her other bodyguard had boarded the elevator. He pulled his hand away and prayed she would acknowledge his presence as the doors slid closed.

"What's the matter with you?" Connelly asked as they headed for the stairs. "Haven't you ever had an asset come back from the dead before?"

Phoenix glanced sharply at her.

"We have cameras everywhere, Bowie. We overheard your conversation with Sandy at the elevators. She's right, you know. You need to keep a level head."

Still trying to get a grasp on his spiraling emotions, Phoenix replied softly, "The last time I saw her, she was bleeding out from a chest wound. I left her for dead, Leslie."

"Then how is she now a bodyguard for Acevedo?" Connelly demanded as she dragged Phoenix into the CIA suite so they could confer in private.

"I don't know," Phoenix said. "That's why I took a walk. I was trying to make sense of it all."

"I hate to interrupt," Schwartz said from behind the control console, "but Zarate's helicopter is inbound."

CHAPTER 14

The **CIA** team clustered around the monitors to watch the president of Venezuela exit his helicopter atop the adjoining BBVA Mexico Tower.

At 235-meters, it was the second tallest building in Mexico City and the fourth tallest in the country. The builders had incorporated a helicopter landing pad into the design at the top of the tower to allow visiting dignitaries and wealthy patrons to come and go with ease. They also had a standing agreement with the Four Seasons to allow its guests to use the landing pad as needed.

Zarate stepped from the Bell JetRanger wearing his customary dark blue suit but without the tie. His thick mustache glistened in the sun as if he'd applied something to it to enhance the sheen. If one didn't know he was a ruthless dictator, they might suspect he starred in tawdry telenovelas as a dashing but gently aging leading man.

The Venezuelan president strode across the walkway from the helipad to the elevator and entered immediately, riding down to the lobby of the BBVA Tower where his vice president greeted her him with a hug and a kiss like a long-lost uncle.

Mark Schwartz and his team had also tapped the cameras in the BBVA Tower, and the CIA officers monitored *El Jefe*'s progress into the lobby of the Four Seasons, escorted by a team of security specialists. While Acevedo had only two bodyguards, Zarate had a dozen clearing his way.

"I count at least two Russians, maybe three," Phoenix said. "Probably Spetsnaz or Wagner PMCs. I'm guessing the other guys are regular SEBIN agents."

"It's a good thing we got here early to wire everything up," Schwartz said. "We'd never get into his suite with all those guards."

"Thanks for stating the obvious," Phoenix retorted.

"At least I was here to do the work," Schwartz shot back. "Where the fuck were you?"

Phoenix glared at the tech but said nothing, keeping his face impassive.

"Knock it off, guys," Connelly said. "We're all on the same side."

Delacroix leaned in closer to the screen to see Zarate step off the elevator and head for one of the two presidential suites set aside by the hotel for him and President Fredricks.

Moments later, Acevedo and her two guards exited another elevator and headed for Zarate's suite.

"You know," Delacroix said. "You might be able to use your past relationship with Blanco to gain access to Acevedo."

Phoenix had a ready retort on his lips but let it die. Stating the obvious and voicing his frustration had led him to be somewhat of a pariah amongst his fellow case officers and handlers, which was why his former lover, Connelly, was his controller. And playing these back-and-forth games to keep everyone happy and appeased was not his forte. Phoenix had been molded from the first day of Army basic training to break shit and kill people.

Not long after Phoenix had left Ground Branch and

moved to LA Division, one of his mentors had sat him down and given him the facts of life. Being a case officer was about finding assets, developing assets, and redirecting their energies toward more important targets. Operation Unicorn was about redirecting Acevedo and bringing her back into the fold, so Phoenix took a deep breath to calm his nerves.

While he *hated* being on a task force, and would rather be in the field, running his own assets, he knew there was also support in numbers. Sure, he had to type lengthy reports concerning his activities and the intelligence he'd gained, but at least the reams of paper didn't make snide remarks or try to measure dicks.

Schwartz was a tech who fancied himself as the next Jack Ryan. He'd repeatedly applied to the National Clandestine Service, but his application kept getting kicked back because he was too valuable in his current position. He carried a grudge and Phoenix could understand that better than anyone.

Delacroix, however, should have known better than to pipe up about his past with Blanco. She had run assets and pitched recruits before becoming chief of station in Chile, and then moved into management at the Latin America Division. A successful Operation Unicorn would be the feather in her cap that moved her to the Seventh Floor. Phoenix could clearly see her motivations and she, like Phoenix himself, wasn't above pushing an asset's buttons to get the job done.

Phoenix took another deep breath and tried to exhale his pent-up emotions then said to his boss, "I need to get Blanco alone."

"Then we need to manufacture a reason for that," Delacroix replied. Straightening to cross her arms and pace the room, Delacroix sounded out several ideas on how to do just that.

"Is she staying in the suite with Acevedo or in other accommodations?" Connelly asked.

Schwartz accessed the hotel's guest list via his computer. "Acevedo's security has an adjoining room."

"Do we have cameras in there?" Delacroix asked.

"No, ma'am," Schwartz replied.

"That's an oversight on your part," Phoenix stated.

"How were we to know your *dead* girlfriend was going to turn up here as Acevedo's bodyguard?" Schwartz shot back.

"Easy guys," Delacroix said.

"He's right, though," Connelly said. "We didn't think her security team warranted a camera."

"Everybody here warrants a camera," Phoenix said with exasperation.

"Chill, Bowie!" Connelly commanded. "We don't have the manpower or the resources to install cameras in every room and watch them."

"I've got to get out of here," Phoenix said, heading for the door.

"Where are you going?" Connelly asked.

"To do my fucking job and get some fucking intelligence on what's happening in his shitty hotel."

He went out the door without waiting for a reply and instead of taking the elevator, jogged down the stairs. Like many of his counterparts, Phoenix wore slacks and a dress shirt, but he'd forgone the tie and jacket. To make himself appear more like a Latino businessman, Phoenix removed his security pass from around his neck and tucked it back into his pocket. He wanted to know what was going on—not just with Blanco but why the defense secretary had been gunned down outside the hotel. Someone had to have reported the man's movements to the *Los Perros Negros* MC, which to Phoenix meant it was an inside job. The timing was just too perfect.

Crossing the lobby, Phoenix spied his old boss and mentor, Chris Miller, at the outside bar but didn't know why the paramilitary officer was horning in on his op. He veered through the door into the hotel's courtyard. He and Miller shared a history all the way back to Afghanistan when Phoenix had been a Green Beret, and Miller had been running CIA capture-and-kill operations against Al-Qaeda leadership.

"Hey, Jim Bowie, want a beer?" Miller asked as Phoenix sat down in the shade of the large table umbrella.

"Sure. What are you drinking?"

Miller motioned for the waiter as he said, "Corona—the Budweiser of Mexico."

When the server arrived at the table, Phoenix ordered a Corona and sat back in his chair to appraise his colleague. Miller was in his mid-forties with a lean body full of ropy muscles. He had a fresh tan and brown hair above thick brows that frequently narrowed to squint, so it was easier for his pale green eyes to read smaller print. The CIA liked to recruit guys like Miller and Phoenix, who could blend into a crowded street from Baghdad to Buenos Aires. Both men were masters of multiple languages and were equally at ease running assets at covert meetings or kicking down doors to bust heads. Miller had recruited Phoenix into the agency, and, like it or not, Miller's name was all over his paperwork and reputation. If Cole Stratten was Leslie Connelly's bishop, then Chris Miller was the one holding Phoenix's hand.

Phoenix had entered the CIA as a paramilitary operations officer and spent his early years with the agency as a member of the Special Activities Center, or Ground Branch, providing the president with alternative options when overt military or diplomatic actions were not politically viable. While part of Ground Branch, Phoenix had also undergone the Clandestine Service Trainee program. As both a spy "handler" and an ass kicker, Phoenix had worked on Miller's teams off and on during his career until he'd transferred to the Latin America Division with the help of Sandy Delacroix.

"What are you doing here?" Phoenix asked.

"Those are my guys out there providing security," Miller replied.

"They did a shit job of it, brother," Phoenix said bluntly. "Who let those motorcycles past the barricades?"

Miller's face tightened with annoyance. "My guess is the local traffic cops."

The waiter brought the beer and after he was out of earshot, Phoenix leaned in closer to Miller. "Why'd they kill Gardoqui?"

Miller shrugged. "Internal politics. A war between cartels and suppliers. Take your pick."

Phoenix nodded. "I heard the same thing. Maybe that's the narrative they want the media to run with."

"What are you up to?" Miller asked. "Delacroix got you under her thumb?"

"She's not so bad. I've been in and out of Venezuela and Guyana for over a year."

Miller let out a low whistle. "With no backup? That's ballsy even for you, Bowie."

Phoenix glanced around to see if anyone was eavesdropping. Miller was the one who had bestowed the codename "Bowie" on him, and while he hadn't liked it at first, the name had grown on him. To augment the mystic of his honorific, Phoenix had started carrying a large sheath knife with a crossguard and a clip point in the tradition of famous knife fighter and pioneer legend Jim Bowie during their Ground Branch operations. The knife had since been retired, but the name had stuck around.

As the two men sipped their beers, a third gentleman slipped into a seat beside Miller. He was distinctly Mexican and forgettable at the same time with his brown skin, brown hair, and brown eyes.

The Ground Branch operator motioned to the newcomer. "Bowie, this is Carl Daniels. He's one of us but stationed here in the city."

"Nice to meet you," Bowie said with a nod, knowing it wasn't the man's real name.

"Shit's going down," Daniels said, keeping voice low. He paused as the waiter arrived to see if the new customer needed a drink, but Daniels waved him away. "The *Federales* are raiding the *Los Perros Negros* compound as we speak."

"I know they killed Gardoqui, but why?" Phoenix asked.

"Party line is the drug angle, but my opinion is that it's a distraction," Daniels replied.

"From what?" Phoenix asked.

"Something happening here," Daniels replied. "We've been hearing chatter about a strike."

"Against whom?" Miller asked.

Daniels shrugged. "That I don't know. Our network just says it's against one of the big guys here."

"Fuck," Miller swore softly.

"What do we do?" Phoenix asked. "I mean, what are you guys working on? I've got my own operation going here, and it's got nothing to do with thwarting whatever the chatter is about."

"We need to tighten security," Daniels replied. "I'm on my way to brief Mike Asbury. I saw you guys here and figured you'd want to know, too."

"Got room for two more in your brief?" Miller asked.

"I don't see why not," Daniels replied.

Miller and Phoenix accompanied Daniels up to the secretary of state's suite and listened in while Daniels gave Asbury a briefing about what the three officers had just discussed downstairs.

Once Daniels had finished, Asbury turned to his Mexican counterpart and asked if they could beef up the security around the hotel. The pudgy, bespeckled statesman said he would speak to the Mexico City chief of police and the General Commissioner of the Federal Police, but he could make no guarantees.

Out in the hallway, as the three spooks were leaving

Asbury's room, a scheme popped into Phoenix's mind. He stopped Daniels. "Can you get me in to see Vice President Acevedo under the pretext of a security briefing?"

Daniels thought for a moment, then said, "I'm sure I can. Why?"

"It would help facilitate my operation if I could speak to her," Phoenix replied.

CHAPTER 15

At seven p.m., Carl Daniels rapped on the door to Vice President Evelyn Acevedo's suite. He glanced at Sandy Delacroix and John Phoenix to see if they were ready for the meeting.

Both case officers knew they would be easily recognized once they walked into the room. Acevedo would know Delacroix as her former handler, and the same went for Blanco and Bowie. Daniels had not been informed of the situation as he hadn't been read in on Operation Unicorn.

The unknown guard answered the door. After Schwartz had run her photo through the CIA's facial recognition program, they'd come up with a blank. She was shorter than Blanco and had a fierce gleam in her eye as if she suspected they were there to cause harm to the VP.

The trio of CIA officers entered the suite to find Acevedo standing by the window in a black pantsuit and cream blouse. She shook all of their hands as they introduced themselves.

Phoenix couldn't take his eyes off Coralina Blanco. Her thick brown hair had grown out, and she'd pulled it back into a ponytail with little curly wisps hanging down on either side of her face to frame it. She returned his gaze without showing any expression, but her warm gray eyes seemed to pierce his soul. Phoenix had to grit his teeth against the pain flaring behind his shoulder blade. He wanted to run over and wrap her in his arms, clearly remembering the kisses they'd shared in Venezuela.

"To what do I owe this pleasure?" Acevedo asked, sinking into an upholstered chair.

Daniels took the lead and explained the heightened security situation to Acevedo. She listened patiently and nodded at the salient points Daniels made. Her eyebrows shot up when Daniels finished with, "And that is why I would like to add *señor* James Bowie to your security team."

Acevedo pondered this for a few silent moments, then said, "I have an all-female detail. I will add Sandy if I must increase my team."

Daniels glanced at Delacroix and Phoenix. "Acceptable?"

"That's works for me," Delacroix said. "However, madam vice president, I would ask that you allow *señor* Bowie to meet with your team while I speak to you alone. There is more information I would like to share."

Acevedo pursed her lips as she inhaled, then nodded. "Agreed. Tranquillo, take *señor* Bowie to your room while I speak with Sandy."

At least we know her name now, Phoenix thought as he moved toward the adjoining room door.

"Uh ... Tranquillo," Daniels said. "May I speak to you outside for a moment?"

Tranquillo furrowed her brow even further, her gaze full of disdain and distrust. She turned to Acevedo and said, "I do not like this separation. There is nothing they have to say which the other cannot hear."

"Tranquillo," Acevedo said sharply. "Do not question my orders. Do as Mister Daniels has asked."

With a sigh of exasperation and a roll of her eyes, Tranquillo led Carl Daniels into the hallway. Blanco headed for the adjoining bedroom with Phoenix in tow. He couldn't wait to close the door and have her spring into her arms. He figured Acevedo knew what was happening the moment Delacroix stepped into the room, and she'd made her choice. Bowie was off the hook as her handler. A feather in Delacroix's cap.

Phoenix closed the door to the bodyguards' room and turned to face Blanco, thankful there were no cameras in the room.

No sooner had the door latch clicked than she ran into his arms.

Phoenix hugged her tightly, a wave of emotion riding through him that nearly brought tears to his eyes. "I can't believe you're alive! You don't know how happy I am."

"Oh, *mi amor*, I love you," she whispered, running her fingers into the hair at the back of his neck.

"I love you, too, Coralina."

"I'm sorry, Bowie. I had to do it," she whispered. "They made me swap the SD card, and they forced me to stay in Venezuela. I had to make you leave without me. It was for your safety and mine."

She kissed him fiercely and then hugged him again. "I'm so sorry."

Phoenix's analytical mind kicked in. Instead of treating her as a lover, his instinct was to pump his asset for more information. Closing his eyes, he breathed in her shampoo and perfume, felt the silky smoothness of her hair on his cheek, and the taste of her kiss still on his lips.

"Who made you play such a terrible trick?" he finally asked, trying to formulate his words into a mild-sounding question.

Blanco stepped back, turning slightly away from him. "A man named Terry Martin. After the SEBIN picked me up at the airport in Piar, he came to me and said I had to work for him."

Phoenix wanted to be pissed at her, but having sex with

her had ruined his objectivity, and all he wanted to do was tear her clothes off and make love to her now.

To fill the silence, Blanco spoke again. "I have been given a job, but it seems you have achieved your goal already. I was to facilitate your meeting with Acevedo."

"Who gave you the job? Terry Martin?"

She shook her head. "No. General Calderón, the Director of the SEBIN."

"Why would he ask you to help us?" Phoenix asked, clearly perplexed.

"Calderón wants change, Bowie!" Blanco whispered with excitement. "He wants to help us—the Venezuelan people."

"How?" Phoenix asked, still trying to determine the angles.

"He didn't divulge the plan, only that I was to help Acevedo meet with you." Her smile at reuniting with Bowie faded into a perplexity. "Why are you not in there, speaking to her?"

"I told you she had been an asset before, right?"

Blanco nodded.

"Warbler, I mean Sandy, was her previous handler," Phoenix said, "and she must have felt more comfortable with her than establishing a new relationship with me."

Blanco's gaze searched his face with a knowing twinkle. "That's understandable. You couldn't stop staring at me."

Phoenix smiled ruefully. "I was that bad?"

Blanco giggled. "Not for me." She turned serious, her eyes suddenly brimming with tears. "I feared you would hate me for what I've done. They brainwashed me, Bowie. It was horrible. They force me to work against you and to fake my own death to drive you away."

"How could I hate you, Coralina? I love you."

She pressed her face against his shoulder and sobbed as he hugged her fiercely. He never wanted to let her go again.

"Tell me," Phoenix begged. "Can you get away?"

"It will be difficult. Tranquillo is highly suspicious of me, but I think Acevedo will allow me to sneak away."

He slipped a piece of paper with his phone number on it into her pocket. "What about during the negotiations? Will you have time off?"

Blanco stepped from his embrace and blew her nose into a tissue. "Perhaps she will let me leave. We have not discussed what Tranquillo and I will do while she is at the conference. Do you have to attend the meeting?"

Phoenix shook his head. "No. I'm only here to recruit."

"Good." She smiled as she stepped closer, wrapping her arms around his neck. "I can't wait to be with you again. Remember the apartment where we made love?"

He smiled. The memories were still fresh in his mind. "How could I forget?"

"I want to make new memories with you, Bowie." Blanco kissed him deeply, and he wrapped his arms tighter around her, luxuriating in the warm, supple feel of her body.

There was a sharp knock on the door, and the two lovers pulled quickly from their embrace. Blanco stepped away, wiping her mouth with the back of her hand and saying sharply, "How could you let this threat go unchecked?"

Phoenix picked up the narrative, understanding the roles they had to play. "We just learned about it. That's why I want to continue working with you and Tranquillo to provide effective security for the vice president."

Tranquillo stepped into the room. After Phoenix finished his narrative, she said, "You must go. The threat is not to the vice president. We have her contained in this building. As long as she doesn't leave, she will be safe."

"I understand," Phoenix replied. "But that is a decision for Madam Acevedo to make, don't you think?"

"I am the head of her security detail," Tranquillo stated. "I will tell her what is best for her safety."

Phoenix could see Tranquillo wasn't going to budge. He

glanced at Blanco once more, then left the room through the door to the hallway without going back through Acevedo's suite. Delacroix and Daniels waited for him near the elevator.

As the car arrived and the door opened, Daniels said, "Tranquillo is going to be a thorn in your operation."

Phoenix discounted his statement. He and Delacroix had already met with their assets, and their mission was moving forward.

CHAPTER 16

Phoenix watched the replay of Delacroix's conversation with Acevedo in the Operation Unicorn suite.

Delacroix had done an excellent job of pitching the vice president, and Acevedo had risen to the bait of the CIA providing a backdoor to the U.S. government. To Phoenix, it appeared that she had anticipated contact with CIA officers and was more than ready to be the star of Operation Unicorn. He reasoning the money and note he'd left in her desk drawer had primed the pump.

"Tomorrow, Fredricks and Zarate sit down to discuss the future of the Essequibo Region," Delacroix said to the team after the recording stopped.

"What's the game plan for Acevedo?" Schwartz asked.

Phoenix had grown annoyed at the little prick's incessant questions about the action plan. Still, even he was curious as to what Delacroix had to say on this point, even though he already knew the marching orders that President Mercia had given them.

Her answer was a bit disappointing when she said, "We wait to see how things play out with the peace negotiations, and we go from there."

While Phoenix didn't think it was a salient answer, he didn't press her for more details, and no one else did either.

"I'm going out," he said, heading for the door. "I want to see if I can pick up more information about what happened to Gardoqui and maybe gauge the mood of our illustrious presidents."

"How are you going to do that?" Schwartz asked.

"If you have to ask, Mark, then you'll never know," Phoenix said. "Maybe you should just stick to pushing buttons, okay?"

Connelly shot a disapproving look at him. He shrugged as if he didn't care. Out in the hallway, Phoenix rolled his shoulder to relieve the ache. At the elevator, he pushed the down button and leaned against a projecting wall corner to jam it into his shoulder. He let out a sigh of relief just as the elevator doors slid open. A little girl stared up at him while holding her mother's hand.

Phoenix winked at her and said in Spanish, "I'm just scratching my back."

She giggled as he stepped onto the elevator and pressed the button for the lobby. The girl looked up at her mom and whispered a little too loudly, "He sounds like a bear."

Phoenix gave her a low growl, and the girl giggled again.

"See, mama, *un oso*."

"*Sí, un oso*," the woman replied absently.

"What brings you to the hotel?" Phoenix asked.

"My husband is Enrique Colon, the Panamanian Minister of Public Safety."

"Is he here for the peace talks between Fredricks and Zarate?" Phoenix asked, knowing full well he was. It seemed everyone wanted in on the action or at least to protect their country from the continuing tension between the warring nations.

"Yes, he is here for the conference," she confirmed.

The elevator doors opened onto the lobby, and they parted

ways as they exited. Phoenix spotted Chris Miller in the lobby bar. He liked to hold court anywhere there was a cold beer. Phoenix slid into the booth across from him.

"You want to tell me exactly what you're doing here?" Miller asked.

Phoenix shrugged.

Miller chuckled. "I should have named you after that stone-faced bastard in the Egyptian desert instead of a fucking war hero. You always have the same blank look on your face as the Sphinx whenever someone presses you for information."

Phoenix glanced around. "You know I can't talk about ongoing operations. Especially not here."

"Then let's go outside, and you can fill me in."

"I can't, Rebar. You know that."

Miller's jaw flexed as he ground his teeth together. Rebar had been the codename Phoenix had known him by in Afghanistan, where Miller had always carried a Leatherman Rebar multitool. He had used it for everything from picking his teeth to fixing a broken-down engine to plucking out an enemy fighter's fingernails. When operating with Ground Branch, Miller used the call sign "Husker" since he'd played outside linebacker for the Nebraska Cornhuskers. What Miller didn't tell people was that he'd only played in one game his entire collegiate career, making an appearance in the Orange Bowl his senior year.

"Let's go outside then." Miller stood and headed for the door with Phoenix on his heels. They walked out onto the street, and Phoenix breathed deeply of the warm evening air. He could smell the scent of cooking meat wafting from somewhere down the block. Faint music drifted in the air, and every building shone with festive lights. Miller clapped his colleague on the shoulder and steered him away from the entrance toward a darker part of the street.

"Talk to me, Bowie. Tell me about Operation Unicorn."

"Never heard of it," Phoenix replied.

"Bullshit," Miller said. "I brought you in. I trained you. I ran ops with you for years. Talk to me."

"You know I can't, even if there was such an operation in play."

"I knew I should have never approved your transfer. Delacroix and Connelly had fucked you up."

"Easy, Husker," Phoenix replied, trying to pump the brakes on the train.

Miller shook his head in consternation. "I should have known that you'd defend those two bitches. They've brainwashed you."

"What's going on, man? This isn't like you," Phoenix said.

"How am I supposed to do my job and protect these people when you're running an op right under my nose?" Miller demanded.

Phoenix scratched his chin. He wasn't going to tell Miller about Unicorn, but he could find out what the guy knew about it, so he asked. "What do you know about Unicorn?"

"That it has something to do with Acevedo. Is she a Unicorn?"

"Where did you hear about the operation?" Phoenix pressed.

"It doesn't matter where I heard about it," Miller retorted.

Phoenix rubbed his chin again as he thought through the logic of how such a highly compartmentalized operation had leaked to the Ground Branch officer.

"Talk to me, Bowie," Miller pleaded.

Phoenix's phone buzzed in his pocket. He was more than thankful for the interruption as he pulled it out. He didn't recognize the number but said to Miller, "I've got to take this. We can talk more at a later time."

"You better *believe* we will," Miller growled.

Phoenix answered the phone as he walked away.

"Bowie. It's me," Blanco said.

"Where are you?" he asked.

"Just outside the hotel entrance."

Phoenix knew better than to turn and look for her. "How long do you have?"

"At least an hour," she said.

Phoenix relaxed a bit, knowing he would finally be alone with Blanco, and he had the perfect spot. "Go north on Rio Elba. It's across the street between the two towers."

"I see it," Blanco said.

"I have a room at the Suites Rio Elba, two blocks away. I'll meet you there." Phoenix ended the call after she confirmed the directions. He'd reserved the room shortly after arriving in Mexico City, hoping he might have a chance to rendezvous with Blanco and to act as a safe house in case things went to shit.

He wanted to race straight for the hotel room, knowing Blanco had a time limit. But he forced himself to stroll in the opposite direction, starting his SDR. As he walked, Phoenix used the reflection of store windows to check for tails, stopped frequently to hide in dark alcoves, and circled around to his back trail. Phoenix found he liked the narrow side streets with large shade trees that formed canopies over the sidewalks. Small cafes with outdoor seating provided places for patrons to relax, and it was nice to overhear the pleasant chatter about their mundane lives.

Turning down Rio Atoyac, Phoenix checked his six by bending down and retying his shoe. Once he'd determined that no one was watching, he quickly pushed aside a plastic sheet and entered a building under renovation. Large drop cloths covered the building's front to contain debris, and scaffolding had been erected over the sidewalk to protect pedestrians.

Phoenix glanced back once more, then pushed through the heavy wooden door to the apartment building. He made his way up the darkened stairwell to the sixth story and exited onto the roof. From there, he hopped down to the roof of the neighboring building. Phoenix didn't need to worry about leaping from building to building as there were no gaps to jump across. All the buildings on the block had adjoining walls, so he was able to cut diagonally across the rooftops toward his ultimate destination, dodging massive air conditioning units and ventilation systems.

At the fire access door to Suites Rio Elba, Phoenix used a set of lock picks he carried in his back pocket to jimmy the lock and then went down the stairs, stopping midway on the last run to observe the lobby. He saw Blanco standing by a rack of brochures and called softly to her.

She walked casually over, and the two of them went up the stairs, waiting until they were in the room and the door had shut behind them before kissing passionately. Phoenix couldn't believe he had her in his arms again as images of the staged death scene replayed in his mind. He pushed them quickly away. They tore off their clothes in a rush and tumbled into bed.

The lovers didn't have much time, nor did they need it. They finished quickly before Blanco nestled in beside him with her head on his chest and leg cocked up on his thigh. Blanco intertwined her fingers with his and let out a sigh of contentment.

"I wish we could stay here and never go back," she said.

He kissed her forehead before whispering, "Me, too."

Again, thoughts of leaving the agency swirled in his head. His days as a warfighter were coming to an end. He couldn't run field ops forever. Eventually, the CIA would saddle him with a desk job, and then where would he be? Phoenix had avoided cubical life for as long as he could, but time wasn't on his side. His knees and lower back ached from years of physical punishment, and the constant knot of muscle behind his shoulder blade reminded him of his ever-present worries.

At least for the moment, he was relatively pain-free, basking in the glow of post-coital bliss.

The clock in his head reminded Phoenix that his time with Blanco was coming to an end. He pressed her for information on Terry Martin, and she told him everything from Martin's interrogation and brainwashing to his swapping the SD cards in the spy pen.

Her naked body shuddered under the sheet as she recounted Martin's threats to her life and those of her family. Phoenix held her close, knowing she needed comfort and reassurance to counter the intimidation she felt.

Phoenix also knew they needed to leave, but his body told him he needed more from her. They made love again before quietly dressing; each lost in their own thoughts and emotions.

He led her up the stairs to the fire door. They crossed the roofs to the building under renovation, and Phoenix told her how to find her way out.

Blanco hesitated at the top of the stairs and turned back to him. "Be careful, Bowie."

"It's John. My real name is John."

"John," she murmured, rolling his name around in her mouth to test it out. "I like it. It's better than Bowie." She kissed him one last time and started down toward the street.

Phoenix moved to the edge of the building, using the skirting from the drop cloths to block the view of anyone looking up from below. He seemed to hold his breath until he saw Blanco step out from under the scaffolding and head across the street.

As she reached the far sidewalk, Phoenix spotted a shadowy figure as he dropped a cigarette and started after Blanco. Phoenix ran for the access door and tripped over the threshold, falling face-first on the landing and sliding down the first set of stairs on his belly. He rolled to protect his head and hit the wall with his rounded back, letting out a grunt.

Pain flared through his arms and legs. He had scrapes on his right wrist where he'd tried to block his fall, and his chest burned from slamming into the concrete.

Ignoring the pain, Phoenix rolled to his feet and charged down the stairs, keeping his hands out to steady himself on the smooth metal railings. At each landing, he'd grip the appropriate rail and spin himself through the turn. Blanco had a head start, and Phoenix had already lost time in the fall. Feeling the need to increase his speed, Phoenix jumped down the final two flights, leaping from one landing to the next, slamming his shoulder into the wall each time. His entire body ached, but he couldn't stop moving.

But Phoenix made it out the door in time to see the follower turn the corner onto Rio Elba by the eight-story parking garage. He ran across the street and charged up the block, reaching the corner before stopping.

Breathing hard, Phoenix peered around the corner and saw Blanco crossing Rio Elba. Instead of fixating on her, Phoenix let his gaze rove over the other pedestrians.

A moment later, he had his suspect in sight. He wore black jeans, a dark collared shirt, and black shoes. The watcher paused to light another cigarette, making him appear as if he was just another guy out for a stroll.

Phoenix took a deep breath and stepped out from behind the building. Cigarette glanced in his direction, but Phoenix had moved behind the trunk of a large tree, almost tripping over the low shrubs planted along the curb. He rolled his wounded wrist as he chastised himself for being so clumsy.

Putting his hand out to steady himself against the tree, Phoenix peeked around it. Blanco had made it onto the other sidewalk, walking south past an ancient church-like building that was most definitely out of place amongst the glass-and-steel towers surrounding it.

Cigarette strolled across the street, flicking his butt away as he jogged the last few steps to avoid an oncoming car.

Phoenix ran across the street in the wake of the car, stepping under the covered patio of a wine bar and staring at his quarry through the stalks of potted bamboo plants.

Blanco must have suspected that someone was following her as she turned into the lobby of the Tower Reforma. The man in black jeans paused at the door and then headed in.

Phoenix stepped out from behind his cover. His gut churned with anxiety, and his shoulder ached at the thought of Blanco being in deep trouble.

CHAPTER 17

A T THE ENTRANCE TO THE SKYSCRAPER, P HOENIX PAUSED TO look through the massive floor-to-ceiling glass panels of the Tower Reforma lobby. Blanco waited by the elevators, staring up at the numbers with the man lurking right behind her.

Once the elevators opened and they'd stepped inside, Phoenix charged across the lobby, slipping into the elevator as the doors began to close. Phoenix slammed the guy up against the wall, pinning him in place with a forearm across his throat. He noted the man was in his late twenties, prematurely balding, with short, cropped hair and brown eyes. Phoenix saw no fear in them. They just bulged with surprise at the sudden attack.

The only sound in the car as the doors banged shut was the soft choking of the stalker.

Once the car began to rise, Phoenix relaxed his grip just enough to allow the man to breathe easier and demanded, "Who the fuck are you?"

"Easy Bowie," the man croaked. "I'm just following orders. I was to follow the girl and see where she went."

"Who ordered you to do that?" Phoenix barked.

"Husker," the guy croaked.

"Fuck!" Phoenix exclaimed and let go of the man. "Why?"

The guy rubbed his throat and took several tentative breaths before saying, "He wanted to know who she was meeting with. I take it that was you?"

"Yeah. It was me," Phoenix replied tersely. "She's my fucking asset."

The guy held up his hands in surrender. "Don't blame me, bro. I'm just doing what I'm told."

The elevator stopped, and the doors opened. Phoenix pulled the balding man out into the empty hallway, saying to Blanco, "Go. You need to get back in time."

Slowly, the elevator doors closed on her. When she was gone, Phoenix turned to the other CIA officer. "If you work for Husker, you must be Ground Branch?"

"Yeah, sure. I'm whatever you want me to be," the paramilitary officer replied.

Phoenix shook his head. He was well beyond frustration, bordering on red-hot anger at Husker for interfering in his operation. "Tell me why Husker sent you after her."

"I just told you, man. I'm following orders. He wanted to know where she was going and why." The Ground Branch shooter smiled lecherously. "Truth be told, I'd be boning her, too, bro."

Phoenix snapped off a punch that caught the other man square on the chin, knocking him back into the window. As the guy tried to catch himself, Phoenix slammed a fist into the kid's gut and doubled him over. He could have kept right on beating his frustrations out on Husker's man, but he pulled back.

"Fuck you," Phoenix snarled. "Get out of here."

Moaning, the man pressed the button for the elevator. Phoenix kicked him in the ass. "Take the stairs, dumbass."

The man wobbled as he headed down the hallway. Reaching the door, the kid half-turned to face Phoenix. Still clutching his gut, he growled, "You'll pay for this."

"Sue me," Phoenix shot back.

After Husker's man had gone, Phoenix put both hands on the railing and gazed out the window at the brightly lit skyline. He breathed deeply, trying to bring his emotions into check. After spending such a lovely time with Blanco, it was rather jarring to find out his own brother-in-arms were spying on him.

Phoenix knew Chris Miller well enough to know the man wouldn't have sent his operator out without a damn good reason, and Phoenix was going to find out why.

———

JOHN PHOENIX GAVE the bald paramilitary officer a ten-minute head start, then rode the elevator down to the Tower Reforma lobby. Outside, he crossed the street to the Four Seasons, flashing his security credentials at the guard by the front entrance.

During his time staring out the window in the tower, Phoenix had pondered how Chris Miller had found out about Operation Unicorn and why he had sent his bald pal to follow Blanco. There had to be a security breach in his operation, and it had to have come from someone in the tight circle of officers involved with turning Acevedo into a CIA asset.

Opening the door to the Operation Unicorn suite, Phoenix found a skeleton crew of night shift workers watching the cameras. He walked over to a young analyst and sat down beside her. Jennifer Newton was a pretty blonde-haired, blue-eyed graduate from Northwestern University. She held a master's in computer science with a minor in Latin American and Caribbean studies, which meant she was fluent in Spanish and Portuguese. Delacroix had handpicked Newton to serve her first CIA tour in the Latin American Division.

"I didn't expect to see you here," Newton said.

"I'm just checking in. Anything new?" Phoenix asked. He

liked Newton's work ethic, putting in long hours to provide critical analysis for other operations he'd been on. While Phoenix wanted to follow the old adage of "never trust anyone," Newton fell into the tight circle of people that Phoenix felt he could at least have some faith in.

Newton nodded to the screens. "Everyone is settled in for the night."

He scanned the suite to see the positions of the other officers, then leaned in closer to Newton. "I want you to run a name through the system."

Newton switched screens on her computer, bringing up the CIA server to run a background check. "What's his name?"

He figured he'd start with the name Blanco had given him, then dive into Chris Miller's team.

She typed the name "Terry Martin" into the search box and clicked the enter button on the keyboard. They both waited silently as the computer worked through the search before it returned a blank. There was nothing in the CIA system associated with that name.

"Try Martin with an 'e.' M-A-R-T-E-N."

Again, the computer found no lead. Phoenix sat back in his chair and put his hands on top of his head.

"I know that look," Newton said. "The surrender cobra. I saw it a lot at Northwestern football games."

"I'm not surrendering," Phoenix replied. "I just need to find another angle."

"Who is this guy?" Newton asked.

"Obviously, he's a nobody in our system." Phoenix dropped his arms and leaned forward.

"Try the word 'dragonfly.'"

Newton typed in the word and hit enter, bringing up a flashing red box that told them they didn't have a high enough security clearance to read the file. It had been stamped "TS/SCI."

"Fuck me," Phoenix swore.

Newton glanced over at Phoenix. "Are you trying to get me into trouble?"

It was just as he figured. He didn't have the clearance to read the file, but Connelly had read him in on Dragonfly at the D/CIA's insistence. "Nobody is going to get in trouble, Jenn. Just forget about it. Can you bring up a list of everyone who works for Chris Miller over at Ground Branch?"

"Sure. That's an easy one." Newton typed on the keyboard, and moments later, a list of names appeared beside headshots of the paramilitary officers.

Phoenix pointed at the balding kid who'd been following Blanco. "Print me out that one."

But another profile that caught his attention was a few photos down—Mark Schwartz.

Newton hit the print button, and Phoenix snatched the sheets off the printer as soon as they came out. He sat back in his chair and read the brief on Riley Richardson. He had a law degree from the University of New Mexico and had worked as a police officer in Albuquerque before joining the CIA. What Phoenix found interesting was that Miller had recruited and trained this kid, which was a deviation from Miller's standard practice of only hiring former Special Forces soldiers for his team. He folded the sheet and asked Newton if there was more information about Richardson in the system.

She shook her head. "I just looked. There's nothing more than what I just printed out. I'm sure there's more behind another TS/SCI label, but I'm not digging around in that mess."

Standing, Phoenix tucked the folded papers in his pants pocket and headed for the door. "Call me if anything strange pops up."

"Define strange. You *do* remember where we work, right?"

"Anything other than people sleeping," Phoenix said.

Newton shrugged as if to say, "Whatever," and Phoenix

left the room. He checked his watch on the way down the stairs. It was almost midnight.

Delacroix and Connelly had bunked in the same room on the third floor, so it was easy enough to wake them both when he knocked on their door.

A sleepy Connelly opened the door partway and asked tiredly, "What do you want?"

"I need to talk to you and Sandy. Can I come in?" he asked, trying to see through the gap in the door to gauge whether the chief was awake.

"Can this wait until morning?" Connelly asked.

"What are you doing in there? Having a pajama and wine party?" Phoenix asked.

"We're just two tired women who want to go back to sleep. I can see from the look on your face that you're not going away, so come in and get it over with." Connelly opened the door all the way and turned to walk back into the room.

Phoenix stepped in and caught the door before it could bang off the latch. Delacroix sat on the edge of the bed, rubbing her eyes. She and Connelly wore fluffy white robes with the Four Seasons logo on the breast.

With a weary sigh, Delacroix asked, "What's the problem?"

"I went out, like I told you I was going to," Phoenix explained. "On my way through the lobby, I spotted Chris Miller. He runs all the Ground Branch operators, providing security for the conference. Anyway, we had an interesting conversation about Operation …" Phoenix put his fist up to his forehead with his index finger pointing out to indicate a unicorn. "He asked me about it and hinted that he wanted me to read him in."

"How did he know about our op?" Connelly asked.

"Mark Schwartz is one of his guys," Phoenix said.

Delacroix cocked her head. "He can't be."

"Yeah. He is," Phoenix confirmed. "He's on Miller's roster. And so is this guy." He removed the sheets of paper Newton had printed from his pocket and unfolded them before he handed them to the division chief.

Delacroix went to the nightstand and retrieved her reading glasses. Slipping them on, she stood by the bedside lamp and read Riley Richardson's cover sheet.

"What am I looking at, John?" she asked, passing the creased top page to Connelly.

"That guy works for Miller, too. He was following my asset tonight. When I confronted him, he said he was doing it on Miller's orders."

"What asset?" Delacroix asked.

"Cobra. She and I had a meet outside the hotel," Phoenix said.

"Seriously, Bowie?" Connelly asked. "How can you still consider her an asset after she turned on you?"

"She's my asset as long as I say she is," Phoenix replied defensively.

"What were you doing, *pumping* her for information?" Connelly asked sarcastically.

"As a matter of fact, I was. Cobra told me that Hector Calderón personally asked her to help facilitate a meeting between us and Unicorn."

"The director of the SEBIN told her to do that?" Connelly said incredulously.

"Yes," Phoenix insisted. "And she gave me the name of the man who brainwashed her—Terry Martin. It was his idea to swap the SD cards in the spy pen, and he helped her fake her death."

"And you think she's being straight with you now?" Delacroix asked.

"I think so," Phoenix replied. "After I escaped from VZ, the SEBIN kept Cobra in a cell in The Tomb until Calderón was ready for her. She said her mind has cleared, and she no longer feels Martin's control over her."

"How does that work?" Connelly asked. "Brainwashing doesn't magically go away."

"I don't know," Phoenix replied. "It's possible that the danger she experienced during the gunfight and the isolation in The Tomb helped to mitigate the effects of whatever Martin did to her."

"Whatever her state of mind, I want you to continue to run her," Delacroix said. "But be careful, Bowie. This could get messy in a hurry."

Connelly snorted. "It already has. You've let this get personal, Bowie."

"I care about my asset, Nightingale. Get over it." Turning to Delacroix, Phoenix said, "What are we going to do about Schwartz?"

Delacroix removed her glasses and ran her fingers through her hair before replying. "We keep him in play and try to figure out how he's communicating with Miller."

CHAPTER 18

Phoenix slept fitfully, dreaming about a shadowy figure chasing Blanco through the dark streets of Caracas, trying to kill her.

He was up before sunrise and ran five miles on a treadmill in the Four Seasons' rec room. Usually, exercise helped him clear his head, and the pumping of endorphins through his system eased all the old aches and pains, but today was different. He couldn't get his mind off Blanco and the terrible feelings his dream had conjured up inside him. All he wanted to do was rush up to her room and check on her.

With the conference kicking off this morning, Phoenix hoped she'd have some free time to slip away and meet him again. He wondered if Riley Richardson had clocked his safe house in the Suites Rio Elba when he'd been following them last night. If he'd followed Blanco there, then he could no longer use it as a meeting place. But Phoenix couldn't figure out how he had known that Blanco would be exiting the building under renovation on Rio Atoyac.

Back in his room, Phoenix stood under the hot water as it rained down on his chest. He held up a small hand mirror to help himself shave, cleaning away yesterday's whiskers and then ducking his face under the water to rinse off. As he stepped out of the shower, he glanced down at his cell phone, and a sudden thought occurred to him. Rushing to get dressed and to the Operation Unicorn suite, he skipped breakfast even though his stomach growled in protest.

Neither Connelly nor Delacroix were in the suite, but Newton still sat behind her bank of computer screens. Phoenix poured himself a cup of coffee, then walked over and sat down beside her. Sipping the hot liquid, he hoped it would calm the gnawing in the pit of his stomach.

"You're here early," Newton said.

"Couldn't sleep," Phoenix replied. "Did anything happen last night?"

"The Brazilian defense minister's wife had a fling with a bellhop in a storage closet, but other than that, everything was quiet," Newton said.

Phoenix laid his phone on the table. "Can you tell if there's a tracker on that?"

Newton picked it up, looked it over, and then shrugged. "There's probably not. I mean, it's too hard to place a physical tracker on these modern phones. I know we usually clone them if we want to track a phone or listen in on a conversation."

"Can you tell if this one has been cloned?"

Newton accessed a program on her computer used to locate various CIA cell phones and typed in Phoenix's number. Staring intently at the screen, she said, "Bad news, Bowie. It's been cloned."

"How can you tell?" he asked.

"We know for a fact that your phone is sitting right there on the table, right?"

"Yes," Phoenix concurred.

Newton pointed to her screen. "According to this, your phone is in the Suites Capri-Reforma Hotel."

"How is that possible?" Phoenix replied, moving closer to get a better look at her computer screen.

After he'd confirmed the location down the street, Newton pulled up a list of phone numbers associated with all the personnel involved with Operation Unicorn and began checking their locations. Phoenix watched in silence and amazement as all but one of their phones appeared at the Suites Carpi-Reforma Hotel. The lone exception was Mark Schwartz's.

"Check one more for me," Phoenix instructed, pulling up Blanco's number and reading it off.

"Yep. It's there," she said.

Phoenix shook his head in consternation. *How are we supposed to run a clandestine op when someone is monitoring our every move?*

"Can you tell what room those phones are in?" Phoenix asked.

"Not without going to the hotel and checking floor by floor," Newton replied. "I have an app for that, though, if you want it."

"Awesome. I want you to go over there and find out which room those clones are in," Phoenix said.

Newton's eyes widened in surprise. "Why me?"

"Because you're the only tech geek I trust, and Schwartz is obviously playing for the wrong team. I never liked him anyway."

Connelly and Delacroix entered the suite and poured themselves coffee, chattering like a couple of sorority sisters on holiday. Once Delacroix had her coffee with two creams and three sugars, she checked her watch and announced to the room, "Thirty minutes to the briefing. Two hours until the peace conference starts."

Phoenix motioned the two women over to the worksta-tion. "There's something you need to see."

As they made their way across the room, he typed his

phone number into the program again and located the clone at the hotel three blocks away.

"What is it, Bowie?" Delacroix asked.

He pointed to the screen. "Tell me where my phone is."

Delacroix leaned closer to the screen and squinted, not bothering with her reading glasses. "Another hotel, it looks like."

Phoenix told them how every phone, but Schwartz's had been cloned and explained his plan to send Newton to find which room the phones were in.

"I don't think that's a good idea," Delacroix said. "It would look suspicious if an All-American girl went traipsing around on every floor. They'll spot her right off. We need a local."

"Do you have anyone in mind?" Phoenix asked.

Delacroix reached for her phone. "I know a woman who will help."

"Well, don't call her on that phone," Phoenix said. "They'll know what we're up to."

Delacroix tucked her phone away. "Good call, Bowie. That's why I keep you around."

Phoenix beamed. "And here I thought it was my charm and wit."

"Not likely," Connelly muttered.

"Who else knows about this?" Delacroix asked, ignoring their banter.

"Just the four of us," Phoenix replied.

"Where's Schwartz, and why isn't he helping you with this?" Connelly asked.

"He hasn't come in yet, ma'am," Newton replied.

"Since he hasn't, let's keep this between the four of us for now," the division chief said. "Jennifer, do we have any spare phones?"

"Yes, ma'am. I'll get one for each of the three of you."

"No. Just get two," Delacroix instructed. "One for here

and one for Bowie since he's our primary operator. Connelly and I will keep using ours to maintain the ruse."

Newton got up, went to a large plastic travel case, and retrieved the new phones. She handed one to Phoenix, who powered it on and worked through the set-up procedure, while Newton did the same with the other. When he finished, Phoenix handed the new burner to Delacroix. "Make your call, Chief."

"Let's go someplace more private. Jennifer, tell everyone that we'll be back in time for the morning briefing." Delacroix led the two case officers out of the room. They rode the elevator up to Bar Four Seasons on the roof. At the early morning hour, the bar wasn't open yet. With it empty, Delacroix could talk privately, with only Connelly and Phoenix listening in.

When she ended the call, Delacroix turned and addressed Phoenix. "Ximena will meet you at the Computacenter beside the target hotel in an hour. She works for Mexico's *Centro Nacional de Inteligencia*. The challenge phrase will be, 'Can I interest you in this laptop?' and the response will be, 'It's a nice model, but I think I'll stick with my old one.'"

"Seriously?" Phoenix asked.

"Repeat it," Delacroix said, and he did.

"She'll make the approach. I told her what you're wearing —charcoal slacks and a lavender dress shirt, which looks nice on you, by the way."

Phoenix checked his watch as he stood. "Thanks for the compliment, Chief. I want to grab some breakfast before I head out. Do you need me for the briefing?"

"No," Delacroix replied, handing him the cell phone.

"I'll leave my old phone in the suite," Phoenix said. "They probably think I'll be there all day, monitoring the conference."

"Let us know what you find," Delacroix said.

"Be careful, Bowie," Connelly added.

He put a hand to his heart. "I'm touched by your concern, Nightingale."

She flipped him the bird.

Delacroix shook her head and muttered, "God, please grant me the patience not to strangle them both."

Phoenix chuckled on his way to the stairs, taking them quickly down to the lobby and heading for the entrance to the BBVA tower. It was in the opposite direction of the computer store, but he wanted to run an SDR to see if he had any tails.

Stepping onto the sidewalk, he turned left and headed for the nearest cross street. At the intersection, he turned left again, paused outside a coffee shop to glance both ways, then went inside and ordered. After collecting his purchases, he stood on the sidewalk while he sipped his black coffee and ate his blueberry muffin, watching the passersby and trying to spot any of Husker's Ground Branch shooters.

Once he'd finished his muffin, Phoenix threw the wrapper into a nearby trashcan, then ambled up the street, sipping his coffee, gazing into store windows, and checking reflections. Phoenix could pick up no one on his tail, but then again, they didn't have to have a human tracker if they could surveil him through his cloned phone.

———

THE COMPUTACENTER TURNED out to be an IT support center and not a retail outfit.

Phoenix walked inside, trying to spot his contact. A young man approached and asked if he needed help. Phoenix shook his head and said he was in the wrong place. On his way out the door, however, a woman stopped him. She was on the shorter side, slender as a reed, and dressed in black flats, a black skirt, and a white button-up shirt. She'd pulled her black hair into a low ponytail, and her shifty brown eyes seemed to look everywhere but at Phoenix.

The woman motioned to a nearby laptop, clearly some-one's personal computer since its owner had covered it with anime stickers. "Can I interest you in this laptop?" she asked,

Phoenix chuckled but gave the expected response, 'It's a nice model, but I think I'll stick with my old one."

"That's too bad," the woman said. "I don't think this one is for sale anyhow. Let's go outside before we attract more attention."

Back on the street, Ximena introduced herself and then opened an app on her phone. "Give me the number of your clone."

Phoenix recited the old number as Ximena pressed buttons.

"Okay. I've got it," Ximena said. "Now, I'm going into the hotel. I'll act as a maid—that's why I'm in this ridiculous outfit—and find out which room this clone is in. I'll text the room number to you, so we won't need to meet again. What's your new number?"

Phoenix gave her the number, understanding her need for caution.

"I understand you witnessed the execution of Minister Gardoqui," Ximena said, pocketing her phone.

"I saw the bikers and heard the gunfire. He was dead by the time I arrived," Phoenix replied as he continued to glace up and down the street for tails. "Are you working the case?"

"I am part of it, but the lead investigator is Joaquín Fuentes. He is the head of the Anti-drug Division."

"Good luck taking down those bikers," Phoenix said.

Ximena tilted her head noncommittally and then turned and headed for the hotel. Phoenix wished he was the one stalking the cloned phones, but he figured whoever was in the room had probably tapped into the hotel's security system and would see him coming from a mile away. Ximena was an unknown player and likely to be overlooked in the innocuous outfit.

As she disappeared through the hotel's service entrance, Phoenix recrossed Sevilla Street, heading west, then turned north and began crossing Paseo de la Reforma Avenue and the access streets that circled the large fountain in the center of a roundabout. Atop the two-tiered fountain was a statue of Diana the Huntress, the Roman goddess of the hunt, aiming her drawn bow at the stars. When the statue had first been unveiled in 1942, the public had thought it too lewd, and they'd draped the naked Diana in a dress. Now, no one seemed to look twice at her bare breasts.

Once safely across the ten lanes of traffic, Phoenix waited for the light on Seville again and went east along the sidewalk before sliding into a seat at a table outside Salón Corona. Fortunately, the restaurant wasn't open yet, so he didn't have to bother with the wait staff or ordering food. Through the tall pines growing in the median of Paseo de la Reforma, he had a view of the lovely Diana in the roundabout, and if he leaned to his left, he could see the Suites Capri tower.

AFTER TWENTY MINUTES OF SITTING, Phoenix stretched his legs by walking east again, this time through the center median of Paseo de la Reforma Avenue, strolling under the verdant shade trees and smelling the intoxicating scents of blooming flowers and exhaust fumes.

A few blocks up the street, Phoenix stopped to admire the Angel of Independence statue in the center of another roundabout. The statue was the most famous in the city, and atop the forty-five-meter column stood a bronze version of the Greek goddess of victory. According to the brochure that Phoenix had read in the lobby of the Four Seasons, the statue had been built to commemorate the centennial of the beginning of Mexico's War of Independence—a vicious bout against Spanish aggressors that had lasted eleven long years.

Sadly, he thought the Mexicans probably weren't any better off, as he turned and headed back toward the Capri. The knot in his shoulder told him the clock was running out. If Ximena didn't contact him soon, he would assume she'd been made, and he'd have to find another way to locate Husker's nest of vipers.

The intelligence game wasn't all glorious action. It was mostly about waiting. Waiting to recruit an asset. Waiting for a meeting. Waiting for orders from superiors. The waiting could drive a person crazy. To kill time during these lengthy periods of inaction, Phoenix liked to scheme out various scenarios in his mind for when the shit hit the fan. Sometimes, in the middle of an op, his schemes manifested exactly as he'd envisioned. And when he saw things spiraling out of control in his mind, he would halt the scenario and begin again, focusing on positive outcomes.

As he walked along, examining the native paintings and jewelry being sold along the sidewalks by various artisans, Phoenix listened to the sounds of traffic and the snatches of overheard conversations. He tried to imagine Ximena pushing a heavily laden maid cart down each hallway of the hotel. In his mind's eye, he saw her phone on the cart and the tracker app signaling whether she was hot or cold like the old children's game.

Phoenix leaned against a tree, contorting his shoulders to find a small knot or a piece of bark to press into the stressed muscles. Hitting just the right spot, he jammed the bark deep into his skin through his shirt. Phoenix closed his eyes and reveled in the sensation of relief no matter how minute. While he might have looked like a bear emerging from hibernation to the daughter of the Colombian defense minister, Phoenix was rock steady otherwise.

There were only two people he'd ever worried about when they'd gone downrange: Blanco and Connelly. Otherwise, everyone else knew the score and took their chances.

Husker hadn't been wrong to call John Phoenix a Sphinx. His finger never wavered on the trigger, whether knocking down a trophy white-tail deer, leading a flying duck, or neutralizing a foreign actor.

Phoenix forced his body to relax and willed away the pain in his shoulder. It didn't leave, but he could focus on other things, like what Chris Miller was doing running a counter-op on his mission. Phoenix should have told Delacroix to get on the horn with D/CIA Stratten and ask him what the fuck was going on. That was a minor oversight on Phoenix's part, and he planned to correct it as soon as he got the chance.

He saw no apparent reason for a paramilitary operation at the conference unless it was part of the audacious plan that President Randy 'Merica had set out for Delacroix and Phoenix in the Oval Office. Phoenix chuckled to himself. His foster father, Paul Schaffer, had been an avid listener of The Rush Limbaugh Show. After the Clinton-Lewinsky affair, Limbaugh had coined the term "Oval Orifice." As Phoenix had sat in rapt attention at the White House, listening to President Mercia, he'd wanted to burst out laughing at the old joke. He didn't think Connelly or Mercia would have found it nearly as amusing as he did.

Walking over to a vending cart, Phoenix stood in the shade of the seller's umbrella and purchased a cup of freshly squeezed fruit juice. The cold, tangy blend of orange, pineapple, and banana went down smoothly, helping to combat the rising heat of the day.

Phoenix moved back into the shade of the trees and lingered on a concrete park bench, sipping juice and watching the pedestrians. He was partway through his drink when his phone vibrated in his pocket.

He pulled it out and read the text message from Ximena. His cloned phone was in Suite 2102, and the name on the room's registration card was Jorge Posada.

Phoenix stood and pocketed his phone, then drained the last of his juice. The name on the registration was obviously fake. Posada was a retired Major League Baseball catcher who'd played for the New York Yankees, but the use of the name fit Husker's *modus operandi*.

Knowing where the cloned phones were, Phoenix now needed a game plan to take down Husker's crew.

CHAPTER 19

Four Seasons Hotel
Mexico City, Mexico

Presidents Fredricks and Zarate stared daggers at each other over the coffee table in the room set aside expressly for their private meeting.

"You are a liar," Fredricks stated. "You have lied to your people. You have lied to the world. And you're lying to me."

Zarate gave a tight, mirthless smile. "The one deceiving himself sits across the table from me."

"I'm telling the truth when I say that you will *never* possess the Essequibo Region again," Fredricks said. "We have history on our side. The 1899 Paris Arbitral Award gave us exclusive ownership, which is, as you know, nine-tenths of the law."

Zarate scoffed. "The victor writes the law."

"Then your country has never been the victor, Michel. You have failed at every turn to reclaim the Essequibo Region, and you will continue to fail to do so. We have a saying in

Guyana, 'Not a blade of grass.' That is how it will be. Venezuela will never own any part of Guyana, and now that we have restored our rightful share of Ankoko Island, we will not let you take it back either."

Michel Zarate leaned back in his chair and studied his counterpart. Fredricks was a slightly built man with a fringe of hair surrounding his balding crown. His short stature had led many to believe he had a Napoleon complex with his sometimes overly aggressive or domineering behavior, despite the picture of calm he liked to project to the world. Today, he wore a brown tweed herringbone three-piece suit with a maroon tie. Zarate knew better than to underestimate the Guyanese president since the man had surprised him at every turn, especially by creating a mercenary fighting force that had run roughshod over his supposedly "superiorly trained" troops.

Zarate hadn't liked Fredricks' tone since they'd shaken hands in front of a crowd of reporters and other foreign dignitaries before entering the suite. The man seemed to gloat about the ownership of the Essequibo, about his mercenary troops, about the American kid who had become a fucking ace on the back of Zarate's air force. And Fredricks had been especially proud of all the countries he claimed would back Guyana if Zarate chose to invade. Truthfully, Zarate knew his position was untenable, but he still had a few tricks up his sleeve.

He thought about getting up and leaving, but outside, the world waited. They demanded the two men hammer out an agreement. But the Venezuelan people had voted to retake the Essequibo Region, and they expected Zarate to do just that— never minding the fact he had rigged the vote and the people had seen right through his sham to jail opposition leaders. Zarate needed to act with a swift decisiveness that would show the world he wasn't fooling around.

Zarate smiled. "My friend, my people have voted, and we

claim the Essequibo as our own. Simply withdraw your troops and allow us to fold *Guayana Esequiba* into Venezuela. Otherwise…" He left the threat hanging with a shrug of his shoulders.

Fredricks chuckled. "Your military has proved inept thus far, and your equipment is in considerable need of repair. I have serious doubts about the cohesiveness of your army. Most of your generals are political appointees who have no military training. How do you expect to overcome those odds, Michel?"

Zarate shrugged again, not wanting to give away his plan. Before leaving Venezuela, he had gathered his military commanders in a secret meeting. He'd ordered the Navy and Coast Guard to deploy, ready to race to Georgetown to set a naval blockade. In addition, the airborne corps had orders to fly into Georgetown and occupy the capitol while his Flankers and F-15 Eagles flew sorties, striking Guyanese military encampments and targets of strategic value.

All he had to do was make one phone call to Major General Alejandro Salazar, and the takeover of Guyana would soon be complete. Anyone with real-time satellite data, however, would be able to see his mobilizing forces, but the ships needed to be in position to move quickly. Even if they steamed at maximum speed from the naval base at Puerto Cabello, it would still take them thirty-three hours to get to Georgetown. That was entirely too long. His fleet was now in the Gulf of Paria between Venezuela and the island of Trinidad or loitered near the mouth of the Orinoco River.

"Are we at an impasse, Terrence?" Zarate asked.

"Do you think I don't know what you're doing by repositioning your ships?" Fredricks asked.

Zarate stood. "Is that your trump card? Telling me the position of my Navy?"

"No, Michel. My trump card is this: If you walk out that door and launch a strike, the world will be with me. You can't hold Guyana hostage and expect our neighboring countries and our strategic trading partners not to act." Fredricks pointed at the entrance to the room. "Outside those doors are the military commanders of the United States, Brazil, Colombia, and half a dozen other Caribbean and South American nations. All of them have assured me they *will* defend the sovereignty of Guyana. You've lost before you could even get out of the starting blocks."

Zarate straightened his suit coat over his barrel chest, then ran a finger over his thick mustache. His hair had left him long ago, and his bald dome gleamed in the sunlight coming through windows. He knew he would never win back the Essequibo Region, but he planned to free his country from the burden of imperialism cast by the U.S. government.

While Zarate didn't give a shit about the people of his country, the lifting of the sanctions would allow him to keep lining his pockets, and by injecting a bit of cash into his social programs, he could keep the poverty-stricken peasants on his side. As long as they depended on him for sustenance, they would keep voting for him. If they decided to rise up, then he'd round up the dissidents and execute them in the street. Dead farmers and miners just meant fewer mouths to feed and more dollars in Zarate's pocket.

The dictator knew the world would eventually force his removal from office, but by then, he planned to have enough money to live comfortably in exile. Until then, Venezuela was his to command, and retaking the Essequibo Region would forever cement his name in the annals of history.

"We are at a crossroads, Terrence," Zarate said. "For more than a century, your country has occupied Venezuelan land. Now, it's time to hand it back to its rightful owner. The crossroads is the path you chose to do so, peacefully or by force."

Fredricks stood abruptly. "How dare you threaten me. I am tired of your constant bullying and grandstanding. If you wish to fight, bring your best warriors. The world will smack you down like the petulant child you are!"

The corner of Zarate's mouth lifted in pleasure as he chuckled. "If it is a fight you want, a fight you will get."

The Venezuelan president strode from the room without another word. His armed security team greeted him as soon as he stepped out and escorted him to his own suite, ignoring the crush of reporters who hurled questions at him.

Once behind closed doors, Zarate pulled out his cell phone and accessed a secure messaging app to contact General Salazar. He typed in a message and sent it across the airwaves before sliding the phone back into his pocket.

Turning to one of his henchmen, Zarate said, "Bring me the vice president. We have much to discuss."

The bodyguard picked up the phone and dialed Acevedo's room as Zarate stepped to the window overlooking the hotel's courtyard. His message to Salazar had told him to activate the war plan. Soon, a naval blockade would surround Georgetown, and his troops would occupy the capital. He would be the victor, and he would be the one to rewrite history.

CHAPTER 20

Operation Unicorn suite

"THE PHONES ARE IN ROOM 2102," PHOENIX REPORTED TO Connelly and Delacroix. "How do you want to handle this situation?"

"For now, we don't do anything," Delacroix replied. "Zarate just told Fredricks to fuck off, and he and Acevedo are pow-wowing in his room."

"What does that mean?" Phoenix asked. "Are they going to war?"

"We'll know more once Unicorn reports in," Delacroix replied.

"Don't we have his suite wired?" Phoenix asked.

"Zarate's team swept it this morning and removed all the bugs," Connelly explained. "There were a lot more in there than just ours."

"Any blowback?" Phoenix asked.

"None that we can't contain," Delacroix replied. "I think they expected us to bug the room."

"The blowback will come from their private meeting," Connelly said. "From the looks on their faces, it didn't go well."

"What about the phones?" Phoenix asked, steering the conversation back to the topic that required the three of them to lock themselves in a room away from the other officers working on Operation Unicorn. "I know you said to wait, but do we have a game plan?"

"I'm not sure what our play is," Delacroix responded.

"With Husker's command suite on the twenty-first floor and our faces well known to them, there's no way we can creep the place," Phoenix stated.

"And it's probably staffed night and day just like our operation," Connelly added.

"I say we wait," Delacroix said again. "I don't have time to run two operations."

"Who could authorize a counter-op like that?" Phoenix asked.

"Stratten for sure," Delacroix replied. "Maybe Rheinhart Constantine."

"Wouldn't the chief of paramilitary ops have to run something like that up the flagpole?" Connelly asked.

"Not necessarily," Phoenix replied. "When I operated out of Ground Branch, the Seventh Floor gave us a lot of leeway. Most of that black bag shit doesn't make it anywhere near the director's desk."

"So, Constantine has free rein?" Connelly asked.

"Not necessarily, but just remember that one hand doesn't always know what the other is doing," Phoenix replied.

The two women lapsed into thought about the implications of a rogue op inside the CIA. It wouldn't be the first time, nor the last. As long as elements in the agency had autonomy and access to black funds, someone was bound to take advantage of the situation.

"My suggestion is to get Stratten on the horn and ask him," Phoenix said.

Delacroix looped a strand of her blonde hair behind her ear. She licked her lips and nodded. "Okay. I'll do that."

"I think it's the smart play," Phoenix said. "Then we don't have to go snooping around in Miller's paramilitary op. I know those guys, and they'd just as soon slit your throat as talk to you."

"And what are you going to do?" Connelly asked her case officer.

"You and the President read me in on Dragonfly. I want to get up to speed by reading his file, but it's stamped TS/SCI," Phoenix replied.

"I got a notification that Newton tried to access it this morning," Delacroix said. "Was that you?"

"Yes," Phoenix said. "Last night, Blanco told me the name of her handler in Venezuela—Terry Martin. Ring any bells?" When neither woman answered, Phoenix continued. "I thought he might be connected to Dragonfly or *be* Dragonfly. While you guys are running this op, I can start on that one."

Delacroix ran a hand through her hair and pushed it all back off her forehead, but most of it fell right back into place as she let go. "All right, Bowie. I'll get you in, but I want updates from you if you find anything."

"Yes, ma'am," Phoenix replied. He shot a grin at Connelly. "See, I'm not so hard to work with."

"Enough with the sniping, please," Delacroix snapped. "I've got plenty of problems without your constant bickering." She didn't wait for either of her officers to reply as she headed for the door. "Come on, Bowie, I'll get you started with the file before I call Stratten."

Delacroix opened a laptop in the main operations area, signed into the top-secret Dragonfly file, and motioned for Phoenix to get started. He sat down at the computer and began reading through it. Despite the high page count, there wasn't much of value as they had no real idea who the guy was, how he operated, or who might be in his network. His moniker, however, had been associated with operations ranging from Afghanistan to China.

The file ended abruptly with a notation about the possibility of Dragonfly working in Venezuela. Phoenix backed up a few pages to the supposed targeting of Dragonfly in Yemen. He read through the supporting documentation again and studied the photos taken by the drone just before the strike. They showed a tall man with brown hair, but there was no clear view of his face, even when he'd glanced up at the sky, as though he knew Hellfire was about to rain down on him.

Phoenix watched the footage of the Hellfire missile strike. One moment, the compound was there with Dragonfly in the open courtyard and the next, the place was a pile of rubble, obliterated in a flash of light and smoke. He'd seen drone strikes up close, having used lasers to paint targets on the ground and then gone in after the strike to do battle damage assessments (BDA) and to ensure their targets were dead.

Based on what he'd just watched, Phoenix was positive that if it had been Dragonfly standing in the courtyard, then that traitorous motherfucker was just a bloodstain on the desert floor.

Paging through the BDA, Phoenix absorbed the intel written by the head of the Ground Branch detachment. There were multiple confirmed kills, but no one knew for sure if they had gotten Dragonfly.

Turning in his seat, Phoenix scanned the room for Delacroix, but she wasn't around. He spotted Connelly and called her over. Pointing at the photo of the man suspected to be Dragonfly, he said, "I want to print this out."

"And do what with it?" she asked.

"Show it to Cobra," Phoenix replied.

Connelly seemed to ponder this for a moment, then said, "What good do you think that will do?"

"If Dragonfly and Cobra's contact are the same, then she's seen this guy up close and personal. I want her to look at the photo and tell me if this guy is Terry Martin."

Connelly pursed her lips, then nodded. "Okay. If she says they're the same guy, then we know he's not dead, and we can start facial recognition to search for him."

"Cool. Thanks, Les. I'd say you're the best, but your head is big enough already." He turned back to the computer and zoomed in on the photo of the man they presumed was Dragonfly.

Connelly leaned forward and whispered in his ear. "Be careful, John. You were always the one with the swollen head."

"You always liked my swollen head, especially when it was inside …" Phoenix let his sexual retort die as Connelly suddenly turned and strode across the suite. He watched her go as the printer spit out the photo.

Something tore at his heart. Instead of feeling like he was cheating on Connelly with Blanco, it was suddenly the other way around.

Picking up the photo he'd just printed out, Phoenix folded it carefully and slipped it into his back pocket. He then texted Blanco and asked if she was free to meet.

She replied immediately, saying she was available for the rest of the day as Acevedo would be busy in the conference room. The VP had taken Sergeant Tranquillo to act as her aide, knowing Blanco might need the freedom to work with Bowie and Warbler, the codename by which Acevedo knew Delacroix.

"Go east into the Chapultepec Forest and walk toward the large monument in the center," Phoenix instructed.

"The Monument to the Child Heroes?" Blanco asked.

"Yeah, that one," Phoenix replied.

The monument, with its six large pillars, honored the six teenage military cadets who had perished at Chapultepec

Castle during the Battle of Chapultepec, one of the last major engagements of the Mexican-American War. The cadets had stayed behind after the military academy had been evacuated, and rather than surrender to the U.S. Army, the boys had leaped to their deaths from the castle walls on September 13, 1847.

"Does it bother you that they honor the dead who fought against your country?" she asked teasingly.

"As long as they don't put up a monument to the drug lord El Chapo, I think I'll be all right," he replied.

Blanco chuckled. "I will head that way," she said. "There are vendor stalls near the monument. I will look for you there."

"Be careful, Cora. Run an SDR like I taught you," Phoenix said.

"I will, my love. See you soon."

Phoenix headed out of the hotel and started his own SDR, eager to meet up with his lover again and possibly gain a new lead in his investigation.

CHAPTER 21

Phoenix found his asset beneath a purple umbrella, examining a selection of colorful masks worn by luchadores, the high-flying Mexican professional wrestlers. The CIA case officer walked past her and stopped at another cart to purchase a bottle of water. While he sipped it, he kept an eye on the people nearby.

Slowly, he walked past Blanco again, whispering for her to meet him on a bench near the Museum of Modern Art, then veered away and paused at another booth selling baseball caps and straw fedoras. He slipped on a fedora, cocked it at a rakish angle, and checked his reflection in a mirror hanging from the vendor cart.

The salesman flashed two thumbs up. "It is perfect, my man. You look cool. Like Indiana Jones!"

Phoenix dug a wad of pesos from his pocket and peeled off twenty, handing it to the man with a touch of the brim. He ambled after his asset, checking for anyone on his back trail. He'd told Blanco to leave her phone in the room to throw off the clone clowns.

Making his way into the trees of the massive seventeen-hundred-acre park, he kept a close watch on his surroundings. The air was fresh with cut grass and blooming flowers. All around him, people strolled and chatted in a variety of languages. The park was one of the largest attractions in Mexico City, filled with statues, monuments, museums, and the Chapultepec Castle that had once been the official residence of the President of Mexico, a renowned military academy, and now the National History Museum.

Blanco sat on a park bench, wearing navy bootcut dress pants, a matching blazer, a white blouse, and black ankle boots. She ran a hand through her brown hair and glanced around, her gray eyes glistening in anticipation.

Phoenix sat on the stone bench beside her with his hands in his lap. "How are you?"

She smiled as she slid closer. "I'm better now that you're here. Why'd you buy that hat? You look absolutely ridiculous."

Phoenix chuckled and tugged on the brim of the fedora. "I thought I looked rather stylish, and the salesman told me I looked like Indiana Jones."

She laughed. "He was just trying to make a sale. Take it off."

"I'm going to keep wearing it just to annoy you."

Blanco ran a finger along the brim in front of his face. In a rather seductive voice, she whispered, "What can I do to convince you to take it off?"

"Let's see if a kiss will work?" He tilted his head and leaned in, gathering her into her arms as they kissed.

Blanco knocked his hat off as she slid her fingers through the hair at the back of Phoenix's neck. To prevent him from reaching down to pick it up, she tightened her grip on his hair and kept her lips pressed to his.

When she finally released him, Blanco laughed as Phoenix picked up the hat.

He reseated the fedora on his head and cocked it like he was Bogart in *Casablanca*.

"Do you have another hotel room ready?" she asked.

"No, but it will be easy enough to get one. I wanted to show you a photo and ask if you know the man."

Blanco pouted her lower lip. "I enjoyed our time together at the last place."

Phoenix reached into his pocket and took out the photo. "I can say most emphatically that I enjoyed it, too, but unfortunately, we have work to do first."

Blanco took the photo and studied it. "Who's this supposed to be?"

"You don't recognize him?"

She handed it back. "No. I've never seen him before."

"That man isn't Terry Martin?" Phoenix asked, refolding the sheet before pocketing it.

"No. I just told you, Bowie. I've never seen him before."

"If I could get you in front of a sketch artist, could you describe Terry Martin so we might know what he looks like?"

"Do I have to?" she pleaded. "I'd rather do anything other than think about him."

"It's important, Cora. Besides, if we can take Martin off the playing board, we can remove the threat to you and your family."

She nodded. "I understand, but do you really think they're in danger now that I work for Acevedo and General Calderón?

"Absolutely, they are. As long as Martin is free, he's a menace to you, me, your family, and maybe even the sovereignty of our governments."

"Is he really that dangerous?" she asked.

"I don't want to take any chances," Phoenix replied. He stood so unnecessary questions or speculation wouldn't prolong the conversation.

He pulled out his cell phone and called Chris Miller as he walked through the park. Once he had Husker on the line, he said, "Do you have a sketch artist on staff?"

"Sorry, Bowie, I don't have anyone here to do that. What are you angling at?"

Phoenix paused at the sight of a young Mexican man drawing caricatures. The case officer figured he was an art student trying to make ends meet since he appeared to be in his late teens.

"I've got to go, Husker." Phoenix ended the call. He turned to Blanco. "We're going to hire that kid to draw a picture of your buddy."

"He's not my buddy," Blanco stated adamantly. "Please don't call him that."

Phoenix took her by the hand and led her over to the sketch artist. He hired the young man with long dark hair and a wispy goatee to draw a caricature of Blanco. It didn't take long for the guy to exaggerate Blanco's features, giving her a long, slender neck, a high forehead, and a wide, beautiful smile.

Once he'd ripped the sketch from his pad and handed it to Blanco, Phoenix asked the caricaturist if he would be willing to draw an individual as described by Blanco. "I'll pay you extra, but not for a caricature. It has to be natural proportions."

"*Sí. Sí.* I can do as you ask." He cast his glance downward. "I must have at least half the money upfront."

Phoenix handed the kid a fifty peso note. "Another fifty when you're done."

"Thank you, sir," the kid said.

"Let's go into the shade, where it will be a little cooler," Phoenix suggested.

The artist picked up his tools, and they headed for a park bench under a large Montezuma cypress tree. As he and Blanco sat down to work, Phoenix roved through the trees and strolled along sidewalks, eyeing everyone around him. He kept walking back to glance over the artist's shoulder to see how the drawing was progressing.

On one of his scouting trips, Phoenix saw a uniformed policeman on a foot patrol. He appeared friendly enough, stopping to chat with other pedestrians, but Phoenix was always wary of law enforcement. On this trip, he carried a black diplomatic passport, giving him official government cover, but Phoenix didn't want to have to wand it for the locals.

As the cop moved through the crowd, he edged toward Blanco and the kid. Phoenix moved closer, wanting to be nearby in case the cop stopped to check out the sketcher's handiwork. His heart rate ticked up a few beats per minute, but his hands stayed steady. He visualized taking the gun from the cop, but Phoenix knew it was a bad idea as soon as it entered his mind. Discarding the thought immediately, Phoenix hoped things didn't go that far.

The cop stopped to gaze placidly over the artist's shoulder, his hands behind his back.

"Move along, asshole," Phoenix muttered tersely through clenched teeth.

Phoenix moved to within earshot. Blanco glanced at him with wide eyes. He tried to smile reassuringly but felt like the wheels were about to come off the mission.

"Do you know this man?" the cop asked Blanco.

"Uh … yeah." She brushed her hair out of her eyes. "He's a friend. I … uh … I wanted to surprise him. You know, with a sketch."

"This man is your friend?" the cop asked suspiciously, nodding toward the sketch pad and raising his eyebrows.

Blanco nodded. "Yes."

The cop, whose name plate said Cartega, cocked his head as he continued to study the sketch.

Phoenix's eyes bulged as he wondered what the fuck was going on. He tried to figure out why the cop was asking so many questions.

"Uh …" Blanco stammered to fill the awkward silence.

"He is my friend from Venezuela. I'm part of the diplomatic mission in town for the peace negotiations."

"How are the talks going?" Cartega asked.

Phoenix felt hope rise that the situation would resolve itself as the cop changed the subject.

"They've just started," Blanco replied. "I'd better get back. May I have the sketch, please?" she asked the artist.

The cop pointed to the drawing pad and asked the artist, "Do you know this man?"

The artist pointed at Phoenix. "That man asked me to draw this for them. He offered to pay me extra."

"Fuck me," Phoenix muttered.

Knowing he'd been busted, Phoenix walked over to the group and handed the kid the promised fifty peso note for finishing his work.

"Can I go?" the artist asked the cop.

Cartega nodded, and the kid scurried off, looking relieved to have escaped.

Blanco started to rise from the bench, but Cartega held out a hand to stop her, saying, "I need to see some identification, miss."

Blanco glanced at him again, and Phoenix nodded. If she refused to show him her ID, then things might escalate. With a sigh, Blanco produced her diplomatic passport and handed it to the cop. Phoenix glanced around. So far, no one else seemed interested in the dynamic playing out over the sketch. He prayed it stayed that way.

Officer Cartega opened the passport and checked the photo against the beautiful woman on the park bench.

"And you?" he asked Phoenix, motioning for his identification.

With no other choice but to comply, Phoenix handed Cartega his diplomatic passport.

Cartega studied both passports, then slipped them into his

back pocket. He motioned to the sketch in Blanco's hand, "You say you are a friend of this man?"

Blanco lifted her head high. "I am a member of Vice President Evelyn Acevedo's delegation."

"That is not the question I asked," Cartega said. "Do you *know* this man?"

"I told you," Blanco stated. "He is a friend from Venezuela."

Seeming to realize he wouldn't get anything else from Blanco, Cartega fixed Phoenix with a stare. "Are you with the delegation also?"

"I work for the U.S. State Department," Phoenix replied.

"Why are you two not at the Four Seasons where the conference is taking place?" Cartega asked.

"The delegates are meeting right now, and our bosses graciously allowed us a few hours to see the sights," Blanco explained.

"But you are not seeing the sights," Cartega said. "You are making a sketch of a known criminal."

Phoenix saw a glimmer of what this interaction was all about. The sketch was a physical link between Blanco and Phoenix and whoever the cop thought was a criminal.

"We know the man in the sketch by the name of Terry Martin," Phoenix said. "Who do you know him by?"

"His name is Silva de Peña Ortega," Cartega stated. "He is a financier of the *Los Perros Negros* Motorcycle Club. And he is a suspect of interest in the slaying of Minister Gardoqui."

"We don't know anything about that," Phoenix said. "From our passports, you can see that we have diplomatic immunity. I'm asking you to give them back and walk away."

Cartega's brows narrowed. "I don't think so. I am placing you both under arrest. Sit down on the bench." Instead of reaching for his radio mic clipped to his lapel, he pulled out his cell phone.

"Let me make a call first," Phoenix pleaded. "You and I

both know you can't arrest us. We are diplomatic guests of your country."

Cartega propped his foot on the bench beside Phoenix and leaned his elbow on his knee, phone in hand. "Tell me how you know Ortega."

"I am a diplomat with the United States government," Phoenix said, slipping on his Sphinx mask. "You have no right to detain or question me."

"I hate diplomats," Cartega muttered. "You are all so fucking arrogant. And you think you can get away with whatever you please. It makes me sick."

Phoenix hated playing the diplomatic card. It made them look guilty, but Phoenix knew his only crime was being an idiot for using a street artist to draw a composite sketch when it should have been done behind closed doors. He could also understand the cop's feelings about visitors who hid behind the diplomatic visa.

Diplomatic immunity dated back to antiquity and had been reinforced by the 1961 Vienna Convention. It guaranteed a diplomat safe passage and freedom to travel, with complete protection against local lawsuits and prosecution, while in the host country.

In some cases, actual crimes had been committed by diplomats, but because of their immunity status, the crimes went unpunished. Generally, the only recourse a nation had to deal with those dips was to kick them out of the country and make them *persona non grata*. If a crime was egregious enough, however, the home country could waive that immunity and allow the diplomat to be prosecuted for his crimes.

"Just because one uses a diplomatic passport does not mean one is a criminal," Blanco replied.

"The investigation into Gardoqui's death is ongoing, and we have been told to pick up anyone we suspect has a connection to it," Cartega finally explained.

"We have the right to counsel," Phoenix said, pulling out

his phone. "While you make your call, I'll make one of my own."

"One phone call because you are diplomats," Cartega conceded.

"Thank you." Phoenix scrolled through his text messages to find Ximena's number. He didn't want to call Connelly or Delacroix as he didn't want to involve more CIA personnel, so he prayed Ximena would pick up as he held the phone to his ear, and it rang on the other end.

"I told you to never call me," Ximena said when she answered.

"I'm in trouble, Ximena. A local cop has detained me and my friend. He wants to haul us off to jail."

"Why?" Ximena asked.

"He thinks we know some guy named Silva de Peña Ortega," Phoenix said.

"Do you know Silva de Peña Ortega?" she asked.

"No. It's a long story," Phoenix said, "but I need your help."

"Fine," Ximena said and ended the call.

Moments later, the cop got a call on his phone. His look of pure disgust didn't rally any feelings of hope in Phoenix. And while Phoenix was thankful the cop hadn't put them in handcuffs, their interaction had drawn attention from others who openly stared as they scurried quickly past.

Phoenix tugged the brim of his fedora down so he wouldn't have to see the cop and sat quietly on the bench. He understood that Cartega was just doing his job, and he had every right to question someone who might be connected to this drug financier, Ortega, but Phoenix knew his only crime had been one of stupidity.

He didn't know how long it would take for Ximena to clear this up, but Phoenix figured it was best to keep quiet until she did.

CHAPTER 22

Cartega ended his call and said, "I need you to come with me."

"Why?" Phoenix asked.

"Your friend Ximena has asked that I take you to her," Cartega replied.

"May we have our passports back?" Blanco asked.

"When we reach our destination," Cartega replied, pocketing his phone.

Blanco and Phoenix followed the police officer through the park to a black Dodge Durango SUV that sat on the sidewalk by the Museum of Modern Art. As he climbed behind the wheel, Cartega instructed them to get into the rear seat.

Thirty minutes later, they were in the heart of Ciudad Neza, the slum dominated by the *Los Perros Negros* MC.

"What are we doing here?" Phoenix asked, watching the rundown homes and businesses as they passed.

Cartega didn't answer. He continued to drive without speaking to his two passengers.

After a few more turns on the winding streets, Cartega pulled to the curb behind a large group of other police vehicles. Exciting the Durango after Cartega had opened the back door, Phoenix glanced up and down the residential street, wondering why Cartega had brought them there. He saw enough cop cars to indicate the place was a possible crime scene. Small knots of onlookers stood along the far sidewalk, staring with morbid fascination.

Phoenix took a deep breath, inhaling the scent of the bougainvillea blossoms coming from the pink-flowering bush hanging over the stucco walls that lined the sidewalk from one end of the block to the other. The residents had painted the security walls to match their homes, and a variety of ornate wrought iron gates allowed access to the inner court-yards. Cop cars blocked both ends of the street, and the first cops on the scene had strung up crime scene tape to ward off unwanted guests.

The air was ripe with cooking meat and a pungent smell of death that Phoenix was all too familiar with. Normally, he swooped in, spilled the blood, and disappeared in the night. He rarely stuck around to see the aftermath of the carnage that he and his fellow paramilitary or Special Forces troops had left behind.

Another uniformed cop stopped them as they approached the gated entrance to a house from which other law enforce-ment officers were coming and going.

"They're here to see Ximena," Cartega said to the other cop who guarded the entry gate.

"Wait here," the beat cop said. He crossed a small court-yard littered with old motorcycle parts to the front door and hollered into the house for the female intelligence officer.

Ximena came out the front door, wearing jeans and a white blouse with an FN FNP-9 pistol on her hip. Phoenix wondered if she'd been carrying the gun when she'd entered the hotel this morning in her maid outfit. It almost seemed too big for her tiny hands. She peeled off latex gloves as she walked and tossed them on the sidewalk with a pile of other garbage left by the crime scene techs and police officers.

"Thanks for bringing them, Miguel," Ximena said to Cartega. "You can give them back their passports now. Hang out for a few minutes, and when we're done, I'll have you take them back to the hotel."

Cartega handed over the passports and headed for the SUV.

"You know him?" Phoenix asked.

"He's my brother," Ximena said. "I asked him to pick you up, but then he spotted your friend sketching Ortega and used it as a reason to detain you."

Blanco handed the drawing over as Phoenix explained who Ximena was and who she worked for but didn't elaborate on the reason for their prior meeting.

"You're lucky I had Miguelito pick you up and not some beat cop," Ximena said. "The man in this sketch is *muy peligroso*—very dangerous." She paused to look up at Phoenix. "What is also dangerous is that hat. Whatever possessed you to buy it?"

"I said the same thing," Blanco said with a knowing smile.

Feeling defensive and ready to snipe back, Phoenix forced himself to remain levelheaded and changed the subject. "Why was your brother following us?"

"I asked him to. He works with me at the CNI. Today, he wore a uniform as we have a heavy police presence in the park and around the Four Seasons Hotel because of the assassination of Minister Gardoqui."

"So, who is this guy?" Blanco asked, pointing to the sketch. "I know him as Terry Martin in Venezuela."

"Here in Mexico, we know him as Silva de Peña Ortega. He is a top financier of the *Los Perros Negros* MC. He uses the drug money to fund other operations," Ximena said.

"Like what?" Phoenix asked.

"Whatever you can name in the criminal underworld, Ortega has a hand in it," Ximena said. "His favorite commodity is intelligence."

"Why did your brother bring us here?" Phoenix asked. "This place looks like a crime scene."

"It is," Ximena said, handing the sketch back to Blanco. She rolled it up and shoved it into Phoenix's back pocket. "Come on. I'll show you."

The trio climbed the four steps to the open front door. Blanco and Phoenix signed the crime scene entry log before they entered the two-story stucco home that someone had painted a garish lime green. The stench of death was overwhelming, and Blanco held her hand up to cover her nose while Phoenix panted through his mouth. Ximena seemed unfazed by the odor.

"We have ten dead men in here," Ximena said. "From the motorcycles left on the street, we think all of these guys were present when they gunned down Gardoqui. The local cops are matching up the bikes to video footage from around the hotel."

"Who killed these guys?" Phoenix asked.

"That we're not sure of," Ximena replied. "My guess—based on the way the limbs have been severed from the bodies and the heads lined up on the table—is that someone wanted to send a message."

"Why send it by killing your own men?" Phoenix asked.

"Silva de Peña Ortega didn't like the fact that these guys killed Gardoqui. They left a *narcomantas*—a message," Ximena said. "Look."

Phoenix stepped into the dining room and gagged at the sight of the ten heads set in two neat rows of five. Sitting on their severed necks, the eyes of the disembodied heads stared blankly at him. The killer had stabbed a bloody machete into the center of the table.

"I do not allow traitors" had been spray painted in black letters on the pale-yellow wall.

Phoenix glanced at Blanco to see her swallowing rapidly as if trying to choke back the vomit rising in her throat. Her wide eyes scanned the scene as tears formed in the corners. She stayed long enough to read the *narcomantas* and then bolted out the front door. Phoenix shook his head sadly. While he'd killed men in battle and had performed numerous wet work ops, Phoenix had never come across such a vicious and brutal slaying of human life. If Terry Martin and Silva de Peña Ortega were one and the same, then Phoenix and his CIA team would need to tread cautiously.

"Do you recognize any of these guys?" Ximena asked.

"All the riders I saw that day had full-face helmets on," he replied, but still, he examined the face of each dead man until his eyes suddenly went wide, and his mouth gaped open.

"What is it?" Ximena asked, reading his expression of disbelief.

"I just found my missing tech guy." Phoenix pointed to one of the heads. "That's Mark Schwartz. He was working with my task force."

"What's he doing here?" Ximena asked.

"I don't know, but we need to find out. If Schwartz was working for Ortega, then he might have been providing him with sensitive information."

"I agree. What do you want to do about it?" Ximena asked.

Phoenix shook his head. "I don't know, Xi. He's dead, so that plugs one leak."

———

Outside, Phoenix found Blanco pacing up and down the sidewalk with her arms crossed as if she were hugging herself.

"You okay?" he asked.

Blanco shook her head. "No. Zarate can be a cruel bastard, but I've never seen anything like that."

"I haven't either," Phoenix admitted.

"It's a drug cartel thing," Ximena explained. "Dismemberment sends a certain message—don't fuck with me."

"But why?" Phoenix asked. "I heard Gardoqui was cracking down drug trafficking operations. If he was cutting into Ortega's profits, wouldn't Ortega want him gone?"

"Not if Ortega didn't sanction the hit," Ximena said.

"So, he's cleaning house. The question is, why?" Phoenix said. "And what did Schwartz have to do with Martin?"

"I guess that's a question for your people," Ximena said.

"We believe Martin also leaked the names of all our case officers and assets in Venezuela to the SEBIN," Phoenix told the Mexican intelligence officer. "We had a pretty good idea of who we were dealing with before, but this adds a new level to things."

"I agree," Ximena said.

"Did you pull any of your people from the peace conference to deal with this tragedy?" Blanco asked.

"I pulled a few, but the Mexico City traffic cops have beefed up their patrols."

"We need to get back to the hotel," Phoenix said. "I'd hate to think all of this was really a distraction for something that might be happening there."

"I don't see how Ortega would benefit from killing anyone else there," Ximena said.

"I don't know either," Phoenix agreed, "but we've been gone long enough."

"And I've been out of touch since I had to leave my phone at the hotel," Blanco said.

"Was it cloned, too?" Ximena asked.

"Do you have a picture of Ortega?" Phoenix asked, deflecting the questioning look from his lover.

Ximena pulled out her phone and texted a photo of Ortega to Phoenix. He held it up beside the sketch. There was a remarkable resemblance that caused Blanco to shudder.

Phoenix emailed Martin's photo to Newton, asking her to run it through the facial recognition database.

"Miguelito will take you back if you're done here," Ximena said.

Blanco and Phoenix got into the Dodge SUV, and Cartega said to his sister through the open window, "Mom wants to have a family dinner on Thursday night."

"I'll try to be there," Ximena said.

"I know you will. See you, sis," Cartega said as he pulled away from the curb.

Phoenix sat back in his seat and watched the scenery. In his mind, he tried to piece together how the events of Minister Gardoqui's death, the slaying of the members of the *Los Perros Negros* MC, and the peace conference all fit together. And then there were the cloned phones.

In Phoenix's mind, it added up to more trouble coming their way.

CHAPTER 23

Four Seasons Hotel
Mexico City, Mexico

"W E'LL HAVE A FULL NAVAL BLOCKADE OF G EORGETOWN WITHIN an hour," Major General Alejandro Salazar reported to his commander-in-chief over the secure phone connection.

"And what is the status of our ground forces?" President Michel Zarate asked.

"The planes are in the air, *El Jefe*," Salazar replied. "We'll have boots on the ground in Georgetown at the same time the ships arrive. A parachute regiment will jump on the capitol building, and other planes will land at Eugene F. Correia International Airport and in Timehri. Not only will we control the seas, but also Guyana's major military bases."

"And air defenses?" Zarate asked.

"All of our anti-aircraft batteries are online, sir," Salazar replied.

Zarate knew precisely what the commander of his armed forces was telling him. Over the years, Zarate and his predecessor had ringed Venezuela with a vast array of Russian-made 20mm and 40 mm anti-aircraft guns, S-125 Pechora and Gadfly surface-to-air missiles, and S-300VM anti-ballistic missile systems to counter any fixed-wing aircraft, cruise missiles, or precision-guided munitions that Venezuela's enemies might try to throw at them. And as a last resort, Zarate's troops carried shoulder-fired 9K38 Igla missiles, similar to the American-made Stinger.

Together, Chávez and Zarate had ensured the sovereignty of Venezuela's airspace with the capability to strike targets deep inside Brazil and Colombia and dominate maritime air space all the way to the islands of Aruba, Bonaire, and Curaçao.

The only fly in his ointment was the Flying Jaguars, who seemed to slip past his defenses whenever they were in the air.

"Swat those pissant Tucanos out of the air if they try to intercept our troop flights," Zarate said, tired of hearing news of America's latest and greatest flying ace, ironically nick-named Dumpster Fire.

A loud banging on the door to the suite interrupted their conversation. Zarate motioned to one of his men to see who had come to disturb him after he'd given that Guyanese bastard Fredricks a piece of his mind.

The bodyguard opened the door, and before he could turn to announce the U.S. Secretary of State, Mike Asbury strode into the room.

"I have to go," Zarate said into the phone. "America's errand boy is here."

Zarate ended the call and placed the phone on a polished mahogany table beside the blue sofa where he sat. He didn't bother to stand as Asbury crossed the room.

"Recall your ships at once, Michel," Asbury blurted out.

Zarate gave the man a small, tired smile as he stood and buttoned his suit coat. "Perhaps it is time for you to face reality, Mister Secretary of State. I will not withdraw my ships nor stand down my military. Guyana fired the first shot. I intend to end the fight and free the citizens of the *Guayana Esequiba*, who have struggled under ineffectual leadership for the past century."

"This is a violation of every treaty you have ever signed," Asbury said through clenched teeth.

"Tell me, Mike, why are you here? Where is your president? Why is Randy 'Merica not here?" Zarate didn't wait for an answer but plowed on. "I will tell you why. He is a weak and ineffectual puppet. You and so many others are the mouthpieces of your Deep State. I would be surprised if Mercia knew how to find the Situation Room without someone holding his hand."

"I am *here*," Asbury stated, "because *you* are in clear violation of international law. Recall your ships at once."

Zarate strode over to the window and gazed out across Mexico City. After a few moments of silence, he said, "No. I will not recall my ships or my troops. Guyana and the world must learn a lesson in leadership."

"I'm warning you, Michel, withdraw *now!*" Asbury said.

"Or what?" Zarate turned to face the Secretary of State.

"The dogs of war will set upon you, and you will lose your office," Asbury stated.

Zarate snickered. "And who would you replace me with?"

"That would be for the people of Venezuela to decide when they have a free and fair election."

"But they have already decided. I have been the victor twice," Zarate replied. "My election has been as free and fair as the ones you hold in the United States. Rigging electronic voting machines is so easy even a child could do it."

"I'm not here to talk about rigged elections, Michel. You *need* to withdraw your ships so we can continue to have peaceful talks."

"My ships are positioned to ensure just that." Zarate

smiled cheerfully. "But there is something you can do for me, Mike. You can call your president and tell him that I will withdraw on two conditions: Venezuela is allowed to reclaim the *Guayana Esequiba*, and all sanctions are lifted from my country."

Asbury pursed his lips and shook his head. "You know that's not going to happen, Michel. The only way we could even start negotiating is for you to recall your ships."

"Then we have nothing to talk about," Zarate said.

The bodyguards flanked Secretary Asbury and escorted him from the suite.

Zarate turned to stare out the window again, wishing he was riding the bow of the *Yaviré*, one of his *Guaicamacuto*-class patrol boats, up the Demerara River into Georgetown as the conquering hero.

CHAPTER 24

Cheddi Jagan International Airport
Timehri, Guayana

WILL POUNDER ROLLED OFF THE READY ROOM COUCH AND SAID into the phone, "I gotta go, Max."

"What's that sound?" Max asked.

"It's an air raid siren, babe," Pounder said. "It's probably just some shitheads screwing around in a light plane. It's nothing to worry about."

"Let's go, Dumpster!" Stitches yelled as she pulled her hair into a ponytail. "We got a whole fleet of inbound Fanboys."

"Be careful," Max said.

"Don't worry, Max!" Stitches shouted. "I'll protect our national hero."

"Love you, babe," Pounder said and ended the call. Things had escalated rather quickly between Pounder and Maxine Gilespie. He'd badgered her for years to go out with him when they'd lived in Hutchinson, Kansas, but she'd consistently rebuffed him. However, as soon as she heard that Gruber and Pounder planned to join Guyana's Flying Jaguars, she was suddenly all in on Pounder. That was all right with Pounder. Max was the type of girl he would want his parents to meet, and they had, except Max had been drunk and belligerent when she'd shown up at their house in the middle of the night. She'd puked in the bushes and then confessed her love for Will.

In her usual blunt manner, made even sharper by the liquid courage, Max had divulged Pounder's plans to his parents. He still couldn't get the look of his father's disappointment and disapproval out of his mind. Pounder had packed in a hurry and driven away from his parent's place, taking Max home before heading for training in Georgia. All that seemed like a lifetime ago.

"Seriously, let's go, Dumpster," his backseater said. "The planes are fueled and armed with Piranhas. We're going to shoot down more Fanboys."

Dumpster followed her out of the ready room, joining the other pilots and navigators in the truck for the ride to the airfield. Pounder could feel the adrenaline singing in his veins, and his hands shook as the truck lumbered toward the airport.

Once it came to a stop, the pilots jumped out and ran toward their planes. Just after the Flanker flight had destroyed the three Super Tucanos on the ground at Camp Stephenson, six more Tucanos had flown in, ballooning the squadron to eight. Every available pilot was taking off today. And while they didn't stand much of a chance of completely repelling the invaders, they'd do everything in their power to try.

Pounder found Cory Anderson leaning against his plane. Five hash marks had been stenciled below the cockpit canopy, marking Pounder's kills. He hoped to add a few more to the tally today.

"She's ready to fly, boss," Anderson said. "Bring her home in one piece."

"Roger that," Dumpster said as he climbed into the cockpit.

Moments later, the flight of eight Super Tucanos was in the air with Colonel Jorge Mansoor as flight leader.

"Our intel says there's a fleet of cargo planes headed our way," Mansoor said over the radio. "They also say the Fanboys have activated their surface-to-air defenses, which can easily cover Guyana. Be on the lookout for incoming missiles, and everyone be safe out there."

Rapid clicks of transmit buttons filled the air as the other pilots signaled their replies.

"All elements, break off," Mansoor ordered.

Steve Gruber and his wingman, Ronnie Abelman, banked away from Mansoor and Pounder, heading off to hunt on their own. Pounder glanced over both shoulders to see the other two ship formations break off from the lead element.

"There's a flight of six cargo planes dead ahead," Stitches reported.

"What's the plan, Papa?" Pounder asked Mansoor over the radio.

"Splash them all," Mansoor replied. "Missiles armed and ready. Fire at will."

Pounder didn't have to be told twice. He locked onto a target the radar identified as a Lockheed C-130 Hercules. Triggering his Piranha, Pounder immediately targeted a second as the two formations of planes raced toward each other.

"Splash one," Stitches called out.

Pounder triggered another air-to-air missile, and it leaped off the weapon's pylon and raced for the next plane.

"Splash two," Stitches reported. "Papa has two confirmed kills as well."

Mansoor and Pounder divided the last two C-130s

between them. Pounder added three more aircraft to his tally, and Mansoor joined him in the exclusive "ace" club.

Linking up with his flight lead again, Pounder wondered how the old pilots from World War II would react to his kills. Those guys had battled with the Luftwaffe and the Japanese Air Force, locking in dogfights that required skill and precision to come out alive. Shooting cargo planes from miles away with missiles was a bit like shooting fish in a barrel, but a kill was a kill, no matter how it happened.

"Fast movers coming in from the north. Angels Ten," Stitches reported.

Mansoor dove for the deck, and Pounder stayed right on his wing. They leveled off just above the carpet of green and flew nap-of-the-earth over the rugged peaks and through the narrow valleys, hoping to avoid radar detection from both the Su-30 Flanker jets and the Venezuelan radar installations that controlled their surface-to-air missile batteries.

Their evasive maneuvers brought them back in contact with Gruber and Abelman, who were doing battle with a flight of three Shaanxi Y-8 transport planes. Gruber and Abelman had already splashed several airplanes and knocked down a couple of Eurocopter AS532 transports.

"We're coming up on your port wing," Mansoor reported to Gruber's second element. "We'll combine forces against the Flankers."

"Copy that," Gruber replied.

After downing the remaining Y-8s, the flight of four Super Tucanos turned to the north, firewalling their throttles to gain ground on an intercept course with the Russian fighter jets.

———

Five minutes later, Mansoor called, "Lead element is breaking to the west. Second element continue north toward the fighters. We'll catch them in a pincher."

"How we looking, Stitches?" Pounder asked his navigator.

"I count six Flankers. I've got tone. We're being painted by a S-300 missile!"

Pounder hauled his control stick back, banking up and to the right, trying to distance himself from Mansoor. He popped chaff and flares to distract the missile at the peak of his climb, then dove to the deck, leveling off just above the treetops.

"There's a Flanker on your tail, Dumpster!" Mansoor shouted.

Pounder pulled the stick back again, driving the Super Tucano straight into the sky. As he climbed past fifteen thousand feet, he popped chaff and flares. Reaching thirty thousand feet above sea level, he let the plane roll over. Upside down, Pounder stared out the cockpit window, searching for the Flanker.

As he nosed the plane over, he saw two jets scurrying along the ground, and the moment the missile lock tone sounded in his ear, he fired two Piranhas.

"I've got missiles in the air!" Stitches shouted, her voice echoing with fear.

"Where?" Pounder asked, rolling his plane upright and leveling off.

"From everywhere!" Stitches responded.

"That can't be good," Pounder said, twisting in his seat to glance over his shoulders.

He spotted another Super Tucano in the distance and banked toward it, throwing the throttle forward to wring as much speed as possible from the Pratt & Whitney turboprop.

Closing in on the other Tucano, Pounder saw it was Steve Gruber's plane. Out of the corner of his eye, Pounder saw a Mi-35 Hind pop up over a rise and fire its machine gun at Gruber's plane. Instantly, Pounder locked up the helicopter in his sights, switching his weapon control to fire the FN Herstal machine guns built into his wings, and ripped the helicopter to shreds as Gruber scooted quickly out of harm's way.

But no one had seen the second Hind hovering just behind the same hill as its squadron mate. It rose ever so slightly to clear the ridge and fired two rockets at Pounder's plane.

The first rocket exploded harmlessly nearby, but the second detonated right under his Super Tucano. While the armored cockpit saved the two occupants from being sliced to ribbons by the shrapnel, the blast knocked two blades off the Tucano's five-bladed Hartzell reversible-pitch propeller.

Stitches jerked the handle on the ejection seat without waiting to be told. The explosives embedded in the airframe blew away the cockpit canopy and then rocketed her and Dumpster from the disabled aircraft.

Martin-Baker had designed their Mk10 ejection seats to a standard that had come to be known in the industry as "zero-zero," which meant the pilot could eject at zero altitude with zero airspeed, and the chute would still deploy. As the Super Tucano augured toward the ground, it passed five hundred feet of altitude. Stitches' chute opened first, and she glanced rapidly around for Pounder, who'd ejected moments later at a much lower altitude. His white chute popped open, and the navigator mentally noted where her pilot would land in the jungle.

———

Tammy "Stitches" Dorn brought her knees up to her chest as she fell through the treetops and landed with a grunt of pain on the marshy ground below. She lay there for a few minutes, trying to catch her breath from the jarring fall.

The sound of a helicopter hovering nearby brought her to her feet. She knew the parachute tangled in the trees above would be a dead giveaway of her location. She dodged under the low-hanging branches and dove to the ground with her hands over her head as the helicopter's nose-mounted machine gun spit bullets into the woods all around her.

As the helicopter buzzed overhead, she jumped up and ran toward where she thought Pounder had landed.

Moments later, she found Dumpster swinging from the end of his parachute lines about ten feet above the ground. His chute had gotten hung up in the heavy jungle canopy, bringing him to a jerking halt.

"Yo, Dumpster. This is no time to take a nap," she said, staring up at his drooping head.

When Pounder didn't acknowledge her, Stitches found a stick and started poking the pilot. She knew she had to get him on the ground before the Hind made another pass and riddled both of them with bullets.

"Wake up, asshole!" she shouted as she whacked him in the front of the helmet with her stick.

The helicopter sounded as if it was right above them.

"I promised your girlfriend that I'd keep you safe. Now wake the fuck up!" she cried again, feeling the pressure mounting as the helicopter hovered nearby.

Stitches dove to the ground as the Hind's machine gun shredded the nearby trees.

A thunderous explosion detonated overhead, and the helicopter suddenly crashed into the trees about two hundred meters away.

The survival radio crackled to life in Stitches' vest. "Splash one, Hind. This is Gruber overhead. How copy Dumpster or Stitches?"

Stitches grabbed her radio. "This is Stitches. I read you five by five. Dumpster is stuck in a fucking tree."

"Copy that," Gruber said with a laugh.

"This shit ain't funny, Hans. Dumpster is out cold. Send us a rescue bird."

"I wish I could," Gruber replied. "They're all otherwise

occupied. You're on your own for now. I'll stay on station as long as I can."

"Roger that," Stitches said forlornly.

She whacked her pilot on the helmet again in a vain attempt to revive him, but Pounder still didn't respond.

Her first job was to get him out of the tree. After that, she'd see if he had any wounds and triage them. Stitches had been through survival training and SERE school in the Air Force when she'd been a navigator in F-15s. After getting out of the military, Stitches had tried flying commercial aircraft and found it rather dull. She'd switched career paths and become an EMT for the city of Denver and had frequently worked with backcountry rescue teams to find missing hikers and skiers. Like Pounder and Gruber, she had joined the Flying Jaguars to have another shot at fighting for a righteous cause.

Tammy Dorn had earned the moniker "Stitches" because she'd put her EMT training to use back in Valdosta, Georgia, when she'd stitched up a fellow pilot who had gotten into a bar fight. He'd received a massive gash in his scalp when one of the other bar fighters had smashed him over the head with a bottle. Working her magic, she'd sewn up the guy's scalp just in time for Mansoor to dismiss him from training for his unwarranted actions.

Taking a deep breath, Stitches glanced around for something to climb on so she could reach Dumpster's shroud lines. When she saw nothing useful, she pulled out her sheath knife and used a roll of electrical tape she kept in her vest to fasten the knife to her "whacking" stick.

With the knife secure, she lifted the stick and began to saw through the lines on the right side of the unconscious pilot. They parted easily as they were taut as banjo strings. It didn't take long to get through all the lines, and when the last shroud line let go, his body swung back and forth, turning in slow circles on his left-side shroud lines.

Stitches started in on them, making quick work of the taut parachute cord. When Pounder was hanging by only a few remaining lines, Stitches cleared his landing area of any sharp sticks, then piled palm fronds and dead tree leaves under the pilot, fearing the fall would break his legs or cause other irreparable damage.

She was about to cut the last few lines when a noise in the brush caused her to whirl around, holding the stick like a spear and praying she could ward off whatever was out there. Her heart thundered in her chest, and she was suddenly conscious of just how alone she and Pounder truly were.

"We are here to help," a native voice called out as four men stepped out of the bushes.

Stitches kept the spearhead leveled at them.

"We are Warao," said the older of the native men. "While we live in Venezuela, we will help anyone who fights against the Zarate regime."

"I need to get him out of the tree," Stitches said, nodding toward Pounder. "He's unconscious."

She was thankful the men spoke English as she couldn't speak a lick of Spanish other than to order a beer and ask for the bathroom, and neither of those phrases were particularly helpful in the middle of the swampy jungle.

One of the men pulled out a poncho, and the four natives each took a corner and stood beneath the pilot, ready to catch him. Stitches cut the final shroud lines, and Dumpster dropped feet first into the poncho. The sudden weight of the pilot caused the men to stagger, and one dropped his corner of the poncho. Pounder rolled out of the makeshift catch net, slammed into the ground, and came to rest on his back.

Stitches dropped her spear and ran to his side. She was about to pry open his right eyelid when the pilot suddenly blinked.

"What the fuck happened?" he moaned, then unbuckled his helmet and pushed it off.

Stitches heard a commotion behind her and glanced up to see the locals melt into the forest, leaving only the poncho behind.

As Pounder struggled to sit up, a group of camouflaged commandos stepped into the clearing with their guns aimed at the two aviators. Stitches caught Pounder as he fell back, cradling his upper body to her chest. Her hand slid toward the Glock pistol in Pounder's survival vest, ready to defend them, but a soldier stepped forward and relieved both Stitches and Pounder of their handguns.

"You are now prisoners of the Venezuelan Army," the leader said.

CHAPTER 25

Oval Office
Washington D.C.

President Randy Mercia stood in the Situation Room, the intelligence management center on the ground floor of the West Wing. He glanced around the room at the array of heavy brass from the Pentagon and top advisors from the intelligence community, all sitting at a table, awaiting his command. Mercia felt like a young JFK, just getting his feet wet as a president when the first crisis struck their administrations.

The Situation Room had been created as a result of a lack of intelligence as the ill-fated Bay of Pigs invasion had unfolded, and Kennedy, pressured by the military and the CIA to throw America's fighting forces into the fray, had told everyone to back down. Now, Mercia faced a similar crisis, but he wasn't going to back down.

Zarate had called him out.

"Play it again," Mercia said, standing behind his chair at the head of the table.

One of the techs pressed play, and the conversation between Michel Zarate and Mike Asbury played on the giant screen at the head of the room. Zarate's bodyguards had been on alert for recording devices, but they had failed to notice the fisheye lens built into Asbury's tie clip as it didn't broadcast the signal live. Instead, Asbury had uploaded the video of their conversation as soon as he'd returned to his room.

Once the recording had ended, Mercia asked for a satellite view to show the positions of Zarate's fleet.

"There are three *Guaicamacuto*-class patrol boats right offshore of Georgetown. We suspect they're positioning for a blockade," Chief of Naval Operations Admiral Adriana Avalon said. She wore her tailored uniform to accommodate her six foot, or 183cm, height, with her long brunette hair pulled into a bun at the nape of her neck. Avalon cut a striking figure, and she could maneuver ruthlessly through the political minefields that often accompanied her position.

"What ships do we have in the area?" Mercia asked.

"Currently, we have two destroyers, the *Farragut* and *The Sullivans*, holding off Barbados, and we have two littoral combat ships, the *Cooperstown* and the *Billings*, stationed near Aruba. Plus, we have LHD-7, the *Iwo Jima*, standing by with a Marine Expeditionary Unit on board as well as a full complement of F-35 fighters and Viper and Venom helicopters."

"Get me Fredricks on the horn," Mercia said.

A moment later, an aide said, "I have him on the line, sir."

"President Fredricks, this is Randy Mercia. I'm sure you're well aware of what's happening."

Fredricks' voice filled the room from speakers concealed in the ceiling and oak-paneled walls. "I am. Venezuela is setting a naval blockade, and my Flying Jaguars are already intercepting their troop transport planes."

"I want to send a message," Mercia said. "With your blessing, of course."

"What is it?" Fredricks asked.

"I have enough Tomahawk cruise missiles stationed nearby to blast every one of Zarate's ships out of the water. Are you game?"

"Be my guest, Mister President," Fredricks replied enthusiastically. "I might also suggest striking his missile batteries. They'll interfere with any land or air mission you might try later."

"Can we do that?" Mercia asked his military council.

"Already pre-plotted, sir," Admiral Avalon said.

"Do it," Mercia said. "The world is tired of being held hostage by Zarate and his thugs. Blast those ships out of the water."

CHAPTER 26

GDFS *Essequibo*
Atlantic Ocean
Off the coast of Guyana

COMMANDER DAVID CLARKE STOOD ON THE BRIDGE OF HIS vessel, staring through a pair of binoculars at the approaching Venezuelan warships. His blood boiled at such audacious actions, and he wanted nothing more than to swoop in and launch his torpedoes in revenge.

But Admiral Mohammed Issacs, head of the GDF Coast Guard, had ordered all Guyanese vessels to steam into the tiny triangle of water between Georgetown and the Suriname border that constituted Guyana's economic exclusion zone not claimed by Zarate in presidential decree number 1787. Clarke had ordered the *Essequibo* to stop just over the line, and from his vantage point, he could see the fleet of Venezuelan naval ships headed for Georgetown.

"They're going to block the port, sir," Boatswain's Mate Glasgow stated.

"I know," Clarke replied dryly. He didn't understand the admiral's sudden order for retreat, but he had his torpedo tubes armed with Raytheon's latest Mark 54 torpedoes. He'd also ordered his crew to man the Mark 38 25mm bow gun and the 12.7mm machine guns. If the Venezuelans wanted to get froggy, he was ready to jump.

"Sir! Radar reports multiple incoming missiles," Glasgow cried.

"Where are they coming from?" Clarke asked.

Glasgow hadn't come up with an answer by the time the first Tomahawk cruise missile slammed into the *Yaviré*, one of the three patrol boats leading the charge for the Demerara River. Microseconds later, more Tomahawks slammed into the other vessels, blasting them to smithereens and sending them to the bottom of the sea.

"What the hell was that?" Clarke whispered to no one in particular.

"Sir, there are smaller patrol boats still headed for George-town. What should we do?" Glasgow asked.

Commander Clarke was about to pick up the phone to call Admiral Issacs when an announcement blared from the radio. "Now here this! This is Admiral Muhammad Issacs. American naval vessels have just fired upon the Venezuelan fleet and sank most of their warships, but there are smaller vessels still at large. To all vessels in the Guyana Defence Force, I say you are weapons-free. I repeat. You are weapons-free. Defend our homeland!"

"You heard the man, Boats," Clarke said. "Flank speed for those patrol boats."

As Glasgow engaged the engines and the GDFS *Esse-quibo* lurched forward like a thoroughbred from the starting gate, Clarke used the shipboard radio to communicate with his weapons teams. All of his crew was ready for action.

"Target the lead gunboat," Clarke ordered his torpedo crew.

"Firing solution is ready, captain," Chief Weapons Officer Allicock replied.

"Fire at will," Clarke ordered.

Seconds later, the 17.3-meter Iranian-built missile boat took a torpedo amidships and detonated in a massive fireball that rained debris across the water and onto the other two Venezuelan gunboats headed for Georgetown.

"Target the second boat," Clarke ordered, and again, his crew fired, scoring a second hit and then a third as the final salvo of torpedoes struck the remaining gunboat.

All that remained of the Venezuelan blocking fleet were small raiding craft armed with machine guns that had been launched by the larger vessels just before the Tomahawk cruise missile strikes had destroyed them.

Clarke ordered his crew to close the gap and to fire at will from the gun mounts. It felt damned good to be in control for once. And Clarke relished the demise of the Venezuelan Navy.

CHAPTER 27

Oval Office
Washington D.C.

"Get President Zarate on a video feed," Randy Mercia said to no one in particular inside the Situation Room.

Moments later, the video screen on the far wall glowed with an image of the Venezuelan dictator, replacing the views of the missile strikes happening across Venezuela as more Tomahawks rained down on the missile batteries.

"This is an act of war!" Zarate shouted.

"No, sir," Mercia replied, facing the camera so Zarate could clearly see his determination. "We have responded in defense of Guyana. By now, Tomahawk cruise missiles have sunk all of your ocean-going vessels, and Admiral Issacs has ordered his Coast Guard to finish off the smaller boats."

"This was an unwarranted action by the United States government against my country," Zarate declared. "I am calling upon my Chinese and Russian counterparts to strike the United States with intercontinental ballistic missiles."

"Stand down, Zarate," Mercia replied. "You thought you faced weak administrations here in the U.S. and Guyana, but you, sir, could not have been more wrong. You have no recourse and no more ships left to fight. As you also know, Tomahawk strikes took out the majority of your missile batteries. I don't wish to do any further harm to the people of Venezuela. I ask that you step down from your command and allow Vice President Acevedo to take over."

"Bullshit!" Zarate exclaimed. "I will never stand down."

The screen went blank as Zarate logged off.

"Your orders?" Rex Scott asked.

"How many Tomahawks do you have left?" Mercia asked Admiral Avalon.

The Chief of Naval Operations glanced down at the tablet on the table in front of her. "Fifty-two remaining in the tubes, sir."

"Strike all the Venezuelan bases along the Essequibo border. I want Zarate to know I'm not fucking around."

CHAPTER 28

Four Seasons Hotel
Mexico City, Mexico

John Phoenix and Coralina Blanco stood in the Operation Unicorn suite, watching the television monitor in the aftermath of President Mercia's Tomahawk strikes on the Venezuelan fleet.

Blanco turned away from the screen and pressed her face against Phoenix's shoulder. He held her tightly as she wept for her fellow countrymen who had just been following Zarate's orders. Now, thousands of sailors and Army soldiers had lost their lives in a needless war. Blanco, as a former Army lieutenant, had known some of the paratroopers and Special Forces operators who had perished in the plane crashes.

Phoenix's phone vibrated in his pocket. He slipped it out and saw Ximena's number on the screen.

"What's going on, Xi?" he asked.

"Where are you?" she asked.

"Why? What's up?" he asked.

"Some of these dead guys aren't in our criminal database. Can I run them through yours? I figured you have a base of operations somewhere in the city."

"We're at the Four Seasons." He gave her the room number and ended the call before pocketing the phone.

"What was that?" Delacroix asked.

"Your friend, Ximena," Phoenix replied. "She has some dead guys she wants to run through the facial recog database." He went on to explain to her about their visit to the *Los Perros Negros* MC stash house, where they'd found the ten headless bodies as a warning to those who had killed Minister Gardoqui.

"How is this relevant to our operation?" Delacroix asked.

"It's a bit of *quid pro quo* since she helped us out this morning with that other errand," Phoenix replied.

———

FIVE MINUTES LATER, there was a knock on the suite door. One of the techs opened it, and Ximena strolled in.

"That was fast," Phoenix said.

"I figured you were here, so I took the liberty of heading over before I called," the Mexican intelligence officer replied. "I have the photos on my phone. Who's going to help me?"

Phoenix pointed toward Jennifer Newton. "She'll fix you up."

After Ximena had her phone plugged into a computer and Newton had the photos uploaded to the CIA's system, Ximena straightened and glanced at the television. "What's going on?"

"The U.S. just destroyed all of Venezuela's Navy and Coast Guard ships and struck air defense batteries across the country," Phoenix reported.

"Is Zarate still in power?" Ximena asked.

"As of right now, he hasn't stepped down," Delacroix said.

"I don't expect him to," Ximena said. "He's got too much of an ego."

"Uh … guys," Newton said. "We've got a hit."

Delacroix, Phoenix, and Ximena walked around to look at Newton's computer screen.

"Did you know Schwartz was among the dead?" Delacroix asked Phoenix.

The case officer nodded. "I IDed him at the scene."

"That should have been the first thing you told me when you walked through the door, Bowie," she said acridly.

"We were all distracted by what was on the television. I was about to tell you when Ximena called," he replied, not feeling any remorse for keeping his fellow officers in the dark. There were too many questions swirling around the death of Mark Schwartz for Phoenix to trust anyone, even the people in the room who he felt closest to. They could all be lying straight to his face.

From the moment Phoenix had met Schwartz, he'd had an ominous feeling about him, but he hadn't trusted his gut. Now Schwartz was dead, and Phoenix couldn't put a gun to his head and ask him any questions.

"Why is a CIA officer operating with the *Los Perros Negros*?" Ximena asked Delacroix.

Delacroix deflected the question by asking Ximena to step away while they read over Schwartz's file.

"Only if you promise to share anything of relevance with me. I'm trying to solve a crime against the Mexican people," Ximena replied.

After Newton and Ximena had moved away from the computer, Delacroix and Phoenix read over Schwartz's file. It basically boiled down to him being a paramilitary operator under Rheinhart Constantine's command. Constantine had been the one to block Schwartz's move to the National Clandestine Service, wanting to keep the technical officer in-house. Phoenix scanned through the pertinent information again, searching for Chris Miller's name until he saw the two had worked together on several operations.

"I'm going to talk to Husker and see what he knows," Phoenix said.

"I don't think Husker was running him," Delacroix replied.

"But he knew him," Phoenix replied. He printed out Schwartz's photo and pocketed it.

"Well?" Ximena asked.

"We're not sure what Schwartz was doing there," Delacroix replied. "Go with Bowie, and you can talk to Husker." She turned to Blanco. "Go see what Acevedo needs. You have Bowie's number. Call if you need anything." As Phoenix headed for the door, Delacroix fired one more shot across his bow. "And, Bowie, take off that ridiculous hat. You're not Cary Grant."

Blanco grinned in triumph as she followed Phoenix and Ximena into the hallway. Phoenix kissed Blanco, and they parted ways, but he kept his fedora seated firmly in place.

Once in the hotel lobby, Phoenix called Husker and asked where the paramilitary commander was since he wasn't holding down a bar stool.

"I see you have that Mexican spy chick with you, so you know exactly where I am," Husker replied.

"Suite 2102, right?" Phoenix confirmed, figuring Husker had his eye on the hotel cameras and could see him and Ximena standing together in the lobby of the Four Seasons.

"I'll see you in ten minutes," Husker said, ending the call.

"I can't believe he just invited you up," Ximena said.

"Me, either, but it looks like we've got a date with the devil," Phoenix replied.

PHOENIX and his female counterpart stood in Suite 2102 in the Suites Carpi-Reforma Hotel. Through the floor-to-ceiling windows, they could see the top of the Four Seasons Hotel but not the street.

"How do you keep an eye on what's happening down there?" Phoenix asked.

"Same as you guys, I reckon," Miller said. "We're tapped into all the surveillance cameras in and around the Four Seasons. First of all, before I ask you why you're here, you gotta tell me what's up with you and that fucking hat?"

"I'm incognito," Phoenix replied.

"As a 1950s gangster or Teddy Roosevelt on safari?"

"It's not a fucking pith helmet," Phoenix shot back.

"Take it off before I lose my freaking mind," Miller said, barely containing his laughter.

"Fuck off," Phoenix replied, pulling the photo of Mark Schwartz from his pocket. "Look at this photo and tell me if you know this guy."

Miller took the photo and examined it. "Yeah. Mark Schwartz. He's one of Constantine's guys. I thought he was working with you."

"He was," Phoenix said.

"This is what he looks like now," Ximena said, holding up her phone to show Miller a photo of Schwartz's head on the table. "Your friend enjoyed Mexico so much that he lost his head over it."

"I don't think Schwartz would find that very punny," Miller replied. He looked closer at the phone. "How many more heads *are* on that table?"

"Ten," Ximena replied. "Retribution for the slaying of Minister Gardoqui."

Miller let out a low whistle. As Ximena explained the grisly slayings to Miller, Phoenix walked around the suite, pausing to glance over the shoulders of various techs at their computer stations. At a table pushed up against the window,

Phoenix found twenty cell phones laid out on it. He dialed his old number with his new phone and watched one of the screens of the burners light up as the phone vibrated across the table.

"What's the reason behind cloning my team's cell phones?" Phoenix asked.

"What are you talking about?" Miller asked, putting his fists on his hips.

"You cloned all the phones on my team except for your boy, Mark Schwartz," Phoenix said.

"What are you accusing me of?" Miller asked.

"I'm accusing you of cloning my team's phones because they're all right here," Phoenix said. "Why are you spying on my op?"

"I am not spying on your operation, Bowie," Miller replied indignantly. "Those are all my spare phones."

"Well, dumbass, they're not all spares. They're the clones that Ximena was looking for earlier when you saw her wandering around your hotel. And if you're not spying on my op, why was Richardson following me last night? He knew exactly where my asset would exit the safe house."

"First of all, Richardson said your tradecraft was shitty, and you telegraphed going into that building," Miller said. "All he had to do was wait to see who came out. When that Venezuelan chick showed up, he knew he'd mined gold. Dumb, Bowie. Just fucking dumb. Second, Schwartz isn't my guy. Constantine brought him in. He recruited Schwartz. He trained Schwartz, and he put Schwartz through the fire. Yes, I operated with him, and I thought he was a good kid, but I didn't put him on your op. If anyone has the authority to do that, it would be Constantine."

"But Constantine had no idea what we were doing," Phoenix said. "The op was need-to-know."

"Well, I'd say Constantine knew, and he put Schwartz on your team to keep an eye on things," Miller said.

"I don't get it," Phoenix said. "If he's Constantine's guy, who cloned all the phones and left them here?"

"And why are they laid out on a table where they would be easy to find?" Ximena asked.

Miller shrugged.

"Here's another question," Phoenix said. "How did you know Ximena and I were working together?"

"Oh, please," Miller replied sarcastically. "If Schwartz is Constantine's guy, then you're mine, and if I see you sneaking around on an op that I'm providing security for, you better damn well believe that I'm going to know what you're up to."

"Is that why you had Riley Richardson follow me last night?" Phoenix asked.

"Look, Bowie, like it or not, I've always got your back," Miller said. "But spying on your op was not on my agenda. I'd read the reports about Blanco, and as soon as I saw her, I knew you two would hook up. I had Richardson track you so I could keep you out of trouble. He told me about the hotel room safe house and about you getting into the SUV with Ximena's brother."

"You're just dialed in all the way around, then, huh?" Phoenix asked.

"What I don't understand is who is running a counter-op, Bowie," Miller said. "You thought it was me, and I thought it was you since you sent Ximena to track the phones. Sorry, Ximena, but it was pretty obvious you weren't a maid when you started going floor by floor, just pushing a cart and never cleaning a room."

"I'm not paid to clean rooms," she replied.

"Then we start by putting together a list of everyone on both our ops and cross-reference them," Phoenix said. "Someone on your team had to be working with Schwartz and know what he was doing. If Schwartz never came up here, then someone else brought in the cloned phones."

"I have what I need," Ximena said. "I'll leave you guys to it."

"Keep me posted if you have any further developments," Phoenix told her.

"I'll have one of my guys walk you out," Miller said, motioning to a nearby paramilitary officer.

"Thanks, but I think I can find my way out. I've been on every floor, remember?" Ximena replied, then she turned and headed for the door.

"Wait," Phoenix said, having a sudden thought about how things connected between Mark Schwartz, Rheinhart Constantine, the *Los Perros Negros* MC, and Terry Martin. To Miller, he said, "Send me a list of names to cross-reference."

"Okay, but what are you going to do?" Miller asked.

"Follow the money," Phoenix replied.

———

"Did you recover any phones or electronic devices from the scene in Ciudad Neza?" Phoenix asked as he and Ximena walked toward the Four Seasons Hotel.

"No, we didn't, and that's highly unusual now that I think about it," Ximena said.

"You have people watching the *Los Perros Negros*, right, like watching the drug cartels?"

"Yes. We do," Ximena admitted.

"Do any of your people collect signals intelligence from the *Los Perros Negros*?" Phoenix asked.

Ximena thought about who would collect SIGINT in Mexico, eventually coming up with an idea. "I have some friends who might be able to help." She went on to explain about a group within the Mexican military called the CMI, an abbreviation for Military Intelligence Center in Spanish. They operated a program called Pegasus, which allowed them to collect cellphone data like the NSA did in the United

States and other countries. "The program basically infects smartphones with a virus that allows the CMI to monitor communications, capture locations, and turn on the phone's camera and microphones to glean real-time data," Ximena explained.

"That kind of spyware has been around for a while," Phoenix replied.

"I agree, but they turn up some interesting stuff from time to time," Ximena said. "I can work my contacts to see if the CMI was monitoring anything at the *Los Negros Perros* safe house or communications between club members."

Phoenix nodded. "I think that's a good plan. We should look for a connection between Schwartz and whoever he was working for and how Martin/Ortega used the funds he received from the motorcycle club."

"I'll see what I can dig up," Ximena said. "I'll call you if I find anything."

"And I'll have Newton, the tech you met earlier, work it from our end—see if we can find any chatter about the beheadings."

Ximena suddenly changed the subject. "Miller said you and Blanco have a history?"

"We do," Phoenix replied, not wanting to elaborate.

"I like her," Ximena said. "She seems good for you."

"In our line of work, relationships don't get much of a chance to blossom," Phoenix replied.

Ximena smiled lecherously. "If that's how you feel, just let me know when you want to see my special blossom."

Phoenix's eyebrows shot up, not expecting that response since he hadn't gotten any sexual vibe from her at all. The only reply he could muster was a stammering, "Good to know."

"I'll call you when I know something," Ximena said with a smile, enjoying the sight of a flustered Phoenix.

Phoenix watched her disappear into the crowd along

Paseo de la Reforma Avenue, wondering what that exchange had been all about.

Inside the Operation Unicorn suite, Phoenix sat down with Newton and asked her to access the NSA database. He wanted her to search the archives for anything about the slaying in Ciudad Neza, including keywords associated with terrorism, money laundering, drug trade, and the names of Terry Martin, Silva de Peña Ortega, and Mark Schwartz.

As Newton compiled a list, she said, "This might take a while."

CHAPTER 29

Fort Tarabay
Tumeremo, Venezuela

Two Venezuelan Army soldiers shoved Will Pounder into a wooden chair and zip tied his wrists to the armrests.

He glanced around after someone pulled a hood off his head, trying to see through the blurry vision of his swollen left eye. He was in a bunker-type structure with solid concrete block walls and a sheen of dampness on the floor. Blinking against the harsh glare of the overhead florescent lights, he saw soldiers in dark green uniforms hovering in the shadows along the walls, armed with automatic rifles.

Moments later, two more goons dragged Stitches in, and zip tied her to a chair beside the pilot. Like Pounder, she had been stripped of her helmet and survival vest, and the laces had been removed from her boots. Pounder shivered at the thought of what was yet to come.

After he and Stitches had been apprehended in the forest by Venezuelan Fanboys, they'd been marched through the dense jungle, then dragged into the back of a truck, and driven to a military base. Along the way, the soldiers had roughed him up and threatened to physically harm Stitches. Pounder had kicked a sergeant in the face when he'd leaned over Stitches like he was going to whip it out and have his way with her. That was when he'd received a savage beat-down and gotten a black eye.

"What do you want from us?" Stitches yelled at their guards.

The soldiers stood stoically at the ready, not bothering to answer her questions.

Once the soldiers had bound the two American aviators to the chairs, more Fanboys filed into the room. Two hung a giant Venezuelan flag on the wall behind the Americans, and two more set up a video camera in front of them.

A man wearing uniform pants bloused at the tops of his black combat boots and a yellow T-shirt stepped through the door from another room. He kept his hand on the butt of his pistol in a drop-leg holster.

Pounder knew instinctively that this man was in charge. He was taller than the rest of the troops and had thick black hair and icy blue eyes. Crossing the room, Yellow Shirt lifted Stitches' head and turned it side to side, then did the same to Pounder, squeezing the pilot's cheeks tightly in his grip.

"Tell me who did this to you," the man said sternly, then turned to the others in the room and shouted something in Spanish that Pounder didn't understand.

When no one answered, Pounder said through gritted teeth, "The guy who did this tried to stick his dick into my friend."

"Is that true?" Yellow Shirt asked in English and then shouted at his men in his native tongue.

One of the soldiers cleared his throat and said, "*Sí, Capitán Gil. Era Juárez.*"

Pounder caught the words "yes" and "Captain Gil."

The captain turned to face Juárez, who hung his head and nodded, and then Gil screamed at the others in Spanish, and they all replied in unison to whatever he'd said.

In English, Gil spoke to Pounder and Stitches. "I have told them we are bound by the Geneva Convention. We are uniformed fighting forces at war with one another, not arresting Zarate's dissenters on the street."

Pounder nodded in understanding, hoping Juárez received a just punishment. Gil jerked his pistol from the holster and shot Juárez in the head, slamming the kid's body back against the wall and exploding gray brains and bright red blood all over the concrete.

Stitches screamed and bucked against her bonds. She toppled her chair over as she continued to kick and cry.

Gil ordered something in Spanish. Two men moved in and quickly righted Stitches, setting her chair back on its feet. They had to put their full weight on her to keep her from tipping over again as she fought with them. More men dove at her ankles and zip tied them to the chair legs to prevent her from falling over again and injuring herself, but she continued to buck and cry.

Bending down, the captain dabbed her tears away with a white handkerchief he pulled from the back pocket of his pants. "It is okay, Miss Dorn," he said in English, obviously reading her name off the patch on her flight suit. "I have made an example out of Corporal Juárez. My men will not hurt you anymore. Please calm down. My president asks that you make a video for him."

"Fuck that guy," Pounder said.

"I am a patient man, *Señor* Pounder," Gil said. "But please do not belittle the president of my country."

"He's a dictator and a complete asshole to make you invade Guyana," Stitches cried, spitting at Gil's feet for effect.

Captain Gil inhaled a long, shuddering breath, visibly trying to control his boiling rage. He exhaled, and his face relaxed as he resumed a disaffected attitude. He spoke softly and calmly to the two aviators. "I don't think you understand. You *will* make this video. I wish for you to be in good health aside from your current injuries sustained during your ejection." He pointed to Pounder's black eye. "That was unfortunate, to say the least. Now, please make this video, and we will take you to your quarters."

While Captain Gil tried to portray a man in control of his emotions and his people, the brutal display of shooting a man in cold blood had wilted Pounder's resolve to fight back. He wanted to get home to Max, and he wanted to protect his navigator from potential harm. The rumors about Venezuelan prisons and the treatment the prisoners received had run rampant through the Guyanese military camps, and Pounder wasn't immune to the tales—tall or otherwise.

And he had seen enough scenarios with captives in front of flags over the years to know that no matter what they did, he and Stitches were in an impossible position. In the Middle East, when a prisoner knelt before an ISIS or Al-Qaeda flag, they usually ended up headless. Pounder would do whatever he needed to keep his head on his shoulders.

Resigned to the reality of the situation, Pounder asked, "What do you want us to say?"

Captain Gil snapped his fingers, and another soldier produced poster-board-sized cue cards with English words written in black marker.

"Are you ready?" the captain asked.

Pounder was *not* ready to read a prewritten speech, but he steeled himself to resist in any way possible. His thoughts harkened back to a conversation between himself and Colonel Mansoor when they had been in flight training in Valdosta, Georgia. They had discussed Greg "Pappy" Boyington, a U.S. Marine Corps aviator with twenty-eight Japanese planes to his credit. Boyington had eventually been shot down, and the Japanese had interned him in several secret prison camps.

The stalwart Marine had done everything in his power to thumb his nose at his captors, but he'd also known when to show respect for his guards.

Will Pounder knew this was a time to show respect to his captors and read the cue cards, but he would slip a few words of his own into the mix, figuring half the assholes in the room couldn't understand a lick of English.

He nodded to Captain Gil to signal that he was ready, and the videographer switched on the recorder.

CHAPTER 30

Four Seasons Hotel
Mexico City, Mexico

"Ma'am!" a targeting officer called out to Sandy Delacroix, drawing everyone's attention to the television at the far end of the suite's living room.

Michel Zarate had gathered the news media in the Four Seasons' central courtyard, where two massive flags hung on the side of the building in celebration of the peace talks. Ignoring the Guyanese "Golden Arrowhead," Zarate had placed his podium squarely in front of the Venezuelan flag with its tricolor yellow, blue, and red stripes. Phoenix thought even the VZ flag was a fucked-up symbol of reclamation. For 195 years, it had remained unchanged, with seven white five-pointed stars glowing proudly in the center, until 2006 when President Hugo Chávez decided to add an eighth star to represent the lost territory of the *Guayana Esequiba*.

The camera angle framed Zarate at the podium with the

flag in the background above brightly colored patio umbrellas and ivy-covered archways.

Zarate seemed to be taking his time in choosing his words, but when he spoke, he was clear and precise. "Two hours ago, American military forces unilaterally attacked warships and military installations across Venezuela in an attempt to disrupt these peace talks and to discredit my presidency. As the Tomahawk missile strikes were taking place, Guyana Defence Force airplanes invaded Venezuela's sovereign airspace. The superior Bolivarian Air Force shot down all the invaders with our strategic air defense systems. You will now see a live video stream of two of my prisoners."

The video of Zarate cut to an image of two aviators zip tied to wooden chairs in front of another Venezuelan flag and surrounded by Army troops holding AK-103 automatic rifles.

"This can't be good," Phoenix muttered as he stood from his seat beside Newton so he could see more clearly.

On the screen, the male pilot with a swollen black eye said, "My name is Lieutenant William Pounder. I am an American pilot employed by the Guyana Defence Force's Flying Tigers. Beside me is my navigator, Tammy Dorn. We are now hosted by the Venezuelan Army. Hosted?" Pounder looked straight into the camera. "Dude, we're *fucking* prisoners!"

The television censors tried to bleep out his curse word but barely caught the end of it.

Someone off-screen shouted at Pounder in Spanish.

"Your English sucks, man," Pounder muttered before fixing his eyes off the camera again, presumably to read the cue cards. "We will be released when the imperialist United States government has complied with President Zarate's demands. If these requesteses are not met ... Who wrote this shit?" Pounder cleared his throat and started again. "If these requests are not met, Lieutenant Dorn and I will be held hostage indefinitely."

The camera feed switched back to President Zarate at the podium in the Four Seasons courtyard. "You have seen the proof of my prisoners, and now you will hear my demands. I *will not* negotiate with Guyana for territory that has always belonged to Venezuela. I *will not* negotiate with the United States for the release of the prisoners, and I *will not* negotiate with any delegation from the United Nations who asks me to step down from the presidency. My demands are simple: Guyana must disband their mercenary forces and give up all claim to the *Guayana Esequiba*. In addition, the United States must withdraw all interventionist forces from Venezuelan Territorial Waters and lift all economic sanctions against Venezuela."

Zarate turned and strode away from the podium, leaving the crowd in stunned silence.

Seconds later, the news feed cut to two commentators at a desk in their New York City studio. Delacroix hit the mute button on the remote before the talking heads could start dissecting Zarate's speech, his demands, or the ongoing hostage crisis with the two American aviators now in captivity.

Delacroix turned and addressed the room. "Zarate's demands change nothing for us, people. Our mission is still Unicorn. She is the priority and our backdoor conduit to Zarate."

"But he just said he won't negotiate with us," an analyst objected.

"I don't care what he said," Delacroix replied firmly. "Our operation is still a go. Start working the cameras and comms to see if we can come up with something new. I need to call Director Stratten."

Phoenix sat back down beside Jennifer Newton.

"I should work on our operation," she said quietly, moving her cursor to close the screen she'd been using to return to Operation Unicorn.

"Everyone else in this room is focused on just that," Phoenix said. "I want you to concentrate on finding something that connects Mark Schwartz to the *Los Perros Negros* MC. Ideally, I'd love to find financial transactions between the club and Miller/Ortega." He paused to gauge her reaction, but Newton just nodded. He picked up again, asking, "Have you gotten anything off the facial recognition scan from the photo Ximena provided?"

"No," Newton replied. "There was nothing in our databases. I scanned CIA, FBI, and Homeland."

Phoenix shook his head and let out a sigh of frustration. He removed his fedora and set it on top of the privacy screen, then rolled his shoulder, trying to ease the tension behind his shoulder blade.

"You should see a *curandero*. I hear they're popular in Mexico City."

"What's a *curandero*?" Phoenix asked, not familiar with the term.

"Oh, they're a natural healer, like a shaman."

"That's just what I need, a fucking witch doctor," Phoenix replied. "They'll probably dose me with some ayahuasca mixed with a dash of peyote so I can commune with my dead relatives."

Newton giggled and said dreamily, "I wish I could commune with my ancestors. Gosh, I miss college. The CIA's zero-tolerance policy kinda sucks."

The hardest drug Phoenix had ever taken was morphine, but he kinda wished he had something to kill the pain and resentment festering in the knot under his shoulder blade. It was all he could do to sit still. With his right arm hanging down, the pain was almost unbearable. If he rested his arms on a desktop to work at a computer keyboard, the pain seemed to disappear magically, but moving out of that position brought it sharply back.

Phoenix wondered who he resented today. Maybe it was

all of the clowns who had made fun of his new hat. Even Blanco had tried to get rid of it when she'd kissed him.

He glanced over at Connelly, who sat at another computer station, a phone glued to her ear. A sudden desire to be with Coralina swelled within him, and he reached for his phone, texting her to ask if she was okay and wanting to know what Evelyn Acevedo's mindset was now that Zarate had thrown down the gauntlet.

Her text came back almost immediately, asking if they could meet.

A rush of endorphins surged through Phoenix. He asked her when and where.

Blanco asked if he still had the hotel room at the Suites Rio Elba. He replied that he did, and her answer was to meet there in two hours. He was glad to have something to do other than stare at a computer screen. Looking at the electronic intelligence (ELINT) data made his eyes want to cross and glaze over. Usually, after just fifteen minutes in front of a screen, he grew antsy and was ready to prowl the streets for some action. Over the years, he'd learned to force himself to work on the computer, but now was not the time to sit quietly.

Phoenix leaned closer to Newton to whisper, "Keep working on the ELINT. I've got to go out."

"Now?" she asked.

"This is the most critical time for a case officer to work with his sources. We need all the intel we can get," he replied.

"But if Zarate is the priority, why am I gathering information on this biker gang?"

"I told you," Phoenix replied. "Follow the money. The gang is connected to other things like all of our officers and agents being outed in Venezuela. Do you remember that?"

Newton nodded. "I had a friend stationed down there. The SEBIN tortured and killed him."

"Hence the need to make this a priority, so we can prevent that from happening again," Phoenix stated adamantly.

He rose from his seat before Newton could offer another argument and went to find Delacroix. She was in a bedroom, sitting on the bed and speaking on a laptop-sized phone made specifically by Klas Telecom to operate on the government's SIPRnet.

Delacroix glanced over her shoulder, then motioned Phoenix into the room. He closed the door behind him to allow for more privacy and moved to the window to peer out through the mesh curtain hung to dampen the vibration of the window glass to prevent electronic eavesdropping.

He listened to the Latin America Division Chief as she conversed with, he presumed, Cole Stratten. She didn't do much talking, just listening and acknowledging.

When Delacroix finally hung up the phone, she said to Phoenix, "I hope you don't have any plans."

"I'm meeting an asset soon. Why?" he asked.

"That was Stratten on the phone. He says President Mercia has green-lit an operation to recover our missing pilots since he has no plans to withdraw U.S. forces from around Venezuela. Stratten wants you to lead the team."

Phoenix rolled his eyes and huffed out a grunt as the knot in his shoulder tightened into an agonizing fireball. He clenched his right fist repeatedly to try to relieve the numbness in his hand. His immediate reaction was a resounding, "Fuck *no!*"

Phoenix resisted, however, knowing the lives of the two aviators were at stake. "I understand Mercia's position. But how are we going to mount a rescue op? We don't know where they're being held, and even if we did, we'd be facing the entire Venezuelan military once we arrived on the ground."

"Stratten has a team of analysts working on that," Delacroix replied.

"Until we have a target, there isn't much use in planning an operation," Phoenix said. His plate was already full of two big servings of Operation Unicorn and Taskforce Dragonfly, and now they wanted him to push those aside and make room for a third entrée.

Delacroix ran a hand through her hair and rubbed the top of her head with her open palm before letting her blonde locks fall back into place. "I agree that it's not ideal, but the president wants options. I guess he didn't account for the Flying Jaguars when he decided to rain hellfire down on Venezuela."

Phoenix mulled over the prospect of going into Venezuela a third time in just over a month. He didn't relish the possibility of becoming a guest of the SEBIN, especially if things went to shit like the other two ops, but those two aviators needed someone to go after them.

Knowing he had little choice in the matter, Phoenix finally said, "I'd need a team. Miller might loan me a few guys."

"What about the contractors you used when going after Cobalt Panther?" Delacroix asked.

"They were solid, but I'd like some operators who have trained for this kind of shit," Phoenix replied. "It's going to be tough, and it *will* get loud." Besides, on the Cobalt Panther op, he had vowed never to take contractors into the field again.

"And if you're caught …" Delcroix asked.

"We'll be disavowed," Phoenix said, filling in the blank.

Delacroix shook her head slowly as if contemplating the consequences of the mission. "I don't like it any more than you do, Bowie."

"You're the boss," Phoenix stated. "You tell me to jump, and I'll tell you to go fuck yourself so that we understand where we're both coming from. In the interest of clarity, I think going back to Venezuela is a really stupid idea."

Delacroix ran both hands through her hair before letting

them fall into her lap. She looked up at her case officer and said, "I get it, but the President wants *you* to jump."

After a sigh of resignation, Phoenix said, "Then you better talk to Acevedo and find out where our guys are being held. I'll go talk to Miller."

CHAPTER 31

On his way out of the Four Seasons, Phoenix spotted Coralina Blanco walking across Paseo de la Reforma Avenue. He let out a sharp whistle, and she glanced over her shoulder. Phoenix motioned with his head toward the east, and she turned to walk along the tree-lined median, paralleling him up the street.

Phoenix didn't care about running an SDR as he knew his team and Miller's had tapped into the security cams, and he figured every other intelligence agency with boots on the ground in Mexico City had hotwired them, too. He did want to maintain some separation with Blanco as not everyone needed to know about their case officer / asset relationship.

As he walked, Phoenix thumbed a text to Blanco, telling her to meet him at the Suites Capri just up the street. Next, he called Chris Miller and asked him to join him in the median at a stone bench near the juice vendor Phoenix had visited while waiting for Ximena to contact him about the cloned phones. The cloned phones still bothered him, but he didn't know how they fit into the picture, especially with Schwartz joining Ichabod Crane in Sleepy Hollow.

It took a few minutes of fast talking to get Miller out of his bat cave without the promise of a cold beer. Phoenix finally dislodged the paramilitary leader by saying, "You know those two aviators? I've got the job."

Five minutes after they ended the call, Miller jogged across the eastbound lanes of the broad avenue and joined Phoenix under a shade tree.

"What's going on, Bowie? Why are you coming to me with this bullshit?" Miller demanded.

"We got a P.D. to go after the Flying Jaguars," Phoenix replied.

Miller nodded, knowing a P.D. was a presidential directive that authorized a covert operation, and using the acronyms in public was better than spelling it all out for all the other spies to overhear. But if they worked in the intelligence community, they knew what the two officers were discussing.

"Sorry, Bowie. *You* got the P.D. Not me. I got a call from R.C., and he told me in no certain terms that I wasn't even to have this conversation with you, but I owe it to you to say this: *no one* in the Ground Branch is going after those two kids. The entire country where they're being held is a no-go zone. If you have a P.D., then you're going to have to find some PMCs. Copy?"

"Where am I supposed to find a bunch of PMCs on short notice, especially ones with the kind of experience I'm going to need?" Phoenix complained, keeping his voice low despite wanting to explode at his friend and mentor. The President of the United States had given their organization a direct order to get Pounder and Dorn, and Rheinhart fucking Constantine had ordered his shooters to stand down, forcing Phoenix to rely on private military contractors. *Again.*

"Honestly, Bowie," Miller said, "I'd go down to Guyana and get a bunch of those cowboys the GDF hired. Most of them are ex-Spec Ops guys and champing at the bit for more action." When Phoenix didn't respond, Miller added, "I know you've got contacts down there, work them, brother. That's all I can tell you."

"Did R.C. give you a reason for telling you to stand down?" Phoenix asked.

Miller glanced around, his gaze straying to Blanco. "That your asset?" he asked, nodding toward her.

"One of them," Phoenix said.

Miller grinned. "I can see why you were boning her. She's gorgeous."

Phoenix didn't say anything about his female companion.

"You were always good with the ladies," Miller said. "Someday, you gotta tell me your secret."

"Don't be an asshole," Phoenix replied.

"I'm not being an asshole. I'd seriously like to know," Miller said.

"No. That's the secret," Phoenix stated. "Don't be an asshole."

Miller rolled his eyes. "I know it's not that hat. It's not doing you any favors."

Phoenix rolled his eyes. He liked his new hat.

Miller chuckled at his friend's discomfort, then turned serious. "There's one other thing I wanted to mention."

Phoenix arched his eyebrows. "Yeah?"

"Your friend, Ximena …" Miller trailed off as a group of boisterous male teens shuffled past, kicking around a soccer ball and laughing loudly at the expense of those they seemed to annoy.

When their ball rolled over to Blanco, two of the youths approached her with catcalls and hollers of admiration for her curvy figure. A kid danced around the ball, showing off his fancy footwork until the ball squirted toward Phoenix.

Just as one kid came running over to retrieve it, Phoenix booted the soccer ball hard, sending it sailing across the westbound lanes of traffic and bouncing it off a window of another hotel. Amid a resounding chorus of boos, one kid called Phoenix an asshole as they sprinted after their soccer ball.

"Yep. Don't be an asshole," Phoenix reiterated.

Miller laughed. "But you are, and I don't expect you to break out of your mold anytime soon, so what's the real secret to your success?"

"What were you saying about Ximena?" Phoenix asked, deflecting the question.

"She wasn't being truthful with you," Miller said, eyeing Blanco as she ordered a juice from a nearby vendor. "There were ten heads on that table in the *Los Perros Negros* safe house, but she neglected to tell you that one of them was Ivan Acosta Serrano."

"Who is he?" Phoenix asked.

Miller scanned the street again, keeping an eye on his sector while Phoenix watched the paramilitary officer's six. Dividing the street into sectors was an old habit, ingrained from years of training and working together, and reminded Phoenix of his days of running Ground Branch ops.

The paramilitary officer grinned. "He *was* the president of the MC, but apparently, he screwed up, and heads literally rolled."

"Why do you think Ximena withheld that tidbit of information?" the case officer pressed amid Miller's chuckles.

Still grinning at his joke, Miller said, "I made some calls. Apparently, Ortega set the MC up in business with the Gaitanist Self-Defense Forces of Colombia, and they were running coke and heroin up from South America."

Surprised, Phoenix let out a low whistle. "The AGC? Ortega has some deep roots."

In the U.S., the *Autodefensas Gaitanistas de Colombia* (AGC) was better known as The Gulf Clan. They were considered a neo-paramilitary group and were currently Colombia's largest drug cartel.

"Yeah," Miller agreed. "The AGC is trying to get a seat at the government table. I guess they control a sizable portion of Colombia and run it like their own nation-state. They even have their own national anthem and police force. Anyway, Gardoqui was blocking the AGC from negotiating a peace deal with the Colombian government that would stop the Army from raiding the AGC's operations. The rumor on the street here is that Serrano got paid to take out Gardoqui, and your boy, Ortega, wasn't happy about being excluded from the deal."

"Okay, I get the reason for the hit, but what the hell was Mark Sanchez doing at the safe house?" Phoenix asked.

"That I don't know yet," Miller said, "but rest assured, I'll stay on top of it while you go get those aviators out of trouble. That Pounder kid is a national hero. It's been a long time since America has had an ace pilot, and we don't need him dying on our watch."

Phoenix agreed with the man's sentiments. "Thanks, Husker."

Miller looked his protégé in the eye as they shook hands. "I wish I was going with you."

"Me, too, brother," Phoenix replied.

Miller spun and walked away, heading east along the broad avenue, disappearing amongst the other pedestrians.

"What was all that about?" Blanco asked as Phoenix moved over beside her.

Phoenix took a sip of her juice when she offered it, savoring the cool, refreshing taste of the pulpy drink. After handing the cup back, he said, "Let's go somewhere more private to talk. We've spent enough time out in the open."

———

"I'm going with you," Coralina Blanco said.

"I don't think that's a good idea."

"I think you need me," she argued. "Technically, I'm still a member of the Venezuelan Army, and I have connections down there that we can utilize. Not everyone wants to be Zarate's puppet, and now, with our Navy toothless and our air defenses shattered, it's the prime time to move."

Phoenix had his reservations. After arriving at the Suites Rio Elba, Blanco and Phoenix had made passionate love. Afterward, he explained to her about the P.D. and his plan to use mercenaries from the Guyana Defence Force to supplement his roster.

"I want you to stay with Acevedo," he said firmly.

"No. I am going with you," Blanco said.

He breathed in deeply and let out a long sigh. Slowly, Phoenix leveraged himself upright to lean against the upholstered gray headboard, where his head found a comfortable divot made by one of the tufted buttons. Blanco slid out of bed, pulled on her panties, and then reached for her shirt.

"Where are you going?" he asked.

"Back to the Four Seasons," she said. "I'll prove my worth to you if you haven't figured out how valuable I am yet."

"Coralina …" Phoenix slid out of bed and grabbed her by the shoulder, spinning her to face him. "You don't have to prove anything to me. I love you, and I just want to keep you safe. Going back to Venezuela is dangerous enough for me, but it would be unconscionable for me to take you as part of my team. After everything you've been through, I don't want to jeopardize what we have together or the safety of you and your family."

"I know you care about me, Bowie. I want to do something other than stand around all day in a stupid suit, acting like protecting Acevedo is doing something proactive."

Despite her earlier voiced preference for his first name,

she still called him Bowie out of habit, and Phoenix didn't mind the lyrical way she said it.

"Hey, I thought you were a pageant queen," he replied. "Shouldn't you be used to standing around?"

Blanco beamed. "I was Ms. Venezuela runner-up. So yeah, I can stand around in anything from a ballroom gown to a bikini."

"So do it, please," Phoenix begged. "Be Acevedo's bodyguard until I can get this wrapped up."

"You need me, Bowie, and you know it. I'm a skilled warfighter, trained by some of the best outfits in the world. You know I can handle myself, and I want to do this. It will be like sticking a finger in Zarate's eye."

"What about your family?" he asked. "There's no way we can protect them if this thing goes sideways, and most likely it will."

"I think they'll be fine. Zarate is not long for the office. Acevedo is already maneuvering to get him out. She told me to help you however I can, and going with you to rescue the prisoners is the best thing I can do to help. We both know it."

"Does Acevedo know where they're holding the prisoners?" Phoenix asked, feeling his wall of reluctance crumbling.

"She said she would relay that information to Warbler. By the way, what codename did you give me?"

Phoenix coughed to cover his hesitation, then admitted, "I told Nightingale to name you Cobra."

Blanco crossed her arms and gave him a hateful look of disapproval. "Why?"

Phoenix shrugged. "I figured you'd like it, and, at the time, it seemed like you were about as venomous as one."

"And now?" she asked.

"Well, the way you're all bowed up right now ..."

"Are you trying to piss me off, *John*?" she asked, peering at him through the corners of her eyes with an angry tilt of her head.

"No. I'm trying to get laid again. Look, Cora, I don't want to argue about this anymore. Let's take it to Unicorn and Warbler, and they can make the call."

Seemingly satisfied by her lover's answer, Blanco smiled coyly as she took his member in her hand. "I might not like my codename, but *I am* a snake charmer."

CHAPTER 32

Four Seasons Hotel
Mexico City, Mexico

SANDY DELACROIX SET THE SIPRNET PHONE RECEIVER BACK IN its cradle and said, "They're waiting for you on Ankoko Island."

After John Phoenix had finished explaining his desire to use mercenaries serving with the Guyana Defence Force to rescue the captured aviators, Sandy Delacroix had gotten on the horn with D/CIA Stratten. The two of them had conferred for several minutes about Rhinehart Constantine blocking the use of Ground Branch troops and then talked about using the GDF mercs. Stratten had then called the head of the GDF, Brigadier General Wesley Patrick, who immediately volunteered his forces for whatever mission the director wanted, feeling as President Mercia did—it was best to strike quickly while they had relevant intelligence.

"I'll get packed and catch the next plane to Georgetown," Phoenix said.

Delacroix nodded, pushing back her hair. Phoenix always wondered why she didn't bother with a clip or a ponytail band, but he had learned long ago not to question a woman's fashion choices.

"I'll keep you apprised of the situation," Delacroix said. "Acevedo has been feeding us some fantastic information about Zarate and his regime."

"Do you think she'll be a decent leader?" Phoenix asked. "I'd hate to think we were replacing him with an even bigger asshole."

"Despite the CIA's propensity to exchange a democratically elected leader for a pro-Western despot, I think Acevedo will be one of the best leaders we've helped put into place."

"I don't know how much we've helped her," Phoenix replied. "I think Zarate pretty much shot himself in the foot."

"That's probably true," Delacroix conceded. She stood from her chair, and the two CIA officers stepped out of the shielded RF tent. Changing the subject, she asked, "Are you sure about taking Cobra?"

"No. I'm not," Phoenix replied. "I'd like her to stay with Unicorn, but Unicorn wants her to go with me, so I guess that's what we're doing."

"Just be careful, Bowie. We still don't fully understand what's going on down there."

"Do we ever?" Phoenix replied.

The chief of the Latin America Division shook her head. "And we won't until Zarate is out of office."

"Speaking of that, do we know what Zarate's travel plans are?" Phoenix asked.

"He's leaving this afternoon for Caracas," Delacroix replied. She glanced at her watch. "You have two hours to get packed and to the airport. There's a jet waiting to take you to Guyana."

Phoenix wheeled around and headed for the door, glancing at Jennifer Newton for an update. She shook her head to indicate she hadn't discovered a connection between Mark Schwartz and the *Los Perros Negros* or ELINT between the biker gang and Martin/Ortega.

He wondered if she was even working on his project. Phoenix had told Delacroix that he thought the ELINT might give them a lead on Dragonfly and asked her to push Newton to find something they could use to stop the death merchant.

In his room, Phoenix hurriedly packed his bags and then headed for the exit. On his way to the elevator, Sandy Delacroix joined Phoenix for the ride to the lobby.

"I'll drive you to the airport," she said.

When the elevator opened, the two CIA officers walked briskly into the parking garage and climbed into a black SUV. Phoenix called Blanco to give her directions to the pickup point as Delacroix drove out of the garage.

Delacroix slowed near the coffee shop where Phoenix had gotten breakfast before meeting Ximena, and Blanco darted out of the Four Seasons maintenance garage and hopped into the SUV.

Before Blanco had the door closed, Delacroix pulled away from the curb.

———

SEVENTY MINUTES LATER, Delacroix brought the SUV to a halt beside a private aviation terminal at Mexico City International Airport. She pointed toward a white Bombardier jet on the tarmac with its door open and airstairs deployed. "That's your ride. Good luck to you. We'll do everything we can to support you from our end."

"Will you run the operation from the suite at the Four Seasons?" Phoenix asked.

"We'll have full operational command and real-time satellite data for you once you have boots on the ground," Delacroix replied.

"Do we have a target?" Phoenix asked.

"Tumeremo," Delacroix said.

"I don't know what its status is right now," Blanco said, "but the 512th Jungle Infantry Brigade is stationed at Fort Tarabay. They've seen some combat against rebel miners that they've been trying to drive out of the Orinoco Mining Arc, but on the whole, most of them are kids with little training or experience."

"*Never* underestimate the enemy," Delacroix said.

"So, my people are the enemy, now?" Blanco asked.

"That's not what I meant," Delacroix snapped. "*You* should know that."

"But we are at war," Blanco said. "Am I the enemy?"

"No, Coralina," Delacroix replied, her voice low and apologetic. "Bowie believes in you, and so do I. The plane is waiting. I wish you the best of luck."

Blanco swung her door open and stepped out. Phoenix grabbed their bags, and they headed for the airplane as Delacroix pulled away from her parking spot.

Once aboard the plane, Phoenix asked the pilot for their intended destination.

"Georgetown, sir," the pilot replied. "We'll have a stop in the Dominican Republic to refuel, but we should land at Cheddi Jagan International Airport in approximately seven hours. Have a seat. We'll be taking off shortly."

Blanco and Phoenix slid into the rich, buttery tan leather seats of the Bombardier Challenger 350 while the steward stowed their bags and then went through the aircraft to ensure it was ready for flight. Not long after the steward took his seat, the plane taxied onto the runway and took off.

Phoenix glanced down at the city known as "the Casablanca of the Cold War" with its notorious nests of assassins, spies, and revolutionaries. Throughout the years, Mexico City Station had been considered one of the CIA's plum assignments, and officers had frequently interacted with the

Soviets, helped run the fateful Bay of Pigs operation, supposedly surveilled Lee Harvey Oswald in the days leading up to the Kennedy assassination, and looked the other way as cocaine fueled the cartels.

No, Phoenix wasn't sorry to be leaving Mexico City, but it seemed relatively safe compared to where he and Blanco were headed now.

CHAPTER 33

Anakoko Island, Guyana

"Welcome to Liberated Guyana," Lieutenant Tyler Verdin shouted over the roar of the helicopter as he stuck out his hand.

Behind Blanco and Phoenix, the rotor blades of the AgustaWestland AW149 helicopter chopped the air as it took off, not wanting to stay in the hostile fire zone any longer than it had to. Verdin let go of Phoenix's hand and then quickly turned his back to protect himself from the pelting debris and dust that swirled around them. Seconds later, the pilot of the AW149 added power as it dipped its nose and flew away.

Once the helicopter was gone, the stifling blanket of humid night air descended on the island again. Verdin turned back to Phoenix, who said, "I'm Bowie, and this is Cobra."

Verdin grinned. "Does that make me G.I. Joe or Duke?" With a wink at Blanco, the cocky lieutenant added, "Cause I gotta say, I might have to change my name to Storm Shadow so I can be Cobra's bodyguard."

While Phoenix had caught Verdin's wink and his references to the infamous *G.I. Joe* cartoon characters, he didn't know if Blanco would.

She shocked both men by correcting Verdin. "Actually, Cobra was a terrorist organization led by Cobra Commander."

Verdin chuckled, seemingly unfazed by her response. "Come on, then. I've got my guys waiting for you in the chow hall. Coffee is hot, but the chow is not. We're still trying to get everything set up here."

"How long have you guys been here?" Phoenix asked as he and Blanco followed the young officer through the flickering firelight left by small campfires that burn throughout the compound, providing just enough illumination to see their path and the rubble of what had once been various buildings that comprised the military base.

"Less than a week," Verdin said. "The fucking Fanboys across the river like to lob mortars at us, and one of them went right down the kitchen chimney and blew the shit out of the place. We're back to cooking over campfires like Boy Scouts."

"And here I thought all you SEAL guys caught fish with your bare teeth and ate them raw by the river," Phoenix joked.

Verdin glanced over his shoulder with a grin. "We only do that during Hell Week. The rest of the time, we try to behave like civilized creatures. Although, we did get to try some gator meat. One of our native boat guides caught a black caiman the other day. That fucker was tasty."

The GDF mercenary leader led the way into the chow hall, one of the few buildings still standing. Phoenix hoped the Fanboys had gone to bed for the night with no further plans to shell them until he and his team had left the island.

Stepping into the dimly lit hall, Phoenix glanced around at the mixture of hired mercs and GDF regulars from the 31 Special Forces Squadron assembled in the building. It seemed all the men had the same dirt-smudged faces and glinting eyes that thirsted for more action, or it could have been just the glow of the kerosene lamps hanging from the exposed rafters.

The first man Verdin introduced was Major Yaw, commander of the 31 Special Forces Squadron. After they shook hands, another man stepped forward, hand extended.

"Hey, Bowie!" Axel, the Guyanese boatman, cried out. "Welcome back to Ankoko Island, brother."

"You know this guy?" Verdin asked Axel.

"Yeah, Fight Club, Bowie and I go way back," Axel said.

Phoenix smiled as Verdin winced at his nickname. When there was a button to push, Phoenix was an expert at applying pressure. He tucked that nugget of information away for later.

"You've been here before?" Verdin asked the newly arrived case officer.

Phoenix just shrugged, not feeling the need to elaborate.

Axel slapped hands with Phoenix, then wrapped him in a bro hug. Apparently, he also knew how to press buttons because he said loudly, "Your girl, Bambi—she said to tell you hello and that she misses you."

"Who's Bambi?" Blanco asked suspiciously.

Axel grinned, sizing up the situation. Phoenix knew he'd have to tell her the story, but instead of doing it in the crowded room, he cleared his throat and turned to the assembled men who, to a man, had perked up at the strange interaction that had taken place before them.

"Thanks for volunteering for this operation," Phoenix said. "We'll have to move quickly. Our intelligence says the Venezuelans will transport our aviators from Fort Tarabay to the new airstrip southwest of Tumeremo in two days."

"Where does this intelligence come from?" a GDF soldier asked.

A heavily bearded man shot back, "Read the room, bro. He's C.I.-fucking-A. You don't ask those kinds of questions."

"What's your name?" Phoenix asked the bearded guy.

Beard smiled, lifting the ends of his thick mustache and displaying brown teeth from the wad of chewing tobacco stuffed in his lower lip. "I'm Moore. My partner, here, is Douglas, and the kid asking the crazy questions is Smittie."

"He's right, Smittie," Phoenix said. "They say there are no stupid questions, but some will get you killed."

Smittie, who had been Verdin's right-hand man since his arrival in Guyana, glanced at his mentor. Verdin just shrugged. Phoenix had no intention of divulging their intelligence source, or that Acevedo had been keeping Delacroix appraised of the events unfolding on the ground in Venezuela.

While Blanco and Phoenix had been flying to Georgetown on the Bombardier jet, they had schemed out various rescue scenarios. They knew they couldn't storm the base at Fort Tarabay since it garrisoned at least six hundred troops. The easiest way to rescue the prisoners would be during a transport maneuver. Unicorn had convinced Zarate that it would be best to house the two American Flying Jaguars in The Tomb under SEBIN headquarters in Caracas. From there, Zarate could more frequently trot them out for display.

Nightingale had called Bowie and informed him of the impending transport of Pounder and Dorn to the Tumeremo airport for a flight to Caracas. If the rescue team missed them there, they would just have to scrub the mission and retrograde back to Guyana, hoping the political situation worked itself out.

The CIA believed that once Acevedo had control of the government, she would release the aviators unharmed, but Phoenix wasn't holding his breath. Apparently, neither was

President Mercia or anyone on the Seventh Floor at CIA head-quarters. Otherwise, they wouldn't have sent Phoenix on Operation Tornado.

"So, what's the plan?" Verdin asked.

"A simple snatch," Phoenix replied. "We'll set up an ambush on the road from Troncal 10 to the airport. From there, we'll have two options to get out. We either drive back or steal a plane."

"How do we get in?" a short, redheaded man asked.

Instead of answering the question, Phoenix asked one of his own. "How many troops are across the river in Ancón?"

"We estimate a force of seventy at the ferry crossing with about eighty more men for reinforcements just down the road in San Martin de Turumban," Verdin said. "For those of you who can't do math, that's one hundred fifty men."

"What about trucks?" Phoenix asked.

"They have a couple of Tiuna light utility vehicles with 12.7mm NSV machine guns on top and Ural 6x6 cargo trucks," Verdin said.

"Don't forget the armored personnel carrier and T-72 tank," Johnson added.

"Where's the tank?" Phoenix asked, surprised to hear about it.

"Just across the river at the other ferry landing," Verdin stated. "The Fanboys trucked it down after we retook the island."

"This is what we're going to do," Phoenix said. "We'll divide our forces. Half will go to San Martin and take out the troops there, and the other half will raid the ferry landing."

"We've been ordered not to go into Venezuela," Major Yaw said.

"We need trucks to get the team to Tumeremo," Phoenix replied. "The easiest way to do that is to raid the enemy compounds, commandeer the vehicles, and possibly some uniforms. Dressed like Fanboys, we should be able to freely move up and down Troncal 10 to our rescue point and back."

"It's too risky," Major Yaw said. "Our force will be greatly outnumbered and outgunned."

"Not if we use everyone we have here," Phoenix replied. "I assume there are quite a few more troops on this island than what's in this room."

"You assume correctly," Yaw said, "but again, I have my orders, which are to hold the island and not provoke the Venezuelans."

"You're provoking them by just being here, Major," Blanco said. "As we speak, the Venezuelan Army is massing for an invasion of the Essequibo Region. They plan to airlift troops into various strong points across the area. If they're allowed to invade, it will be the end of Guyana as you know it."

"How does going across the border prevent that?" Yaw asked.

Phoenix didn't know what Blanco was talking about, but he figured he'd go with it. A good bluff could usually win a hand. "Rescuing the prisoners will show the Venezuelans that you aren't pushovers, and it's my understanding that those kids put their lives on the line to defend you when you needed it most, Major. Maybe you should consider doing the same. If you're not comfortable with that, I'm sure Lieutenant Verdin would be happy to lead the charge."

"I need to consult with General Patrick," Yaw answered, meaning the head of the GDF.

"We have his authorization," Phoenix replied.

"I'll check with him just to be sure." Yaw stepped out of the building to make his call.

"How do you prevent the Fanboys from reporting up their chain of command once we attack?" Verdin asked.

"We use the element of surprise to overwhelm them and leave behind radio operators to maintain their checks," Phoenix said.

"This is getting complicated," Verdin replied.

Before they could continue their discussions, Major Yaw returned and handed a satellite phone to Phoenix. The case officer put it to his ear, and he immediately got chewed out by General Patrick, who told him in no uncertain terms that he'd authorized a rescue mission, not the wholesale slaughter of Venezuelan troops. Patrick ended by saying, "Find another way," and terminating the call before Phoenix could argue.

The CIA officer handed the phone back to Major Yaw and said, "I want ten men. Verdin will lead one team of six, and the other four will be with me and Blanco. Major, I need rockets and rifles. We'll leave tomorrow at first light, cross the river, and commandeer vehicles. It will be a quiet strike, not a full-scale invasion."

"My supplies are at your disposal," Yaw said agreeably now that Phoenix had altered the plan.

Phoenix checked his watch.

"You heard him, gents," Verdin said. "Johnson, the Beard Twins, and Nascimento, you're with Bowie on Red Team. Smittie, Hollenbeck, Mankowitz, Franks, Kelso, and Basker, you're with me on Blue Team. Let's get kitted up and ready to rock."

As the men stood to go about their assigned task, the lone woman on Red Team introduced herself to Blanco and Phoenix as Bianka Nascimento, Red Team's dedicated sniper. At six feet tall, or 183cm, Nascimento was fit and athletic. She kept her long black hair in a tight bun, and her blue eyes seemed haunted by decades of pain. Nascimento and Smittie would be the only Guyanese regulars accompanying them on Operation Tornado.

Axel approached as Nascimento steered Blanco away, and the two women went to prepare for war. "I've got an idea," the boatman said to Phoenix.

"What is it?" the CIA officer asked.

"We go by boat up the Cuyuní River to El Dorado. You

can find some civilian vehicles to use there. It would be better than raiding an entire military base."

"How long will it take to go upriver?" Phoenix asked.

Axel shrugged. "It's about seventy-five kilometers along the winding path of the river, perhaps four hours. From El Dorado, it's a short drive to your destination."

"Do you have any intel on El Dorado? What's it like? How easily can we acquire vehicles? Are there Army troops there?"

"The main problem with El Dorado is Marco González Morello," Nascimento said, appearing at their sides like a ghost. "He is known locally as *Rubio*, or Blondie, for his penchant for Clint Eastwood movies. He's the local *pran*, or godfather, as you would call the head of a mafia. Rubio and his men engage in gold smuggling, trafficking, extortion, and kidnapping. He can muster around four hundred men on motorcycles and around one hundred and twenty to man riverboats. They attack in groups of one hundred to one fifty."

"Great," Phoenix muttered. "This country just keeps getting better and better."

While he'd been in a lot of hot spots around the world, Venezuela seemed to take the cake as far as corruption and armed paramilitary groups. At least in the Middle East, they had Islam as a guiding force. In Venezuela, there didn't appear to have any other god than the almighty dollar, and they didn't give a fuck about who they trod on or abused to get it.

"We can get a couple of vans in El Dorado and drive to Tumeremo," Blanco said. "The point is to rescue the aviators, not engage in a war with the local *pran*."

When no one rose to defend the lawlessness of the neighboring country, Phoenix turned back to Axel. "Can we get everyone in one boat, or will we need two?"

"I can get one boat to haul everyone, but I will need to go to Eteringbang to retrieve it," Axel replied.

"Do it," Phoenix said. "Take Cobra with you and introduce her to Bambi."

"That does not sound like a good combination," Axel mused. "The snake and the fawn. You keep interesting company, Jim Bowie."

Blanco glanced quizzically at her handler as Axel headed for the door. Phoenix figured the guy wanted to get laid and drink a cold beer before returning to the island. Phoenix nudged Blanco and nodded, silently signaling her to go with the boatman.

Once Axel and Blanco had left the building, Phoenix and Nascimento headed for the area where Blue and Red Teams were staging their equipment. Each team member had geared up in their camouflage BDUs, chest rigs with plate carriers packed with grenades, combat knives, and plenty of spare mags with 9mm for their Glock pistols and 5.56mm rounds for their M4 rifles. Resting on a plastic tarp on the ground were two SLIM shoulder-fired rockets.

"You need gear, Bowie?" Verdin asked.

"Cobra and I brought our own gear," Phoenix replied.

"Special spook shit?" Johnson asked.

"Shoe phones and dick mics so we can hear your lover whisper sweet nothings to you while he's on his knees," Phoenix replied.

Moore spat tobacco juice on the ground. "He knows you pretty well, huh, Red?"

"Real cute, Bowie," Johnson said.

"That's what your girlfriend said when you dropped your drawers," Nascimento joked.

"You, too, Bianka?" Johnson said. "And I thought we were friends."

"All right. Can it, everyone," Verdin said. "That goes for you, too, spook. This is your team. Don't piss everyone off before the mission."

"It's just a bit of friendly banter, Fight Club," Phoenix replied.

Verdin shook his head in disgust. "You spooks are all the same. A shady bunch of hairy assholes."

"You can stay here while the rest of us go have fun," Phoenix said.

"And let you get all my guys killed? I don't think so," Verdin said.

Phoenix checked his watch again, then glanced around at the rest of the team. "We have about six hours before dawn breaks. Axel will be back with a boat before then. Let's get some sleep before we ride."

As the men disbursed, Phoenix found himself alone with Verdin. "Sorry, man. I saw the look on your face when Axel called you Fight Club, and I couldn't resist."

Verdin smiled. "Don't worry. I get you, Bowie Knife. We're cut from the same cloth. Let me show you where to bed down."

The two men walked through the darkness to a row of tents. The merc pointed to a tent and then disappeared into the night. Phoenix sat by his new abode, listening to the lull of the insects and the cries of the night creatures. Low fires crackled along the paths running through the old base buildings, casting flickering shadows across the encroaching trees and rubble.

The last time he'd been on Ankoko Island, the Venezuelans had controlled the camp and had invited Russian advisors to help construct a new concrete runway to accommodate fighter jets. Between the raid and the continuing mortar attacks, the place had been nearly destroyed. Those were the casualties of war. Buildings and men turned to dust—ashes to ashes and all that shit.

Phoenix found a comfortable position to reduce the stress on his shoulder and breathed deeply, trying to meditate away the pain. He strained his ears for any sound that signaled the return of Axel and Blanco, suddenly wishing he hadn't dispatched her to help find a larger boat to handle the twelve-man rescue team.

He tried to envision the scope of the mission from the trip upriver to finding vehicles in El Dorado to ambushing the Fanboy transport team. Once the prisoners were secure, the team would either race down Troncal 10 and recross the Cuyuní River or steal a plane to fly straight to Georgetown.

In his mind, he studied how the Venezuelans would form the transportation convoy. Typically, the prisoners or executive principals would be in the middle vehicle. A good ambush team would take out the lead and tail vehicles and then assault the remaining convoy. Phoenix had directed numerous ambushes in much the same way, and he'd go over the guidelines with the rest of his team before they found their hiding spots.

Phoenix's phone buzzed in his pocket, interrupting his train of thought. He pulled it out and answered, knowing it was Connelly on the other end. She made him say his identity verification before proceeding.

"How's the plan?" she asked.

"They took the bait," Phoenix replied. "I pitched the invasion gambit, and they immediately balked. Major Yaw even called General Patrick like you figured he would. We're headed for El Dorado in the morning."

"That's good news," Nightingale replied. "Everything is set on my end. Unicorn said the prisoner transport is a go, and we reached out to Rubio. He's agreed to meet you and provide you with vehicles and extra manpower if needed. Do you still have the payment for him?"

"Yeah, I do," Phoenix replied, not happy about having to negotiate with another heavy-handed thug to accomplish the goals of the U.S. government. It seemed that intelligence work made for strange bedfellows, all the way back to the original OSS and Operation Paperclip when America had integrated former Nazi scientists and engineers into the highest echelon of its civilian and government programs. While the technology that stemmed from those partnerships had led to the products of modern society, Phoenix sometimes felt those Germans had instilled a yearning for socialism within American politics.

But he wasn't fighting Nazis, and he couldn't stop the slow erosion of American liberties. What he could do was put a stop to Dragonfly's treason and the murder of U.S. intelligence officers and assets. During their flight to the DR, Delacroix had flashed a photo of Terry Martin to Unicorn. Acevedo immediately confirmed that she had met Martin in General Calderón's office but had never learned his name. Calderón had claimed that Martin had assets within the U.S. and Venezuelan governments.

One of the things Phoenix had always admired about Connelly was her ability to play the long game. She had taken the information gleaned from conversations with Unicorn and Cobra and then pieced together an action plan that would not only put Acevedo into the Venezuelan power seat but also ingratiate Bowie with Dragonfly. Putting him undercover would hopefully expose the agency mole and allow Phoenix to take down Dragonfly and his organization.

Phoenix hadn't liked the plan at first, and there were a lot of factors about it that still bothered him, but he had agreed to it.

And he hated himself for it.

"Are you still good with the plan, Bowie?" Nightingale asked.

The pain radiating from the knot in his shoulder caused him to grind his teeth as he replied glumly, "Yeah. I'll make it work."

There was a pause on the line, and Phoenix could hear Connelly take a deep breath as if steeling herself. The words she said next would echo in his ears and carry him forward.

"Good luck, Bowie. I love you. We'll get you back safely, I promise."

The connection went dead as Phoenix kept the phone pressed to his ear. He strained to hear more from Nightingale, but she was already gone. From downriver came the sound of boat motors. Phoenix stood, slipping the phone into his pocket, but his legs were shaky, and confusion filled his head.

Why? he pleaded silently. *Why now, Nightingale? How could you say that to me on the eve of this operation?*

His only reply was that of insects humming in the trees, and the low murmur of soldiers gathered around the campfires. The boat motors grew louder, signaling the return of Axel and Blanco. The muscle knot tightened with the knowledge that Blanco was just a placeholder for Connelly, no matter how much Phoenix tried to convince himself otherwise.

Phoenix stood in the darkness, trying to gather his strength for what was to come, for he knew danger lurked at every turn.

CHAPTER 34

"HOLD FAST!" AXEL SHOUTED OVER THE ROAR OF THE TWIN Mercury engines on the back of the twenty-five-foot boat.

They were in the middle of the frothing, brown Cuyuní River, pitching up and down through a series of rapids. Axel stood at the wheel in the stern, just in front of a bulkhead that had two blue plastic fifty-five-gallon drums strapped to it as fuel tanks. The team crouched over upturned five-gallon plastic buckets that they used as seats with their combat gear and equipment wrapped in tarps to keep it all dry at the bottom of the boat.

A wave of white water broke over the bow, soaking everyone to the bone.

"What the fuck, Axel!" Johnson screamed from the bow. "Who taught you how to drive a boat?"

Axel just grinned, maintaining the breakneck pace he'd started the day with after leaving Ankoko Island. The Guyanese boatman seemed to know every bend, sandbar, and rock in the crooked river, and Phoenix wondered how frequently Axel had made the trip to El Dorado. After all, the guy had to earn a living doing something other than being the CIA's huckleberry in the Guyanese hinterland. Phoenix knew he sold fuel to the miners along the river and smuggled out the illegally mined gold they processed with mercury and cyanidation. Not only were they killing the environment, but the miners were also poisoning themselves just to eke out a meager living.

It took another two hours of intense backbreaking jolts on the river to reach the Eiffel Bridge on the eastern edge of El Dorado. The old metal suspension bridge was a work of art. Like many projects throughout South America, the citizens falsely attributed its design to the famed French architect Gustave Eiffel. After the government had constructed a modern concrete bridge to accommodate the heavier truck traffic along Troncal 10, they abandoned the Eiffel Bridge. Mother Nature had covered it in leafy green vines and corroding red rust. Still, it was a marvel in the middle of the jungle that tourists flocked to, and it was also a symbol of everything wrong with Venezuela or any other civilized culture that neglected its critical infrastructure.

Just past the old bridge was another series of rapids, with the water tumbling and swirling around massive boulders that jutted ominously from the river. Axel navigated the raging white water with skill and ease before pulling the boat up onto a beach behind a row of rundown block buildings. Many had laundry flapping from wires strung between trees or half-naked children playing in the dirt yards.

"Verdin and Johnson, stay with the boat. Keep your guns out of sight but ready to deploy," Phoenix ordered, reaching for a waterproof briefcase to take with him. "Cobra, Axel, Nascimento, you're with me."

The four of them climbed from the boat. Franks, another former SEAL, manned the helm and kept the outboards idling, ready to depart if the shit hit the fan.

Everyone in the landing party had pistols tucked into the small of their backs except Axel, who preferred to let his gregarious nature defuse any potentially hostile situations.

As the team approached an abandoned building behind a concrete block wall that surrounded three sides of the property, a short, fleshy man with a front left tooth covered in gold stepped out of the shadows. He carried an AK-47 with inlaid gold accents and had an ammunition bandolier draped around his shoulder and across his belly.

Phoenix, who had been on high alert already, felt the hairs on the back of his neck stand up. He didn't know if the guy was trying to evoke a modern-day Pancho Villa, but, in his opinion, it wasn't working. This encounter wasn't the first in which Phoenix had dealt with such men, but he was always aware of how out of place he was in their presence. The key to such situations was to project confidence and to have a well-thought-out game plan or even a rehearsed speech.

Gold Tooth nodded to Axel as if the two men knew each other, and Phoenix knew it had been the right move to bring the boatman along.

Stepping forward, Phoenix said in Spanish, "We're here to see Rubio."

Gold Tooth glanced around at Phoenix's team and frowned at the show of force, but he calmly said, "He sends his greetings and asks that you provide your *present* before further negotiations take place."

Phoenix set the case he carried on a tree stump and opened it for Gold Tooth to look inside. The emissary smiled appreciatively at the sight of the stacks of American dollars.

"There will be no negotiations," Phoenix stated authoritatively. "This is the agreed-upon price. Where are my vehicles?"

"The price has gone up," Gold Tooth said. "We know what you are after."

"Two vehicles and passage to and from Tumeremo, that's what was agreed upon. That's what you will provide," Phoenix said.

"The deal has changed."

"Fuck you," Phoenix snarled. "We agreed to a deal, and if Rubio is an honorable man, he will abide by it."

"Still …" Gold Tooth hesitated.

Phoenix closed the lid on the case, snapped the latches shut, and turned to his companions. "Let's go."

"Why are you leaving?" Gold Tooth asked. "Don't you want the prisoners?"

"Not with your help, asshole," Blanco replied, understanding as Bowie did that they couldn't capitulate in the face of this gangster.

Gold Tooth opened the bolt on his AK and let it snap closed in a menacing gesture.

Without hesitation, Phoenix pulled out his Glock and shot the negotiator in the forehead.

Before the echo of the single gunshot had died away, more armed men emerged from the abandoned building. The instant Phoenix had pulled his gun, his teammates had done the same, and now everyone in the abandoned lot had their guns drawn and aimed at one another in a Mexican standoff.

"Who's in charge?" Phoenix shouted.

Out of the corner of his eye, Phoenix saw the rest of his Blue and Red Teams glide into position in shooter crouches, M4s up and ready.

"Who the fuck is in charge!" Phoenix shouted.

"You are all dead men!" one of Rubio's gang members shouted back.

"I had a deal with Rubio," Phoenix said. "This asshole tried to change the terms. Get Rubio out here, *now!*"

"What the hell are you doing, Bowie?" Verdin asked quietly. "I don't know what you guys are talking about, but we are *way* outgunned here."

Phoenix ignored the mercenary and shouted, "Does anyone speak Spanish here, or are you a bunch of dumb mutes who can't think for yourselves?"

"*Bowie*," Blanco cautioned.

"She is right, you know," a man said in English as he stepped through the line of gunmen. He wore black slacks, a pink dress shirt, and alligator-skin cowboy boots. He had long, flowing brown hair and a tightly trimmed beard and mustache. Phoenix's gaze was drawn momentarily to the black semi-automatic pistol in a cross-draw rig on the man's left hip. The dude looked more like Fabio from the romance novel covers than he did Clint Eastwood.

"Are you Rubio?" Phoenix asked, not lowering his weapon but shifting the sights to center on the man's chest.

The spokesman chuckled. "What if I told you that you just shot Rubio in the head?"

"I'd call you a liar," Phoenix said. "No one would take orders from the fat pig."

"All of these men did." The man spread his hands to encompass the totality of the armed men around him. "I think they would like to kill you out of revenge."

"They can try," Phoenix replied tersely, "but we'll take a whole lot of them with us."

The spokesman advanced to the center of the clearing and extended his arms out before fluttering his hands up and down. "Please, everyone, lower your weapons."

No one moved.

"Enrique," the long-haired man said calmly to a man who had advanced with him. "I said lower your gun."

"He killed Tuco," Enrique said. "I can't let that stand, Rubio."

"I said lower your weapon, Enrique. Your brother negotiated in bad faith. I would have killed him, too."

"I cannot put my gun down," Enrique fired back. "I must avenge my brother's death."

"Everyone lower your weapons!" Rubio shouted.

Phoenix lowered his gun, and his team followed suit. Everyone on Rubio's side did as Rubio had ordered, except for Enrique.

"Enrique, I am warning you …" Rubio muttered in Spanish. "Lower your weapon. *Now!*"

Enrique glanced at Rubio but kept his gun on Phoenix.

Rubio swiftly pulled his pistol from the holster and shot Enrique in the side of the head, dropping him beside his brother. The *pran* holstered his gleaming chrome Colt 1911 replica and, leaving his hand on the butt, tapped his finger against the leather of the holster like some Old West gunfighter. He sighed. "I hate to kill my own men, but when they do not listen, it is best to put them down before they start a revolt."

"Solid plan," Phoenix said.

"You and I understand each other," Rubio said. "I have made a deal with your superiors, and I will honor that deal, but if you *ever* come to El Dorado again, I will personally skin you alive."

Phoenix tossed the plastic money case at Rubio's feet. The *pran* snapped his fingers. A man darted forward to scoop up the case and then ran back to his own skirmish line.

"The vehicles you requested are waiting in the driveway," Rubio said. He turned to Axel. "You and I are through, my old friend. I trusted you, and you brought this locust to my doorstep."

"He had nothing to do with this," Phoenix said.

Rubio jabbed his finger menacingly at Phoenix. "*You* are the locust, feasting upon my country." He turned to face Axel. "And you are no longer welcome here. Once your business with the aviators is complete, you must not come back here. The warning I gave to your friend applies to you."

Turning on his heel, Rubio circled his hand in the air with his index finger extended to signal his troops to mount up. They kept Phoenix and his team of mercenaries under their gunsights as they retreated behind the wall. The roar of engines filled the air as the gang started their motorcycles and escorted Rubio's SUV from the scene.

"Axel, after we get our gear, take the boat downriver. I'll call you when we're on the way back," Phoenix said. "If you don't hear from me, we aren't coming via the river."

Tight-lipped, Axel stared at the case officer for a long moment. "I will do as you ask, but you have cost me everything."

Phoenix turned to head for the boat to retrieve his gear without replying to the boatman. At the water's edge, he pulled on his assault gear and checked his weapons. "Let's go. Someone grab those SLIMs."

After seeing Phoenix's ruthless display of aggression and sensing his hostile attitude, the team moved quickly and quietly to gather their equipment and head for the awaiting vehicles.

Phoenix was the last to leave, pushing Axel's boat off the beach. "I'm sorry for screwing up your operation. That wasn't my intention."

Axel nodded but didn't appear to take the man's apology sincerely. He started the outboards and left Phoenix in their burbling wake.

"What the hell is wrong with you?" Blanco asked as she and Phoenix walked through the yard past the two dead men.

"I did what had to be done," he replied.

"But it didn't have to go down like that," she insisted.

Phoenix stopped abruptly, dust swirling around his boots. "You know better than anyone that I had to show strength, or else we wouldn't have walked out of there alive. The mission is to rescue the aviators, not pussyfoot around with warlords."

"But you've declared war on all of us," she said.

"We have safe passage," Phoenix said. "That's all that matters."

"What is going on, John?" she demanded. "This isn't like you."

"You don't even know me, Coralina," he said, walking off.

It was best to put some distance between the two of them. Phoenix had his orders, and they didn't include her. He tried to fix in his mind that she was an asset and nothing more, but his heart ached.

By the time Phoenix walked around the block wall, the other ten team members had divided themselves evenly between two flat-nosed Daewoo Damas minivans. Phoenix and Blanco climbed onto the bus hauling Red Team, and they set out silently for Tumeremo.

CHAPTER 35

Tumeremo Airport
Tumeremo, Venezuela

"Convoy is inbound," Nightingale whispered through Phoenix's earpiece. "Four vehicles total—a Tiuna at the front and rear equipped with machine guns, and two SUVs in the middle. The second contains the principles."

Phoenix acknowledged with a short, "Copy that," knowing she was watching a satellite feed in the Operation Unicorn suite at the Four Seasons Hotel in Mexico City. Using a local frequency, Phoenix relayed the information to Blue and Red Teams through their comms unit.

The drive to Tumeremo Airport should have taken the two vans just over an hour, but it took almost twice that. Not only had the Blue Team had to stop and change a flat tire, but Troncal 10 had been long neglected. Heavily used by semi-trucks that carried mining equipment, unprocessed ore to the smelters, and cargo containers from Brazil packed with food and supplies, the asphalt had all but broken down, leaving large potholes and long sections of wash-board dirt.

Once they had reached the airport, Phoenix and Verdin had studied the layout, determining an L-shaped ambush would be their best option. Two dirt roads led into the airport, one through a residential area, and the other stemmed directly from the main highway. The roads converged less than one hundred meters from the tiny terminal building. While it was less than ideal for an ambush spot, the rescue team had to make do. Otherwise, the Venezuelans had a chance of escaping the coming carnage by driving through the tall grass on the northern side of the road as a chain link fence surrounded the runway to the south.

Phoenix wished they could have used the fence to their advantage. Along with the runway, the fence also enclosed the tiny parking lot in front of the terminal building, but there wasn't enough room within the terminal building enclosure to stage the ambush and ensure the American aviators remained unharmed. Based on the geographic location, the team had been forced to take a weak position, and Phoenix acutely felt the lack of intelligence and planning.

After spending a restless night in a large copse of trees just off the main airport artery, the Red and Blue Teams had moved their vans into position near the road junction, and everyone had dismounted. Both teams carried a SLIM to take out the lead and tail Tiuna utility vehicles.

Phoenix chaffed at the delays as he lay in the grass. He kept clenching his fist in frustration and in a vain attempt to make the stabbing pain in his shoulder go away.

"Convoy has passed the first turn-off," Connelly reported.

Phoenix cherished the sound of her voice in his ear. He relayed the information to his teams. With the convoy coming straight from the highway, it shifted Verdin's Red Team to the assault element with Blue Team in support.

Verdin dispatched Kelso to the terminal to hide behind a

car with his SLIM so he could hit the lead Tiuna head-on with his shoulder-fired rocket just as it went through the front gate. Phoenix radioed Johnson to strike the rear Tiuna.

A column of dust rose in the air as the prisoner transport convoy roared toward them. Phoenix's body thrummed with anticipation, and the endorphin high seemed to push away all the pain in his shoulder. He clicked off the safety on his suppressed M4.

The lead Tiuna bounced and swayed as it traversed the dirt road, and the gunner had to keep a firm grasp on his 12.7mm machine gun to keep from being tossed violently about. As the convoy approached, Phoenix heard the distinct sound of helicopter rotors.

"Inbound Mi-35," Connelly said into Phoenix's ear.

"Where the fuck did that come from?" Verdin asked as the helicopter buzzed low over the runway.

"Is that what they're flying the prisoners out on?" Phoenix asked Connelly.

"Negative. There's a Cessna 208 lining up on the glide path now," Connelly reported. "The Hind appears to be combat support."

Phoenix clicked his comms. "Kelso, you stick with the lead Tiuna. Johnson, you knock that fucking helicopter down. Verdin, use a couple of your M203 grenades to take out the rear Tiuna." He heard his teammates acknowledge the change in game plan and settled back to fret. The pain in his shoulder was back with a new intensity that nearly made it impossible to hold his gun steady.

"Uh … Bowie, what's going on there?" Connelly asked.

Phoenix eyed the convoy. It seemed to have slowed to a crawl. His gaze shifted from the lead Tiuna to the Hind helicopter coming in fast and low from the east. His gut tightened. Something was terribly wrong.

He glanced at the Red Team's van parked beside the runway fence. The team lay in the grass, spread out at ten-foot intervals to provide a maximum field of fire. Bile rose in his throat.

"Why has the convoy stopped?" Connelly asked.

Phoenix saw a twinkling of light under the nose of the massive Russian attack helicopter. Red Team's van disintegrated as the Hind spit 12.7mm rounds from its Yakushev-Borzov nose cannon. The Daewoo Damas van exploded in a roaring fireball, flashing a searing heatwave across Phoenix's face. He blinked back tears and tried to focus on what was happening.

"Verdin! Verdin!" Johnson screamed.

"Talk to me, Bowie!" Connelly shouted in Phoenix's other ear. "Bowie!"

Johnson stood and fired his SLIM at the Hind as it crabbed past, flying sideways to their position, nose gun swiveling for targets. The Mi-35 banked, and the SLIM munition, not designed as a heat-seeking projectile, flew harmlessly underneath it. At the same instant, the gunner on the lead Tiuna fired his machine gun, and the 12.7mm bullets sliced Johnson in half, separating his torso from his legs.

Members of Verdin's team jumped up and ran away from the burning van. Phoenix tried to count the moving figures to see how many had escaped the helicopter attack, but the black smoke from the burning van obscured his vision.

"Bowie!" Connelly shouted again.

"Shut up, Leslie," Phoenix snapped. He'd lost count of how many Red Team members he'd seen make it to their feet.

Phoenix tried to plot a way out of this clusterfuck. If it was just him, he'd cut and run, but there were too many unknowns and too many team members for him to abandon during this crisis. He targeted the Tiuna gunner in the holographic sight of his M4, but just as he let loose a burst of fire, Kelso triggered his SLIM. The rocket exploded in the grill of the Tiuna, lifting the heavy vehicle off its front wheels and blasting apart the engine bay.

"Cease fire!" someone shouted through a bullhorn.

Phoenix glanced around for the speaker, twisting to look over his shoulder at Kelso's position in the parking lot.

The helicopter moved farther away, remaining at a hover, the distinct smack of its rotors keeping everyone on high alert.

"What's happening, Bowie?" Connelly demanded.

"Cease fire!" the bullhorn speaker squawked again.

The Tiuna that had been at the tail of the convoy drove down the grassy verge of the road and positioned itself sideways across the road in front of its burning twin.

Connelly screeched in Phoenix's ear again, and still, he ignored her as the wind moaned through the trees along the chain link fence behind the ambush team. The sound sent a chill through Phoenix, reminding him of winter storms in Texas.

He clicked his comms. "Verdin? You there?"

"Yeah. I'm here," came the terse reply. "I might be bleeding out, though. I caught some shrapnel in my leg when the van exploded."

"Hang tight, buddy. I won't let you die in this shithole," Phoenix promised.

With a laugh, Verdin said, "You're a fucking liar, but I like your spirit, Bowie."

"Bowie. It's a setup!" Connelly shouted in his other ear.

"No shit," Phoenix mumbled.

"No," Connelly said. "SEBIN troops loyal to Zarate just arrested Unicorn."

"Listen to me, Les," Phoenix said. "You hear me?"

"Yes!" Nightingale replied.

"Listen to me. We're done here," Phoenix said. "I've got wounded troops, and we're pinned down. I know this wasn't the plan but stay the course. I trust you, Leslie. Come get me." Phoenix pulled the CIA's encrypted satellite comms unit from his ear and fished the wire out of his vest. He placed the sending and receiving unit and earpiece on the ground in front of him, and then he hammered everything into tiny pieces with the butt of his pistol.

"What are you doing?" Blanco whispered.

Phoenix turned to face her. "I'm sorry, Coralina, but it's time to give up."

CHAPTER 36

Four Seasons Hotel
Mexico City, Mexico

Leslie Connelly couldn't believe her eyes. John Phoenix had just surrendered to the Venezuelans.

Nightingale leaned back in her chair and threw her headphones onto the desk in front of her. She rubbed tears from her cheeks with the palms of her hands as she stared at the real-time satellite feed of Tumeremo Airport playing on the screen in front of her.

"They'll be all right," Jennifer Newton said.

Sandy Delacroix, who stood behind Connelly, rested a reassuring hand on her colleague's shoulder.

They watched as Phoenix and his team stood on the road in front of the Tiuna. Connelly counted eight living members of the former rescue team. Three had died in the initial helicopter attack on the van, and the other had been gruesomely cut in half by gunfire.

Connelly's heart ached in her chest, and she didn't feel she could breathe enough air.

Phoenix and a woman that Connelly assumed was Cobra remained standing with their hands in the air as the rest of the team sank to their knees. The two SUVs in the convoy pulled out of line and drove along the verge, following the Tiuna's tracks. One came to a halt beside the group of prisoners, and the other continued toward the terminal.

"Zoom out," Connelly said. "Keep both vehicles in the frame."

Newton pressed a button on the keyboard, and the picture expanded. Connelly kept the moving SUV in her periphery and concentrated on the SUV near Phoenix. A rear door opened.

Phoenix shook his head.

The gunner in the Tiuna's turret swiveled his machine gun barrel and shot one of the rescue team members in the head, spraying a cloud of mist as the giant bullets pulverized it to mush.

More tears spilled down Connelly's cheeks. She had sent these people to die. All of their plans had turned to blood and excrement, and the man she loved was now a captive of the Venezuelan army.

Phoenix and Blanco climbed into the SUV, and it sped away toward the terminal where the other SUV had stopped.

Connelly winced as flame belched from the end of the Tiuna's machine gun and ripped apart the helpless, kneeling prisoners. She bent forward and puked into a waste can.

Newton held back Connelly's hair as she heaved and heaved, feeling as if her stomach would come out through her throat. It was a stunning defeat after the sweeping victory of American shock and awe against the relatively static Venezuelan navy ships and missile batteries.

Once she'd stopped puking, Connelly set down the waste can

and refocused on the monitor. Newton zoomed the satellite feed in on the four shackled figures marching across the tarmac in front of several men with guns. Phoenix looked up at the sky, and Connelly's heart skipped a beat as she saw his battle-weary face.

Then, they were all inside the Cessna 208 Caravan.

"Can we track that plane?" Delacroix asked.

"Yeah," Newton said. "It's squawking a Venezuelan military code, and we're already in their system … There."

As the Cessna lifted into the sky, one of Newton's screens displayed a map of Venezuela with the plane icon tracking across it.

"Shut off the satellite feed," Delacroix ordered.

Newton hit a button, and the screen showing the feed turned black.

Connelly stood and ran from the suite, banging violently through the entry door and slamming into the far hallway wall. She could barely see through the curtain of tears streaming down her face. Phoenix was a prisoner. The team was dead. They were all *gone*. She knew it was part of the job —a hazard they endured to keep their country safe—but she never believed it would end like this. Everyone dying was *not* the plan.

Fishing her room key card from her pocket, Connelly slapped it against the electronic lock and tried to shove through the door, but the lock didn't budge. She had to swipe the card twice more before the tiny light changed from red to green. Connelly burst through the door and threw herself onto the bed.

Curling into a ball under the covers, Leslie Connelly cried herself to sleep.

CHAPTER 37

Sandy Delacroix didn't have the luxury of running away.

She entered the shielded RF tent and answered the ringing phone with, "This is Delacroix."

"Can you tell me what just happened?" D/CIA Stratten asked calmly.

"Unicorn has been compromised, sir," Delacroix said. "Zarate arrested her just as Bowie was about to spring the rescue ambush. The Venezuelans got the drop on us, sir."

"How did our op get blown?" President Randy Mercia asked.

"I don't know," Delacroix admitted. "I can tell you it wasn't from any of us on Operation Unicorn."

"How do you know Mark Schwartz wasn't the leak?" Stratten asked. "I read your reports, and between his death and the cloned phones, we don't know who learned about Unicorn."

"True, sir," Delacroix admitted. "We need to do a full review, but we can't entrench right now. We have an officer in the field who needs our help."

"I agree," Stratten replied. "Do you have a plan?"

"This is just breaking, sir," Delacroix said. "We're tracking the plane, but I'll go out on a limb and say it's headed for Caracas."

"I don't think there's anything you can do straight away," Stratten said. "Close up shop and get your team back to Headquarters."

"Yes, sir," Delacroix replied. "I'm sorry, Mister President. I hoped to have better news."

"I agree. The footage was hard to watch," Mercia replied. "I like Bowie. We'll get him back, and the same goes for the aviators. I want a full briefing as soon as you return."

"I'll see you soon, sir," Delacroix replied and ended the call.

Stepping from the tent, she called the crew together. "We're packing up and going back to Washington." Delacroix wished Connelly hadn't bolted, but she understood the reason for her disappearance and decided to give her protégé some breathing room.

As everyone started to pack up, Delacroix pulled out her key card and slipped it to Newton. "Take your laptop to my room. Monitor the Venezuelans' communications for any mention of Bowie or the Flying Jaguars. While you're running that in the background, keep working on that ELINT between Martin and *Los Perros Negros*. We need something to turn this pile of shit into a rose."

Newton hurriedly packed her bag and slipped out the door as Delacroix shouted orders and kept everyone's attention on her. She wasn't immune to the carnage she had watched take place in Venezuela as the army soldiers had mowed down her paramilitary force. Even though she didn't know the men or women operating with Blanco and Phoenix, she knew her officer and asset personally.

Delacroix had always taken personal responsibility for her officers and their actions in the field, which was what made her such an excellent station chief and now chief of the Latin American Division. Delacroix wanted to mourn the loss of the team with Connelly, but it was a luxury that would have to wait until she had everything packed and ready to go home.

And even then, Delacroix knew she wouldn't find any rest with her officer in the wind.

———

It took several long hours to break down the SIPRnet consoles, collapse the shielded tent, remove the special window shades, and pack all the computers and gear.

By the time Delacroix closed the door on the empty suite, she could barely keep her eyes open. Yet, with the images of the paramilitary team's death still fresh in her mind, Delacroix decided she needed a drink. The bar was the best place to go as Connelly and Newton were in her room, and she wanted to be around happy people who weren't mourning the loss of a lover.

Sandy Delacroix wanted the company of a man, but her husband was back in Virginia, probably out screwing one of his young interns while their daughters were fast asleep under the watchful eye of their nanny. She ran a hand through her hair and gripped it tightly, pulling the skin of her scalp painfully back just to let herself know she was still alive and not completely numb.

Sliding onto a bar stool beside Chris Miller, she ordered two fingers of Dewars' twenty-one-year-old whiskey.

"That bad, huh?" Miller asked.

"Fucking devastating," she replied.

"What happened?" he asked.

"We lost ten contractors. Your protégé and his asset got picked up by forces sympathetic to Zarate."

Miller let his head drop between his arms as he leaned unsteadily against the bar and let out a deep sigh. After a moment, he straightened himself up and asked, "What can I do to help?"

Delacroix sipped her drink, then said, "Nothing. My team has been recalled to Washington. We leave in the morning."

"I looked through the security footage around my suite," Miller said. "I caught Schwartz bringing in a bag that I assume he had the cloned phones in. When he left, he didn't have the bag."

"I still don't know why he did it, but there was a leak somewhere," Delacroix said. "Someone knew what we had planned."

Miller put his hand on her wrist. "Let me help, Sandy. You know I'm here for you. Whatever you need."

Delacroix didn't move her hand from under his touch but sipped her drink. "I need someone to sit with me for a while."

Miller took his hand off hers only to signal the bartender for another round. After the guy took their order, Miller asked, "Did Bowie ever tell you about when he escorted your husband around Afghanistan?"

"I didn't know he'd ever met Phillip," Delacroix said. She was used to Washington insiders bandying about names as if dropping them would move them to the head of the line, so it was surprising that Phoenix had never said anything to her about knowing her husband.

Miller chuckled to himself. "I guess he's got more class than I do."

"What's so funny?" Delacroix asked.

"You've *never* heard this story?"

"No." She sipped her drink. "Let me guess, Phillip did something stupid?"

"It's kinda legend in the SF community. I'm surprised you've never heard it. Anyway, Bowie and his team were sent to escort Phillip on a handshaking mission with some of the old Northern Alliance commanders up in the Panjshir Valley. Their interpreter, who'd been with Bowie's team for almost a year and had worked with U.S. forces for decades, suddenly stopped their convoy at a road junction and suggested they take a different route. Bowie trusted his advisor, and they deviated from the planned route. Phillip wasn't happy with the delay. He berated our boy for wasting his time, and instead of having faith in what their terp said, he claimed the new route had made them extremely late for the meeting. And, of course, when the terp advised of a second course change, Bowie graciously allowed Phillip to make the call.

"Your husband chose the planned route like the true dip that he is, and they got hit with multiple IEDs. During the ensuing firefight, Bowie pulled Phillip out of their vehicle to keep him safe and basically knelt on him to keep him from running off into the bush.

"After the SF team mopped up following a wave of air strikes, Bowie pulled Phillip to his feet and found your husband had literally shit himself. I mean, it was *everywhere.* The entire backside of his pants was covered in shit from his belt to his cuffs."

Delacroix burst out laughing.

Laughing himself, Miller continued, "The SF team had to pull security at a river crossing so Phillip could clean his ass off in the creek. Bowie said Phillip wanted to save his trousers because they were some expensive brand, but Bowie wouldn't let him put them in the truck because they smelled so bad. Phillip walked into the meeting with his dress shirt tucked into a spare pair of camo BDU pants. He was still wearing his suit jacket and tie."

Miller took a sip of his drink to compose himself. "Of course, when they get to the meeting, the chiefs are kinda pissed that Phillip is late, and they start muttering to themselves about the outfit he's wearing. The terp tells them the entire story, and by the end, everyone in the compound is rolling on the ground laughing."

Tears filled Delacroix's eyes as she laughed. It took another moment before she could compose herself, having to dry her eyes with a bar napkin. "Thank you, Chris. I needed to hear that story after my rough day. And truthfully, that sounds exactly like something Phillip would have done. He always wants to be in control no matter what the consequences." At the beginning of their courtship, Phillip's brashness had been one of the things Sandy had found endearing about him, but now it was just tiresome, and it had cost him rank and privilege with the State Department.

"I'm amazed you've never heard that story before," Miller said, still chuckling.

"Bowie never said a word, probably for the best," she said.

Miller smiled wryly as he shook his head. "That kid's a real asshole, but sometimes he can be a class act." Miller reached over and squeezed Delacroix's hand. "We'll get Bowie back, Sandy. I promise."

Standing abruptly, Delacroix shot back the rest of her liquor. "You got a private room we can review that video footage in?'

Miller smiled gleefully and tossed money onto the bar for their drinks. "I've got a room upstairs."

It wasn't the first time they'd hooked up. Delacroix had liked the self-assured paramilitary officer from the moment they'd first met many years ago. If Phillip was going to screw around, then Delacroix felt she had a right to a piece of side action herself. She and Phillip were only together for the kids. Delacroix already had the divorce papers drawn up for the day her youngest daughter graduated from high school.

She hadn't planned to jump into bed with Miller on this trip, but Sandy Delacroix needed to feel comforted by her lover's arms on this day of such personal tragedy.

———

DELACROIX GLANCED at her watch the next morning after zipping up her boots. It was still early enough for her to have time to shower and change before catching the plane back to Washington, D.C.

Miller exited the bathroom with a towel wrapped around his waist as she reached for the doorknob. "Hey, lover," he said. "I'll see you when I see you."

"Thanks for last night, Chris. I needed that." She rose on her toes to kiss him, tempted to rip off his towel and make herself even later than she already was.

On the way up the stairs to her room, Delacroix's phone vibrated in her pocket. Figuring it was Connelly calling to find out where she was, Delacroix ignored it. The buzzing stopped and immediately began again as Delacroix entered the hallway to her room.

Pulling out her phone, she put it to her ear and said, "Hello?"

"Sandy, this is Jenn … Newton. I have an important call for you on the secure phone."

"I'll be right there," Delacroix said, approaching the room. "In fact, open the door for me."

Newton had the room door open as Delacroix walked up.

"Is everything okay, ma'am?" Newton asked.

Delacroix brushed past her into the room. "Fine. Where's the phone?"

Newton pointed to the SIPRnet case on the dresser below the television with the receiver on the table beside it. "I had it brought down after you left last night."

"Where's Nightingale?" Delacroix whispered.

"She took her luggage down to the SUV. She should be right back. I'll be outside if you need me." Newton stepped into the hallway and closed the door behind her.

Delacroix picked up the phone and put it to her ear. "This is Delacroix."

"Warbler, I presume?" a male voice purred into her ear.

"I don't know anything about songbirds, sir. This is Sandy Delacroix."

"Yes, I'm well aware of who you are. You're chief of my sector … and Unicorn's handler," the man stated, still in the low purr.

Delacroix straightened as she wondered just who the hell was on the other end of the line. "Why are you calling, and what is your name?" she asked sharply.

"You know me as Saber," the man said.

"Saber! You're Hector—"

Calderón cut her off by saying, "Enough, Mrs. Delacroix. Call me Saber, please."

When Vice President Evelyn Acevedo had sat down with Delacroix for a private conversation about the state of Venezuela's political affairs, she'd begun to refer to the Director General of the SEBIN as Saber. However, it would have been more serendipitous to refer to Zarate as Saber since he was the one actually rattling the saber. Apparently, the name had been the first to pop into Acevedo's mind, and it had stuck.

"Are you on a secure line, sir?" Delacroix asked.

Calderón chuckled. "I'm using the encrypted phone you handed to Unicorn."

Delacroix ran a hand through her hair and dug her fingernails into the top of her scalp. "I have so many questions right now. But tell me, *Saber*, why are you calling me?"

"We don't have much time," Calderón said. "But rest assured, things on my end are well in hand. I had no control over the army's actions yesterday. Our friend Dragonfly put a crimp in our plans."

Delacroix's eyes widened at the mention of the intelligence purveyor's name. Her mind shifted gears and concentrated on the more pressing question. "What about the aviators and …"

"They are alive, and I am holding them in The Tomb. I will contact you again soon."

Calderón signed off before Delacroix had a chance to ask

another question. Stunned, she set the phone down in the cradle.

"Who was that?" Connelly asked as she and Newton stepped inside the room.

"Uh …" Delacroix's gaze shifted to Newton and then back to her lieutenant. Newton had been read in on Operation Unicorn, and she'd witnessed firsthand the demise of Bowie's private contractors at Tumeremo Airport, so Delacroix felt safe speaking in front of her. "That was a new asset—Saber."

Connelly's eyebrows shot up.

"You know who he is?" Delacroix asked, reading her expression.

"Yeah. I read the reports you sent to Stratten," Connelly replied.

Newton shrugged as if she didn't know or care.

"Needless to say, Bowie and Cobra are in custody. Saber is holding them and the aviators at The Tomb," Delacroix said.

"At least it's not *El Helicoide*," Connelly said with a sigh of relief. *El Helicoide* was the SEBIN's main prison in the heart of Caracas, but it was hell on earth and infamous for its horrific human rights abuses, torture by the sadistic guards, insufficient food and water for the prisoners, and rampant drug use and crime.

And as a former American CIA officer John Phoenix didn't stand a chance of leaving there alive.

CHAPTER 38

The Tomb
Caracas, Venezuela

Phoenix felt like he was going to die.

He heaved and choked and fought, but the water pouring across his face caused his brain to believe he was drowning.

A prison guard had stuffed a cloth into his mouth while another doused him with water from a hose.

Phoenix didn't know how long they had been waterboarding him, but it seemed like an eternity. Suddenly, the man ripped the cloth from Phoenix's mouth. He spat out water and tried to inhale a giant breath of air, but someone jammed a cattle prod into his belly.

The CIA case officer writhed on the concrete floor. His vision blurred in and out under the hot intensity of the bright lights that constantly flooded his prison cell. Whoever had the cattle prod in his hand kept it glued sadistically to Phoenix's belly, causing his spine to arch and eyes to roll back in his head as his mouth opened in a silent scream and his lower jaw quivered.

Just as quickly as the guard had lit him up, he removed the prod. As the crackle of electricity faded from Phoenix's body, his muscles began to relax. Lying on his back, Phoenix closed his eyes and tried to do nothing but breathe. His body had switched into survival mode, and there were no other thoughts in his mind other than the pain of the prod and the taste of the rusty water at the back of his throat. And he knew the guards would give him no relief.

No sooner had he caught his breath than the guard draped the wet cloth over his face again and stood on both sides of it to pin Phoenix's head to the floor. He shuddered as water splattered on the floor from the end of the hose. The guard laughed as he flicked the water over Phoenix's face and then pulled it back. He kept doing it, letting the water stay on the cloth just long enough for Phoenix to draw in a deep breath of water vapor and then flick it away.

Phoenix kicked and bucked, flailing away with his loose limbs, slamming them into the concrete, and busting open his knuckles.

In the back of his mind, he wondered just how long they would keep up this relentless torture. If the SEBIN baited him with the carrot of no more punishment for revealing classified information, he knew he would probably break down and spill the beans. The problem was that it would never be enough. No matter if he told them every last detail, they would demand more.

And everyone broke. It was a case of retaining one's identity in the face of the enemy and not becoming brainwashed or falling under the psychological phenomenon known as Stockholm syndrome, where a victim aligns with and shows empathy toward their captor's objectives. Phoenix had been brainwashed by the CIA a long time ago, and while he didn't agree with all their causes, he was still a staunch patriot.

As Phoenix was trying to catch his breath from the latest round of water and shock therapy, the door to the two-by-three-meter cell opened, and a stranger in a tailored suit stepped in. Sucking in deep breaths of air, Phoenix glanced up at the guy, then did a double take as he recognized the director general of the SEBIN from the man's visit to Evelyn Acevedo's apartment after Phoenix had tried to blackmail the VP by stuffing a satchel full of cash into a desk drawer in her apartment.

Phoenix hacked out a giant glob of phlegm, trying to hit the toe of Calderón's expensive Ferragamo shoe.

Calderón kicked the end of the hose, so the flowing water washed the phlegm down the drain, and then he shut off the wall spigot. He put his hands behind his back and peered at the prisoner for several moments. He spoke softly in Spanish to the guards. Phoenix couldn't hear him over the ringing in his ears from the physical abuse and remnants of the gunfire and explosions from the lopsided firefight at Tumeremo Airport.

Phoenix just lay on his back, naked and wet, and clenching his muscles to prevent his body from shivering. The clenching helped to distract him from the pain radiating from the electrical burns on his stomach and thighs. He appreciated the fact that they hadn't zapped him in the balls —yet.

The case officer's heaving chest was the only thing that moved. His brown eyes took in the director's well-coifed black hair and the dark circles under his eyes. Phoenix made no move to cover himself nor to assume any sort of upright posture. The abuse had been too hard and plentiful, sapping his body of any reserve strength he might normally have been able to muster.

"Do you know where you are?" Calderón asked in English.

Phoenix didn't care. It hurt too much to move, and really,

did it matter if he knew the geographic location of hell on Earth?

"You are my guest in The Tomb," Calderón said after a few silent moments.

Phoenix closed his eyes. His body demanded rest, and he knew sleep would come quickly if the guards left him alone.

"I brought you here," Calderón said. "You, and Lieutenant Blanco, and your precious aviators."

Phoenix's eyes snapped open at the mention of his lover.

"Ah, that got a reaction. Blanco and your friends have been listening to you scream. You are the last to break."

Phoenix's eyelids fluttered closed, and he did nothing but breathe. There was nothing else in the world besides the cold, damp concrete beneath him and the steady rise and fall of his chest. He didn't have the strength to challenge Calderón nor the current mental capacity to debate with him. Leslie Connelly was safe in Washington, and that was all that mattered.

He wondered why he'd thought about Connelly and not Coralina Blanco, but even that mental arithmetic seemed too taxing at the moment. Trying to conjure up an image of Blanco produced an image of Connelly instead. The two intelligence officers had been on an op in Argentina and had gone out to dinner at a fancy steak house in Buenos Aires. She had worn a royal blue sheath dress with her black hair down and wavy. Connelly had never looked more lovely, and the time they'd spent lingering over delicious grass-fed steak and red wine pressed from local grapes had only cemented Phoenix's deep affection for her. And they'd made love that night like the end of the world was coming, and they might never get enough of each other.

"Are you with me, John Phoenix?" Calderón asked, leaning forward to see if the prisoner was still awake.

Phoenix slowly opened his eyes, and he silently blamed Connelly for his daydream since she had professed her love for him over the phone. He wondered why she'd put that curse on him on the eve of the mission. If Phoenix was a superstitious man, he'd say she was the cause of Operation Tornado going to shit.

"Good. You're still with me." Calderón squatted beside Phoenix. "In situations such as these, there is always a deal to be made."

Phoenix blinked, trying to comprehend the man's words. He wondered if this was why they had tortured him without asking any questions. Maybe Calderón wanted him to soften up for this very moment. Phoenix swallowed hard, knowing there was only one way to find out. Licking his lips, he croaked out, "What deal?"

Calderón's face genuinely glowed as he smiled. "The deal will free your friends and make you a wanted man. Will you give your life for theirs?"

CHAPTER 39

Hector Calderón had his answer when he clanged shut the door to Phoenix's cell. He flipped off the wall switch and plunged the prisoner into darkness. Phoenix would need his rest for what lay ahead.

Stepping to the cell beside that of John Phoenix, Calderón slid open the slot in the door and peered inside.

Sergeant Tranquillo came to the door and stared up at the director of the SEBIN. "Why am I here?" she asked. "I did exactly what my president asked of me."

"President Zarate is pleased with your actions. You discovered a dangerous coup attempt by Vice President Acevedo and Lieutenant Blanco. We must ensure you have not chosen their side over that of our glorious leader, *El Jefe*."

"Never. I will stand by President Zarate until I die," Tranquillo stated adamantly.

"That is an excellent answer, Sergeant," Calderón said. "However, you must know that as a former guard here, time spent in these cells has a way of making one repentant of their actions."

"Always loyal. Never traitors," Tranquillo responded in reference to Zarate's tweet about traitors in the military, who he claimed had sold out their interests to the United States after opposition leader Juan Guaidó and U.S. officials had urged Venezuela's armed forces to withdraw their support for Zarate in order for Guaidó to strongarm his way into the presidency.

Calderón chuckled. "It is a blessing to have troops as loyal as you."

"I have *always* been loyal," Tranquillo insisted. "I don't understand why I am being treated this way. Why am I naked and alone in a cell when I should be punishing that traitorous Coralina Blanco and her CIA lover?"

"There will be plenty of time for that. For now, enjoy your rest, Sergeant." The director appraised the woman's thin figure and small breasts before smiling wickedly. "It's a pleasure having you as my guest."

Calderón slid the cover back into place, blocking his view of Sergeant Tranquillo. He hoped Tranquillo would be as loyal to the new regime as she was to Zarate when this was all over. He reflected on why so many of the remaining airmen, sailors, and soldiers remained loyal to the president. After more than forty-three hundred National Guard troops had deserted their posts, Zarate had forbidden his active duty and reserve forces from leaving the country. But that didn't stop them from fleeing the oppressive tyranny exerted by Zarate's regime.

There was, however, a great deal of the military who had pledged their allegiance to Zarate. The president and, to an extent, his predecessor, Hugo Chávez, had understood that to protect and defend the sovereignty and legitimacy of the Venezuelan government, they needed to permanently mobilize the military and operate it as a political action arm of the regime. Once the troops had been indoctrinated into the government's intellectual and political philosophies, they fostered a zealous defense of the homeland and a commitment to the regime that prevented mass desertions and bloody coups.

Calderón's SEBIN and the military leadership also maintained a tight grip on the troops. If they learned of a coup plot, they tapped the dissenter's phones and detained their family members for vigorous "questioning." If a soldier were to discover a coup and turn the plotters over to the proper authorities, the snitch might receive a new car or home as a reward. The fear of punishment and the value of the reward kept everyone under the regime's thumb.

If Tranquillo had been the one to turn over Acevedo and Blanco to Zarate's cronies, Calderón wondered what her reward would be if he ever let her out of prison. As far as Calderón was concerned, Tranquillo was part of the reason why they couldn't enact regime change and rid themselves of that bastard Zarate. There were too many like her who would rat out their compatriots for the gratuity. Calderón knew Tranquillo hadn't sold out the prisoner exchange. Even before he'd sent her to Mexico City as Acevedo's bodyguard, he'd had her phone tapped and agents monitoring her movements. Tranquillo hadn't contacted anyone since leaving on the peace delegation, and Calderón wondered who had known about their plan to free the hostages.

Calderón shuddered as he strolled down the bleak concrete corridor of what had once been designed as the building's underground parking garage. It could just as easily be him in the cell. He had pulled Blanco from The Tomb and dispatched her to Mexico City with Acevedo. And he had suggested that Acevedo and Blanco reach out to their CIA contacts to open a back channel to the United States government.

Zarate had been furious about Calderón's recommendation of Acevedo for the VP slot after he had learned of her involvement in the hostage rescue plan. The man's bald head had turned beet red as he'd screamed at Calderón for his incompetence. Only Calderón's friendship with Major General Salazar had saved the SEBIN director from being permanently entombed in his own prison. Salazar had argued for his friend's loyalty, claiming that even the mighty SEBIN could not always know the inner workings of the most devious minds, which Acevedo obviously had.

Yet, Calderón knew he walked a thin line. He had marshaled his friends to face down his foe, but it was a one-time shot. He had no more silver bullets to fire. If Zarate discovered his duplicity, Calderón would face two choices if the coup failed—run or die.

Calderón's liberty rested in John Phoenix's hands.

CHAPTER 40

Oval Office
Washington, D.C.

"THERE ISN'T MUCH WE CAN DO," D/CIA COLE STRATTEN SAID.

President Mercia paced across the presidential seal as he typically did when conducting strategic meetings about the future of the world. He figured that by the end of his four years in the White House, the interior designers would have to replace the carpet after he'd worn it down to the floorboards. He'd never paced this much as the governor of Oklahoma, but the stakes hadn't been quite so high either.

Randy 'Merica was facing what he called his "JFK moment." Kennedy had the Cuban Missile Crisis, and Mercia had Venezuela. Kennedy had a back door to Nikita Khrushchev, while Mercia had hoped Acevedo would be his ace in the hole. Unlike Kennedy, who had fought the CIA and their attempts to undermine his concepts of change—and some might say they silenced him permanently to keep him from doing too much damage to *their* country—Merica had a supportive D/CIA and Secretary of Defense.

Slowing his pace, Mercia turned to Leslie Connelly, who sat beside Cole Stratten, Sandy Delacroix, and Rex Scott. "You're supposed to be the expert on the region. What's your take?"

"We're in uncharted territory, sir," Connelly replied. "Zarate is a caged animal. We've backed him into a corner where he feels he has no other recourse but to hold our people hostage until we meet his demands."

"I don't get it," Scott said. "If we had a guy like that in office here, we'd have given him the boot a long time ago."

"You did," Connelly replied. "President Brandon was as corrupt as we've ever had, but everyone sat on their hands while he ruined the economy and decimated the Southern Border. And it was for the exact same reasons that Zarate is still in power. Brandon weaponized the media to demonize anyone who spoke out against him, and he dispatched his minions to hold sham trials against his primary political rivals. We, fortunately, have the option of somewhat free and fair elections every four years to change the balance of power. Zarate, however, is in control of Venezuela, and he's entrenched behind his military and the SEBIN."

"What about military action to remove him from power?" Mercia asked. "Is sending a coalition force viable?"

"I think we would have another Iraq or Afghanistan on our hands," Scott said. "We might be able to wipe their aging military equipment off the map, but there's still a large fighting force that can wage a guerrilla war against us, just like the FARC have done in Colombia."

"And the Taliban, and ISIS, and whatever other Iranian-backed force you want to name," Stratten added.

"Regardless, a war in Venezuela would be a long and protracted one with no end in sight, and the American people are quite sick of those," Scott said.

"Okay, I get it," Mercia said. "War with Venezuela is not a smart idea. What about Unicorn? Where do we stand on that mission?"

"Nowhere," Delacroix replied. "She's in prison. Zarate had her arrested for her part in the attempted rescue of the Flying Jaguars."

"So, we either comply with Zarate's demands or do nothing," Mercia summed up.

"Then I vote that we do nothing," Connelly said. "We know for a fact that President Fredricks won't give up any part of his country, even if it meant the recovery of mercenary forces that he hired."

"We can't do nothing," Mercia said. "There's got to be a solution to this fucking problem. What if I called Zarate?"

"He might take your call, Mister President," Stratten replied, "but he's not going to back down from what he's already said at the news conference. He can't. Otherwise, he'll lose all his power."

"And you said we should take what he says at face value, sir," Chief of Staff Crowley said.

"You're right, Tabby," Mercia said. "I've always said we should listen to what guys like Putin, Xi, and Zarate say. Generally, they'll tell you exactly what they're going to do well ahead of time."

Rex Scott stood and buttoned his suit coat. "I know what I just said about long wars, sir, but we need military options. I want to reach out to our allies to build a coalition."

Mercia nodded. "I like the proactive approach, Rex. Let me know what you come up with." He turned to his CIA team. "I want the same from you. Appoint someone to work with Rex and get a game plan in place. I expect something on my desk within the next twenty-four hours."

CHAPTER 41

The Tomb
Caracas, Venezuela

The intense glare of the overhead light brought Phoenix awake.

He blinked rapidly, trying to remember where he was. Then reality settled heavily upon him. Phoenix still lay on his back on the cold, wet concrete—naked and very much alone.

Rolling to his left side, the CIA officer groaned in pain. His muscles had stiffened from inactivity and the cold. He glanced around the cell. There was a stainless-steel toilet, sink combination, and a concrete bunk with a single wool blanket. There were no windows and only a single steel entry door.

While Calderón might have shut off the light when he'd left, someone else had found the switch, and the extremely bright panel of overhead LED lights caused him to shade his eyes as his pupils adjusted to the glare.

Phoenix levered himself into a seated position and then scooted backward until he could lean against the wall. Just that minimal effort had taxed his waning strength. His head dropped between his shoulders, chin touching his chest as he slept again.

He dreamed he was in a different prison. The multistory building was rectangular, with all the cells open to the elements. Phoenix could look down into the central courtyard from his cell and see the daily fights and riots. A bookie took bets on all fighters, and today, the courtyard hummed at a fevered pitch as two female combatants circled one another.

Knowing instinctively that something terrible was about to happen, Phoenix made his way down several flights of stairs and then pushed his way through the crowd of dirty, shirtless men. Some elbowed him back, but Phoenix squeezed through the gaps to the front of the pack, where the inmates held a hastily erected circle of rope to delineate the fighting ring.

The crowd undulated around the women and screamed for them to fight. Phoenix glanced around, trying to gauge who the crowd thought would be the winner. There was a distinct difference between the women. Each feature registered with Phoenix—Blanco's slightly taller height with her brown hair pulled into a clip at the base of her skull versus Connelly's thicker figure, the darker espresso color of her skin, and her jet-black hair. He realized in horror that his two lovers had squared off in combat.

Phoenix tried to shout for them to stop, but his voice came out in a whisper that was quickly drowned out by the cheering crowd. A shrill whistle sounded from the bookie, a wiry Black man with long dreads and a white wife beater to go with his tan prison pants. He shuffled his shower shoes through the dust to the center of the ring. Pointing at Phoenix, the man shouted, "Behold! The prize. These women fight for his honor because he has none. He is a traitor to his country and a ruthless murderer. And that is why he is in prison with us. *We* are his people!"

Suddenly, the faces of the crowd turned to haunting specters of every man Phoenix had ever seen killed on the battlefield, including Tyler Verdin and the team of GDF mercs that had accompanied him to rescue the Flying Jaguars. They all jeered at him and began to chant, "Traitor! Traitor! Traitor!"

The bookie waved his hands, and eventually, the crowd fell silent. "We have two challengers! Nightingale versus Cobra. Whoever wins will get to be with the traitor. Whoever loses … they're just fucking dead."

"No!" Phoenix shouted, trying to catch the attention of the two women.

Connelly slid her left foot back, bringing up her fists in a classic boxer's stance. Blanco moved into a Brazilian Jui-Jitsu crouch. Phoenix knew both women were highly skilled in hand-to-hand fighting techniques. He had no idea who would come out as the victor. Another whistle sounded, and the women began to circle each other again.

As Connelly faced him, she said, "I love you, John."

Blanco would face him as they circled and fixed him with a hateful glare. "*You* are *my* asset. *I'm* the one in control."

Then, the women attacked each other—screaming, clawing, biting, punching, and kicking. They used every trick in the book to try to gain an advantage. When it appeared they had come to a stalemate with Blanco locking Connelly in a Jiu-Jitsu hold, Bookie sent two men to break up the fight. Once the women were back on their feet, the bookie handed them long, wicked-looking Bowie knives.

Blanco, blood streaming down her face from a cut over her left eyebrow, raised the knife above her head. She let out a soul-piercing scream and ran forward. Connelly raised her knife to parry, and metal rang against metal.

Phoenix jolted awake and glanced around, blinking against the harsh light. His heartbeat seemed to mimic a galloping horse smacking out a staccato tattoo as blood roared in his ears.

The sound of clanging metal that had awakened him was the opening of the food slot at the bottom of the cell door. The guard shoved a plastic tray heaped with rice and beans through the slot and then slid his hand in to flip the bird at Phoenix before closing the slot in the door.

The case officer rolled onto his side, then levered himself up on all fours, crawling across the floor like a feral animal. His knees ached from grinding against the concrete, but he didn't care. The guard hadn't provided any silverware, so Phoenix leaned down on his elbows, face close to the tray, and scooped the food into his mouth with his fingers. Despite his awkward eating position, Phoenix knew he needed the nourishment to rebuild his strength for what lay ahead.

After finishing the meal, he slid the tray up against the door slot and leaned against the wall. He slept again, thankful he didn't dream about Blanco and Connelly fighting.

Reviving from his dreamless sleep, Phoenix moved to the concrete shelf designed as a bunk and pulled the blanket over his body. The fighting dream loomed large in his subconscious, with the women savagely pounding on each other and slicing each other with the big knives. Blanco kept screaming at him that it was all his fault. They wouldn't be in this mess if he had just taken her to the U.S. when they'd first met. Instead, he had turned her into a double agent and made her a traitor. Sitting astride Connelly, Blanco raised the knife over her head, ready to plunge it into her heart. She looked directly at Phoenix and said, "This is all your fault."

Phoenix woke with a start. He lay on the bunk, panting hard, and his heart pounding in his chest. He buried his head under the blanket, trying to block out the images of Blanco and Connelly fighting.

Once he decided he would get no more sleep, Phoenix sat up and rubbed his face, thinking about what he had agreed to do. Hector Calderón had given him an ultimatum. Phoenix and his people could rot in these cells, or he could put a stop to the suffering of all Venezuelans. The answer had come quickly and easily to Phoenix's lips, knowing that what he agreed to would make him an international fugitive.

Calderón's plan wasn't that different than the one the Nightingale had concocted. Her plan had been for Phoenix to rescue the aviators, then fade into the bush and make his way toward Caracas. He would then link up with an agent working for Acevedo and figure out the best way to eliminate Zarate. Once he'd assassinated the president of Venezuela, the agency would disavow him, and he'd go on the run.

The plan, however, was to put him in touch with Dragonfly once he was *persona non grata* at the CIA. With Phoenix a wanted man and proving he was capable of being more than just an agency asset, he could penetrate Dragonfly's organization and bring him down from the inside.

Maybe.

Phoenix huddled under the blanket, but with no natural light to set his cycadean rhythms by, it was impossible to tell when he should sleep or be awake. At least the guards hadn't been back to torture him.

He wondered when Calderón would send someone for him so he could start his new mission. While Connelly had assured him that she would provide backup when he needed it, he didn't believe he could count on any agency support if they disavowed him. And he didn't know if Calderón would keep his word and release Acevedo and Blanco once he had killed Zarate. Calderón could be planning to ascend to the throne himself and keep just as tight a fist on Venezuela as Zarate had.

Phoenix would only know the answers once he had completed his new mission.

CHAPTER 42

"It's time," Coralina Blanco said, stepping into Phoenix's cell.

Phoenix stared at his former asset. She wore urban camouflage BDUs complete with black chest rig and a black baseball cap with the word SEBIN printed across the front in white letters.

"Let me guess," Phoenix said dryly, "that's your Halloween costume."

"You're not as funny as you think," she replied.

Sliding his legs off the bench, Phoenix righted himself to a seated position. "At least Calderón freed you."

"It was my second stay in The Tomb, and neither was pleasant. Come on. Let's get you dressed and ready. I'll be your handler on this mission."

"It's like a dream come true," Phoenix muttered. He stood unsteadily on his weak legs and asked, "Got any clothes for me?"

"In the next room," she replied, heading down the hallway.

Phoenix followed her to a shower area, passing more cells with closed and locked doors. A fresh towel, soap, and shampoo had been laid out on a bench beside a pile of folded clothes. Taking the toiletries, he stepped under the scalding water. After washing his hair and body, Phoenix dressed in the provided SEBIN uniform, matching the one Blanco wore.

He settled the chest rig on his torso and strapped it down tight, noting the empty pistol holster and mag pouches. He pointed to it and asked why he didn't have a weapon even though Blanco carried a Beretta Px4 Storm in her rig.

"You'll be provided what you need when the time is right," she said. "From now on, you take your orders from me and speak only in Spanish. Everyone must believe you are my subordinate."

Phoenix grinned. "I like it when you're on top."

Blanco rolled her eyes. "This is not a joke, John. This is a matter of life and death."

"Okay, so what's the plan?" he asked.

She motioned for him to follow her and remain silent.

Phoenix walked behind the Special Forces lieutenant through the eerily quiet hallway of The Tomb and onto an elevator. The car rose from the basement cells to the lobby of the SEBIN headquarters. Blanco led him through the spartan lobby, where two men in black uniforms with balaclavas and Kalashnikov AK-103s stood guard.

Stepping through the entrance onto the street, Phoenix drew in a huge breath of relief. By far, the torture in The Tomb was the worst thing he'd ever experienced, and he never wanted to repeat it.

Blanco continued down the sidewalk and into a parking lot, stopping at a white Ford Explorer. It was a newer model body style that Phoenix thought the company had stolen from Land Rover. Blanco chirped the alarm with the key fob and told Phoenix to get into the passenger seat.

"I hope you know your way around Caracas better than you knew Maracay," he grumbled, remembering how her shitty directions had nearly gotten them lost.

"This is my home," she said.

Phoenix got into the SUV and buckled his seatbelt. He glanced at Blanco, who refused to meet his gaze. She started the engine, pulled on her seatbelt, adjusted the air conditioner vents, and then put the vehicle into gear.

"Where are we going?" Phoenix asked.

"Let's get one thing straight," she said, leaning forward to check cross traffic before pulling onto the street. "I am your handler, and you will do as I tell you."

"You ratted us out, didn't you?" he asked, unable to explain how he knew she had. Possibly, it was her cold demeanor toward him or her brisk, businesslike attitude.

"My *job* is to protect my country," she stated firmly.

Phoenix closed his eyes and forced himself to relax. He found he was clenching his teeth. The knot of muscle behind his right shoulder radiated pain all the way to his fingertips. It wasn't Tranquillo or Acevedo who had sold out the rescue mission to the regime—it was Blanco.

How could you be so fucking stupid, John?

He tried to come up with a reason why she had betrayed everyone on Operation Tornado as they rode in silence through the streets of Caracas.

Blanco slowed the SUV as they approached a crowd in the street. They waved anti-Zarate signs demanding he resign and chanted protest slogans. SEBIN agents and National Guard troops stood in a line behind clear battle shields. Other police officers patrolled on horseback or stood in the back of pickup trucks, ready to fire teargas and bullets.

Finally, Phoenix could stand it no longer and asked, "Why?"

"Because I needed you here, *guapo.*"

Phoenix knew she was stroking his ego by calling him handsome. Still, he liked that she had given him a pet name. It made it seem as if they were still lovers. He figured he would never see her naked again, but he could always hope.

It's what a man clung to with women like Blanco. They knew how to hook a guy with the good nookie, then withhold it in return for favors the lover might perform.

"So, what's the plan?" he asked.

"The same as it was before. You are to kill Zarate," she replied, not taking her eyes off the road.

"If that's still the plan, why did you leak the intel about our raid?"

"It needed to be done," she replied.

"I don't get it, Cora," Phoenix said. "I already had a plan. Why did you change it?"

"Your plan was selfish. You wanted your people back, and your president wants Zarate dead so he can have oil. *Our* plan is to fix our country."

"Okay. Explain it to me, then," he said.

"Now is not the time," she replied, honking the horn at a group of protesters blocking the street. "Trust me. It had to be this way."

"Can I call Nightingale?" Phoenix asked.

"Your agency has disavowed you," Blanco said. "She can no longer help you. I am your handler now, John. Your orders come from me."

Phoenix knew he was in trouble. She kept using his Christian name. Even though he'd told it to her after a fantastic rendezvous in Mexico City, she had continued to call him Bowie. He preferred it because he didn't like the way she now said his first name. She put too much hard inflection on it with a hint of ridicule and sarcasm.

"Did we have this conversation in my cell?" he asked, feeling as if his dream was coming true even if there was no fight pit and Connelly was a thousand miles away.

"No," she replied flatly.

Phoenix wondered why it seemed so real. He idly pondered the thought that the SEBIN had used some sort of mind control technique on him, burning the belief that Blanco was his new handler into his brain. If that was the case, he didn't know how well it had worked. He felt the need to reach out to Connelly to let her know he was still alive. The two of them had frequently used back-channel communication techniques when they'd been in the field together before she'd become assistant chief of the LA division. Phoenix figured he could find a way to open one of those again. Hopefully, she would be on the lookout for them now that he'd dropped off the radar.

Blanco let him stew in silence as she tried to navigate around the protestors blocking the streets. She pulled into a curbside parking slot and shut off the engine. "We'll have to walk from here. The crowd is too big, and I'm afraid someone might be tracking the SUV."

Phoenix and Blanco stepped out of the vehicle. He felt conspicuous in his SEBIN costume and naked without a handgun to go with it. The agitated crowd surged and chanted. Most protesters marched in the opposite direction, but a few spotted the disguised asset and handler and headed toward them.

Approaching a cluster of about ten people, Phoenix picked out a likely target to pickpocket. Before he and Blanco reached the cluster, the crowd turned on them. A man in his early twenties attacked Phoenix. The embattled case officer wrestled with the man as another charged in to join the scuffle. Blanco jerked her pistol out and smacked the butt of the Beretta against the man with his arms around Phoenix.

Phoenix shoved the kid away and turned slightly to prepare for the next attacker, who was just a half meter away and closing. The others in the group started shouting vehemently at Blanco and Phoenix, calling them traitors and criminals. In their eyes, anyone who wore a uniform represented an oppressive government and was no friend of the people. The uniform became a dehumanizing element, allowing the protesters to see state-controlled automatons and not human beings just trying to scrimp by.

Suddenly, whistles sounded down the street, and more cops ran toward the crowd around Blanco and Phoenix. She had backed them off by brandishing her pistol, but they had yet to escape the madness. Behind him, combat boots pounded on the street. Blanco turned to look. Phoenix kept his eyes on their assailants.

A man stepped through the crowd, carrying a stick like he was the designated hitter about to step up to the plate. Before the guy could swing the stick, Phoenix kicked him in the side of the knee, and the guy went down with a scream. They couldn't afford to duke it out with the protesters when their lives were in jeopardy.

Swiftly, Phoenix reached out and snatched a phone from a nearby protester who'd been recording the entire confrontation. The guy started to protest, but Phoenix jammed his elbow into his solar plexus, and the guy fell to the ground in pain as his diaphragm locked up. Blanco turned back from looking at the other SEBIN troops running their way. She swung her pistol in an arc, attempting to cover the crowd.

"We need to go," Phoenix urged.

Blanco glanced over her shoulder again, then down at the prostrate man clutching his knee and screaming in agony. She seemed to reach a decision and nodded. Phoenix took off running without hesitation and, several meters down the road, glanced back to see Blanco giving pursuit.

The two ran to the nearest street corner. Blanco shouted for Phoenix to turn right. He had about five meters on his handler, and as soon as he rounded the turn, he stopped and pressed his back against the building, hiding himself from view. He reached into his pocket and pulled out the phone. It was an older iPhone that was still recording and hadn't switched off yet. Phoenix opened the control panel and changed the password.

Blanco came running around the corner, gun still in hand. Phoenix stuck out his foot and tripped his former lover. As she sprawled face-first on the concrete sidewalk, Phoenix set the iPhone to silent and then stuck it back into his pocket. Blanco was just coming to her knees. Phoenix grabbed the pistol that had skittered away during the fall and holstered it in his vest before reaching out to help her.

Lifting Blanco to her feet, Phoenix glanced around to see if there were any potential hostiles. Blanco brushed her palms together to get rid of the grit and quickly examined a cut caused by a pebble. Phoenix tugged at her elbow, urging her to move.

After a glance over her shoulder, Blanco took off up the street. Phoenix saw no reason to run, but he followed her lead, and they put some distance between themselves and the riotous crowd. He wanted to ditch their uniforms, but he had no other clothing. Although, he thought going naked might attract less attention than the camouflage uniform of a government official at that moment.

When Blanco stopped running, she put her hands on her knees to aid in catching her breath. Phoenix was in no better shape. They both huffed and puffed for a few moments before Blanco straightened and said, "We need to get out of here. I have another car farther down the street."

They started walking and had only made it a few meters before Blanco suddenly stopped. She turned to face her asset. "You tripped me."

"You fell, and I helped you back up," Phoenix said nonchalantly. "I think there was a lip in the concrete."

"Why were you waiting around the corner?" she asked.

Phoenix took a deep breath. "I'm still trying to catch my breath. I'm out of shape."

Her gaze shifted to the pistol in his holster, and she put out her hand, palm up. "Gun, please."

Phoenix wanted to unzip his fly as a joke but knew better.

It wasn't the time to play around. He handed her the Beretta butt first.

"I don't know what game you're playing, but I don't appreciate it," Blanco said. "Stop fooling around. We don't have much time."

Phoenix motioned forward. "After you, mistress."

Blanco moved quickly through the city streets toward their awaiting vehicle. Phoenix kept trying to run an SDR as they walked, but it wasn't easy with the pace Blanco had set. He just hoped the altercation with the protesters hadn't blown their cover.

CHAPTER 43

"Get in," Blanco said as they approached an older Honda sedan parked along the curb on a residential street a few blocks off Bolívar Avenue, the main artery through Caracas.

Phoenix climbed into the passenger seat, and Blanco got behind the wheel. He tried to play out various scenarios in which he could derive some private time to use his new phone to check in with Connelly at Headquarters.

"Is this car clean?" Phoenix asked, wondering if it had bugs or tracking devices installed on it.

"My tech checked it two days ago, and no one has been near it since. There's a doorbell camera on the house over there." She pointed to a nice-looking home with a high wall and shrubs. "We've been watching it the entire time. No one has been near the car since we parked it here."

Blanco started the Honda and put it in gear. She pulled away from the curb and drove a zigzag pattern through the city streets. Phoenix was glad she'd decided to check for tails.

After another twenty minutes of strenuous city driving, Blanco pulled down a ramp into an underground parking garage. She got out, opened the roll-up gate, and motioned for Phoenix to bring the car through. He did so, and Blanco closed and locked the gate behind him. She climbed into the passenger seat and directed him to drive down one level.

Phoenix glanced around at the gray concrete walls, the thick gray support columns, and the gray electrical conduit. His skin crawled at the thought of how much the garage resembled his prison cell in The Tomb, and he wondered if he would ever look at a parking garage in the same way.

No lights were on in the garage, and Phoenix had to find the switch on the Honda's dash to activate the headlights. Blanco told him to park by the stairs, and once he found the right spot, he switched off the car.

Blanco used the flashlight app on her phone to dig out a key and insert it into a lock on a gray steel door.

Once inside the narrow stairwell with the door locked behind them, she led the way up.

"What is this place?" Phoenix asked.

"It's not The Tomb, John," she replied.

There it was again. The use of his first name was like something hostile. He paused on the steps, leaning against the wall for support, one hand on the railing. He was still feeling the effects of the torture and their sprint through the street. "Why are you so angry with me, Coralina?"

She stopped and turned to face him. "I'm not *angry*, John. I'm your handler. We're not supposed to be overly familiar with each other."

"You can stop calling me John, then. Only my friends call me by my first name."

"What would you like me to call you?" she asked.

"Anything *but* John. You know, since we're not supposed to be overly familiar with each other." He grinned at her, feeling a kick of satisfaction at throwing her words back into her face.

"Okay, asshole, let's go." Blanco started up the stairs again.

Phoenix followed at a safe distance. There was a reason he'd given her the codename Cobra: he was afraid of her venomous bite. Still, he couldn't help himself; he caught up to her and pressed her to the wall. He looked deep into her brown eyes. They had once shown love and adoration, but now they were hard, dark orbs without a glimmer of a soul behind them.

He nodded his head in understanding. He'd been there. Phoenix knew how to set aside emotions, too. Releasing Blanco from his grip, he straightened her uniform and motioned with both hands toward the rising steps.

He counted fourteen landings—seven flights of stairs in total. Phoenix followed Blanco into a long, narrow hallway with windowless doors on the left side and large banks of windows on the right that overlooked a courtyard. Phoenix glanced down, expecting to see children playing or lovers necking on park benches, but there was nothing but over-grown trees, shrubs, and grass that formed a silent green blanket. A creeper vine had attached itself to the corner of the building and had spread out to create a living wall. The place had an eerie, creepy, deserted feeling, like something out of a horror movie.

After reading about all the homeless and the squatters in Caracas, Phoenix was surprised that the building was empty. Someone had been inside, though. There was brightly colored graffiti everywhere, making the exterior not as gray as the rest of the shithole. He glanced down at his feet and the gray concrete showing through the worn and chipped puke-green paint.

Blanco stopped at door number seven and knocked.

Phoenix noticed a pinhole camera set into the doorjamb and imagined someone staring at them through the fisheye lens.

The door lock clicked, and Blanco pushed through, urging her charge not to linger outside. Phoenix saw no reason for urgency as no one else was around, but he did as Blanco ordered.

They entered an empty room. Phoenix closed the door behind him and heard the lock seat in place. Before Phoenix took his hand off the knob, he tested it to find it didn't move. Once again, he felt like he'd been locked inside a cell.

Blanco either didn't catch his actions or didn't care. She went to a door set off to the right, and someone buzzed them in again. This time, they entered a warm white room housing multiple computer stations and staffed by a short, skinny brunette with thick glasses and a man in his late thirties.

"John Phoenix, meet Arika and Joel," Blanco said. "We're here to help you complete your mission."

"Nice to meet you," Phoenix said to both.

"How did you get into Acevedo's apartment?" Joel asked.

Phoenix shrugged. Apparently, his reputation had preceded him. "I picked the lock when she was at work," he said as he appraised Joel. The guy had a compact, muscular body, buzz-cut black hair, and black eyes. Turning to Arika, he asked, "We're all operatives. What do you do?"

Arika glanced at Joel, then shifted her gaze to Blanco and back to Joel.

"I can tell, Arika," Phoenix said. "We're kindred spirits. And from the way you're eye fucking him, I can tell you've been sleeping with him. I hope that's a good thing—meaning you care about him and don't want him to die." He glanced at Blanco. "Or are you just using him for sex?"

Her brown eyes widened in shock.

"I'm also guessing you're the computer geek," Phoenix said, changing the subject when she didn't answer. "So, what are we doing that needs three paramilitaries and a technical officer?"

"We're here to help you complete the mission, Bowie," Blanco said.

"Good. I hope you have a plan." Phoenix stepped over to

a map pinned to the wall and examined it. Someone had used pink, orange, and green markers to trace routes over the streets.

"Is this a planned event for Zarate?" Phoenix asked.

"Yes, it is," Joel said. "I've been scouting potential locations for a hit."

Phoenix turned to address the room. "How many people are involved in this plot? There are six that I know of. Any more than that, and someone higher up will get wind of it."

"This is as big as it gets," Blanco said.

"Who's in charge?" the disavowed case officer asked.

"I am," Blanco replied confidently. "I have the full trust of Director Calderón. How do you think I was able to walk you out the front door of The Tomb with no questions asked."

"What about the guards there?" Phoenix asked. "At least three guys had a hand in torturing me."

"You've been marked as transferred to *El Helicoide*," Joel said. "I put in the paperwork myself."

"Are you all SEBIN?" Phoenix asked.

"We're patriots." Blanco pointed to the map. "Joel, go over the routes with Bowie."

Joel began explaining the various colored routes to Phoenix. "Zarate will travel from the Miraflores Palace to the Bolivarian Military University at Fort Tiuna to address the troops. We won't know which route he'll take until he leaves the palace. We'll station Arika outside it so she can phone us with the route number. You, me, and Blanco will be on motorcycles, so we can quickly access any of the routes."

"I like it so far," Phoenix said. "What about the hit itself?"

Joel motioned for Phoenix to join him at a low workbench set against a far wall. He picked up a metal canister about four inches around and six inches long. "This is an EPF. I assume you're familiar with how they work."

Phoenix nodded. He had seen firsthand the damage an explosively formed penetrator (EFP) could do. The insurgent fighters in Iraq and Afghanistan had become masters of building the low-tech charges to disable American armor. Phoenix took the bomb from Joel and examined it. At the top sat a remote detonator that, when triggered, would explode the plastique inside the metal tube. Rolling the charge, the former Green Beret saw Joel had used copper to cover the base. Once the charge detonated, it would deform the copper plate into a slug and shove it through the armor. There were several types of EFPs, but the one Phoenix held was meant to be attached to a vehicle via three electromagnets spaced evenly around the base of the cylinder.

"The pack on the side of the cylinder supplies energy to the electromagnets and the detonator," Joel explained. "This is a two-part charge. The first blows the EFP through the armor, and the second sends a wave of steel pellets into the vehicle."

"Should do the trick," Phoenix said. "Now, how do we deploy it?"

"That's your job," Blanco cut it. She explained the plan in detail to Phoenix and the others. Phoenix walked back to the map and examined it as he listened to his handler speak.

Phoenix rubbed his chin thoughtfully. The plan had come together.

He had one shot.

And he had to make it count.

CHAPTER 44

Phoenix sat alone on a cot in a separate room off their operations center.

Blanco had locked him in shortly after they had discussed the plan to kill Zarate. Thankfully, she hadn't bothered to search him, or she would have found the phone he'd stolen from a protester. He glanced at the pile of clothing she had left for him. The uniform was similar to the one he still wore, but it bore the insignia of the Presidential Guard, an elite force comprised of Cuban paramilitaries since Zarate didn't trust his own people to protect his life. Phoenix didn't look Cuban, so he hoped the black, full-face motorcycle helmet would disguise his identity enough for him to blend in with the other troops.

He got up and pressed his ear to the door. No sound came from the other side. This was his chance to phone home.

Pulling out the iPhone, he put in his PIN and dialed Leslie Connelly's cell number in the States. She didn't answer. He considered leaving a message and thought better of it.

He made his next call to the main switchboard at CIA Headquarters. Phoenix asked to be put through to Sandy Delacroix, chief of the Latin America Division. He prayed she would answer, but his call went to voicemail once again. He hung up and dialed the switchboard again. This time, he asked for Jennifer Newton. Moments later, the technical operations officer came on the line.

"Jenn, this is Bowie," he said in a whisper.

"Why are you calling me?" she said hastily. "I'm not supposed to be talking to you."

"The plan is going forward tomorrow for when Zarate addresses the troops at Fort Tiuna."

The line clicked and buzzed. Phoenix figured it was the long-distance connection to the States.

"What do you want me to do?" Newton asked.

"Tell Nightingale and Warbler." Phoenix ended the call before she could ask any more questions. He had been on the phone long enough. At least he'd passed the message along.

Phoenix checked the phone's battery to see it was at sixty percent. He considered shutting it off but decided to leave it on in case Connelly realized her missed call had been from him. After stripping down to his underwear, Phoenix examined the cattle prod marks on his inner thighs and belly. They appeared black and blue but probably wouldn't leave a permanent scar. His time in The Tomb, however, would leave a mental scar.

He felt it had made him more ruthless and less caring. He flashed back to the guy with the stick in the crowd. Kicking him in the knee had probably blown out the joint. Before his prison stay, Phoenix might have found another way to deal with him, but like Gold Tooth, putting them down had been about sheer expediency. He'd do whatever it took to keep his ass out of The Tomb.

The phone screen winked on, and Phoenix scooped it up. A text message from Connelly said, "Good luck."

THE FOLLOWING DAY, Phoenix examined his burgeoning beard in the polished metal mirror above the bathroom sink. He decided not to shave since he only had bottled water and disposable safety razors. His thick stubble would dull one of those cheap things within two passes. His eyes had bags under them, and his skin looked sallow. He needed some sunshine. The Maldives always had sunshine. And no extradition treaties with the U.S. The islands would be an excellent place to start a new life.

"You ready, Bowie?" Blanco asked through the closed door.

"Yeah. Just a sec." He straightened his BDU blouse and rolled his shoulders to loosen things up.

They were about to put the hammer down.

He opened the door and entered the tiny kitchen where someone had brewed coffee. Reaching for a mug, Phoenix poured himself a cup of strong black brew and sipped it, enjoying the rush of caffeine burning down his throat. Joel had brought *arepas*—little cornmeal pancakes—from a bakery. They had two each, and then the bag was empty. Phoenix's stomach growled for more. At least it was a distraction from the knot in his shoulder and the constant worry of the mission ahead. If the holistic doctor was right and the knot was where he carried resentment, then every time he glanced at Blanco, the pain should have been crippling.

Yeah, he thought, *the Maldives sounded really nice.*

Blanco must have caught him glaring. She faced him with crossed arms. "It's like this, *John*."

The knot tightened. Phoenix's right hand went numb.

"I called Zarate and told him about the rescue plan. I even told him Acevedo had okayed it and that she was talking to the CIA."

Phoenix rolled his shoulder and gritted his teeth.

"It was part of the plan, *John*. We wanted Acevedo tucked away in prison so she wouldn't get caught up in the conspiracies that will inevitably come out after you kill Zarate. She needed the insulation. I needed to be seen as a team player. Terry Martin knows where my mother lives. Out of the three of us—you, me, and Evelyn—you're the expendable one, and since you'd already cooked up an assassination scheme with Connelly, I figured we could make it better."

"What was the point of the torture?" Phoenix asked.

"As you know, there are lots of Cubans helping Zarate run the government. They wanted to see how far they could bend you before you broke. Luckily for you, Calderón interceded before they started pulling your fingernails out."

"And the Flying Jaguars? What happened to them?" Phoenix asked.

"Calderón is shielding them from harm," Blanco said. "You were fair game as a rogue CIA agent."

"*Officer*," he corrected.

"Disavowed is the key," Joel interrupted. "If you guys want to go in the back room and grudge fuck, be my guest, but we're playing on the same team right now. Let's get it together."

Blanco ran her fingers through her hair several times and then used a band from her wrist to capture her hair in a ponytail. "You're right. We have work to do."

Phoenix shouldered the backpack that contained the EFP. Blanco carried the detonator, but she wouldn't be able to trigger the improvised explosive device until after Phoenix had placed it on the vehicle and activated it.

Blanco handed a smartphone to Phoenix. "There's Bluetooth built into the motorcycle helmets."

In the parking garage, Phoenix, Joel, and Blanco each mounted a blue Kawasaki KLR650 dual sport motorcycle decked out to look like those of the Presidential Guard. Arika climbed into the Honda and followed the three bikes out of the parking garage. As the bikers pulled away, she locked the gate and headed for her position outside Miraflores Palace.

For the cyclists, the ride across town to their staging area by Plaza O'Leary, at the western end of Avenue Bolívar, was uneventful. They stationed themselves in a parking spot along San Martin Avenue and waited for the call from Arika to tell them which route Zarate was taking to Fort Tiuna.

They were all dialed into the conference call and listening for the signal from Arika. As Phoenix waited, he pulled out the iPhone. There were no new calls or text messages—nothing from Nightingale.

He dialed her number with the smartphone Blanco had given him. The conference call automatically went on hold as Connelly's phone rang on the other end. It went to voicemail. Phoenix ended the call without leaving a message and then texted her.

Mission is a go. In position now.

CHAPTER 45

Oval Office
Washington, D.C.

Randy Mercia looked up from the paperwork on his desk as Tabbitha Crowley entered.

"Can you believe this horseshit?" he asked, tapping the papers. "I sent over a recommendation for a new energy bill that increases drilling and productivity, and the Senate sends back hogwash about solar fields and offshore wind generation plants. They listened to what those rich assholes at the World Economic Forum had to say and literally wrote it down almost verbatim. What a waste of perfectly good trees."

Crowley smiled tritely. "I would love to commiserate with you, sir, but I have Michel Zarate on the phone. He wants to talk to you."

Mercia leaned back in his chair and smiled with satisfaction. "Well, isn't that a surprise? Put him through."

Crowley's smile turned to one of amusement. "I've kept him on hold for a few minutes just to let him know he's not as high on your list as he'd like to think. Don't be too eager, sir. We have him over a barrel."

"Thanks, Tabby," Mercia replied.

"Would you like me to sit in, sir?" she asked. "You know, as a second set of ears."

"Yes. I'd love that. And see where Stratten is," Mercia replied.

"He's waiting outside, sir. I called him as soon as I put Zarate on hold."

The president breathed deeply, trying to stabilize his nerves. He glanced at the clock, wondering how Stratten had made it from Langley to the White House so quickly. Then he decided it was better to let spooks do spooky shit and not to question their methods. Crowley opened the door, and Stratten and Leslie Connelly stepped inside. The Chief of Staff and two CIA officers took seats around the Resolute desk.

Once everyone was set, Crowley pressed a button to activate the speaker phone and said into it, "Thank you for waiting, President Zarate. I have the President Mercia for you."

Mercia leaned forward and placed his forearms on the desk with his fingers interlaced. "President Zarate, what a pleasure it is to finally speak with you. How can I be of help?"

"I have been advised …" Zarate paused to clear his throat as if what he was about to say was extremely painful for him. "I have been advised to resign from my office. I have a plane waiting to take me to Cuba, where I will live out the rest of my days in exile from my beloved country."

Mercia glanced at the others in the room. The news Zarate had just imparted was as shocking to them as it was to him. No one on the world stage had expected the man to relinquish his power. The U.S. president nodded, then said, "Okay, Michel, how can I help you?"

"The sanctions imposed by the U.S. have frozen several of my personal bank accounts. I want to consolidate my assets and use that money to furnish a comfortable lifestyle in my new home. This is all I ask."

"Can I ask what made you decide to leave?" Mercia asked, noticing Connelly was looking at her cell phone.

"It was not an easy decision to make. Believe me," Zarate said. "I realize my position here in Venezuela is untenable. I made some bold moves to try to better my country, but that has not been the case. You have destroyed much of my military, and my soldiers are deserting in droves. There is a large crowd demonstrating outside Miraflores Palace as we speak. They have been rioting since my return from Mexico City. I have lost control of my nation. And my security apparatus has heard electronic chatter about an assassination plot."

Mercia focused on Connelly. She stared right back at him, but there was something about the eyes. She knew more than she was letting on. Mercia's gaze shifted to Stratten. His face was open and alert, listening attentively to the call. Connelly glanced at her phone.

"I understand, Michel. Once you land in Cuba, I'll have my people release your funds," Mercia said, partially distracted by Connelly's thumbs flying over her phone screen.

D/CIA Stratten shook his head adamantly as if to tell Mercia that releasing the funds wasn't an ideal thing to promise.

"Who is going with you to Cuba?" Mercia asked.

"My wife, our three children, and my mistress," Zarate replied.

Mercia chuckled to himself, wondering how that dynamic would play out. He refocused on the call, thinking of safely getting the man out of Venezuela. "Would you like a fighter escort, sir? I have jets that can accompany you to Havana if you'd like."

"I don't believe President Díaz-Canel would appreciate your jets flying over his country. However, if you were to escort me to Cuban airspace, I would welcome the gesture of goodwill."

"How soon will you be in the air?" Mercia asked.

Connelly leaned over and whispered something in Stratten's ear, showing him the phone screen. Mercia wondered what was so fucking important that she had to disrupt his phone call.

"We are leaving immediately for the airport and will take off in one hour, Mister President," Zarate said. "I will notify my military to turn off the S-300 missile shield so as not to shoot down any of your jets."

"Thank *you*, Mister President," Mercia replied. "I look forward to hearing from you after you've landed safely in Cuba."

Zarate hung up, and Mercia smiled triumphantly, leaning back in his chair with his hands behind his head.

Mercia felt like the king of the world. He'd made that cocksucker, Zarate, blink, and now the dictator was ghosting his country.

Victory was at hand. Kennedy would be proud.

Connelly shifted in her seat. She kept glancing at the phone. With the call from Zarate over, she said, "I need to excuse myself, sir. We have a developing situation that I need to handle."

CHAPTER 46

Plaza O'Leary
Caracas, Venezuela

"He's coming out now," Phoenix heard Arika say into the
phone.

"Which direction?" Blanco asked.

"West on Urdaneta Avenue," Arika said. "He is in the white Rhinoceros."

"What is a rhinoceros?" Phoenix asked.

Joel came on the line to explain. "It's a Chinese VN-4 APC —armored personnel carrier."

Phoenix checked the image of the map he'd memorized in his head. "He should come back east, and we can catch him on the North-South Highway before he enters the Paradise Tunnel."

He punched the starter button on his motorcycle. The smartphone Blanco had given him sat in a cradle on the handlebars. Battery power at ninety percent and charging through a corded connection to the bike. There were still no calls or texts from Connelly. Mission go.

"I've got the lead," Joel said, rolling away from the curb.

Phoenix had no problem letting the younger man take point. He knew his way around Caracas better than Phoenix did, and Phoenix was glad he'd let him lead. Joel made a right turn and then a second right to put them on Baralt Avenue. Phoenix had no clue where they were going. He would have stayed on San Martin Avenue, but he would have been wrong as San Martin ran under the highway with no ramp access.

The three riders roared down Baralt, weaving in and out of traffic. It was the intersections that slowed them the most. Drivers blatantly ignored traffic lights or any hint of others having the right of way, sometimes causing blockages that took minutes to resolve. The three bikers, however, didn't have the luxury of waiting. They honked their meager, tinny-sounding horns and flashed their lights to get people to move. Some kid threw rocks at them as Phoenix shot past.

Again, Joel led them into a series of turns, and they came out on the Francisco Fajardo Highway, an elevated freeway that ran through Caracas. Moments later, they were on the exit ramp and leaning through the sharp ninety-degree curve, which would connect up with the North-South Highway.

"Let's stop at the junction," Phoenix suggested, eyeing the long triangular strip of pavement between the ramp and the main lanes of the highway.

They came to a stop and backed their motorcycles up to the barricade, marking the split in the elevated roadway. Phoenix glanced at the time on the phone. Their ride had taken eight minutes off the clock. That was plenty of time for Zarate's convoy to join the North-South and begin their journey to Fort Tiuna.

Ahead was the Paradise Tunnel, cutting under a mountain

with brightly colored houses stacked in tight and packed atop one another.

"That's called Cota 905," Joel said. "After Zarate took office, he sent in Special Action Forces to clean the area up, but all they did was start a war between the government and the gangs. They negotiated a peace deal, and the slum became off-limits to police. The crime didn't go down. Until a couple of years ago, it was run by a guy named *El Koki*. The police killed him in 2022, but his gang is still active. Many dead bodies have been dumped in the tunnel since."

Phoenix didn't give a shit about the local history. He had a clock in his head, timing Zarate's arrival. "Arika, are you following the convoy?" he asked.

"Yes," the tech replied. "Zarate is still on the North-South Highway. The convoy didn't turn south. They're headed north."

"Change of plan, guys," Phoenix said. "Arika, stay on them. We're coming to you."

He kicked his Kawasaki into gear and roared toward the tunnel. Just before he would have entered it, Phoenix spotted a break in the high curb and downshifted, signaling to the others to follow suit. He glanced at the phone screen as he made the U-turn to head north. No new messages. He figured Connelly had disavowed him, too, and wanted no part in the assassination of the Venezuelan president. Phoenix couldn't blame her. The less involved she was, the more protected she would be from reprisal. She had her career to consider, and John Phoenix now operated outside the law.

"Where are they, Arika?" Phoenix demanded. "What's the closest kilometer marker?"

Arika hummed and muttered until she saw the next marker and gave them the convoy's location. Zarate had a five-kilometer lead on them.

"How fast are they going?" Phoenix barked at Arika.

"One hundred kilometers an hour," she replied.

Phoenix made the calculation—sixty-two miles per hour. He glanced at the bike's speedometer as they entered *La Planicie* Tunnel with more colorful slum housing terraced into the mountainous terrain and interspersed with trees. The speedometer needle hovered at 125 kph. He glanced in the side mirror to gauge how far back his companions were, but the vibrations caused by the wind made everything blurry. He tucked himself in and twisted the throttle all the way open, urging the big dual sport machine to its maximum speed of 144 kph. The entire bike vibrated, and the wind off the cars he passed buffeted him around. Phoenix let off the gas, afraid he might lose control of the motorcycle. If he went down, he just might kill himself, or worse, Zarate would live.

After another three minutes, the bikes entered a sweeping left-hand curve that arced the elevated freeway toward the west, running parallel to the mountains of the Venezuelan Coastal Range. The road was fairly level, and the three bikers increased their speed to the maximum.

"Marker?" Phoenix called out.

"They're crossing the Second Viaduct," Arika reported.

"How far?" Phoenix asked, not knowing where the viaduct was in relation to his position.

"About four kilometers," Joel shouted.

They had gained some ground, but not nearly enough. Phoenix considered asking Arika to block the route but decided it was a suicide mission. The armored car would plow right through the little Honda or blast it out of the way with its 12.7mm machine gun. He cranked open the throttle, and the bike shot forward. The motorcycle's gearing limited its top speed, and Kawasaki hadn't intended the dual sport bike to be a crotch rocket.

"They're slowing for traffic in the tunnel," Arika said.

Phoenix muttered, "How many tunnels does this fucking road have?"

"Two more before the coast," Arika said. "They're entering *Túnel Boquerón I*."

"Two kilometers," Joel called out as they passed over the Second Viaduct.

A minute.

Phoenix had to prepare to place the EFP, but first, he had to catch the convoy. And he was almost there.

Ahead was the mouth of the tunnel, and Phoenix could see Arika's Honda. Beyond it was the white Rhino. He passed her quickly and joined the other Presidential Guard motorcycles surrounding the convoy. It was a weird sensation slowing to fifty kilometers an hour. The speed almost felt too slow, as if the bike wouldn't stay upright or respond at the lower speed, but the vibrations that had buzzed through the handlebars had disappeared.

Phoenix had reached the trickiest part of his mission. He had to pull the EFP from his backpack and place it on the Rhinoceros.

He accelerated hard and caught up with a box truck traveling behind the convoy. He closed within a meter, then let off the gas, allowing the truck's slipstream to pull the bike forward.

Reaching around to his backpack for the cord he'd attached to the zippered compartment, he jerked at it several times before he felt the zipper give way. Once the pocket was open, he reached back with his right hand and grabbed the EFP. The bike was slowing precipitously, losing ground on the truck. A car honked behind him, letting him know he'd lost too much speed.

Phoenix tried to pull the EFP free. It caught on the fabric of the pack. He let go of the bomb and grabbed the throttle again, cracking it open and racing forward until his front tire was almost at the truck's rear bumper. Phoenix reached behind him again and grabbed the EFP with his right hand. The bike slowed. *I need cruise control!*

Phoenix managed to pull the EFP free of the backpack. He placed it between his legs, gripping his thighs tight to the bike to keep it from falling. If he dropped the EFP now, he would be royally screwed.

Looking forward, Phoenix saw the light at the end of the tunnel. The Rhinoceros had four bikes around it. He would need to dart in and slam the EFP onto the cargo compartment of the armored vehicle, then quickly back off. Hopefully, Blanco would wait to trigger the blast until after the Rhino had left the tunnel, giving Phoenix a chance to escape the carnage.

He visualized his actions—riding up to the truck, reaching between his legs to grab the EFP, holding it out, flicking the switch for the electromagnets, watching it suck to the steel. Activating the magnets too early might attach the EFP to the motorcycle's gas tank. If that happened, he'd have to waste precious seconds deactivating the battery and go through the motions all over again. By then, the Presidential Guard might be on to him, and he might not get a second chance.

Phoenix glanced down at the bomb. The tunnel's overhead lights flickered as they raced through. The tunnel had a slight bend toward the end of its two-kilometer length. The road surface was smooth, black asphalt against white tiles stained by exhaust fumes. Phoenix smelled the diesel exhaust from the Rhino and felt a little lightheaded. It was now or never.

The disavowed case officer shot past two of the Cuban Presidential Guards. He came almost abreast of the driver's door, glanced up at the gunner in the turret behind the 12.7mm gun, and flashed him a smile. Phoenix let go of the throttle, grabbed the EFP, and held it out toward the white Rhino. He flicked the switch for the electromagnets, and the bomb practically leaped from his hand as the magnets activated and sought the first available metal surface to attach themselves to. He'd planted the EFP right between the two windows of the armored personnel compartment.

Phoenix tapped the rear brake on his bike, slowing it to allow the APC to gain ground.

The mission was almost over. All Blanco had to do was press the button. The remote would trigger the explosives in sequence. The first would shove the penetrator through the vehicle's thin armor—probably shoot the copper projectile straight through both sides. Then, the second explosion would send a hail of metal balls into the compartment.

Everyone would be dead.

The shock wave would hit first, rippling through their supple bodies, damaging organs and brains, maybe killing someone sitting close to the initial blast. And then the steel hail would rain down on them, ripping and shredding and tearing everything in their path. They'd bounce around the metal interior, magnifying the effects of the damage.

Zarate would meet his untimely end and bring some peace to Venezuela.

Phoenix's phone rang in its cradle. He glanced down. Connelly!

Before he thumbed the answer button, he said into his Bluetooth comms, "The EFP is in place. Hold until he's clear of the tunnel."

Blanco's voice came back hard and flat. "Copy that."

Phoenix tore off his glove with his teeth so he could touch the phone screen. He activated the new call and then pulled the glove from his mouth. "This is Bowie."

"Call it off!" Connelly shouted. "Whatever you're doing. Stop!"

CHAPTER 47

THE RHINOCEROS PUSHED OUT OF THE TUNNEL INTO THE OPEN air. Ahead, the mountain dropped away to the west and rose high above them to the east. A carpet of majestic green spread out across the valley. It was breathtakingly beautiful.

"What?" Phoenix screamed into the phone, trying to understand what Connelly was trying to tell him.

"Zarate has given up. He's going to the airport to catch a plane to Havana. You gotta stop whatever you're planning!" Connelly shouted.

"Fuck!" Phoenix screamed into the onrushing air.

He threw down this glove and switched back to the conference call. "Don't activate the bomb!" he yelled. "Zarate is fleeing the country. Hold fast."

Without waiting for a response, Phoenix swapped calls again and then hit the gas. He didn't know if Blanco would heed his warning. Phoenix had to deactivate the EFP.

Racing forward again, he heard Nightingale in his ear. "What's going on, Bowie?"

"I've got to stop it!" he shouted. "I've got to kill the bomb."

"Do whatever you have to do, Bowie," Connelly said. "If you kill him now, he'll be a martyr. We have to let him leave!"

"I know!" Phoenix shouted back.

He crouched behind the meager windscreen, streamlining his body with the bike to gain speed. The highway curved around the mountain in a sweeping right turn—a giant 180-degree arc carved into the mountainside.

Approaching the Rhinoceros, Phoenix saw one of the Presidential Guards trying to pull the EFP off the APC. Phoenix knew he'd never succeed unless he tripped the energizer switch hidden on the battery pack.

As Phoenix got closer, a guard edged toward him, trying to block him from moving alongside the APC again. Phoenix stuck out a foot and kicked the guy's kickstand down. On the kickstand was a tiny switch that disrupted electrical power to the engine with the bike in gear. The guy's motor shut off, and the bike wobbled as he glanced down to see what had happened. Without maintaining a visual on the road ahead, the bike followed the lead of the rider's head and turned to the left. The kickstand dug into the asphalt, and suddenly, the rider and bike were cartwheeling head over heels across the pavement.

Phoenix kept the throttle pinned, wishing he had a gun so he could shoot the other rider and get him away from the EFP. He came alongside the guy, reached over with his foot, knocked the kickstand down, accelerating quickly to move away from the wrecking bike. With two guards down, he eased off the gas and allowed the Rhinoceros to gain on him.

He didn't know if Blanco had heard him or if she was waiting for the right moment to trigger the EFP. Maybe she wanted Phoenix to be in the blast radius, so he'd die, too.

Out of the corner of his eye, Phoenix saw another motorcycle coming up fast in his mirror. The rider had a pistol out and tried to aim at him with their left hand and keep the gas pinned with the right. Riding and fighting from a motorcycle took a lot of skill, which was probably why the Germans had used so many bikes with sidecars during WWII. One guy steered while the other guy fired his weapon.

Phoenix tried to ignore the rider, but it was damned hard to do with bullets chirping off the steel body of the APC. He reached for the EFP, intent on tripping the switch to shut off the flow of electricity to the bomb.

Ahead, the twin mouths of the *Túnel Boquerón II* yawned at them with bright yellow and black vertical markers on each side of the opening in the cast block wall. The handgun thundered again, and Phoenix veered away from the APC, hooking his finger in the wiring coming out of the battery pack. He felt the wires give, and the EFP fell away from the Rhinoceros. Phoenix shook his hand to rid himself of the bomb, and the EFP bounced and rolled on the pavement behind them just as they entered the tunnel.

Phoenix must have only pulled loose the wiring that had activated the magnets because a sudden detonation sounded behind him, followed by the rush of wind from the twin explosions, just milliseconds apart. Beneath him, the Kawasaki wobbled dangerously, the bars swapping back and forth in what was known as a tank slapper. The front wheel wobbled, and if Phoenix didn't get control of the bike, it would throw him off.

The only way out of a tank slapper was to accelerate and get the weight off the front wheel. Phoenix grabbed a fist full of throttle and wicked it all the way open. Slowly, the weight came off the front end as he slid his ass back to hang off the rear of the seat and change the bike's center of gravity.

Just as the bars stopped twitching, the rider with the pistol came alongside him. Phoenix saw the wind whipping at the brown hair hanging below the helmet at the base of the rider's neck. It was Blanco! She extended the gun across her chest while keeping her right hand on the throttle. Phoenix thrust out his leg and kicked her bike.

Blanco veered away, having to use both hands on the bars to gather the bike back up. Phoenix glanced over his shoulder to see if she had wrecked into the wall, but she kept coming. Blanco had the gun up and pointed at him again. He chopped the throttle, pulled the clutch lever in, and stomped on the back brake. The big Kawasaki bucked under him as he tried to control the skid. Blanco shot past without getting off a round.

Just call me Maverick, baby! Hit the brakes, and she'll fly right by!

Phoenix let off the brake and slipped the clutch. With power to the rear wheel again, he cracked open the throttle and hauled ass toward Blanco. He couldn't let her prevent Zarate from getting on that plane.

He reached up and activated the conference call on his phone again. "Cobra. Knock it off!"

"You're a fucking liar!" she screamed.

"It had to be done," Phoenix replied. "There's a change of plans. Have you thought about why he didn't go to Fort Tiuna?"

"Shut up!" Blanco shouted. "We had him, and you took the bomb off the APC."

"Listen to me, Coralina," Phoenix shouted. "Zarate is going to the airport. He's getting on a plane to Cuba."

"What?" she demanded, still not relinquishing her grip on her Beretta.

Phoenix accelerated to match her speed. They rode beside each other, letting the Rhino speed away from them. The Presidential Guard kept pace with the APC, not bothering to stop to see about their brethren who'd crashed or to interfere with Blanco trying to shoot Phoenix.

"Zarate cut a deal. He's going into exile in Cuba."

"Are you sure?" she asked.

"Nightingale called as we were coming out of the first

tunnel. That's why I rushed to deactivate the bomb, but you blew it anyway."

"I thought you had changed your mind," she said.

"I did. We have to let Zarate leave," Phoenix replied. "The power transition will be peaceful this way. Put the gun away, and let's go watch the asshole get on a plane."

Blanco holstered her weapon. "I need to call Calderón."

She clicked off the line, and Phoenix said to Arika and Joel, "I assume you heard our conversation?"

"Is he really leaving?" Arika asked.

"Yes. We'll follow him to the airport and watch to make sure," Phoenix replied. "Joel, let's close ranks with the Presidential Guard and sneak through the gate."

Seconds later, Joel was beside Phoenix and Blanco as they caught up to the tail end of the procession.

Phoenix dialed Connelly, who had let the call drop during his chaotic ride.

"Hey, Nightingale, what's cooking?" he said when she answered.

"I take it that you stopped whatever you planned to do," Connelly replied.

"At the very last second. Zarate is safe. We're entering the airport grounds now."

"You have eyes on?" she asked.

"We're right behind his APC as part of the mounted guard," Phoenix replied. "Want me to smile and wave at the satellite?"

"No. Don't do that," Connelly said. "Why are you such an idiot?"

Phoenix could practically hear her eyes roll. He, Blanco, and Joel bunched up at the airport entrance gate with the other riders. Within seconds of stopping, the gate pole rose, and the Rhino proceeded through with its formation of riders.

"We're at the PDVSA hangar," Phoenix said. "I might lose you, but I'll call back as soon as he's off the ground."

"Be careful, John," Connelly said.

"Aw, you do care about me. Thanks, Leslie, you're the best." Phoenix ended the call and climbed off the bike to join the other guards.

They milled about for a moment and then formed a tight knot behind the APC. The rear door of the troop compartment opened, and Zarate's wife, an older, heavyset blonde, stepped down, then reached back to help her children. Instead of letting her assist, the guards grabbed the kids and pulled them out. The oldest, Phoenix noted, was a fourteen-year-old girl with glossy black hair, pursing her thin, pale lips as if the thought of moving to Cuba had caused her to be physically ill. He could easily imagine her stamping her foot and screaming at her papa that she wanted to stay in Caracas with her friends.

Zarate's mistress came next, a former Miss Venezuela who didn't look like she'd aged a day past her eighteenth birthday even though she'd been servicing Zarate for nearly a decade.

Maybe there's something to be said about good, regular sex, Phoenix mused.

He glanced around at the other guards. They had pulled off their helmets but wore balaclavas underneath. Phoenix removed his helmet, thankful Arika and Joel had gotten the uniform details correct. Even with the balaclava in place, it was much cooler without the helmet. Blanco and Joel followed suit just in time to see Zarate step out of the APC. He wore a pressed blue suit with a wine tie. He'd shaved his head that morning, and it gleamed in the sunlight.

The Presidential Guard didn't waste any time escorting their charges into the hangar with Blanco, Joel, and Phoenix moving with them.

"What did Calderón say?" Phoenix whispered to Blanco.

"He had no idea this was happening," she replied. "He said he would release Acevedo and the Flying Jaguars as soon as the plane takes off."

Phoenix nodded. They walked through a wide hangar with sparkling white floors and soaring ceilings. The mechanics had removed the cowlings from a small private jet, and a twin turboprop plane sat on jacks, missing its wheels.

Without hesitation, the group continued out of the hangar onto the apron. A sleek, white Dassault Falcon 2000EX sat with its passenger door open and engines running. The Cubans walked Zarate and his family to the plane and climbed on with him.

"Aren't you going?" an older man in greasy coveralls, holding a wrench, asked Phoenix.

"Not to Cuba, I'm not," Phoenix replied. "Your president is defecting."

The mechanic's mouth gaped open. "*El Jefe* is leaving?"

"Exile in Havana to smoke cigars and drink rum with your money," Phoenix said.

The pilot closed the door to the Falcon after one last look around, and moments later, the plane rolled forward.

The Falcon headed for the west end of the runway so the pilot could take off into the sultry sea breeze blowing in off the Caribbean Sea. Phoenix walked out onto the taxiway to watch the Falcon continue its roll. It turned at the end of the taxiway and aligned itself with the center of the main runway. The powerful jets rose in pitch, and the Falcon shot down the runway, lifting off into a cloudless azure sky.

"Good riddance," Joel crowed, throwing up a double middle-finger salute.

CHAPTER 48

Simón Bolívar International Airport
La Guaira, Venezuela

SEBIN Agent Marcus de los Rios had liked Hector Calderón from the moment they'd met, but he'd been infatuated with Evelyn Acevedo from their first meeting in the bowels of the University Hospital. He would do anything for her, and Calderón had played his emotions like a master violinist.

De los Rios was a tall, affable-looking fellow with wavy black hair, warm blue eyes, and a quiet, professional demeanor. Like most Venezuelans, he'd known poverty, despair, and heartache. He'd grown up in Cota 95, joined the police force to help combat the rise of crime in the slums, and then Calderón had recruited him into the SEBIN. He ran errands for the director, worked physical security for high-value principals, or whatever else Calderón needed, including pulling out fingernails and performing extrajudicial killings.

In his heart, de los Rios knew he wasn't any better than *El Koki*, but he considered himself a part of the law and not above it. He had learned early on that life was about compromise. Working for Calderón had its perks, and Calderón had filled de los Rios' coffers with enough cash that he'd never have to go back to the slums.

Calderón had dispatched de los Rios to Mexico City to shoot down Zarate's helicopter. Yet, he'd been unable to get into place with the rapid decline of negotiations between Zarate and Fredricks. After the SEBIN had captured John Phoenix during the failed rescue of the Flying Jaguar aviators, Calderón had altered his plans, hoping to pin the blame on a rogue CIA officer and install Acevedo into office. Marcus de los Rios hoped to be by the new president's side in whatever capacity he could.

Once Calderón had learned through his own spies in the Miraflores Palace that Zarate had decided to defect, he'd sent Marcus de los Rios ahead to the airport as a standby precaution to Coralina Blanco's mission. Should she and John Phoenix fail to assassinate Zarate, de los Rios was the failsafe.

At his feet was a green plastic case containing a 9K333 *Verba* man-portable infrared homing surface-to-air missile. The Russian-made weapon had an effective range of 6.5 kilometers. It used a multispectral optical seeker that combined ultraviolet, near infrared, and mid-infrared sensors to make it deadlier than its predecessors.

As de los Rios glassed the PDSVA hangar across from him with high-powered binoculars, he wondered why Zarate had chosen one of the oil company's jets instead of departing from the presidential hangar at the western end of Runway 27. It was not his mission to question Zarate's motives. It was his job to ensure Zarate didn't leave Venezuela alive.

The phone rang in his pocket, and de los Rios lifted it to his ear. "This is Marcus."

"Blanco has failed. It's up to you now," Director Calderón said.

Peering through the binoculars, de los Rios said, "The target is boarding the aircraft now, sir."

"Shoot it down," Calderón ordered. "We cannot let Zarate live and continue to wreak havoc on our country from afar."

"Yes, sir," de los Rios said before ending the call and pocketing the phone.

He lifted the *Verba* from its case. Crouching in the shrubbery to stabilize and camouflage his position, de los Rios activated the missile. He watched Zarate's Dassault Falcon taxi onto the runway and then accelerate into the wind.

De los Rios lined up the sights of his missile on the departing jet, waiting for the tone to sound, which meant the missile had locked onto its target. Once he heard it, de los Rios stroked the trigger.

The missile launched from the tube with a whoosh and roared away. Seconds later, Zarate's Falcon blossomed into a raging fireball and fell into the sea.

CHAPTER 49

John Phoenix stood with Coralina Blanco and Joel outside the PDVSA hangar. All three stared in disbelief as Zarate's plane fell from the sky.

"What the hell just happened?" Nightingale shouted into the phone. Phoenix had called her as soon as the Dassault Falcon had started to taxi and held the phone to his ear, giving her a play-by-play.

Slowly, Phoenix shifted his gaze along the length of the runway to the high bluff at the far side. It was too far away to see anyone on it, but it would make for the perfect sniper perch.

"I'd say someone just hit the plane with a heat-seeking missile," Phoenix said into the phone. Then he turned his face up to the sky and smiled. "Are you watching from a satellite?"

"Yes. I was just in the Situation Room with Stratten and the president. Holy shit, Bowie, tell me that wasn't you."

"Wasn't me, Les. If you look outside the PDVSA hangar, you'll see me waving."

"Why are you such a wiseass, Bowie?" Connelly said. "This is a critical situation."

"For whom?" Phoenix asked. "The way I see it, someone just did the job for us. Shit, I feel like Indiana Jones in *Raiders of the Lost Ark.* Those Nazis were going to die without Indy finding the ark, and Zarate died without my help. I could have stayed home."

"I guess someone wanted him dead more than we did," Connelly agreed.

"Yeah. I just feel bad for those kids," Phoenix said. "They didn't deserve that."

"No, they didn't," Blanco replied softly.

It wasn't lost on him that he'd been about to do the same thing. His EFP would have killed everyone inside the Rhinoceros, but he hadn't known the kids were in there until he'd seen them hauled out of the APC by the Presidential Guard.

"Can I come home now?" Phoenix asked.

"You're still burned. Let's stick to the plan and see if you can get close to Dragonfly," his handler said.

"I don't like that plan, Nightingale. Bring me back in, and I'll work with agency cover."

"I'll help you any way I can, John," Connelly said. "I don't have the power to change your status. Let's nail Dragonfly, and we'll go from there."

Phoenix ended the call and dropped the phone on the concrete. He was about to smash it under his boot when he thought better of it and picked it up. If he destroyed it on the flight line, some guy like that mechanic he'd talked to would have to come out and pick up all the pieces, so a jet engine didn't suck them in and damage the turbines. Phoenix carried the phone into the hangar and set it on a workbench. He picked up a nearby ball-peen hammer and smacked the phone violently, taking out his pent-up aggression on the electronic device.

"Why did you do that?" Blanco asked as he dumped the pieces into a nearby trash can.

"I don't want that bitch to ever call me again," Phoenix said, looking the venomous Cobra in the eyes. "Let's get out of here." It was a complete lie. More than ever, he wanted to spend time with Leslie Connelly, and the bitch was Blanco.

The three operatives left the hangar and walked nearly half a kilometer to exit the airport, passing the gate they'd come through with Zarate's Rhinoceros. After crossing Airport Avenue to a small strip mall, they found Arika waiting for them in the Honda.

She climbed out and stood in the open door, watching them approach.

At the car, Blanco popped the trunk, and the three stepped out of their uniforms and pulled on civilian clothes. Phoenix had to admit that Blanco had chosen well for him, providing sleek, charcoal gray ripstop cargo pants, a blue guayabera with a vertical white stripe on the left side, and a pair of running shoes. He changed right there in the parking lot, stripping down to his underwear and pulling on the new clothes, not caring who bothered to stop and look. Blanco and Joel did the same.

"Was that Zarate's plane?" Arika asked when the others finished dressing.

"Yes," Joel said. "We think someone shot it down with a surface-to-air missile."

She shook her head sadly.

"I need something to eat," Joel said. "I'm famished from all the riding. You guys want to get something?"

Arika and Blanco headed for the restaurant door being held open by Joel. Phoenix remained by the car. Blanco turned back to him, telling the other two she would join them inside.

"Want to get a beachfront hotel room and roll around in the sheets?" she asked.

"Weren't you just trying to kill me?" he asked, leaning against the Honda.

"Yeah, well …"

"How about you call Terry Martin and tell him I'm looking for work," Phoenix said.

"I don't know how to contact him," Blanco said. "He always came to me."

Phoenix glanced away, tired of watching her microexpressions give away her lies. He sighed, wondering where all the love had gone from just days before. Shifting his focus back to her deep brown eyes, Phoenix said, "Tell you what? I'll call you in a few days, and you can tell me what Martin has to say."

He pushed off the Honda and started walking east.

"Where are you going?" Blanco shouted.

Phoenix raised the stolen iPhone above his head. "Don't worry, I'll be around."

Once he was out of sight of the restaurant, Phoenix threw the phone into the bed of a parked pick-up truck. He wasn't going to call Blanco. He wasn't going to worry about Terry Martin. The CIA had burned him, and now he was on the run.

Phoenix no longer enjoyed the protection of the Central Intelligence Agency. Any enemies he'd made in the past could now consider him fair game. He would have to watch his back, but that was an old habit he'd never be rid of.

As he reached Sublette Avenue, Phoenix stuck out his thumb, hoping to catch a ride.

For the first time since the police had arrested him for arson in Abilene, Texas, John Phoenix was a free man.

He felt like celebrating, but first, he had a few scores to settle.

ABOUT THE AUTHOR

Evan Graver is the author of the Ryan Weller Thriller Series, the John Phoenix Thrillers, and the stand alone Liberty Brigade. Before becoming a writer, Graver worked as a motorcycle mechanic, property manager, and in the scuba industry. He also served in the U.S. Navy as an aviation electronics technician (AT) until they medically retired him following a motorcycle accident that left him paralyzed. Graver lives in Hollywood, Florida, with his wife and son. His passions are fishing, scuba diving, and writing.

To see his full biography, visit the About Section at www.evangraver.com.

While you're there, sign up for his newsletter and receive the free Ryan Weller Thriller short story, *Dark Days*.